T0354814

INSCRIPTIONS
— ON —
A BELT
"Life Is About Relationships"

CURTIS &
KATHLEEN BENT &
W. P. LEAR

authorHOUSE®

AuthorHouse™
1663 Liberty Drive
Bloomington, IN 47403
www.authorhouse.com
Phone: 1 (800) 839-8640

Published by AuthorHouse   11/14/2016

ISBN: 978-1-5246-5016-2 (sc)
ISBN: 978-1-5246-5015-5 (e)

Introduction

Moments in days like today I had come to cherish with snow piled high to the window, in soft swirling drifts to the roof of my oaken weathered shed. Franklin stove glowing orange hot coals. Rudy, the best Yellow Lab in the world, dream twitching on his dog pillow. I knew when I started the chop saw the motor would cause his eyelids to feign alertness. Rudy was hanging in there despite his twelve years, could still jump into the back of the truck, more than I could say for myself.

The shed, besides woodworking tools, was filled with my memorabilia. Everything from my Founder's athletic teams to all that screams Red Sox to a shelf dedicated in honor of my Dad. I'd had a sign made for Dad's section that read, "Dedicated to Bill Reynolds: Husband, Father, and Great Garage Man." A bunch of his old tools and fishing gear adorned the shelf as well as a couple of pictures, one from his college days and another with the fifty-two pound bass he had caught on a trip to Ohio. Good guy. Good Dad.

I noticed, through the window, that it had begun snowing again, wind was picking up. I glanced at a large framed picture of the regal Victorian. I recalled the first time I had seen it and how I had looked at the stylish towering Victorian from across the shaded street. It had never been grand in the classic embellished baroque manner of gabled spired gingerbread. The Victorian that had housed Valley Oak School held a solid, weathered appearance. The columns that formed the corners of the spacious front porch were formidable though in need of a good sanding with some color coordinated fresh paint. The four beveled bay windows on the street side first floor were rectangularly tall displaying elegant ornate trim that could certainly benefit from some elbow rubbing. When you entered through the imposing front door you were greeted with a winding cherry-wood staircase that twisted up to the bedrooms of the second and third floors. The first floor was comprised of five rooms, including a spacious combination living room/dining room area with a massive stone mantled fireplace that could have heated a drafty medieval castle. There was a fourth floor that opened up to the steeply pitched roof that must have made a marvelous secret place for a youth desiring to hide their personal thoughts and sacred possessions.

The Victorian was the largest house on the block and, as a corner house, was on a double lot with large leafed forest green ivy growing up its back fences. Maple and Elm trees stretched embracingly to its fourth floor attic, enticing any adventurer to swing down or scrabble up.

Rudy growled in a dog dream and brought me back. What good memories that structure held, if not uniquely bizarre. I laughed to myself as I lifted my old weight belt that was overhanging the picture of the Victorian. It was filled with student inscriptions carefully burned into the leather. I had a new belt now because this one was completely filled with charred insignias of students who had graduated from Valley Oak. I held the belt with pride and took in the names, each a vivid memory. I caught sight of a large lettered massive scrawled signature....JAMES............ He had been Valley Oaks first student.......

Valley Oak School
Psychoeducational Intake Summary

Laura Rosso: LCSW
Name: <u>James Lucas</u>
DOB: <u>10/3/76</u>

County of Residence: <u>Bay County</u>
School District of Reference: <u>BAY TREE USD</u>
Date: May 2, 1992

Physical Description: James is five feet six inches tall and weighs three hundred and eighty-seven pounds. Although his stature qualifies as obese, James is very active and enjoys bike riding, swimming, fishing, and observing team sports. James states that he enjoys "mall hiking" and knows every vender at the Willow Creek Mall. His goal is to become a comedian/actor like his hero John Candy.

Referring Criterion: Review of school history and interviews with Martha and Hank Lucas reveal that James has had difficulty in public school since enrollment, which was at the age of six in first grade. James' large frame allowed others to easily ridicule him. James response to this teasing was to become verbally and physically assaultive to his peers. As James determined he was able to physically dominate and intimidate his peers, his assaultive issues became a recurring theme of his school participation and brought about a referral to Bay County Day Treatment Program.

James' physical escalations were not limited to the school day. At the age of nine, James' destruction of property and physical threats to his parents prompted an out of county residential placement. To date, James has been in fourteen placements.

James is referred to Valley Oak School with a history of noncompliance, poor peer relationships, verbal assault, physical assault, and a general inability to be successful during the school day. During the past six months James has stabilized his acting out and has earned the right to return home to his parents.

Family History: James is the youngest of six children. Martha and Hank Lucas have been married for thirty-six years. Their five other children have all completed college and have families. James' birth, although unplanned, was without incident. His closest sibling is twelve years his senior. Martha and Hank have stated that they became concerned as James' size continued to increase and he did not attain the expected developmental milestones in speech, motor, and relational skills.

Martha and Hank sought specialists to assist them in providing a quality home program. Martha took a leave of absence from her work to provide for James, which continued, until he entered school and was subsequently placed in a variety of residential treatment programs. Martha and Hank are ecstatic with James' return home. They are willing to be involved with James treatment at Valley Oak in order to contribute to James' growth and ultimate success.

Psychiatric History: James began working with school district specialists at the age of six. At this time he was seen by Occupational and Speech Therapists. During his first year of public school, James was referred to the school psychologist for the Red Rock USD. Within the same year he was referred to Bay County Mental Health where he was seen by Dr. Jean Leer. (These reports are available in James' cumulative record.)

The reports and following clinical work ups present that James has had numerous medication trials over the years. The medications have included individually or in combination; Ritalin, Depakote, Imipramine, Haldol, Clonidine, and Trazadone. James' current regimen includes Haldol, Depakote, and Wellbutrin. James has been psychiatrically hospitalized three times, all of which were initiated due to danger to self and others.

DSM:

Axis I	299.80 Pervasive Developmental Disorder Not Otherwise Specified
Axis II:	V 71.09
Axis III:	Obesity
Axis IV:	Recent discharge from out of home placement; academic problems;
Axis V:	GAF-40 (Current)

Recommendations: School Program needs to be aware of James' needs in terms of physical health. A structured exercise program is strongly suggested for James to improve his physical/mental health and to act as a release for his frustration. In addition, treatment goals should include anger management counseling and social skills building. The rationale is based on the likelihood that James will need a structured, supportive living environment throughout his life. Services need to work together to begin to link James and his parent to adult transitional services.

Given James effective efforts to stabilize his aggressive actions over the previous six months and his parents willingness to engage in family treatment, I support James admittance to Valley Oak School.

Signed_____Date_____

Laura Rosso LCSW

Chapter 1

JAMES: A ROOM OF HIS OWN

May 6, 2000

The stairs. Always the stairs. Two flights up. I knew them from the time I was four. Twelve years ago. Sixteen to the landing. Just like my age, fifteen to the top. New carpet now from last year's remodel. At least the glue smell was gone. Can't believe I use to snort that stuff. Ugly brown carpet. Carpeting over years of my stumble dragging footsteps following mother, one step at a time, up the forever never ending stair well. My stairway to hell. Why couldn't Marianne move her office to the first floor? Always the narrow walls pressing in at me tagging behind good old mom to the second floor, turning right and stopping at the last of three doors, which opened to Marianne Walker's office.

I stood before them, again, the stairs, not wanting to begin the trudging climb. Once, at a circus, I had watched the elephants performing, and there was this young elephant that must have felt just like me. He was straining with his trunk extended towards his mother. His feet were stumbling as fast they could to keep up with his mother elephant, who never looked back. At least Dumbo could fly. Oh well....here I am...on my own. I let go a long, huge yawn. Pulled back the heavy black sleeve of my sweatshirt to check the time. Moisture clouded the dial. I wiped at it. Two-o'five. Big deal, I thought. I'm always late. I like to keep Marianne and whatever she has lined up for me waiting. It was OK by me. I felt like another yawn, but it wouldn't come. I'm here, might as well start up. I pulled the sleeve back over my watch, grabbed the rail, and began the climb...

I sat in Marianne Walker's remodeled office, waiting. Last time I had been here was over two years ago when I was making contacts to establish Valley Oak. The frumpy forties era motif had been replaced by clinical

1

high tech glass topped secretarial desks, Astrobrite filing cabinets, television sized computer screens. I wasn't sure if it felt like an improvement, though I greatly appreciated the upgraded air conditioning.

I was always early for my meetings. Marianne was busy on the phone as the silver door knob so slowly turned, the pastel door soundlessly slid open. I stiffened as James entered the second floor office. His presence filled the room. The day was going to be a boiler. James' chest heaved. The room began to reverberate with his panting. Sweat dripped from his undulated chin like a slinky going down stairs. Each drop fell in an ever widening, darkening blotch upon his black tent of a sweatshirt, clinging like an overextended water balloon to his bulk. I sat there wondering why a sweatshirt on a day like today, ninety-one degrees, humid and barely two o'clock? An East Coast swelter that could only radiate up. The office was cool enough inside with the new air conditioning so that some of the staff had light sweaters on. James just stood there, teetering Humpty Dumpty like, after coming up the stairs to Marianne Walker's office.

I shuddered as James' eyes suddenly rolled back, all three hundred and eighty-seven pounds of him heaved and collapsed, enveloping a Naugahyde stuffed chair. My gasp was covered by the chair sinking to the floor with an air groaning moan. My immediate reaction was to jump up and save James from injury. The budget of the Bay County Mental Health Department was not stipend to provide chairs substantial enough for James' unprogrammed burden.

OOOOeeeeeeeeee So Sweet!!! God I enjoy blowing people's minds with my patented Chair Smush Move! The WWF was waiting for me! Where was my name in lights?? How many times had I tortured this poor chair? Jot that in your notebook new dude. James is in the house. Ready To RuuuuuuuMMMMMMbllllllllle??!!

Marianne kept the old chair around just for me. Felt it gave me comfort, like my old blanky. Look at that guy's eyes. Freaked him out!! Gotcha! New Dude. What now?

I was knocked back. James was huge, not tall, five feet six inches at most. His head rotated like a lazy susan on shoulders with no visible neck, His skin was an eruption of festering zits that lay scattered like oozing volcanoes on a scarred alien landscape. The eyes were skulking, immersed in fat-sunken sockets, scanning for a focal point to latch onto. He had thick, pink lips that protruded like he was in a perpetual pout. White foam collected and crusted at the corners of the mouth open, gaping, gasping in air as the tongue alternately lolled to the side or lagged over the lower lip. The image of Jabba the Hut came to me. Maybe Jabba the Pizza Hut. The teeth were amazingly even. Somebody had a good health plan and an orthodontist had earned his money there. James was entirely dressed in black. Black sweatshirt. Black pants. Black shoes. Black socks. Missing was the black cowboy hat.

I glanced towards Marianne, she was securely unruffled. Marianne had known James since his lunch box was being crammed with Ho-Ho and Ding Dongs. She ended her phone conversation. Marianne placed the phone down in the holder and neatly squared it with her porcelain Kleenex box. She was the only therapist James had known. She provided us with a lustrous gentle nod that let you know her full attention was yours. Marianne intoned in her clipped chiming British accent,

"James, I would like you to meet Lou."

"Hi James," I managed, standing and reaching over to shake an extended hand that could not have formed a clenched fist. I wondered if the fingers could touch?

I flashed back quick-like over the years. How many meetings, countless group brainstorms? How many? How many people had Marianne introduced me to? I couldn't begin to remember the ke, stupid? But, good old Marianne just kept them coming. One after the other I just kept climbing speech therapists, psychiatrists, nutritionists, occupational therapists, psychologists, social workers, physical therapist and that's not counting the doctoral acronyms. There had even been a psychic hypnotist! That was fun. Really blew her mind with my fake trances. Got her to believe I could really see blue termites with green eyes. Was she li the stairs. But this guy was different. I studied him. There was something about him. I could feel it in just the way Lou had greeted me. Something ok about the way he reached out to shake my hand. Like he was a good guy. Like, maybe, he had been where I am. Maybe I was becoming desperate for a cure or tired of my act. Both? But I decided to see what this Lou guy was selling.

"Pleased to meet you, Lou," James emitted in one forceful gasp of air as he stood and shook my hand.

Quick! The guy was quick? No, he couldn't be. Maybe I just was not prepared to accept total torso movement, just how smoothly he had risen and shaken my hand. I watched as James reclined back down into the Naugahyde stuffed chair. This time he held his weight on the arms of the chair, balancing as he lowered his bulk into the cushion. The first collapse had been for my appreciation. Thanks mucho James. Now there were no dramatics. James was letting me know this. He was aware and had solid social skills. But that head. The guy had a buzz that looked like he was getting ready for the summer carnival circuit or the WWF. A name in lights like "Two Ton Tony Talbert" lit up before me. The reality was that it was hard enough for him just to maintain equilibrium between gasps of oxygen while seated. The stairs had wiped him out. If he had any stamina he would make a great nose tackle for the Patriots in a three/four defense. He was intimidating, even scary. If I got lucky, he'd be my first student.

"James," Marianne continued unfrazzled by the moment, smoothing out the folds of her long, lacy therapeutically appropriate skirt. Marianne had advocated eloquently for the establishment of Valley Oak School in Bay County. She had written letters, attended meetings, and was prepared to recommend the placement of students so that they might remain in their county of residence. In Marianne's words, "A less restrictive environment," close to home was preferred rather than some far away program. With regards to James' entry to her office, I was sure that there was little that James or any other of her clients could do that would surprise her.

Marianne properly continued, "James, I invited you up to meet with Lou so that you could ask him some questions about his school." I had always thought that Marianne's British accent made her seem so impenetrably cool. "I have told Lou that you have attended several programs (Fourteen I recalled from Marianne's briefing.) and that, for the past six months, you have been on home teaching."

OK, now I get it. Lou has a school. Marianne wants to get me out of the house and the home teaching. Can't say that I'm not bored there. I've had enough of Frank. Comes in every other day to check my work and give me assignments, which I never do. Like I care about proper nouns. As if I am ever getting a diploma. Keeps showing up. Keeps giving me the same stupid assignments. I just stare at him until he leaves. Like he even cares. Just a number on his case load. I shrug and switch positions. Hmmmmmmmmm. OK, I'll check this Lou guy out.

The lazy susan swiveled and eyed me. The sunken sockets found a focus. My heart rate quickened. Beads of perspiration began to form on the sides of my forehead. I could feel myself becoming a fixed object in space. James was checking out placement number fifteen.

As I hurriedly got out of the Bay County Mental Health building, I continued to sweat, and it was not due to the heat. Sure, I had lots of experience working with the ED population but my work had been with students eight and under. James, as an individual, weighed as much as my entire primary classroom of six ED children! How do you physically restrain or "keep safe" a sumo wrestler nose tackle? Additionally, I would be stabilizing his escalations without the backup services of a Quiet Room! Time Out Room. Chill Room. Safe Room. Stabilizing Room. A God Help Me Room! Whatever you called the purgatorial isolation. The room could be padded or just surfaced in one inch plywood with a single fireproof metal door with an "unbreakable" window to view the occupant. Legally, there could not be a lock on the door. Staff had to hold it against the ramming assaults of the thoroughly raging youth that had been assisted inside. I had witnessed three staff having to hold the door shut against the seething energy from within. I had heard screams and threats like, "I'll get scissors and stick them in your fat fucking gut and open them up!" They would take off their clothes and yell, "Hey Lou, c'mon in and suck my cock you gay nigger fuck!" They would urinate on the floor. You name it. They said or did whatever contorted spite they could conjure up. But the thing was, and, they knew this. Whatever act they performed, however long the process took, staff would wait for the student to begin a six minute stint standing, staring at the wall away from the door, arms at their side, not fidgeting in order to defuse, stabilize, earn the right to return to program. Which, of course, entailed the cleansing of the room from their deeds. The effort around a "Purgatory Room" was exhausting, for staff and students.

Now what was going to come down? How would James work out? What had I opened myself up for? How desperate had I been to have the famous Laura Russo come aboard the good ship Valley Oak? Damn that Laura. Marianne had told me I needed to hire her. So I hired her and like,

Bingo, no padded room! Valley Oak was going to be a Relationship Based Day Treatment Room!? I had just nodded. Relationship based? Say what? I couldn't wait for the mellow dialogue training.

Outside, I bounced up and down a couple of times to clear my head of the images. I climbed into the safety of my trusty five year old Honda Civic, windows were down. My buddy Rudy the Labrador seemed almost happy to see me. I made him get over to his side, he was six years old and not showing any signs of speeding up. Sometimes I thought that he had more Hound in him than Lab. But, it was Spring. The Yankees were in town. I was meeting up with my buddies in the bleachers. I had a few days to sort out how to work with James, not to mention this Laura shrink. The Yanks were enough for now.

I watched from the waiting room as Lou hustled through the front doors and James, about five minutes later, lumbered past me. Marianne had asked that I meet with her after James and Lou were introduced. Teachers, what can one do with them? I thought. Lou, as most educators, is foremost concerned about control of their student population. How are they going to get the student to remain in their seat and focus on the lesson at hand without that seven lettered word, "control?" In the traditional Day Treatment format, if the student has a history of physical and verbal assault, how does the teacher provide for a safe classroom without the behavioral tools of a Quiet Room or "Hands On?"

For me, Laura Russo, the "you were told to hire me therapist" for Valley Oak, a student such as James is going to enter program completely out of control, or, at the very least, with a history of public programs not being able to stabilize their assaultive behavioral patterns. The reason James is being referred is because he has not internalized a framework of skills to soothe his escalations. His acting-out has made him a danger to himself and others in a manner that is outside the boundaries of public education. Public education has authorized Valley Oak and other such programs in our state to meet the needs of more than eight thousand IEP referrals. The work of Valley Oak will be to provide James with the tools for him to be successful in a less restrictive environment, such as a Special Day Class on a regular school site. That was the role of Valley Oak as I understood it.

I was prepared to assist Lou in figuring out how to offer James boundaries and insights into courses of action and techniques for stabilization. We would do this by coordinating education and mental health services to offer a Relationship Based Program, which, currently, was not within Lou's scope of thought. I knew that the task would be daunting. In fact, I was coming to accept that my most crucial work might, in all actuality, be with Mr. Lou Thompson.

JULY 22   On Task

"Let's add the mileage, James." I went over and got the calculator from the rickety roll top desk. I noticed there were six new calls on the answering machine.

"I rode for twenty minutes Lou," James huffed, his face a maze of rivulets splattering to the wooden floor of the front porch. He mopped his neck and placed the sopped bathroom towel over his shoulder. His undulated chin was vaporizing.

James' head and arms were a bright red and stuck out of his lime green tank top like extended tomatoes on a vine, the gray sweat pants were completely soaked though. James was going into the sixth week of riding the stationary bicycle. He enjoyed the spectacle he commandeered from the wide front porch of the Victorian, he was quite a sight. Neighbors and passing university students would stop and strike up a conversation. They all lavished positive encouragement upon him. James was in his element and relished the adoring attention.

We had decided to chart his mileage and had mapped out a route through fourteen states that would land him on the Golden Gate in San Francisco. We never pressed James on his weight, you could tell he was thinning down. Anyway, our scale only went up to three hundred, but there was hope that James would be able to soon make use of it. What we did focus on was time on the bike and distance, just try to keep it consistent. James did his part for every day, sometimes even twice. James was recording his distance and time. The arrival date at The Golden Gate would be determined by the effort he put in. I had to admit that the exercise bike and mapping was one of my greatest innovations.

James shuffled back to the bike and peered at the odometer. "I went five point three miles or five and three-tenths miles, almost a third of a mile to six total miles!"

James had become a wealth of too much information. I found James to have sixth grade level academic skills that were enhanced by a broad array of trivial surface information that he employed with staff and the general public. James said he enjoyed the History Channel and his folks listen to NPR when traveling in their Cadillac. James was breathing deeply and his clothing just clung in a spongy, soggy mass. Time for a shower. He leaned against one of the pillared columns moaning, "Boy, Lou, do I feel tired."

James should be tired. He was proud of his accomplishment. We all were. Since the first week he had ridden over two hundred and forty miles. A trail of blue stick pins marked his progress on the large wall map of the US that hung in the main dining room. We kept James' ride safe as he could only peddle on the "Blue Highways" made famous by William "Least Heat" Moon. Least Heat had toured the US in an old clunky pick up on the highway system marked in blue, these were the least traveled. I had read his book and mapped out the route in blue ink on the US Map. James and I had skimmed through the book and looked over Least Heat's route. James thought that it would be cool to peddle his own "Blue Highways."

Up to this point, James had peddled through three states and written letters to eleven county seats. In the letters James had described how he was riding a stationary bike to become healthier, and was mapping his way across the United States sticking to the "blue highways" He asked, in every correspondence, if they had heard of the novel by Mr. Moon, or <u>Blue Highways.</u> Thus far, no one had.

"Why do you think no one has read <u>Blue Highways, Lou?</u>" James asked on a pleasant summer morning as were walking back to the Victorian from the hardware store.

"Well, maybe people are in such a hurry they are only interested in the interstate red ones."

"C'mon Lou," James grinned at me.

"Or," I ventured stoically, "They didn't attend Berkeley."

James thought that one over, "Nah, don't think so."

We walked a bit more. James stopped, "What do you really think Lou?"

Now, that was a really good question. As Program Therapist I needed to understand, I did not have to know, but I did need to understand the process by which Lou really thought. How did Lou think? This was a major concern to me. If Valley Oak was to be a relationship based program, Lou would have to model the skills. That was a work in progress. Right now, for instance, my basic concern was whether Lou could ever give a concrete straight ahead response to a basic question. Not just to students but to anyone! If I asked him what time it was, I did not need to hear that it was five o'clock somewhere. If I brought up that he was risking James' emotional well-being by his "grandiose brilliant idea" of peddling across the US. I mean, why not just to the tip of Cape Cod, I did not need to hear that Horace Greeley said it was time for all young men to head West. Did Lou always have to come back with something oblique that left the other person hanging, trying to figure out where he was coming from.

I had broached this subject with Lou more than once. He had blown my insight off the first couple of times but I would not let up. The issue was crucial to a relationship based dialogue-enriched therapeutic program model. Sure it was fun to be witty and quick and turn things around, especially if you are the one doing it. Our students had been having that done to them all their lives. If it was not their parents, then there were the peers. They were always the odd ones out. The ones left hanging. The ones devalued with wounded egos. Maybe Lou did the language play to keep himself from being the one who was left hanging. Maybe…

No! Don't rip! As I fashionably tumbled out of my car seat, grabbing the door handle to steady my departure from my parked car on the side of the Victorian. God, I wished I had learned to swear like my father! My favorite layered skirt caught on the bottom edge of the car door! Why I felt it necessary to wear therapist garb instead of jeans, I just did not know. Such a girlie my father would say! Maybe I should concentrate more on exiting a parked car than processing Lou's issues. Then too, maybe it is easier to look at Lou and get frustrated on snagging my skirt than my own issues. I took a breath, what the hell. DAMN IT!! Thank you Dad. (Lou would have sarcastically commented that "damn" was what a fish said when it bumped into concrete.)

I made my way to the sidewalk without falling down, praise the lord, and walked alongside the Victorian to the back entrance. I briefly admired the tall climbing pole beans attached to the south side of the home. Beautiful green foliage ascending toward the second story. As I carefully scaled the steps to the back porch, I spotted one of our staff, Fred, with our ten year old student Sam. in the backyard garden gathering zucchini and tomatoes and waved to them.

The back porch was, actually, an enclosed sun room that now, looked more like a greenhouse with all of the Golden Pothos snaking in and out of everywhere. Lou only grew one type. Felt it would be easier to get it right. Of course, this was another of his "brilliant ideas." Once a week the staff and a couple of the students would walk over to the Farmer's Market where Lou had negotiated a free booth, and sell some of our plants and hand painted pottery containers. It was good community based instruction. (CBI's as Lou termed them.)

From the back porch I entered the spacious, although dated, kitchen where Jake, Valley Oak's Culinary Artist Supreme ruled. Per usual, he was stirring up something healthy and aromatically tingling as I passed through and said hi. I was fragrantly reminded that I had skipped breakfast and one of the benefits of Valley Oak was Jake's lunch. I continued down the hall to my office, closed the heavy wooden door, and glanced at the answering machine. There were already nine calls on it and it was not even 11:00! With all of the scheduled IEP's and tentative placements, Valley Oak was getting ready for a student surge! I needed to consult with Lou about increasing my time on site. I opened my office door and looked down the hall where James and Lou were absorbed by the wall map.

James and I stood staring at the map, town by town, county by county, state by state, stick pin by stick pin. As James passed through, he sent the county seats self-addressed envelopes to be returned full of local information. Thus far, he had received five of them back. James had sifted through the contents and posted some of the material on the bulletin board.

There were chamber of commerce proclamations from Worcester, motels to stay in from Northampton, the natural beauty of Berkshire County, where Pittsfield was the county seat.

Fred came swaying up to the back porch from the garden. Sam and he had their shirts stretched out, forming a bowl for the string beans, zucchini and cherry tomatoes from the garden. Sam and James comprised two-sevenths of our student population.

"How far did you get today, James?" Fred called from the kitchen as he emptied his red and green produce filled T-shirt into a colander in the sink.

"Well, let's take a look." James sauntered back through the high entry hall, past the stairs, laboriously searched his damp sweats, and then, remembering, reached over to the stairwell rail where he had perched his glasses before his workout. He wound them around his face. The stems did not reach to the front of his ears. He returned and squinted at the AAA road map of the United States that was laminated and mounted to the stairwell wall. He leaned forward, placed both hands on the map, braced himself thoughtfully, his forehead wrinkling, forming a topographical map of its own.

"Let's see, yesterday, the day before here. Before that…." He wiped his face, stepped back and cleaned his glasses. "Whew, it's hot." Then he rattled off. "Made it through Mechanicville. Went around Schenectady. Came down a bit into Cobleskill." James scratched his cheek, paused, cleared his throat. I could tell he was going for effect, "Lou, which way do you think I should go now?"

James knew which way I desired him to go.

"I could just continue on alongside 88 through Schoharie or I could head into, how do you say this town?"

Fred chimed in, "You wouldn't mean Cooperstown, would you James?"

"That's how you say it? Who'd want to go there?" They both laughed and looked at me.

Saved by the clanging triangular bell from further harassment, lunch was called and we wandered back to the kitchen where Sam was assisting Jake in the final needs of Culinary Arts. James headed for the shower, leaving a puddled remembrance in the hall by the road map. Sonja and Gerald, two other students, began setting the dining room table for lunch.

August 4   Splish Splash

James and I paid the fee and entered the community pool. I ignored the gawking stares with young fingers pointing at James' presence. James was oblivious, a composed jolly white giant amongst the multitudes. A Gulliver in transit. He entered the pool arena and wrestled off his sweatshirt to rinse in the shower. Small mesmerized urchins looked on in awe, not believing all the rolls of creamy flesh cascading from James' chest to his thighs. James, for his part, continued to posture a practiced indifference to the crowd's reaction as he lathered on suntan lotion. James was partial to Coppertone Coco Bronze. He had endured eyeballing crowds forever, no big thing to him. James had told me that he liked to swim and the water exercise would augment the cycling. Finally, he had convinced me to take him over to the Greater Bay County Community Pool, which was the largest complex in our area.

"Hey James," I asked feigning fear, "You're not going to pull a <u>Sand Lot on me,</u> are you?"

James paused, slowly looked around the huge Deep Pool at the six lifeguards now seated in their chairs, four were female. All no more than two or three years older than James. All physically attractive in their county approved one piece red bathing suits. He looked me in the eye, lowered his voice, "What a ya think Lou? How about the one in the corner chair?" Then he winked.

<u>Sand Lot,</u> was there a better coming of age movie? How many children did Squints and The Lifeguard have?

We laughed and James asked. "Lou, can I jump in?" His feet were perched over the edge of the pool tile.

"Sure," why not I had thought. Although I might be missing something, seemed OK. It would have been safer to have started out in the shallower pool, the one that went up to six feet but James seemed confident.

James immediately drew a deep breath and avalanche toppled into the Deep Pool. The Deep Pool had two high diving boards and two lower ones. No pool depth less than six feet. Thankfully, he did not hit the side of the pool as he heaved in. A tsunami tidal wave surged from the point of entry. I looked on as James drifted meanderingly towards the aqua blue bottom. He was at the twelve foot depth. I stood waiting, hoping not to appear too concerned. I mean, could he really swim? Moments slowly passed. I donned my shades to have the "cool no biggee present." Again, as in Marianne's office, I had been caught off-guard by his quickness. Presto! Like the chair, into the pool. My anxiety increased. Maybe he had caught his head on the side. Maybe the cold water on this hot day had caused him to lose consciousness. I fervently hoped that he would start to come back up. Bulk floats, I knew that. How could he stay down there without a weight belt? Why had I so readily agreed to his jumping in? Why not the Shallow Pool? I mean, could I have made a better decision. Maybe checked

James out for ability to survive in water in the Shallow Pool. Did I have a brain? (Don't answer that Laura.) From his indistinct image, bubbles arose to the surface in a continuous vapor trail noting his existence. I checked the sky for clouds, polished my sunglasses. Seeing my feigned lack of concern, swimmers in the area went back to their activities. James remained a stationary blur. I continued to peer at the underwater form for some signal that he would surface. I distinctly remember looking away and offering a solemn prayer, at the same time wondering if James might not be enjoying my high anxiety? He had years of practice in stressing adults out. Why should he stop now? He had me on a string with the possibility of great crowd interaction.

Then, praise the gods, in slow motion, the imprecise object ascended. Gradually he gained definition. I could make out the arms, head and with a sudden burst he breached! A three hundred plus pound birth! James' head bobbed on the surface. I suddenly loved that shaven skull, teeth gleaming up at me with eyes shut in a toothy Crest smile. I felt my body relax as he began wiping water from his eyes, floating comfortably without holding onto the edge. "Baby Beluga" came to mind. The lifeguards looked at both of us and smiled.

"Gotch ya, huh?" He grinned.

"Totally." I managed, once more becoming cool behind my shades.

Lou took chances. He had disclosed some of them with me. Lou did not like to admit to his willingness to take on risk, but he did. Look at Valley Oak. He could have remained within the public system and moved into a comfortable administrator's salaried position. Again, Lou would rather tell stories about his fear of heights or hating to go fast or his inability to sing on key, but that did not stop him from doing it. When he was not sitting in right field at Fenway he would find cliffs to climb where a fall would drop him into the Atlantic. Three years previously he had stuck his Harley into the side of a left turning car and flipped over the trunk. The responding officer had said six inches and he would have been strained spaghetti through the rear window. Then, his songs! From "Six Little Ducks" to "I'm Going Bowling with My Friend Burt." Where did he come up with these things? I could appreciate "Fisherman's Blues." I mean, even my father knew Taj Mahal's song, and, fortunately, my father could sing on key. For Lou, for all of his professional composure, he relished James' limit pushing as much as James did.

Three weeks had now passed, James had developed a regimen. We, as a program, were now coming down to the pool every day. What better activity on a summer's day? There is simply more to education than academic levels. Get real! We were all involved in the swim and healthy exercise. It was good for staff too. James always went through water aerobics before free swim.

As we finished his aerobic leg raises, I said, "OK James, today you start with five laps. After five laps you can have some earned swim time."

"Can I dog paddle for my laps?" James asked.

"Sure, but no barking" I answered. If he could make five laps, I didn't mind if he walked on water.

By the end of August, James was up to fifteen laps. Before he swam his fifteen laps, he had to complete his extended water aerobics, now up to twenty minutes, in the Shallow Pool. The greatest depth in the Shallow Pool was six feet, which was just right for James. He was fluid in the water. His bulk was balanced and he was able to relax and move with ease. He was an Apatosaurus, confident in his ability to be successful and enjoying the workout. His outdoor water activities had allowed his body to rejuvenate. His skin tanned and darkened. His complexion cleared. He no longer needed to soak himself down with sun block. For sheer crowd pleasure James now completed his pool sessions by doing cannonballs off of the low dive. James' cannonballs stopped all pool action. James loved it. I was so proud, you'd have thought the Red Sox had drafted him to play left field!

August 23   Too Good

"Laura."

"Yes James?" We were seated in my office. James had asked to meet with me in addition to our weekly hour of therapy. I was interested to see what was going on. James continued to sit straight up with shoulders back on my much rumpled couch. He looked uncomfortable. A sense of gloom was upon him.

He shook himself, as if trying to start up. "Ok, here it is," he struggled,. paused, then looked away from me and uttered in a stilted monotone. "Laura, where…. am ………I going?"

That was a statement! Not that I had not expected a concern in that direction. James was introspective and had been involved in psychotherapy for most of his life. He was familiar with the phraseology and intonation. I presented the standard response, "Where do you think you are going, James?" He shifted in the couch. Reclined a bit.

"I mean, I'm doing all this stuff," Quickly adding, "It's good stuff, everybody tells me so, but, I just don't know what's in it for me?"

James was correct, he had been involved in activities and positive socializing at a level of success beyond any of our projections. He had more than met with program expectations, never presenting his history of escalations and noncompliance. James had developed friendships, become physically healthier, and was working to develop living skills that would assist him throughout his adult life. His parents, who I met with every other week, were enthralled with the positive turn of life James was undertaking.

What James was presenting to me was his vulnerability. He had been able to present a façade of confident success for an incredible stretch of time, and now his internal, personal issues were beginning to come to the forefront. That James was able to share his concerns with me was an indication of the maturity he had achieved and the trust he had forged in our relationship. I knew that the next few months would be critical. This is when my work would really begin.

SEPTEMBER 23   Termites

"He what?" I was incredulous. This could not be happening!

Fred was always so matter of fact. He was on the phone. "James just kept saying, polished mahogany. Polished mahogany. Over and over. Just the phrase polished mahogany. He perseverated and was getting louder and louder. It was totally weird."

Fred had taken James, Sam, and Tony to the GM Auto Museum for an Earned Activity. Jake and I had stayed back at the school with four other students who were not into vintage autos. Fred's call was really a shock because, even if we had read about James' escalating issues in his cumulative folder, he had not had one instance of acting-out since coming into Valley Oak and James had been with us over four months.

"Say what? Polished mahogany?"

"For whatever reasons, the tour guide was talking about some of the older cars and how they had this polished mahogany dashboard in them. I think I'm losing you."

Static was breaking up the car phone connection.

Fred came back on. "Hear OK?" I could. "Anyway, the next thing I knew, James was chanting polished mahogany.. He had this maniacal look on his face. His lips were in a sneer. All teeth showing. I've never seen him like this. Then he started growling out the words polished mahogany and getting louder and louder. People were looking at him and moving out of his way."

Unbelievable. "What did you do?" I don't know what I would have done. Out in public with three hundred pounds of chanting polished mahogany.

Laura had presented to us at a staff meeting that this could be coming down. We could have pro-acted by sending two staff. I could envision her subtlety listening head nod as I gave her the details. Damn, I was going to have to get use to her being right.

Fred's course of action was to immediately leave the tour and get out of GM Museum with the three students. James had acquired a fixed grimace, his hands were moving agitatedly in front of his face, his eyes shown with the glint of one possessed. Fred was concerned but felt safe enough to drive the students two blocks to an adjacent park for lunch. James had laughed and giggled during the short ride, but settled down once out of the car. As they set up for the picnic Sam and Tony, the two other students, had continued to ignore James. Even they were embarrassed by the public display. When they had finished lunch, James had calmed down and Fred decided it would be all right to return to the school site, which was a distance of twelve miles.

"Where are you now?" I lost Fred with more static. The hills in the area made cellular communication inconsistent. I heard the University bells begin to ring the hour time. Fred came back on.

"I got off on the Livingstone ramp." There was a pause. Fred came back on with more concern in his voice, "Now James has started talking about termites with 'blue-green eyes.' He says he can see them outside the van. Now he wants to drive the van." I heard Fred tell James that student driving was not part of the curriculum.

I could imagine the scene in the van. Fred's perpetual calm was embodied by a steady gaze. I use to wonder if he blinked. Fred was always so under control, at least on the outside. Reality, just what the hell to do?

Ooooooeeeeee this is fun! Got everyone going. That old man in the museum almost had a coronary. Probably thought that I was going to put a smudge on one of his vintage beauties. I should have left some teeth marks on the upholstery. Polished mahogany, that's a good one. Have to remember it. I've used the blue green termites before, but not with these guys. Got Fred sweating. Mr. O'So Mellow.

I'm not going to push this too far. Just see how they'll react. I forgot how much fun I could have doing this. Maybe Sam and Tony can learn a few things from me. Look at those duds, they're petrified. Probably think I'm going to steer us into an eighteen wheeler. OK, enough good times. I'll go back to being Sweet Baby James. That's what my mom used to call me.

I had taught for over twenty years, held four credentials, a masters, was a Physical Assault Response Trainer. I should have some sort of clue. Maybe call 911? Definitely stay off the highway.

"Hey, Laura," I yelled. Hoping not to sound too desperate..

Laura's door slowly opened, and she said in that pervasive "I'm such a centered therapist voice,"

"Yes, Lou?"

I don't think she'd ever heard me yell. "There's an issue with James off site. I'm going to have to go meet the van at the Livingston exit."

Fred came back on the phone. "Problem's over. James just apologized for his actions. He says he hopes he hasn't caused too much trouble. He just wants to get back to school." I could hear the relief in Fred's voice. "I should be there in fifteen minutes, if termites don't attack."

So much for my expertise. I shook my head. There was just so much vulnerability to program when involved in off-site activities or transportation. I couldn't come up with any good answers for it, except being more aware of who was going where and over staffing. It was just plain risky, even with three staff. Yet, how could you have predicted this event. Maybe the risks just came with the off-site territory.

When Fred and the students arrived back at Valley Oak, James clambered out of the van and headed straight for me. "Lou, I'm sorry." He was panting with anxiety. "It won't happen again. Please, I don't want a level drop. I'm just really sorry. I don't know what happened. Sorry Lou."

James was sweating. There was the mark of white crusted foam at the corners of his mouth. His eyes were pleading. I decided to let it go. "Come on in and relax James. No one died. Let Laura, Fred and I talk, see what we can work out."

Well, I, for one, knew what James was looking for, and that was boundaries. Where was the Valley Oak containment net for actions, he knew, were not socially appropriate. Any of his other programs would have found him stabilizing in a Time Out Room, after a prone restraint. Valley Oak, working from a relationship base, just wants to dialogue. In between swimming and peddling and Culinary Arts and Tool Time and...... James is needing to know how much could he get away with?

James had run his course in meeting up with social expectations. He knew he could maintain, Valley Oak had allowed James to see and present a positive side of himself. What James was experiencing was that he was not able to enjoy the same adrenalin rush he received when he acted out. Having friends, feeling healthier, moving on to have more self-determination, just did not rate for attention getting when put up against property damage and physical assault.

James' history of physical assault and property damage was extensive and had become more destructive in his adolescence. Through the creative and relationship based program of Valley Oak, James had experienced another potential aspect of his personality. He was capable of pulling together the social and emotional skills needed to be an appropriate student and young man. James knew this and his success challenged his ego framework because the transition would demand his leaving the womb that had nourished him through his dysfunctional formative years. By acting-out James imprisoned his family and placed demands on social services to meet his needs. He could orchestrate an array of adults to congregate and console and hold meetings and develop behavioral plans and place him on a pedestal of attentive offerings. James would lose all this worshipful focus if he continued to develop successful skills through Valley Oak. As his therapist, I just did not know if he would be able to tolerate this level of social appropriateness and individuation.

As Lou had bemoaned, without a Time Out Room, where was the ultimate containment that James was seeking. What type of intervention did James need to resolve his issues?

October 25   Pumpkins

The Valley Oak program offers door to door student transportation. I had taught in several county day treatment programs and they had always had issues with the yellow buses. Some of my six year old students might live three blocks from the school and, due to district routing, would spend as much as two and a half hours going from home to school. To say that they had issues on the van was to minimize the lack of restrooms, level of yellow bus staff training, or the impact of the "restrictive coats" some earned the right to wear to stabilize their behavior in transportation. Add to this menagerie the fact that the students arose from lower socioeconomic no breakfast struggling households and the concoction that poured forth from the moving yellow cell block into my room was a torrent of pent up tortured turmoil. Fortunately they had an immediate target, us. We would need to spend the first hour of program just trying to calm the students down from their ride in.

The different variations of student vs. van driver are too numerous to comprehend. As educational cohorts, of course, we needed to posture solidarity with van staff in order to empower drivers for a safe van ride, which only added to our student's frustration. The students knew what was going on and felt further victimized as they did not get support for the outlandish situations that the van drivers would impact them with. The most flagrant violation, to me, was the disclosing of personal information from the drivers to the students. Time and time again one of the students would share with us something like,

"Did you hear that Jeanie's daughter got raped the other night," or "Did you see that black and blue mark on Susan's shoulder? She said her husband hit her when he was drunk. They made up though."

"She said make up sex is the best."

Why should these children, any school children have to be exposed to such a hideous needy adult communication? Where were the boundaries? Where was the supervision?

I had vowed that, should I ever run a program, students would not be on a van for longer than forty-five minutes and, secondly, the staff that drove the vans would work the day school program. I figured that in having staff work both areas of program there would be consistency of communication between home and school. Our drivers would have good training as they were the day program staff, and we could process the "he said they said and then she said" information and make van transportation safer. And, finally, our vans would not be yellow! Another of my many brilliantly luminescent ideas!

This evolved into Valley Oak School which was a day treatment program whose staff drove and worked in the classroom. As I had foreseen, this allowed for direct communication with the home or residence concerning events during the school day or in the neighborhood. As owner-teacher-custodian-transportation director, I had not counted on the opportunity I would, personally, be offered to transport students to and from school, in some cases a distance of eight miles. So much for my "Louuminous" ideas.

Thus far, my brief transportation experiences had allowed me to gain a great deal of admiration for the yellow bus drivers. Nothing like sharing the same steering wheel to gain a more relevant perspective. I had never given much thought to the issues that came at the driver. Being alone, the vulnerability of driving fifty-five on an interstate with two to five emotionally disturbed children. Your only support was a cell phone. What if there was a fight? What if a student took off their seat belt and went for the wheel? What if........ What came one's way to process when in transportation left me with considering a sane administration position for some school district. I had to admit, if Valley Oak ever became large enough, my transportation responsibility would be immediately delegated.

My van route brought us through the rolling farm country our area was famous for, the three year old Voyager making the ride very comfortable. The picturesque scenery is postcard certified gorgeous with the fall cold snap orchestrating a resplendent chorus of color. Morning or afternoon runs home without students would allow me to choose the least traveled roads. Where was Least Heat? With students, I was on the intrastate, I didn't mind the tolls. Need for speed. But for now, there are scattered orchards, fields of alfalfa, stands of pine and hardwood trees, small parcels with horses, and general truck farming enterprises with most of the front yard fruit stands now boarded up. I thought about how people were saying that maple syrup might be out of the stands in a few years due to global warming. Quebec was now producing more than New England. Things do change and, although I treasure the Victorian home and small town University atmosphere that houses the Valley Oak School, someday I envision having the program located in a rural environment. The students could more readily build their self-esteem and work skills through hands-on experiences. Maybe we could get a truck farm with a fruit stand going.

At the outset of transportation, I had shared the back roads with James. Taking this one route, we would go by an immaculately white painted with green trim farmhouse and barns. The fences were New England sturdy and a pristine white. The entry road was a multi colored cobblestone with birch trees on either side. Our ritual was for one of us to ask, "What's your choice today? A Ferrari or the farm?" Depending on our mood, it was usually the farm.

Well, that was then. No longer did such thoughts or conversations come to mind as James' behavior had plummeted. No longer was transportation a remotely pleasurable activity.

I drove up to James' single story middle America brick home. Mr. Normal Rockwell could not have chosen a more "This is New England" Fall multicolored leafed neighborhood. I got ready.

"Morning, James," I greeted him with the same upbeat greeting as in the good old mornings when life was full of promise. James broodily stood staring at the sidewalk. In a despondent effort he grasped the latch and swung open the passenger door of the van. I had made it a point to stop a distance from the curb so the door wouldn't stick on the ground when he came aboard. His menacing scowl, disheveled, stained clothing portended another," this is going to be a too much fun ominous day."

I always held out hope that this might be a good day, because, some days there was an unexpected positive change, as if James was toying with us. Letting us know that he was in control. Or, sometimes, he might have seen a good movie that lifted his spirits. However, this was not going to be an uplifting day. I prepared myself to offer a lot of positive energy and accept personal abuse. I continued, "Just sayin' good morning, James" I tried, "It's a social nuance that people participate in. Even people that root for the Yankees"

"Don't say nothing to me you slimy turd. Just drive the fucking van."

"James....."

He sneered, "Shut the fuck up or I'll fuck you up!"

Well, that would be a bit of a reach, but that I was accepting assaultive language from a student and still transporting him in? Had I become Gandhi the Driver? Or, was the stipend from his attendance the motivating force?

"Has he ever assaulted you?" Laura had asked.

"Not physically, but the language gets the point across. What about personal safety. Would my blood on the windshield suffice to leave him home?"

Laura donned her soothing, perplexed look. "What would you like to occur when James makes these statements?"

Give me that opportunity!! What I would like to do to this Humpty Dumpty cracked egg wannabe was to get a wide Velcro belt and strap it around his ugly mug with a slip knot and cinch it thoroughly up in a "trucker's knot" ever so tight around some maple tree. However, given Laura's terminology and my desire for meeting up with a therapeutically relationship dialogue based program, I profoundly stated.

"What I would like to do is to be able to offer James some alternatives to redirect his escalating behavioral decisions in a manner that would assist him in stabilizing his issues during transportation." I was learning to talk the talk! Maybe I could even don the therapeutic garb. Comfortable, bit rumbled, sport coat. Collared long sleeve pastel shirt. No tie. Maybe a matching vest. Of course slacks with some worn, though well-polished, leather shoes and matching socks. Suited up! Ready to dialogue and listen!

Laura laughed, because she knew that I did not mean one word of it. "That was good Lou! If you practice more positive self-talk you might even believe it."

I leaned against the door frame, "Golly gee Laura, thanks. Maybe in the next life I can come back a therapist."

"Only if you move up the food chain."

Funny lady. Not only was Laura, easily, smarter than me, but she was ten times better looking. Her Italian olive smooth complexion was strikingly framed by thick blond locks that, more often than not, she wore up. She admitted to rinsing to keep the gray out. At least she was honest about it and laughed at her ego needs.

Laura got her therapist cap back on. "Now, let's review James' issues and see what we might offer."

I attempted, in a civilized manner, to communicate the experience James was bringing my way. His weight was back up, that was obvious. When I arrived to pick him up in the morning, I watched as he belligerently heaved his ponderous frame into the seat, willing it to give up its fabricated form. The act reminded me of the chair in Marianne's office on the first day I had met James. Once in the passenger seat, James struggled with his seat belt. Grunting, his eyes were slits in an erupting swollen, reddening face. Gone was the well-being and tanning of a water healthy summer. His facial hair had been allowed to grow out and there were inch long strands dangling among his multiple chins. His shaven head gave him the look of a wanted felon, #492 on America's Most Wanted.

In her most soothing servile voice, "Well, Lou, he is willingly coming into program."

I nodded. THE THERAPEUTIC NOD OF UNDERSTANDING......
..... meaning, this just sucks!

Another day...............

James sat back, panting from his exertion. Then gutturally blurted, "You need to do it."

Like hell I needed to do! Yuk. Was this part of the job description? Was my Master's in baby sitting or strapping in the Incredible Lunk? I turned and reached across James to grab the seat belt and prepared to buckle him in. I processed to myself,......... I hate doing this. I hate doing this. I understand that the issue is not personal. That, until last month, he had always been able to buckle his own belt. His eight inches of overhanging flab on his expando shorts expressing, as Laura would say, his vacuous neediness, was not developed in anger towards me. In spite of my drenching the van in Fresh Air, James' body odor was omnipresent. But, I am just part of a life that is not sweet for an emotionally disturbed child with an eating disorder.

Making sure to avoid physical contact, that would set James off, I reached over and grasped the seat belt and buckle. God, I would need a Duct Taped Elastic Velcro strap to secure him in if he continues to bloat and a hoist to get him in and out.

On the ride into Valley Oak we pick-up one other student, Sam. James acknowledges Sam's presence by hissing at him and donning a Cheshire Cat faced grin with his right hand held up in front of his face like a claw. His fingers begin twitching up and down. James starts to giggle. I recognize this as the start of his escalating. Although he has not been physically unsafe in transportation, James chose bizarre dialogue that was, at best, uncomfortable and, definitely, socially inappropriate.

Why couldn't James ever be ill or miss a day of school? Why act-out in this manner and continue to participate? There is no chance of getting him into conversations about raising vegetables or who the Red Sox might be trying to bring aboard. Now he's with the finger stim-stuff and giggling. Then he will start asking disquieting questions that have no basis in reality. Why don't humans have signal lights instead of eyes? Every now and then bringing back the blue green termites. Then he will begin rocking back and forth, making ethnic slurs. Black, white, yellow, he took them all on. Didn't matter. Each of these specific actions had developed over a period of time, like James was testing to see what was going to happen. Determine where the boundaries and consequences were. I wondered if I would be privileged with a new behavior today.

We enter the town through the tree laden outskirts. I was taking the scenic way in instead of going roundabout to avoid the highest concentration of the university student population. As we begin passing the occasional peddling college students on the way to morning class, James laughs and targets a group of Asian students riding their bikes into the University.

"Ching-achong-chinks! Chop suey monkeys!" James yells out.

"Chingy-chong-chingy-chong-chingy-chong, chink-a-dink chinks!!"

"James," I state, "It's refreshing to hear that you are aware of the ethnic diversity that forms the basis of our representative democracy." I had long ago stopped attempting to have him cease his nauseating acts of racial harassment. I should have taken a more roundabout way in and avoided all this turmoil.

He just ignores me, "Yellow bellies. Chinks or Japs, you're all slant eyed yellow bellies! Kill them all. Kill all of those yellow bellied World War Two slant eyed Japs. I hate Japs. I hate your monkey parents! Put them in Concentration Camps! Take the Rainbow Division and shove it!" (I had offered James the perspective of Japanese internment during World War II and the history of the Rainbow Division in Europe in the hope that it might increase his racial awareness.)

Now, he begins coughing. His yelling has run him out of breath. His face is flushed. Drool is oozing onto his shirt. We are stuck at a red signal light. Again I ask myself, why was I not enlightened enough to take an even more obscure way into town? Next time around and through the industrial section. How many times do I have to learn this?

I look on as James puts his face to the window, opens his mouth, and crams his tongue against the glass. Saliva runs down the pane and onto his arm. Fortunately, the students who are stopped at the light, are unaware or are kindly ignoring his sickening behavior. Likely the latter. I know that he would roll down the window and scream if he could. Sometimes his weight is a blessing. The window handle is buried beneath an avalanche of thigh tissue. There is no way that he can get to it. I make a note to pay a little more and get electric windows with locks for our next school van. The light changes and we move on.

With no further duress, we finish our ride and arrive at the stately Victorian home that is Valley Oak School. I have already called ahead to alert staff. Jake and Fred are sitting on the front steps watching our van pull in, they know the drill with James. I unlatch the seat belt from James and he struggles to open the van door. Fred comes over to open it from the outside to keep it from swinging out and grating on the concrete curb.

"How's it going James?" Fred asks.

"Fuck you guys. I can open my own door." James grunts and positions one foot on the curb outside the van. He grudgingly oozes sideways out of the vehicle and totters for balance. Several times in the past he has fallen trying this maneuver, but he won't let anyone help out. Fred and Jake look over at me for some direction as James trudges towards the front porch.

"Typical morning. Just full of good humanity and insight." I catch a side glimpse of James dropping his back pack and picking up one of our Halloween pumpkins. I struggle to suppress my rage, search for the proper response. I was not in Laura's office, I was on my own.

"James, we've talked with you about making poor decisions with the pumpkins."

James has picked up one of the Jack O'Lanterns that are lining the front porch rail that we had painted a bright green. He eyes Jack and Fred who are moving out of range as he raises the pumpkin above his head. We have seen this dance before. James has proven not to have the physical energy to maintain his assaultive acting-out behavior for any duration of time. He can neither hold the pumpkin for long nor chase staff. His face is turning a bright red from the physical effort. We await his next move.............

"James," Jake asks, "Why not just put the pumpkin down, get some juice, and get on with the day?"

I agreed, "Really James, what's the pumpkin ever done to you?"

Look at those assholes. They don't know what to do. They're just waiting for me to tire out. This time it's going to be different. I'm fucking through with their sweet be so kind talk. What a bunch of crap. This is a job to them. Just like all the other suck staff I've known. They come and go. Me, I stay the same. Same fat ugly body. Nothing changes for me. But this time I have a plan. I'm ready. I'm going to take this into Laura's office and smash it on her computer. Can't wait to see her scream! That'll show'em to fuck with me.

I nod for Jake to go around through the back to head James off if he goes into the Victorian. I watch as James struggles up the front steps, the pumpkin precariously balanced overhead. This is a new direction. Each time a further step in acting-out. Laura stated that a likely reason for James' acting out is that we were getting more students in program. James is missing the early center of attention he had received in being our first student. He's looking for ways to come back in and, unfortunately, he's only able to choose negative ones. James had chased us with the pumpkin, smashed the pumpkin on the sidewalk, thrown the pumpkin against the house, and now, he was going into the Victorian to wreck havoc. Just like in the van, raising the ante as events materialized. Where's the boundary? Where's the containment?

Fred approaches James as Jake slips around the corner of the house, "James, let's take a breath and go for a walk. It's a good weather day. Let's get some space from this place." Fred liked to rhyme.

James will not respond. "On second thought," he giggles through a fiendish grimace, "I think I'll toss this pumpkin into the therapy room. Laura can use some pumpkin therapy!"

With that James pivots and wheels towards the front door. I rush the front porch, glancing at the row of pumpkins neatly spaced and somehow wondering why I have never moved them. I mean, how many times does James have to grab one? How 'bout "Clueless?"

James has stopped, pumpkin is held head high. Eyes popping with the effort. Jake has come around through the backdoor and is blocking the front entryway.

"Fuck you! I'm going to smash this pumpkin into your face!" James screams as he rears back to fulfill the prophecy. Strange how moments like this can slow down. I can see James' neck, which is not an anatomical property normally viewed, strained with veins. Fred calls for "team control" as I wrench the pumpkin from James' grasp. James is spun and brought off-balance by the effort to control the pumpkin. He half turns around, closing his fist to punch me in the face. I back out of harm's way as Jake and Fred position themselves on either side of James, take hold of his arm and shoulder, lock their inside feet together in back of his knees to form a stable base, and raise James' arms towards the wall for a standing restraint.

We are all PART Certified (Physical Assault Response Training). The key to being PART trained is that a restraint is the last thing you want to employ in stabilizing a situation. We have practiced the PART maneuvers in our team meetings, but this is the first, for real restraint in Valley Oak history. In other programs I had done as many as five per day. We had managed to avoid actualizing a restraint at Valley Oak as we sought to offer other alternatives. However, when events escalate, as they had with James, where an individual may be a danger to himself or others, a restraint is necessitated.

I stand ready to assist Jake and Fred as, with James, there is no chance of continuing the standing restraint. James' weight dictates his slowly sliding to a prone position on the floor. The pumpkin is dropped and rolls against the open front door. As he is settling down, Jake and Fred move away to give James space to stabilize. There is no reason to keep hands on. Momentarily, James' negative behavior has run its course. Hopefully he will not continue to escalate when he catches his breath.

As I stand to the side of James, Marianne Walker is formally marching up the front walkway, seemingly oblivious to the situation. With British good cheer she greets her child prodigy, "James, how is it going?"

James wearily lifts his head and gains a focus. "Fuck you! Fuck you Marianne! Leave me alone bitch!"

So begins another day at Valley Oak School............

NOVEMBER 21

"Where is he?"

"Usual place."

I had just returned from a district IEP meeting. All was well at Valley Oak. Students at task. Staff involved. James in the second floor bedroom.........

I went down the hall to Laura's office and knocked, softly. She could be a hellion if intruded upon.

"Doors unlocked," she answered.

As I entered I noticed that her hair was down to her shoulders and she was wearing blue levis.

"When did you start wearing jeans." She did look good in them. Not as formidable as in all those layered skirts and vests.

"I don't know," she laughed, "About three weeks ago or so." She tossed her hair back. "That's when everyone else noticed."

"C'mon Laura, give me a break," I asked, "I'm not as dumb as I look."

She just nodded waiting for me to go on. She might not wear the mental health uniform but she still wore the pants with that therapeutic silence. I sat down, which was fairly bold as I usually waited for her to ask me to have a seat. Her office always had the scent of a florist's shop. It was like a cool fresh scent after a mist had just been turned off. I liked the fragrance but it just didn't seem right to ask what it was. Anyway, where was I?

"James," I almost stammered. Was I brain dead? Why was I always so stupid-awkward when I was in her office? "We need to do something to get him going."

She looked right into me. Damn those lipid blue eyes. "OK Lou, what would you like WE to do?"

I looked away to the pictures on the walls. Mostly of the West Coast and San Francisco, where she was from, Nothing of family, Nothing really personal. For therapy being such a personal thing, Laura sure didn't put anything out there. Myself? I had loved the Left Coast. Laura said family pictures were not appropriate for a therapeutic setting. Therapy was about the client. Maybe I felt like a client in her presence.

"Look Laura, James has been here, what, about six months. For the past three weeks he just comes in, goes up stairs, and sleeps in the third bedroom. It's just not OK"

The phone rang. Laura let the answering machine take it. She sat back in her swivel chair. Why were therapist so laid back. She folded her arms.

"Lou, I know this is hard for you to accept, but James needs to work through his issues at his own pace. That he comes in to program every day is a positive statement."

Laura could find a positive statement in the Spanish Inquisition. "OK, ok, ok. It is hard for me and we both know that. The thing is, the school districts don't look for Valley Oak to be a bed and lunch resort. The only time James comes down the stairs is for lunch. Wait!" I interrupted Laura before she could target me with another positive. "I know what you're going to say, he is choosing to have positive social interaction and maintain the relationships!"

Laura smiled. "Lou, you just are getting to know my M.O. too well." She shifted in her seat and leaned over, looking at her planner, "Why don't we get the IEP Team together and see what they think."

January 23   Where Are the Boundaries?

Through Federal Law 95-172 students are determined to be eligible for special education services through a meeting of the concerned parties. The

Individualized Education Plan Meeting or IEP Meeting is "The Event" in evaluating the participation and progress of a student involved with special education services. The initial referral for special education consideration might be from a parent or teacher to the School Psychologist or Special Education Teacher for evaluation. When the evaluation is completed, the individuals schedule an IEP meeting to determine possible services for the referred students.

Well, when students, such a James, were lacking success in their Nonpublic School placement, then, guess what? You got it! An IEP (Individual Education Plan) Team meeting was called. I have had the pleasure of participating in pleasant and successful IEP meetings that have lasted forty-five minutes. I have had the opportunity to attend IEP meetings that have found reasons to exist for three days, involving twenty adults representing mental health; occupational therapy; physical therapy; speech therapy, the juvenile court system, attorneys, parents, aunts and uncles and fourth cousins. Somewhere in there, the student.

At James' January 17, IEP, there were seven adults, no attorneys. Marianne Walker represented Bay County Mental Health. Mike Dawly was the Henderson Joint USD Program Specialist. The role of the Program Specialist is to record the meeting, making sure the proper protocol and four part NCR forms are followed and filled out. As James' family lived in Mike's school district, he would be chairing this IEP meeting.

Martha and Hank Lucas are, of course, James' parents. They had attended IEP meetings since James' was in pre-school. James was their youngest child, by twelve years, of their six children, two of whom were local doctors. The Lucas's, from my perspective, were good, earnest people who were trying their best. Laura Rosso, James' therapist, and I represented the Valley Oak Day Treatment Program. Since it was after school, we all sat around the large table in the dining room.

Mike asked if we all knew each other, which we did, and then stated, "Let's begin with the education component." He swiveled towards me. "Lou, how's James been doing during the school day?"

I presented, as we all knew, how James had started out well in program. He had participated in summer biking and swimming activities, culinary arts, community based instruction and had been very successful. However, with the addition of other students, his behavior had decompensated. He had begun by acting-out at the GM Museum and this had been followed by his setting-up other students, verbally assaulting staff, committing property destruction, creating an environment that was a danger to himself and others that had culminated in a restraint. In general, James was having a difficult time being successful in program. Although he attended consistently, we were having a tough time figuring out what to do to meet his needs.

Marianne asked, "Doesn't he still care about the Monetary Reward? I thought, at one time, that he had nearly three hundred dollars in his account?"

I briefly explained the Monetary Reward System to Mike, who was not familiar with the program. "Basically, we pay our students to be successful. They can earn up to one hundred and fifty dollars per month be being on-task and working program successfully." I handed Mike a copy of the Monetary Reward Program.

Monetary Reward System

A bank account of $50.00 is established for each student.

Students earn additional money based upon their performance (See below.). Students may withdraw any money above $100.00 in their account.

Student's bank account will never fall below $50.00.

Student's Reward Day is on Friday for rewards earned in the preceding week.

Students may choose to withdraw earned rewards each week, or save in their account for later withdrawal.

Students may earn:

$3.00 for school day of 27 points or more

$4.00 for school day of 30 points

$3.00 for successful week (M-F) of all 30 point days.

$2.00 deduction for each point below 27

$7.00 deduction for each step drop

$20.00 deduction for each level drop.

Students will receive all money in their account when standards of the Matriculation Process are met.

Students who transition for any other reason are entitled to all funds above $50.00

I continued, "But James has stopped caring about whether or not he earns any money. He believes that he can get everything that he needs at home. There is just not any incentive for him to be on-task in our program."

At this point Laura spoke up. She always offered a positive insight when our meetings turned towards a negative perspective, like when she wanted to stop me from blaming the home for James' issues.

This was a serious IEP and Laura had attended professionally attired with her hair up in a braided bun, pastel flowing layered skirt that skimmed the floor when she stood. She wore a matching neck high three-quarter sleeve sweater with a gray vest. I thought of, Marianne the Librarian, in "The Music Man."

Laura intoned, "I must say that the Lucas' and I have been working to come up with some alternatives for redirecting James at home that could benefit his school program."

The Lucas' nodded in agreement.

"To everyone's credit, there is the realization that James needs to earn his rewards in the home and not just be given money because he wants it or threatens to act-out." She shared a look with both Martha and Hank to assure agreement and continued, "Hank and Martha have been extremely pleased by James' activities in the Valley Oak program and his willingness to attend school consistently. How to work through this current period of disengagement and decompensation is something that we, as the IEP team, can hopefully address today."

I felt the need to state the obvious, "Speaking for the staff, their concern is that when James escalates, he only has so much energy and he will stabilize. This may take a restraint and he will calm down for the moment. However, when he gets his wind, he will continue with the assault and property damage. It just goes on throughout the day, unless he finally runs down and falls asleep." I kept rushing on. I'm sure Laura would have liked to have cordially asked me to stick a sock in it. "And now, for the past two weeks, James has been spending most of his time sleeping in the upstairs bedroom."

Admitting at an IEP that a student slept in my school, in an upstairs bedroom, was dysfunctional, but we were out of ideas. What was not being spoken was that staff, maybe me, felt we needed a Time Out Room. The TO Room had always been available to students such as James in their other programs and he might be asking for that form of containment.

What the IEP Team came up with was a direction that would shape student behavior policy at Valley Oak School, not only for James, but for all other students. In fact, this decision would impact on the staff that were hired into the Valley Oak program because they would have to accept the therapeutic values of this direction. The decision was made to continue to find ways to address James escalations in a nonconfrontational manner. We would not construct a TO Room. Instead, as a primary intervention, the IEP team determined that we would offer James one of the rooms on the second or third floor. The room would be his own! No other student had one. He would be special. That room would be available on an as-needs basis and James could place things in his room that would assist him in calming down. Television, not a problem. Stereo, for sure. If James desired to take a walk or bicycle to stabilize his anxiety, that was O.K. too. Basically, it was going to be up to James to determine the success of his program.

We would consult, offer alternatives, provide expectations, but we would seek to avoid drawing a line in the sand and engage in conflict over these issues. This did not mean that he could pick up pumpkins or create any form of "danger to himself or others," but, within these parameters, Valley Oak School would be a vehicle to meet James' needs.

How did I feel about this? How about no respect! Was I Rodney Dangerfield? I mean, a student being able to lay down and take a nap during my riveting lecture on the cultural make-up of Australia? Maybe, if I was a good teacher I could watch "The Price is Right" with him? Or, say, excuse me, I would like to go for a bike ride, when I was computing two function, whole number, math word problems for independent living skills? Or, I would just back off when he might haughtily demand to speak with their therapist instead of gaining further mastery of home base on the keyboard? Had the Curse of The Babe descended upon me! Did I feel devalued? My position as educator diminished? Something whispered in my ear that I was not bringing my twenty odd years, Masters in Reading, and four credentials worth of educational insight into the equation. I mean, teachers teach. That's a given! That's what we do! That's what we're about!

But, with the IEP Team's blessing, the reality? "Take a nap. Have a nice day. James. The pillow ok?" Now, that's what I call a Time Out Room

How did I feel? I needed a good shrink…………..

Fortunately, I am Lou's good shrink. I watch his reaction at the IEP meeting as the team continues to move away from confronting James on his escalating issues. Lou's body language is one of discomfiture as I direct the dialogue towards the antecedent actions that James presents prior to his acting out. Marianne was invaluable in this discussion because she was able to frame James' events in other programs. She continued to extol Valley Oak, which soothed Lou's ego, and the promise Valley Oak held for James to progress in his own manner while residing in his home community. As Marianne elaborated, the respect that Valley Oak held for the individual student and their relationship needs was what Bay County and James needed.

After the meeting, as I was driving back to my sanctuary of a home, I thought of Lou and the changes he was going through with Valley Oak. Lou was a good guy. He was passionate about teaching. He had twenty years in the field and still carried the torch. I had watched him hold our students' attention while delving into the impact of facing up to a Roman Legion and then showing Kirk Douglas and Spartacus to vividly reinforce the concept, skills I certainly did not possess.

For all of his immediate presence and humor, (Lou hated the term sarcasm.) Lou was old school. He dressed casual, liked to wear cut offs and T-shirts. Drove a marked up Honda. Had an old Labrador as a buddy. He did lesson plans. He showed up on time. He worked hard and enjoyed it. How many times had I heard him singing while mopping the kitchen floor or vacuuming? I had teased Lou about being a rah-rah because he always had some Red Sox or Cal Bears hat, shirt, bandana about him. His curls no longer fell to his shoulder, his hair did have a hint of gray, which he stated he would never Grecian Formula out. I could respect that.

Good bod for a forty-two year old. Wonder why he had never married? Attachment disorder?

I shook my head, was I getting attracted to this guy? Maybe I should ask why I had never married. I know my family did. Enough! Good day. Positive meeting. Time to get home and get my comfies on, say hi to my two adorable Jack Russell's, Bonnie and Clyde. My garden awaited. I sighed, Valley Oak was meeting James' primary need, letting him know he was special, with a room of his own.

Chapter 2

SAM, A CAN OF PAINT

Valley Oak School
Psycho/educational Intake Summary

Laura Rosso: LCSW

Name <u>Sam Stowe</u>
DOB <u>6/12/81</u>

County of Residence <u>Bay County</u>
School District of Reference <u>BAY TREE USD</u>

Date: May 28

Physical Description: Sam is a pleasant looking, slightly obese eleven year old biracial (African American & Caucasian) male. His speech is monotone and eye contact is very poor. Sam is an identical twin and states that he enjoys playing Nintendo, watching television, and eating pizza. He prefers solitary activities and voices concern that his brother is his only playmate and that they often fight. His goal is to be wealthy and invent interactive video games.

Referring Criterion: Review of school history and interviews with Rebecca, Sam's mother, reveal that Sam has been extremely depressed over the death of his father five years ago as manifested by overeating, isolation, irritable mood, aggressive acting out, and school failure. His depression seemed to have increased following his mother's re-marriage and subsequent birth of a half-brother. Sam is referred to Valley Oak following a psychiatric hospitalization which was precipitated by an assault on his 3-year old half-brother and suicidal ideation. He has a history of poor peer relationships, inconsistent school attendance, noncompliance with school rules, verbal assault toward adult staff, particularly males, and a general inability to be successful during the school day.

Family History: Sam is an identical twin born to Rebecca and Rick Stowe. There were no reported complications with the caesarean delivery and developmental milestones appear to have been met within normal limits. When Sam was six, his father developed pancreatic cancer. As the family had minimal insurance, Rebecca elected to provide for Rick's health needs in the home. As Rick's health deteriorated, Sam became increasingly irritable and withdrawn. He began to have issues in school with peers and staff and, at age seven, was placed via IEP in a special education Resource Specialist Program. Three months before his father died, Rebecca gave birth to Sam's half-brother, Joe, whose father was known to Sam only as an "uncle." Sam currently resides with his mother, Rebecca, step-father, Mark; twin brother, Seth; and half-brother Joe in a small two bedroom apartment in the Bay County Housing Authority. Rebecca has stated that, while Mark is totally unwilling to be involved in family therapy, she will do whatever is necessary to help Sam through this difficult time.

Psychiatric History. Sam was evaluated by Dr. Jean Leer during his recent two week hospitalization prior to his referral to Bay County Day Treatment Program. Dr. Leer notes that Sam has never been medicated and that this was his first psychiatric hospitalization. He was discharged from the hospital medicated with Paxil to control his depression and anxiety.

DSM:

Axis I: 296.22 Major depressive disorder, single episode, moderate.

Axis II: V71.09 No diagnosis

Axis III: Moderately Obese

Axis IV: Problems with primary support group; death of father.

Axis V: GAF-40 (Current)

Recommendations: School Program needs to be aware of Sam's fragility over the recent events impacting his life. Working from Sam's individual strength areas around electronic games, it could prove positive to employ Nintendo as part of the reward system with many, other academic activities being computer directed. Activities with peers should not be an expectation for Sam at the outset of program.

Sam will continue with Dr. Leer for medication evaluation. Given Rebecca's willingness to participate with program and Sam's consistent attendance, I support Sam's admittance to Valley Oak School.

Signed_____Date_____
Laura Rosso LCSW

June 3 Which Is Which

I peered through the frayed lavender laced curtains of the Victorian's elongated rectangular front window as the family of our second perspective student lingered on the walkway. Bit of a scene coming down out there. The mother was shaking her fist in the face of one of the boys, both boys were hefty. Blond locks curled in disarray, almost touching their stooped shoulders. Their skin was the dusty colored smooth of a racially mixed pairing. Handsome young guys. The children of these relationships just seem to have an unfathomable hold on physical attractiveness, in spite of all that might swirl around them.

Both boys continued to rock from foot to foot in an agitated manner as if they were barefoot on a gravel path on a sweltering summer day. They wore similar, though not matching, faded gym clothes that, like their hair, were in need of a wash. Their faces were pinched, brows furrowed in irritation. I began to feel like a dentist observing his waiting room. From where I observed, either could have been Sam, the referred twin.

I recalled Sam's thick, worn cumulative folders, there were three. The mom was assertive and, according to the psychological evaluations, a recovering meth user. She had been clean for six years, how that played out on the lives of her children, one needed only to watch the local news. However, to her benefit, the mom had sought support for her twins from the get go. I could respect that.

I went over to the large, weathered, wooden, someday I would get around to sanding it, glass paneled front door which swung open easily as I extended my hand to the mom, "Hi, I'm Lou. You must be the Stowes."

The mother spoke right up. She looked to be in her early thirties. Hair cut short. "You got that right. Lou, I'm Rebecca Stowe, and these are my three sons, Seth, Sam, and Joe." Shaking my hand firmly, an in charge lady. From her smile I noted that she had a full tray of new dentures.

Rebecca reached behind her, "Now stop the shoving Joe."

At first glance I had missed Joe and I had caught no mention of him in the cumulative folders. He looked to be about five years younger than the twins with a sprinkle of freckles across his cheeks, as he peeked from around Rebecca's Levis and smiled up at me. His red hair stood out from Rebecca's and the twins.' Not only the color, but Joe's hair was neatly combed, in fact parted, and he was wearing a starched yellow collared shirt. Pretty spiffy for a five year old. Like, who was getting the attention in the family?

"Hi guys," I nodded.

Joe peered in around me and spotted the Nintendo System. He nudged by as Rebecca started to grab him, but I said it was fine if Joe went into the "Chill Room," which is what we had named our game room. He expertly snapped in a NHL cartridge and turned on the system as if this was his home. Rebecca started to say something but I just shrugged, it was no big deal.

Seth whined a moan, "Sam's the fat one. He's why we're here! Can I just go now? Puuleease, This is too embarrassing!"

Well, I knew which one was Sam. Nice to see hefty supporting heftier, no intervention from the mom. I have always, readily, admitted that the easiest thing to do was to make recommendations to an adult on how to raise their children. It's pretty presumptuous to do when you do not go home with them. Just ask grandparents. Being on my own with Rudy gave me all the right answers. Then too, I had been tight in a couple of relationships with women who had young children, but they had never worked out and the fact wasn't on the kids.

"Ohhhh, be quiiieeeet," Sam whined his nose puckering into a forlorn forehead. "Why does it always have to be meeee?"

I totally agreed with Sam. I was sure the Victorian had room for two.

Just then Laura opened her door and walked down the hallway. I did the introductions. Seth and Sam stopped their complaining and held a respectful silence, waiting to see what was next. Laura had that kind of presence.

I stopped reviewing my notes on the Stowe referral when I heard the voices outside the Victorian. I could hear Rebecca threatening to belt Sam, when they got home if he did not get his fat ass up the stairs. If I had ever said that to one of my brothers and my parents got wind of it, I would have gotten a belt. Fortunately, for me, Dad only gave it to my brothers. I breathed a sigh of relief as Sam made the decision to enter the Victorian. I organized my desk in preparation of doing an intake with Rebecca and Sam, then opened the door to meet the family.

After Lou had concluded the introductions, I said to Rebecca, "Come on into my office for our intake, which should take about thirty minutes."

I turned to Lou. "Lou, you want to show Seth and Sam around? They can wait in the Chill Room with Joe while we finish up."

Rebecca followed me into my office. I had the packet of intake papers awaiting her signature but she, with my door closing, let go a taut rambling stream of consciousness that set me back into my cushioned chair.

"Laura...I can call you Laura....it's ok..........right?" I nodded. "I just don't know what to do....where to turn...how to get through the day" Rebecca's facial expressions were so distraught "There are moments I just want to drain a bottle of Tylenol. Sometimes I stand on the walkway over the train tracks and just think about throwing myself down I have so destroyed my life Everything is in disarray My children's'......." She caught her breath and rushed on. "I know you have read about my past, the drug abuse, jail time. In and out of rehab, but I have been clean for six years! I totally have....really........"

Her eyes pleading acknowledgment.

"I have been trying to put it together and I find myself scratching to hold on. Seth and Sam hate me. They blame me for Rollie's death. Like I gave him cancer. The older they get the meaner they become to me, and they have never accepted Joe. Joe is a curse to them. A weight they have to bear because I was so desperate for someone to listen.

I sat there for the next twenty minutes holding Rebecca's anguish. My training had taught me to not interrupt at these moments. Marianne had stated, from her point of view, Rebecca was the key individual to stabilize in order for Sam and, ultimately the family, to make progress. Rebecca and her family had been receiving county mental health services for the past eight years and it was time for another alternative, which meant Valley Oak. I could hear from Rebecca's desperate plea that echoed Marianne's concern, that past interventions had not been successful in providing for a positive direction for her family. Whether the issue was substance abuse, Asperger's Disorder, ADHD, inutero drug issues, PDD, an Anxiety Disorder, any or all of these, Rebecca just wanted a clue to regain a bit of sanity for herself and her family. Rebecca's fern d pain had overwhelmed both she and her family. I heard Rebecca out then let her take the paperwork home. More than enough for one day.

September 4 A Time Out Room?

Tuesday, a good day. I bounded up the steps of the Victorian after my early morning gym workout. Turned on the lights. Got the computers humming. Started the coffee. Tuesday was a good day for two reasons. One, I was not driving a van into program. Two, there was no Laura on site to scrutinize my every move. Well, Laura may have stopped me from building a Time-Out Room, but I still had some weapons at my disposal. She could contain, but she could not dominate!! No one dominates The Dude. For sure too much "Big Lebowski." One of the local university book stores had an entire basement section dedicated to his shirts. Never could drink White Russians. Bowling was cool. I had never divulged to Laura that I carried a one eighty-seven league average when I was eleven. I had agreed to extend Laura's on site time to three days per week, which left just two for my total control with my own methods.

One of my best tried and true actions was a "time-out" or "time-away," which is a classic manner of stabilizing student escalations in the behavioristic day treatment industry. This was time tested, almost ritualistic. The manner in which this technique is employed needs to be consistent amongst staff in order for the students to internalize the expectations and consequences. For instance, I have been in programs where there was no such thing as an accident. Zip. Nada. You did not accidentally bump into Sharon. You did not accidentally drop your pencil. You did not accidentally knock over Jeff's drink. You were held accountable for everything you did. Tough luck if it was an accident. Take a time-out. Bummer on you. Wanna argue? How about a looooong timeout?

I knew what Laura hated about time-outs, was that they eliminated dialogue through a strict, hardened concrete doctrine. Laura held The Evil Male Empire responsible for the imposing of these nondialogue interventions. Her perspective was that "guys" (Like me!) have such a limited vocabulary that our intervention technique was based on limited phrases such as, "do as I say" and, "do I have to repeat myself, " or "do I need to get the belt" kinds of righteous male dogma.

I just have to wonder what Laura's upbringing was like? I mean, if the relationship model was so hot, how'd it work in her home with five younger brothers? Who waved the magic wand or was that a leather belt? There is not another program in our state that was offering "The Relationship Model" with the sexualized, violent, aggressive population that Valley Oak was accepting? (I had reviewed several programs.) Were we so right that everyone else was wrong? Any books to read up on Relationship Success? For now, for me, what worked from the get go was directing a student to a time-out. A time out was good stuff. The students got the message.

Now, for the time out to start, staff might state to a student to take a time-out for provoking peers. The student must, immediately, disengage from whatever they are doing and go to a space that is not involved with any activity, preferably a corner wall in the room. If the student does this in the correct manner, which means to the wall. No talking. Feet together. Shoulders military erect. Staring straight into the joint. The time-out is for a short duration, approximately two minutes. Should the student make a poor decision such as turning around, talking to peers, arguing with staff, just grimacing-twitching-breathing hard, the time automatically extends to six minutes and the student does not earn two points on their behavioral chart. Clear enough. When either of these time-out methods is completed, the student must appropriately state to staff what their time-out was due to: For instance, I was setting up peers. I dropped a pencil. I was not being on-task. I was swearing. I was blowing spit bubbles. Basically, making them state what they would do differently the next time.

I was furious, frustrated and close to just losing my therapeutic perspective. Maybe the time was right for me to get my dad's belt out? (Lou could relate to that.) I sat there, looking at Lou and asking him, in as understated tone as possible, "What was occurring Lou, was he breathing too hard?" There were moments when I just wanted to strangle this jerk. It was like getting one of my brothers to make a better decision when they were enmeshed in denial.

I looked at her. I knew she was really pissed off. The sign was Laura's fiddling with the necklace around her neck.

"What's the big deal Laura? There were no hands placed on him. He came back and did his work, still earned a positive day."

Damn her, if she ever had to do something besides ask them how they were feeling? Did they have fun over the weekend. What game would they like to play? She'd have a clue as to why students needed some clear boundaries.

43

I took a breath. Lou and I were sitting in my office following a long day with Sam being off-task, behaviorally oppositional, and being directed to take a time-out due to four different occurrences, the longest one being for almost an hour!!

"Lou, there needs to be another way of working with our students other than having them on a time out for over an hour a day. Our program is about the Relationship Model." I wanted to add, you moronic-testosterone-filled control- freak- imbecile!

I let some measured time pass. I was looking to model Laura's interaction strategies. Give her some of her own stuff. She was coming at me, and the staff, again and again about our intervention. Did they work or did they not? Did everyone else use them? Were we out of bounds? What was I missing? OK Laura, where are your brilliant interventions? What would you have done? I mean, just what the hell do you want from Valley Oak? Were we some Holy Relationship Grail?

The phone rang and Laura picked it up. She seldom did that. Obviously, our conversation was ended. I got up and firmly closed her office door on the way out. (I did not slam it!) Maybe I should head over to the gym and ease my pain. I mean, okokok, I get her point. A time-out is devaluing. Embarrassingly difficult. How difficult? Well, let's see. Here's an example of what might be going on in a student's head when the teacher says, "Ok, you're on a time-out for side-talking."

The student could be thinking some like, I didn't do shit you fucking rule freak!! I know I can't say it. Just suck it up. Can't even look at that fuckhead Lou. I just need to begin walking towards a corner of the room without looking at anything. So I'm on a time out for side talking. Big f'ing deal. Shit. Gotta ignore Paul, that kiss ass puke flipping me off. Then there's Tyler, as I squeeze by his desk, smirking cross eyed, picking a bugger. If he flicks it at me I'll kick his fucking ass. OK the wall. I'm staring at the god damn corner of the wall from one foot away with my feet together and shoulders back. How old am I? How many year have I been doing this? C'mon, puker up Lou. Get ready to kiss my ass. Wonder if Lou's family had a Nazi background. Shit. There's the spot where Alex wiped the snot from his nose yesterday. OK. Relax. Get focused. Like my therapist said, get a time expectation. This was not forever. Begin counting to one hundred and twenty. Maybe I should count to two hundred and forty by twos. It would be a change. Even when I get there, that pussy Lou might forget to call on me. Remember the last time. How long was that? Did it bother Lou? Like, fuck no. It was like tough shit. What's that?? What the fuck you saying to me Conrad? There's his heavy breathing, like he's giving someone a blow job. His breath smells like fresh shit. I'll kick that fat fuck's ass when we get back to residence. What?? You've got to be shittin' me?? What did I do? God damn it! What the fuck you saying to me? My head turned! Eat shit and die Lou! My head turned your ass! Now, a long time-out! God Damn it. Gotta chill. Get cool. There went two points! Fuckingsonofabitch! Now Lou has me on a long time out with nothin' coming down on Conrad. A long timeout. Six fucking minutes of looking at Alex's snot and Conrad's throat snorting blow job. Listening to Little Lou Dickless talk about fractions. I am pissed off! Why does this crap happen to me? Bitches. Who the fuck are they to put me into a corner for a long time-out!? I'll clean their fucking ass clocks! Dickweeds. Mother fucking Lou. I am pissed off. Oh yeah, better pissed off than on. How many mother sucking jokes you gotta make Lou? Isn't life just one funny fucking rip? Why does this crap happen to me……………..

Ok, I do understand a kid's point of view. Been there. Heard that. I had never done time in the Time Out Room or been restrained. But do you think this is easy on staff? Hell no. Now, take a restraint from the teacher's point of view. For the teacher it's the same everyday vigilance. He has a class of dysfunctional, school hating, teacher baiting, anti-social, non- compliant, happy go lucky students. Here's what's in the teacher's head. This has happened to me too many times.

I can see Jim talking out for the second time. Whenever I want to give them some room and not just come down behaviorally, they push it to the next level. Just can't stop themselves. Happens every damn time!

I address the student, "Jim, take a time-out for side talking."

Jim's getting up and going straight to it. Thank you Lord, no big blow, maybe make it to lunch break. He'll be able to blow off some steam outside. Jim's in the corner straight up. I put down the walkie talkie and get back to the class. I turn back to the math problem.

"Let's look at problem number three on the board."

Do I have enough staff available for a possible restraint? Jim's head just turned, just upping the ante. "That's a long time-out." The punk sociopath, now I have him up there for six minutes. "Mark, come up to the board and work the fraction problem for the class." Hopefully I can avoid a restraint. Did I hear Conrad say something to him?

I have participated in time-outs that have reached over an hour in duration. I know what goes through a staff's control demanding mind that you can not share with the acting-out student. Nobody likes time-outs or restraints, but they sure allow staff to vent their negative frustration, flex some muscle. The issue for me was that these long time-outs could turn a classroom into a dysfunctional disaster. Holding a teacher-directed board lesson on addition of improper fractions becomes a layered ordeal. What Laura has to accept is that passive-oppositional-escalating students need to be contained in a manner that allows the classroom to continue. An inappropriate student's consequences had to take place outside of the academic classroom. Academics come first!

How does the teacher ensure the learning environment with an emotionally disturbed behaviorally disordered student population? How was this done? Let's face it, 0-65, like, Bingo! All escalating activity is terminated in a prone restraint, quiet-room stabilization, or 911 call for a handcuffed free do not pass Go or collect two hundred dollars ride to placement at Juvenile Hall. This was a fact that everyone knew, understood, and accepted. Staff knew the drill. Students expected the negative consequences. Just part of program. The decision was up to the student as to how far the escalation would go. IT was crowd control by Prone Restraint. For the teacher, the almighty academic lesson came first. Relationship model, yeah, right. Send me a postcard. Bottom line, time-outs and restraints are needed.

My personal favorite phrase in providing for a safe classroom was the preparatory statement with proper intonation, "Can we assist you in being safe?" had all the empathic warmth of a concrete floor.

The time was 10:59 A.M. Sam was now beginning the twenty-seventh minute of his time-out. I sat on the stool in the kitchen, watching Sam's actions from a distance but close enough that he felt my presence. I could watch the pendulum on the living room clock stroke out the seconds. All the other students, except for James, were off-site on activities. Laura was nowhere near. Thank you God.

"Can I stop noooooowwwwww?" Sam howled like a coyote at the moon.

I wish we could. From across the town center chapel bells on the university campus struck eleven times. This was the first time that I could recall hearing them since we started to have more students. When I was sprucing the Victorian up I could mark the hour through their toned timeliness. Lunch would be coming up. Sam couldn't hold out that much longer.

"You'rrre so meeeaaannnn!! You and my mutheeerrrr! Sheeeee ooooowes me moneeeeeeeey!" Sam's face screeched up in a contorted scowl as mucus sucked up from his throat oozed spittle down to a glossy puddle on the floor by Sam's feet. James continued pedaling his stationery bicycle on the front porch, ignoring the escalating behavior.

Throughout my teaching experience with programs employing time-outs and restraints, I have observed this form of detached response of students to a peer's acting-out. On numerous occasions a unique separateness would occur. The detachment has always boggled me how a student might be going on in a huge verbal fashion or earning a prone restraint and the rest of program will just continue on with their work, disconnect from the chaos. Although, to this date, no student pronations had occurred, I felt the inevitability.

"Team control! Three staff charge at the student. "Keep him standing! Standing restraint!"

"Mother fuckers!! Let me go you fucking pieces of shit!"

Arms, legs, hands, fingers, shoes in a tangled gumbo.

"Clear the desks!" A mad scramble as other students and staff move the desks in the immediate area for safety.

"Watch his legs!" Shoes kick off.

"He still has a pencil in his left hand!"

"Get your knees locked with mine!"

"To the wall!"

"Can't hold it! He's spitting!" Saliva goes into your face.......

"You pussies! Takes three of you!"

"Prone restraint!" Staff positions, grasping shoulders, leaning the torso forward.

"Got the shoulders."

"Let him down forward!"

"Watch the teeth!"

"Knees are down."

"I've got the legs.

In a tumultuous matter of seconds three heaving sweating adult males comprising six hundred plus pounds of straining flesh clamber onto a fourteen-year old writhing adolescent pronating him to the linoleum, like a pinned insect for display.

Then the screaming verbal assault becomes personal and begins with,

"Feel good fuck heads? Feels good to me! Who wants me first? First is always best! Rub it in pecker head. Can't wait to call CPS! My attorney will fry your asses. You motherfucking gay pricks!!

About this time you are able to get your adrenaline rushed breath back and check in with the restraint team. Make sure everyone is secure, employing correct technique. No pressure on the joints, ability for the student to breathe, no one injured. You take in that the rest of the class has detached from the restraint and is taking space until the situation is stabilized. Support staff is supervising. The students' message to the restrained peer is clear. It's like, this is on you. Dude, this is your problem, not mine. You brought the restraint down you dumb sucker. Excuse me, but I have academic assignments to take care of. I plan on earning break time. No time-out room for me. I know what's coming down on you and, no thank you, I'll pass this time. Catch you on the rebound, got some math to do. It sucks to be you. It sucks to be me watching you. Too close to home.

Sam returned to his standing time-out, "Do you enjoy torrrrrrturiiiing little children? Are you diabolicalllll?"

Good question I thought. This was Sam's third week in program. During the second week Jake and I had placed "hands on" Sam to redirect him to his time-out. (Laura was off-site.) Sam did not like to be touched and willingly accepted his time-out space. His M.O. now was to become agitated and verbally assaultive to staff throughout the time-out period.

Jake walked by and mouthed, "Quiet room?"

"Don't we wish," I smiled back.

Was Lou diabolical? Did he enjoy torturing children, there were moments I wondered. He certainly believed in his techniques. They were industrial standard comfortable. Tried and true. Familiar. Time-outs were standard "proven" methods of stabilizing escalating youth in both educational and mental health programs. In a Day Treatment Program, their implementation was never questioned,. just documented. Was the Spanish Inquisition diabolical? Not to those who were in charge. Not to those who were supervising the consequences for individuals making poor decisions.

I had to, in some manner, get Lou's buy-in regarding other methods of implementing responses for intervention. He, and therefore the staff, was so enmeshed in traditional culturally-accepted techniques of intervention to non-compliance. I was relieved that water boarding was not part of the practice. I knew I had to start with Lou to get to the staff.

This had been an on-going issue. Every program I had previously worked in had a Time-Out Room. Hell, even therapists advocated for them! Time-Out Room. Such an euphemism for what amounted to a cell. These rooms were square, contained a single door with a minute window for staff to observe, and allowed a student to act-out their frustrations in a "safe manner." The door was non-locking and staff was required to hold the door shut. Sometimes it would take two or three staff to hold the door closed against the onslaught of some of the more determined (terrified?) adolescent. But worse than any physical challenge, were the verbal attacks that were hurled through the door.

"I'm taking my clothes off!"

"Wanna see my cock?"

"I'm going to pee all over the door!"

"You can suck my dong!"

"You eat shit Lou!"

"Jack-off on the asphalt Lou!"

"Take scissors and cut out your guts Lou!"

"Fuck yourself with a hose and blow it out of your weenie!"

All students quickly learned to talk the talk. How to push staff's buttons, their parent surrogates. The ability to make these comments endearingly personal was always a joy. The language and expressions were quickly absorbed by new referrals and passed on in the living language tradition of incarcerated institutions. Staff had to learn to disengage themselves and not take these words personally. This fact was a necessary requirement of working with this population and a Time-Out Room.

Sam sniveled, "I'm ready to starrrrt my time-oouutt!"

"You understand how to show me you're ready Sam," I intoned, even though I knew I should not have broken the silence.

"I am readyyyyyyyyy!" Sam moaned, smearing snot from his nose in lines on the fresh paint. Looked like he was getting ready for another game of tic-tac-snot. He must have been doing this for years. I wondered if he was familiar with Chinese Checkers?

Well, this was turning into a record breaking marathon. I looked over at Jake in the kitchen, he signaled fifteen minutes. James was continuing to peddle his exercise bike on the front porch. I checked the camcorder to make sure the tape had not run out. I knew Marianne and Laura would be interested in reviewing Sam's activity during the looooooong time out. They would wonder about my part in the consequence as well.

September 9 Wishes

As I waited for Sam to enter my office, I thought of my five younger brothers and how I had assisted my parents in raising them. My brothers were loud, aggressive, entitled, and brutally direct in their communication and, of course, I loved them to death! One could not have had a thin skin and survived in our household! Sam was just the opposite. He was closed, withholding, and cynically devaluing when he did communicate. His issues were clouded in a depression that was impenetrable.

"Hi Sam," I called catching a shadowy movement in the ajar doorway. "Come on in and have a seat."

Sam failed to make his appearance. Reluctantly, I rose from my squeaking swivel chair to assist him. I formally opened the door and ushered Sam to his seat, into which he sullenly slouched. I assumed my therapeutic demeanor as I slid my chair out from behind my desk to begin our session. Early on I had accepted that there would be no humor or lightening of the mood with Sam, his armor was this brooding silence, we were now into our sixth meeting.

"How's it going?" I began.

Sam ignored me. His body twisted stiff away from me, towards the large, open window that I had first heard him from, which was ushering in a slight crisp fall breeze.

"Did you bring the paper back?

As a form of initiating communication, I had given Sam an assignment the previous week. An assignment was not my usual tactic, but after five meetings of sitting across from one another, I was getting desperate. Sam would not produce any drawings. Refused to color. Hated Uno. Forget Yahtzee not to mention any of my vast array of therapeutic games. The sand tray was for babies. Lou had suggested paint ball guns at twenty feet. To my pleasure, without looking at me, Sam begrudgingly reached into his shirt pocket and brought out a crumbled ball of paper. He held it out to me.

"Thank you Sam. I am pleased you remembered."

"Whatever," he inaudibly muttered looking to the ceiling.

I reached over and regally gathered the page in, as if some treasure could fall out, I took my time unwrapping the gnarled wad. Sam continued his indifference. As I had suspected, the paper was blank.

I smiled to myself, "Sam, I want you to know that I appreciate your bringing back this paper to our meeting." I paused. "I also want you to know that I gave you a tough assignment, that assignment being a blank page of paper to write your thoughts on."

Sam invisibly shrugged.

I reached over and took my note pad. "This time I will give you a more specific assignment. I call it The Three Famous Wishes." I took my legal pad and wrote:

1. I wish I could _____
2. I wish I could be a _____
3. I wish Valley Oak would_____

I showed the page to Sam. "What do you think of these questions Sam?"
Sam actually read them. "Alriiiiight, can I goooo now?"

I removed the sheet from the pad and folded it over. Sam took it from me and wedged it into his shirt pocket. "Unless you have any further questions for me, I will see you next week."

"Well." It was like he was having a cerebral wrestling match between commit and noncommittal. "Well. why are these questions so famous?"

""Good question, Sam. Tell you what, when you get them back to me, I will let you know"

Sam struggled up from his chair and slowly made his way toward the door. At the door he paused and asked, "Would you like it open or closed?"

"Open would be fine Sam. Thanks for asking."

I had never, ever, done anything like The Three Wishes.

I had just made them up on the spot. I looked forward to seeing what Sam would do with them. I hoped that his door would continue to open.

September 28   Monopoly

"The concern Sam," I articulated, "is how to be involved in positive peer interaction while participating in community based instruction. You may find this difficult to accept, but I will not always be at your side to give you direction."

That set him off, "I don't want to walk with youuuuuu. You walk toooo fast," he slurred as he slowly revolved in a foot dragging, stumbling circle.

I turned to James, who stood and grinned like a huge jack o' lantern overhearing the conversation. James was really pleased with himself. He was approaching three hundred pounds in weight! I hoped his bulk would continue to disappear as summer was coming to an end. His bicycling expedition now had him entering the realm of the Cincinnati Reds and Louisville Sluggers, "James, do you think you could slow down for Sam?"

"Sure Lou," James smiled. "That wouldn't be a problem."

Sam agonized, Why do we have to walk togetheerrrr? This is soooo embarrassing." A late summer thundershower had just passed through leaving a trail of steaming sidewalks.

I looked back at Sam. This was not personal. He was continuing to have difficulty associating with humanity. Then too, if I had to witness my father slow die a cancerous death over two years in my home while my mother divorced him and gave birth to a child of a man who had quickly left town, I might feel a bit different. I might not want to be around people much either.

I chose one of Laura's interventions. I put the decision back on Sam. "It's up to you, Sam. You can continue with us or return to The Victorian and work on your history assignment with Jake."

As with James, the Valley Oak Day Treatment Program had become more and more about not finding lines to draw in front of the students. Fewer to almost zero time outs. Hope you're happy Laura. Offering our students other behavioral alternatives, with their own decision-making, was what we were working towards. Laura Rosso would say that this was a Relationship Model as opposed to a Behavior Model. I believed that Marianne and Laura had reached an agreement that, although I was from Education, I was trainable material. They had gotten me to agree to not construct a Time-Out Room in the Victorian. Their main point played with the words of one of my favorite baseball movies, "Field of Dreams," by saying, "Lou, if you build it, they will come." So we didn't build it. Laura seemed continually present to absorb my male maniacal education directed control needs and massage my concerns about our program's lack of negative consequences for inappropriate student behavior and lessening of academic expectations. Maybe we should just get a spa and a massage therapist.

For instance there was the time I had said:

"Look Laura, Ruby told Sam that he could kiss my white ass."

"Really? Why would she say that?

It was now late afternoon. Students were gone and transportation was taken care of. Laura and I were debriefing the events of the day.

"Like, all I did was to ask her to clean up and put away her lunch dishes because it was time to move into our next activity." I sat there. I was getting use to this. I knew what Laura was doing to me. She was getting me to look back at the antecedent actions that precipitated the oppositional behavior. Like it was on me for what came down. I reached desperately for more ammunition.

"Actually, she told me she wasn't my house nigger like Oriole Sam was. If Sam wanted to be the good Negro, he should start by kissing my white ass!"

Laura paused, then offered, "Ruby certainly internalizes a great deal of anger. How did you respond?"

I thought a moment. Actually, I thought I had done pretty well saying, "Well, I asked Ruby if she could have chosen other words, like, give me five more minutes Lou and I'll be ready. Or she could've let me know she needed more time."

"I'm impressed Lou, that certainly was a holding response. You should congratulate yourself," Laura beamed, knowing how hard this was for me. "Now, tell me what you were thinking."

Thinking? Oh-no! Been down that road before. She was starting to shrinkasize me again. I hate this dialogue based relationship process. Process-process-process- process.........! What I was thinking I did not want to own for. Ruby and her entitled attitude could just take a flying leap! Talk crap after gorging lunch into her two hundred and fifty pound cavern for over an hour! Were we an all you can devour food kitchen or a school? Just who the hell did she think she was?

"Lou, you don't have to tell me your thoughts."

Did I miss something? Who said I was?

"I can read them in your body language. I'm sure Ruby could too." Laura stood up and picked up a mirror. "Take a look at your face Lou. What message do you think you were giving Ruby?" Whether the emotion was anger or humor, you could see Lou coming a mile away. When joking or teasing, his lower lip would tremble. Someday I might let him know this. I would bet he was a horrible card player!

Lou, think about this. Was there a restraint? Was anyone injured? Was this a hill worth dying on?

The issue was, did I care?

Laura and Marianne were right, they were always right. I was getting tired of their always being right. I didn't fully understand what was going on or why I always felt stupid. Maybe, just dumb. Just wrong for expressing my frustration, but if "taking a pause to refresh" kept me from having to be involved in restraints and long time-outs. They had my undivided attention.

Marianne and Laura would go on and talk at me about how our students needed to make good decisions at stoplights without our being there to assist them. They had to go on the green, stop on the red, and make good decisions on the yellow. They needed to make decisions without fear. They needed to do it for themselves. The best way to develop these skills in the student was for the teacher to allow them to make, and then own for, their decisions, and, no, you could not restrain them just because you were really ticked off.

Random heavy drops splattered around and down as we awaited Sam's dawdling indecision. I knew that he would continue to earn all of his points and would not be negatively consequenced for his lack of success in participating in the community based instruction. He would just need to return to The Victorian for academic, maybe some therapeutic, intervention. His decision. Right Laura?

Well, what would I do if Sam chose to just walk off or go on a sit down strike? How did we provide for the safety of students and staff when off-site. Maybe we just weren't a safe program? Maybe we were always vulnerable. We all carried walkies or cell phones with us. I could bring in more staff to make sure that Sam would be safe. It's not like we didn't talk about our vulnerability. At the end of the day we would debrief and review how we came to determine that Sam or James or any of our students could be successful off-site.....with Laura always giving her concluding two cents. What was coming at me was that figuring this out was more than difficult because a core theme to our program was that the students did not know how to accept success. They were placed with us because they had a long history of not making good decisions. If there was one thing our students knew, it was how to fail, that was their comfort zone. It was like me trying to do anything in art, I just didn't go there, didn't even want to try.

For me, I've suffered a life of devaluing failure in the realm of creative art. That's how our students felt about success. It was up to us to continually provide them with positive situations. Again and again and again, even when they had not earned them in the traditional sense. Our students did not understand how to enjoy success. They knew how to create defeat and relish decline. They had perfected the art of inadequacy on a grand scale. Valley Oak was about learning to accept and enjoy achievement and accomplishment. Don't ask me about my art thing.

Somehow, Sam discovered that he had the ability to keep up with the rapid pace that James and I set as we shadily traveled our route over the root split sidewalk. Large droplets caught by our overhead canopy continued to splatter down on us as we approached the railroad crossing. Valley Oak was located just two blocks and a series of railroad tracks from the town center. The railroad tracks were part of a major line that carried Amtrak along with four diesel switch engine trains of a hundred cars or more as they headed into or returned from the westerly mountain passes. It was late summer with fall just around the corner. There was a university football game this Saturday that annually marked the beginning of the fall school term.

A clanging bell and red lights marked the approach of a train as the guard rail came down in front of us. "How many cars do you think, James?' This was a ritual, trying to see who came closest to guessing the number on the passing train. Since we were on a bend in the tracks, there was no way of seeing to the end of the train, unless it was very short.

James pondered, tapping his forehead with one beefy finger. "Fifty-seven, that's my lucky number for today. Fifty-seven Lou."

It was James' lucky number today because I was showing the Sixth Inning of Ken Burns' documentary on baseball. This inning featured Joe DiMaggio and his hitting streak. The Streak stopped at fifty-six. In the documentary, Joe is quoted as stating his fifty-seventh hit would have been worth ten thousand dollars because "The Heinz People" were following him. James bonded with Joe because his parents had always told him that he was a "Heinz 57 Kid" due to the array of ethnicities his ancestors had passed down to him. He liked the tie in with Joltin' Joe. (Does everyone know that Joe then hit safely in the next twenty-seven games!)

In the Valley Oak curriculum, I taught baseball as a subject. Not with the bat and glove, though that would have been a kick. Someday we might field a team. I used baseball to address the basic academics from a different tact and one that I thoroughly enjoyed. We had cut up large construction paper replicas of the fifty states and pinned a map of the United States on the ceiling. From the ceiling map colorful banners with mascots hung of all twenty-eight major league teams that we had made from the Banner Mania computer program. We studied the history and statistics of the game in a manner that gave the students something to talk about other than the dysfunctional histories they were products of and enmeshed in.

I enlarged the major league standings and asked questions of the students that would have them working with percentages. Determining states and capitals. (James was now peddling along the Ohio River between Ohio and Kentucky.) spelling, math, and just good conversation. Like, what about #42'? I did the same with major league leader statistics from home runs to leading pitchers. We watched video presents such as the Ken Burns production or rented others that might have Earl Weaver talking about managing strategy. We attended major league games twice a month. Often we listened to the radio, keeping a box score or caught some out of town day games on television. (No, Laura, I am not enmeshed in meeting my personal needs!)

I had long believed that if a teacher enjoyed what they were teaching they did a better job of it. If the teacher liked what they were doing, chances were, the students could pick up on the same enthusiasm. If we taught basic academics in the traditional manner, we would have gotten the students' traditional basic negative response. Our students could as easily been taught plumbing or sewing as much as baseball. I just wasn't so hot at the other two.

The train was beginning to pass by. "Sam, James says fifty-seven. What do you think?"

"Do I haaaavvvee to?"

"As always, it's your choice."

"Oh, alllllrigght. If I have to," Sam enjoyed games. Although Sam would never admit to having fun, we knew a highlight of his day was the red light blinking and guessing the number of train cars. He looked down the track to see if he could see the end of the train. It was still coming around the bend, but Sam always tried to play the angles. "Forty-three," he finally emitted.

"What's your guess Lou?" James asked.

I held an imaginary crystal ball in front of me and went into a trance.

"Swami says seventy-six." I swallowed my competitive urge, knowing my guess was far too many for this time of day with the traffic patterns.

We stood there counting as the cars slowly rumble-clanked by. We could easily read the names such as Northern Pacific, Santa Fe, Rock Island, B & O, Cotton States, Southern Pacific. James and I had talked about making a chart and graphing the number of a specific railroad cars that came over our tracks to see which one or type might have the largest representation.

"I the cars continued to slowly clatter by I asked, "Who can name the four train companies in Monopoly?"

"That's easy," answered James. "B & O, Reading, Pennsylvania, and ………."

James contorted his brow and pondered.

"James, it's the Short Line," chimed in Sam.

"That's right guys. Now let's see who gets curtain number three."

The last car passed. "There were forty-seven Lou." James stated.

"What did you count Sam?"

"Forty-seven."

"Well, guess Sam won that one Lou."

"We'll get him next time James."

We walked across the tracks. James went philosophical, "That's right, Lou. Can't win them all. Even baseball is about losing. How to deal with loss. Isn't that right, Lou?

Ken Burns couldn't have said it better. Sam had no problem keeping up with us.

October 23, 2000   A Deal

Here I sat in my second floor newly remodeled bedroom office, with windows open, soaking in a brilliant New England fall day. The trees surrounding the Victorian were shrouded in rainbow hued leaves, awaiting the first coming of a Fall gust to billow a carpet to the ground. I had left the safe haven of Bay County Mental Health to enter the ambiguous field of private practice and the projected services of Valley Oak. Not one of my friends or family had supported my vocational change, except for Marianne. Where was I working? Who was I working for? Lou who? Well, guess what nay sayers, at the moment, I now have eleven students with Valley Oak and a case load of twelve private clients. I, smugly, feel pretty darn proud of myself! Maybe I should raise my private client rates? Maybe I should demand a raise from Lou?

The door squeaked open, "Hi Laura."

"Hey there Sam. Right on time."

"When haven't I been?"

I laughed, "You are correctomundo. I could not tell you the last time."

So changed in attitude. Sam's confidence had bit by bit been building. Lou, who was with Sam every day, even noticed the gradual transformation. I, who met with Sam once a week, was consistently astounded.

Sam was grinning. "Hey Laura."

I sat down on the couch opposite Sam. He had chosen the leather chair. I watched as he confidently pushed back the lever to recline.

"Yes, Sam."

"Remember The Three Wishes you had me answer?"

Did I ever. Sam's answers had been the key to his emergence. They had allowed Sam to open his personal door of emotions to me. Sam had written articulately, in complete sentences:

1. I wish I could have known my father when he was well.
2. I wish I could be a doctor so that I could cure all the diseases.
3. I wish Valley Oak would keep helping me make friends.

"I sure do remember Sam. That was a real break through for the two of us."

Sam was grinning. I knew he had something up his sleeve. He gushed, "Laura, how about you answering the same three questions?"

I considered the options. Sam's question was fairly invasive and he was testing the limit I would go with him in being open. I thought of Lou's phrasing, of how we were all equal but just not the same. Sam's vote counted as much as mine, but I was not an eleven year old twin male. How to negotiate and remain believable to my young client as he stretched his wings.

"OK Sam, here's the deal." I was scrambling, but the conclusion felt right. "When you graduate from Valley Oak and return to public school full time, I will write you my three answers."

Sam rocked in the recliner, contemplating my response. "You promise?"

"Cross my heart." I answered laughing. "Now, Sam, can we talk about you for a bit?

"As long as you cross your heart with your right hand Laura!"

"Got me!" As I used my right hand, An old habit I had used forever on my brothers. "Now, do you want to begin where we left off last session?" That had been a difficult closure.

"Not a problem," he answered.

I waited. There was no squirming, just perplexed thought.

"Could you help me start, Laura?"

"Sure Sam. As I recall, it was a dark and stormy night, the ship was sinking, and you turned to me and asked, tell me a story Laura. And so I began, it was a dark and stormy night, the ship was sinking…

"Laaaaaurrrra!" Sam bellowed laughing. "That's not true."

I laughed with him. Help me lord, I was turning into one liner Lou. "How about, then, something to do with your brothers?"

"That's right. Now I remember." Sam began, "Like I was saying, I wish I could have been Joe."

I nodded affirmation for Sam to continue………………

December 12 Lunch Bunch

Where to this Monday? Downtown beckoned with pesto pizza at Woody's. Gyro sandwiches from Marcie's Deli. Pot stickers and Kung Pao Chicken at The Wall. The list seemed endless. One of the benefits of dwelling in a fast food frenzied eating-out university town. Healthy? Maybe not? Now, for some tough choices.

In order to earn Lunch Bunch a student had to have a Successful Week. I had, previously, called this a Perfect Week but Sam had pointed out that nobody was perfect. How could there be a Perfect Week? I agreed so we changed the name to Successful Week. A student still needed to earn ninety-five per cent of their points throughout the previous week, which included returning their home communication book signed by an adult and doing their weekly homework assignments. However, they no longer had to be "Perfect." I had given up that personal quest many moons ago.

Four of Valley Oak's students had earned Lunch Bunch this week. Our program had grown to a total of twelve students. It was Sam's ninth consecutive week with the Lunch Bunch group. He had made a turn and was doing well throughout program. I noted how he joined in the walk with the other students, like no big thing with keeping up. He still did not participate in the general conversation and yet, he did not miss a beat.

Downtown was a beach boardwalk of bright activity sun lit and crisp this December day. The students and townspeople walked briskly along decorated sidewalks colored in their Christmas holiday attire. There had been a light snowfall over the weekend, but two days of sun had quickly melted the white stuff. Any moment I expected to hear Bing break out in "Silver Bells." The university was over two hundred years old and many of the elms, oaks, and ash trees canopying the business district were, at least, half that age. In the night their bare branches glowed with interlaced lights braceleted to sparkle with the stars.

Our group dawdled along, peering into the variety of shops and stopping to look over the vendored tables of belts, jewelry, pottery, and other entrepenueared organically homespun made gift items for the holidays. While wandering through this carnival of activity, we discussed where we should have lunch. Usually the students would vote and, sometimes, just to introduce a new type of food such as Thai, with its tasty satay peanut sauce, we would dictate where lunch would be held. Anyone for Sushi?

Valley Oak's favorite place was Red's Barbecue. Red's was so popular that we had made a rule that we could only go there every other week. Otherwise, our Lunch Bunch group would not have tried any other cuisine. We had often discussed whether the barbecue was called Red's due to the color of the owner's hair or the fire that was in his sauce. I even thought that Red might bleed Indiana Red, he was a Hoosier fan, then too, nobody was perfect.

We pushed open the heavy glass encased stainless steel edged doors to Red's Barbecue. The familiar aroma immediately warmed us as we walked, single file, along the narrow tile and mirrored corridor, lined with many of the framed notables that had graced Red's. The corridor opened to the compact barbecue dining room that held eight red and white Formica table and chair sets with four seats to a set. The counter had six revolving pedestal seats. Red said you always needed the sixth man. Each seat was named after the current starter on the Indiana Hoosier team, his name being applied to the circumference of the cushioned seat. Over the iron gates of the barbecue, made from the same material, was inscribed "The General," which Red had named after the former IU coach, currently on furlough to Texas Tech, Bobby Knight.

Red looked up and smiled in the way that just made you feel glad to be there. His velvet deep base voice greeted us, "Hey there Valley Oak! You almost have enough for a team today if Lou could suit up."

"I'll tell you this, Red, I could play for some of those teams Indiana pads its record on."

Red gave me a menacing scowl," You don't worry yourself about my Hoosiers, we always know how to get to the dance."

Red would have been a Hoosier fan in Outer Mongolia. That he was one in our university hoop-crazed town and could still draw a waiting line for lunch was a testament to the quality of his menu. He was one of our university's biggest boosters and, for the past sixteen years, had held four seats eight rows up behind our bench. He enjoyed inviting his friends to sit with him or giving them to a local school to use as rewards for deserving students. Red never hollered much at the games but, goodness, did he like to recruit! The university would often "employ" Red to visit the home of a sought after recruit. Red's love of barbecue was a great entry point into the home and, being Black, did carry some sway thereabouts.

I had never asked him, but he must have gotten hooked on Knight when he was coaching at West Point. The military academies, except when Navy had The Admiral, (Seven feet tall and in a submarine?!) never did much in basketball so it was natural for Red to follow "The General" when he moved to the high profile program at I. U.

Since you asked, Bobby Knight, from my point of view, any coach who tossed chairs and berated his players did not get my vote, and, winning didn't count. I was not from Indiana nor did I have a military background. Red's story was something like, after serving two tours in Vietnam, Red was asked to conduct courses at West Point Bobby Knight was his man. Me? I just wanted Red and his barbecue sauce on my side.

In his best military jargon, "What'll the Lunch Bunch Platoon chow-down on today?"

We placed our orders from a menu that featured Gumbo, Chili, Pulled Pork, Chipped Beef, Jambalaya, Hot Links, Chicken, Pork or Beef Ribs, and they came, as Red liked to say, with all the fixin's. Red gave us a special deal to keep our purchase under the five dollar maximum that each student earned for Lunch Bunch. He said he appreciated that we came in before the lunch rush hit. He just refused to hire any help, unless it was someone he had recruited for The U hoop team and wanted to keep an eye on. From the size of the helpings, you just knew he couldn't be in the business to clear a huge profit. Red wouldn't allow us to tip, saying the "pleasure was all his."

At various times I would find myself wandering into Red's without the students. I enjoyed the peace of Red's closing rituals. Neither Red nor I ever chose to go back into our past history. Our roots ran deep and were forged together. Just being close was good enough.

When I was here with the students, I didn't get much into Red's background or his support of a person such as Knight. I looked around at the autographed pictures on the wall. I knew most of them. In one corner there was a black and white photo of some teenage basketball prodigy wearing a Founders uniform while flushing an elbow deep two hand dunk. The caption read "Team Captain Jack Reynolds: Founders vs. Power Memorial." I knew Jack on a personal level. Not all the photos were sports related. Some went back to Red's military days. Red had told bits and pieces about some of them. Red didn't forget his past. I was proud to be part of his history.

One of these times after hours, Red was scraping down the barbecue. "Well Lou," he went on that late afternoon, "I kind of see it that you have to have equal parts love and lash to motivate your Valley Oak Team."

I was chewing on my hot links that I had dumped Red's beans over. I wiped my mouth with the buttered white bread. Red simply refused to offer wheat. I looked up.

"Now, take that Miss Laura, you should bring her around more often. She might even get you to therapeutically see the love in Mr. Bobby Knight."

Here we go again, "Red, listen to you? (Say what? Did he just mention Laura?) Did you ever consider the fact that Knight is committing child abuse? Of course, if they're over eighteen, we could just make the charge felonious assault." I took a bite of the coleslaw. "How can you back such a charlatan?"

There was no one else in the place, Red had always closed down by 3:30. I was honored that he let me hang around. Maybe, if I put more of the hot sauce on, he might even offer me a ticket to the game.

"I tell you, Lou since you're throwing those polysyllabled terms around with my beans," He continued scraping down the barbecue grill, "I tell you, all life just comes down to one thing."

I waited. Red was always teaching me.

Red paused as he flipped the grill over, winked at me and said, "The Usufruct."

The what? I looked at him. Say usufruct? Was that a new zone defense? "Usu- what? Never heard of it Red. How do you spell it?"

Red laughed his deep "got you" laugh, meaning he knew something that I did not have a clue about.

"You look here Mr. Lou, 'I know everything about you Red,' Thompson. There are some lessons that need be offered at the appropriate time."

I could see that Red was serious. I put down my fork.

"Look it here." He came around from behind the counter and pulled the white pant leg above his right calf. On the scarred, muscular calf was a sideways eight, which I knew was some Eastern Religion sign for eternity, with some scrawl along the lines. Though wrinkled and bled out, I could make out the word usufruct, forming one of its strands. I wondered where else Red was hiding tattoos.

"I'll tell you the long story Lou," Red looked out his door to make sure the closed sign was up and the blinds pulled halfway down, "If you don't rush me."

Me? Rush Red? Fat chance.

He returned to scraping the grill. "When I was a teenager I read a lot. Just not what was current, but I, whenever I could, I would wander around the city library looking for the thickest book I could find, just to prove I could read the thing. Books like <u>War and Peace, Tale of Two Cities,</u> Books that I could never talk to anyone I knew about. My friends just kind of left me alone with my books. I was in my own private world. I simply loved being alone with the smell of so many dusty books. Then, one evening I saw this itty-bitty book at the end of the shelf that had the name Henry Steele Commanger on it. Now, I didn't know who Henry Steele Commanger was, but somewhere I had heard the name. Sounded like he should be somebody. So I picked up this little book and looked at it. The book was entitled <u>Jeffersonian Democracy.</u> I opened it up and read some of the pages. And there was this word that kept coming up that I couldn't figure out. The word was usufruct." Red walked around to the other side of the counter and continued wiping down. "I didn't know what usufruct was but, when I met a word I did not know, I always looked it up. So I looked it up in a big old thick dictionary in front of the librarian. Now, the librarian, Mrs. Shaw, had become a friend of mine because I spent so much time there. She had never heard of the word and came around the counter to look it up with me. We found usufruct and it had only one definition but it was eight lines long!"

Red looked over his shoulder at me to see if I was still doing more than just chewing his food. "Eight lines long, basically said: <u>The right to use or enjoy the fruit or labor of another as long as the substance is not altered or diminished in any form in regard to its composition, character, or potential.</u> Sort of comes from the Latin to mean something like you can eat another person's fruit as long as it remains the same."

Red went over to his deep sink. "To me, that's what life is about. That's what my tattoo says. We are here with the right to do whatever we want as long as we do not diminish whatever the other wants. That's me, you, and Mr. Bobby Knight. "Because Lou," he smiled that sweet hard eyed smile of his, "Because Lou, when it comes down to crunch time, we all want to put the rock in the hole." He laid his wire scrapers on top of the oven grill and closed The General's iron doors.

I was not at all sure what the hell Red meant. Usufruct? Rock in the hole? Every now and then he left me feeling like my brain was warming the bench. I just shook my head. That Red accepted Knight's credo was up to Red. That Knight was still accepted by Indiana or Texas Tech or Martians, that was up to them. That this was the concept of the usufruct, I'm enlightened. To me, whether teacher, coach, or parent, the time of throwing chairs and physically intimidating children or six foot ten basketball players was coming to an end. Right Red? Or, what the usufruct?

Sam sat across from Mark, Ruby, and Scott at the red Formica table. He had ordered the chipped beef with the mild sauce. Red just shook his head and asked if he might not want some catsup instead. Red was muttering that McDonalds was two blocks down, on the right. Sam gathered a handful of rectangular napkins from the chrome dispenser, being sure to place one on his lap. I watched as Sam paused, knowing he was designated to initiate the ritualized dialogue with Red.

Sam twisted slowly on his red Formica seat, turning his head and asking with respect, which was the only way one addressed Red, "Pardon me, Mr. Red."

Red shut the cast black iron barbecue grate, saluted The General for affect, and walked to the red marbled counter. He leaned forward, resting on his elbows. "Yes Sam?"

I could see the other students eye each other. They smiled over at me. They knew the drill. How these traditions start, I just don't know.

Without hesitation Sam asked, "Could you please tell me your barbecue recipe?"

Red recoiled as if he was being interrogated by Charlie to give up the location of his platoon or, worse yet, game plans to Kentucky. He took a faltering step back from the counter appearing shell-shocked. Then he flashed that Red's smile that only a kid could bring out. His eyes went soft. Red reflected, hands on his white-aproned hips.

"Sam, you're a friend of mine. I would consider myself derelict of duty not to pass on to you the secret of my success. I have no children. No will." Red raised his arms to the ceiling. "Lord knows what crazy skin-headed monkey is going to dismember me with his skateboard. My moments could be few. I surely need to pass on the secret of my success. Here, let me get you a pad and pencil."

With that he reached under the counter. "I never wanted glory for myself, but this could make you rich and famous!" Red handed the writing material to Sam, then he folded his arms and said, "Since we have a few moments." As Red folded his large dark arms, his Special Forces Seal peeped out on a bicep below his starched short-sleeved white shirt. "I want to make sure you get the words right."

Red was all business when the talk turned to barbecue sauce, his or anyone else's. He arched his left eyebrow and began, "First, he cleared his throat, "First I scare me up two cans of thick," He looked at Sam hard, "Thick mind you. You paying attention Sam?'

Sam stammered a smile and nodded.

"Then why aren't you writing, young man?" Sam began to scribble. Red continued, "The first thing, I don't like to repeat myself, the first thing is to get some thick, red, paint. Not interior either. Interior's too runny. Has to be exterior to weather the elements. You got that?"

Sam, unblinkingly, nodded.

Red wandered on, weaving his recipe spell. I marveled at Sam's smile, hand no longer writing, eyes following Red. Welcome to the human race Sam. Every now and then, we can be OK.

Lunch Bunch, what a concept.

Thanks Red.

January 23 Three Wishes

For the last time, I sat across from the Stowes. All four of them and what a difference six months can make! Both Seth and Sam had begun to sprout up into adolescence, their chubby cheeks becoming tighter with a soft down emerging on their chins. They were such handsome young men with their blond hair tied back in ponytails and making funny faces to Joe, who sat between them on the couch. It was as if my younger brothers had entered the room, with dad eyeballing them.

Rebecca was her gushing self, "Again and again and again I, we just can't thank you and Valley Oak enough Laura."

"Sure we can Mom."

"Yeh, Mom, let's not over do this good-bye."

I marveled at how this divergent, dysfunctional, group had transitioned into a family.

"Seth and Sam, allow your Mother to express herself." I chided. "For me, I love hearing the good things."

"OK, OK, Laura." Seth mockingly grimaced. "You're wonderful, great, the best, now can we please go?"

"Compliments will get you anywhere, Seth." I assured him. "How about you, Joe, and Rebecca give Sam and I a moment?"

Seth, Joe, and Rebecca walked up to me as I stood for a group hug.

"Can we still stop by and see you?" Joe asked looking up hopefully.

"Anytime you like," I promised.

Joe hugged me again saying, "You sure are pretty Miss Laura."

Rebecca blushed. "Enough, enough. Let's get out of here before we all start crying!"

I am sure I was blushing as well as we parted and the three of them made their way onto the front porch. I turned to Sam. Even the worst good byes leave me sad. Sam remained seated on the couch. I sat down next to him. My rule with not touching clients and being aware of appropriate space refrained me from giving Sam a big hug.

"Watcha thinkin' Sam?" I playfully asked because we both knew what he was expecting.

"You know Laura," he smiled. "What you promised me."

"You are right Sam. A promise is a promise." I stated as I reached into my shirt pocket and produced a gnarled mound of wadded binder paper.

Sam's eyes expanded in surprise as I handed it over to him. He carefully, cautiously unraveled the paper and flattened it out on the couch.

"Laura," Sam sighed turning the paper over, "There's nothing written! You promised me your Three Wishes."

"That I did, that I did." I muttered, as I reached over and handed Sam another paper that was folded in half. Sam, carefully, took it from me and read aloud,

"One, I wish I could be invited to Sam's high school graduation."

Sam stopped and looked directly at me.

"C'mon Laura, this isn't about me."

"Sam," I assured him, "Nothing would please me more and you must read the other two before passing judgment."

Sam continued, "Two, I wish I could play saxophone in a jazz band." Sam screwed up his face and shook his ponytail in disbelief.

"I guarantee that is the truth, Sam," I moaned. "I played in elementary school and for two years in junior high school, but there was so much going on in my life that I had to let the horn go."

"Really?"

"Really truly," I nodded. "Read the third one."

Sam cleared his throat. "Three, I wish Valley Oak would be there for all the Laura's and Sam's of this world." Sam gave me a quizzical search.

"You see, Sam, I, also, gain so much by being a part of Valley Oak." Which is as far as I could go with Three Wishes and disclosing to a twelve-year old client. Sam nodded and folded the paper crisply to fit into his coat pocket. We stood and, automatically, I gave Sam a hug as I walked him to the front door. Sometimes you just have to let those boundaries go.

"Laura."

"Yes Sam?"

"Thank you for everything."

"Sam, thank you. Make sure to drop by."

He beamed, "For sure, and, maybe, I'll bring a saxophone."

"I will look forward to that," I laughed, waving good bye to the Stowes as they headed down the street to Red's to celebrate Sam's graduation to public school, where Lou and the crew were waiting there for them.

Valley Oak School
Psycho/educational Intake Summary

Laura Rosso: LCSW

Name: <u>Mike Adams</u>
DOB: 5/5/86

County of Residence: <u>Bay County</u>
School District of Reference: <u>McCormick USD</u>

Date: July 20

Physical Description: Mike is an attractive, slender five foot six inch one hundred and twelve pound fourteen-year-old youth. In our initial interview he described himself as a "skater" wearing baggy clothes with his hair shaved. He had a difficult time remaining in his chair, frequently getting up to touch items on my bookshelf and, in his words, "needs to be on the move." Mike's physical posture is one that displays anger and a willingness to challenge anyone who might enter his space.

Referring Criterion: As yet, I have not made contact with Mike's mother, Sharon Adams, but his school records clearly record his behavioral issues. Mike has a school history of physical assault to peers and noncompliance with school expectations. His first suspension occurred in the third grade for fighting. He has had several other suspensions for the same issue and has been transferred to three different school districts. He has been placed in juvenile hall several times for petty theft and assault. Due to his repeat offenses, Mike has been classified as a 602 and assigned a probation officer.

Family History: Mike is the second son of Sharon and Jesse Adams. Mike's brother, Steven, is eight years older. Jesse, when Mike was two, left the family and moved to the West Coast. Jesse has never complied with child support expectations and has not remained in contact with his children. Mike states that he has no memory of his father. Sharon has been employed at the same insurance company for twenty-three years. Her commute and work requirements often left her two sons unsupervised with Steven being left in charge under the distant supervision of neighbors. Steven and his peers were soon employing Mike to assist them in stealing from local stores and acting as a look out for their activities. Mike states that Steven, who is now serving time for a manslaughter conviction, is his hero.

Psychiatric History: Mike's file does not present any psychiatric evaluations. This is due to Mike's unwillingness to work with the Mental Health offerings of Bay County. He is not on any medication other than his purported indulgence in alcohol and marijuana.

DSM IV TR Diagnosis:

Axis I:	313.81 Oppositional Defiant Disorder
	R/O Conduct Disorder
Axis II:	Traits of Narcissistic Personality Disorder
Axis III:	None
Axis IV:	Father uninvolved; family stressors
Axis V:	GAF-40 (Current)

Recommendations: Given Mike's unwillingness to accept assistance from the Mental Health resources offered him as well as a long history of anti-social conduct, I am dubious about Mike's ability to have his needs met by the Valley Oak School Relationship Program. I do support his being interviewed by Lou Thomas prior to making a decision regarding intake.

Signed_____Date_____
Laura Rosso

Chapter 3

MIKE: MEAN TO THE BONE

July 23

There are some things that just tick me off. At the immediate top of my list are bullies, prejudice, the Yankees, hypocrisy............ Especially the hypocrisy you get sitting across the dinner table from your family. Then too, you could count yourself fortunate to have a dinner table or a family. Being an only and an adopted child with good parenting, this didn't come my way much. But I can hear the noise coming down in the extended fragmented families with "uncles and aunts" showing up at odd moments to soothe their off spring. Not only that, I've seen hurt. For instance, can you remember when you would ask your father or aunt or some adult in your family if they had a favorite daughter or son or niece and they would answer "we love them all the same" or "sure they're different, that's what makes each special in their own way" or, "there are times one might seem a little more special, but the love is always equal."

Yeh, right. You know that picture. That sort of traditional Hallmark Greeting kind of prose: "To my Special Daughter/My Most Beloved Son." You hear it so much that you even believe the myth must be the truth. They all say the same thing so it must be so. All children are loved equally.

Well, do I have a news flash. Forget about it! Everyone has favorites. I am not being jaded, just facing the mirror. You know it. I know it. The checker at Piggly Wiggly knows it. You have a favorite candy. A favorite hamburger. A favorite pasta sauce. A favorite pet. A favorite book. A favorite bicycle. Get real. Having a favorite is human nature. Stop the B.S. This is not heavy disclosure. I still have my favorite bat stowed away in the garage.

Nature/nurture? A dash of this. A sprinkle of that. Bibbity Bobbity with a wand. Sometimes you just do not have a choice. Sometimes heredity and environment just shut down the options to favorites. Gotta stick with your starter, because the bullpen's used up. Curve's not workin'. Hit the corners with my change up? Jump shot's not splashing. Drive. Make do with what you got. Take me. Raised in New England, what were my chances? What choices were open to me? With Red Sox Mania there is no free will.

Take my all time favorite baseball player, Ted "Ballgame/The Splendid Splinter" Williams. I didn't choose him. Somehow my dad imprinted him on me. I could have gone with Yaz or Jim Rice. But The Splendid Splinter was my man. Dad had his pictures and stats up in the garage and I saw them all the time. I didn't even see Ted play a game. He had retired by the time I got into sports. I mean, I thought I chose Ted. But, if I had been drafted by the Indians Little League Team and we lived in Toledo, I might have chosen Rocky Colavito. Rocky who? You know, the guy they traded to Detroit for Harvey Kueen. Forty home runs for one hundred and sixty singles. Impressive nonessential and too much information. Do you know how much time you have to waste kneeling at the statistical altar of baseball to know this stuff? But that's what makes them special. That's why they mean something to you. All those years away from it all. The past is like you're still right there. Space and time have not occurred. Heroes do not age.

I can still see Ted knocking the sphere out in the '41 all-Star Game. I swear, if I see him walking down Church Street I'm going to say, "There goes the best damn hitter in the history of baseball." In fact, I'd add "the first Hall of Fame Hispanic ballplayer." Betcha didn't know that. My dad passed away without knowing that fact.

Can you relate? Is this clear or, like Harry Belafonte would calypso, "......clear as mud but it covered the ground, the confusion made me brain go round."

Try this for dealing with favorites. Teachers. Take teachers. We all know they have favorites. I know I struck out on being a favorite student, "the adopted tag" of a mixed marriage stenciled on my forehead. But recall your favorite teacher. Bring back the events and the good times. What made them special? The way they showed up everyday. The insights shared.

I know I can immediately recall my third grade teacher who was not even my favorite. But don't be bummed if you ever bump into them in later life and they don't remember your name. OK, so that might have happened to me, but you have to give them a break because, if they teach for twenty years at the high school level, three thousand students might have passed through their grade book.

For me, though, it's easy. I have a great memory for faces and numbers. I held my students close like I did my baseball stats. More specifically: What decade? What league? What team? What position? To teachers the call is like: What school? What grade? What subject? What year?

I have these favorites. I admit to honesty! I'm a teacher and a baseball fan, fan being short for fanatic. Baseball: The Fifties; American League; Boston; Teddy Ballgame. (What can I say about cryogenics and his son.) Teacher: Mrs. Bodine. 3rd grade: Riverview Elementary: Boston. Student: Craig Murray1989; Lincoln Elementary; 6th Grade: Berkeley, god that kid could hit!

If I ever have children, I hope they never ask me which one is my favorite! Probably have to say that I love them all the same. Of course! Each is special in their own way.

Lou, Lou, Lou............ Such a hyperventilating rant of fear-based justification for the avoidance of developing relationships that differ amongst individuals. I want to tell him that a human being (Even Red Sox genetically charged.) has the right to establish different expectations with those we interact with in our society. One must not hold fear of experiencing the value of relationships. Take a breath.

For Lou, as I was coming to know him, taking a breath was not a part of his mantra. Take, for example, his rant about favorites and the hypocrisy of the family dinner table. From my perspective, Lou was overflowing his thoughts with the frenzied activity of perpetual motion. Lou was willing himself to not consider the family unit that he had lost due to misfortune. Admittedly, I can respect his remorse and reactive nature to that foundation of well-being having been so brutally taken from him through a car accident.

What I have yet to fathom was Lou's underlying current of anger that he masked with one-liners and surface conversations. Even his "right field buddies" were of a surface relationship. Lou would participate and laugh with them but he held himself back from joining in with family dinners, graduations, and all the other cultural events that form the basis of the community fabric.

Marianne and I did welcome the gradual change that was occurring in Lou's relationships with our students. I, also, know that Marianne was not sharing all that she knew about Mr. Lou Thompson, as she remained so overtly optimistic with regard to the direction of Valley Oak.

For myself, I needed to wait and process.

This brings me to my subject, which is the opposite side of the coin. What do you say about a kid you did not cherish? As a teacher the one you could easily live without. You know the type. The kids who are smarter than you. The ones for whom the only hope you hold is that they will be transferred to another classroom, like forever.

Ask any teacher. You become self-conscious when such an individual enters the room. You spell words wrong on the board, bump into furniture, drop the chalk or dry eraser. If the student you abhor is absent you silently rejoice as you know this will be a pleasant day in the room. This is the type of kid you always want to get rid of. You keep your eye on them. You watch them anticipating that one false move. You wait for them to screw up and you know they will! Patience. Timing. Get them before they get you. This is survival of the fittest!

Then I find myself sitting across from the cosmic crystal ball that lies on Laura's shoulders and fixates me in space and vent, "Damn it Laura, these are the mean kids. The bullies. The ones who get what they want by intimidating others. Peers, adults, insects, it doesn't matter. They are the kind that feed on the sheep of your room. Like a preying mantis perched and predatory with a voracious endemic appetite consuming all joy. A Shakespearean Tragedy that, although the evil is defeated, leaves such a shattered good you end up questioning the concept of public education.

My, my,.my....... How Lou's Berkeley English Major supports his waxing eloquent in polysyllabic venom. Do I sooth the beast or allow him to sputter on? How about some ownership?

Against my better judgment, I attempt to reason with the guy. "Lou, I have clearly stated that I am completely willing to accept your decision as to Valley Oak's ability to meet the needs of the warlocks and druids of our universe."

I thank Laura for her wisdom and, being conscious of not stomping, disengage with the blue-eyed serpent of calm and walk out of the Victorian into an afternoon thundershower. Ok-ok-ok fine…….. The Shakespeare bit was a tad much, but we know who I am talking about. I am talking about the Mike Adams in our lives. The kind of kid who, if you did not have him on your roll, you would have the perfect class.

Do I need Mike's kind of energy in my life? Does my decision really count?

July 16 Who's in Charge?

I sat there with Mike's cumulative folder spread out in front of me on the living room coffee table. I had read through six IEP's, four behavior intervention plans, three psychological reports, juvenile hall records. The time was Wednesday, around 4:30. Laura came in and settled her gown in the overstuffed chair. I'd been waiting for her. She was never on time. Not real late. Just fashionably. Her timing had nothing to do with me. Whether it was an IEP, a staff meeting, you name it, she always made the many-layered entrance. Might be a good nickname for her, Fashionably Late Laura.

I was much more comfortable having our conversations outside of her office. Takes some of her omnipresent righteous pompous power away.

I was on track to be late for my private therapy appointments. Need to get this conference over and done with Lou. As I enter into the living room lair of my employer, I can primordially feel Lou preparing to pounce on my recent referral.

"So, Lou, have you had a chance to look over Mike's file?" I ask as I flop into the soft chair.

Obviously Low has and he has determined to disconcert me by bringing me out of my therapeutic office comfort zone to voice his concerns. Lou's being so sanctimoniously proud of his devious intent that I find I must challenge my demeanor to keep a straight face. I pointedly run my fingers over my necklace so Lou will think that I was becoming anxious and vulnerable to his machinations. Lou never should have told Marianne that he was aware of my necklace habit.

I want to say something like, "duh, Laura. Do you think I'm making a scrapbook?" Why can't she just say "what do you think about bringing Mike into program?" Why all the prelims? Didn't she state that Mike's admittance was on me? I lean back into the worn leather couch, watch her tug at her necklace. I'll have to get her out of that office more often.

I responded with, "Sure have. Quite a read." We continue gazing off, waiting for the other to venture an opinion.

I need to move this meeting along. Lou is learning the dance, but I have clients coming in that do not enjoy waiting to discuss their issues.

"Lou, I know there are red flags concerning Mike's aggressive behavior and social skills."

How about a ship load of them. I go for it, "Laura, why bring in a student who has been verbally and physically assaultive to peers and staff, carried weapons into his school, has a history of drug and alcohol abuse, and…"

I need to put closure to Lou's defiant surge. "Lou…"

"Hear me out Laura. You said Mike's coming aboard was my decision. He has been in juvenile hall on four different occasions." There, I finished. I was gaining confidence in talking through Laura's interruptions. Ms. Divine Therapeutic Process didn't have all the answers.

This was not the time to get into a battle of wills. Decisions had already been made and Mike was headed our way. I did value Lou's opinion, but I was the gatekeeper. I was the one who did the intakes and, with Marianne, the placements. There were referrals that Marianne and I had reviewed and determined other programs would benefit the student rather than Valley Oak. Lou was peripheral to these placement concerns. With Mike Adams, I had offered Lou to review the folder in order to pro act to, what I knew would be, Lou's negative response

. "Lou, Marianne is bringing Mike by Valley Oak to review program and meet with you. A final decision will be made after the visit."

That should be enough to quell Lou's ego apprehension. "Just be willing to meet him with an open mind. Marianne has said that Mike is ready to make some changes in order to remain in his home placement."

I picked up my briefcase and stood to head for the door. Meeting over. I note that Lou looks forlorn at the brevity of our discussion and the fact that he will have to meet face to face with Mike.

"Make sure you lock the file cabinet when you put Mike's folder up." I decide to leave one more tidbit for Lou to conjure on, "By the way, Marianne said that Mike was quite an athlete. Made River Dale Little League All-Stars two years in a row." I whisk myself away to the door with a wave.

I follow Laura to the door and I watch as she fumbles in her purse looking for the car keys and dropping them on the walkway. I know Laura's just softening me up. She knows that I knew that Marianne and she have already made the decision. I'm not as dumb as I look.

I call out the front door to her, "Laura, this is not going to go down well."

Damn, the guy is just relentless. I turn and reply, "Watch out for your wish fulfillment. Gotta go."

I finally grasp my keys and make it into the car without further protestations from Lou. Before I drive off, I call my first client to let her know I will be just a tad late.

June 29   Conduct Disorders

Mike Adams. I remember the first time I looked at him. Fourteen years old, five feet, nine inches skinny mean-eyed head shaven wannabe. A multi-colored ferocious dragon tattooed sleeve covered his left arm. He swaggered into the Victorian with Marianne, from Bay County Mental Health, leading the way. I had bad vibes right away. This was not going to go well.

No acknowledgements, just, "Hey, yo. Like dude, I need a smoke. Got some sticks?"

I found myself wanting to punch out the jerk from the get go. I'd seen his type enough. Youth Authorities and jails were filled with the likes of him. Who did he think he was? What a punk, like, I should find him a match. Just oozing with entitlement. This dude -slinger. Dude this and dude that. Depersonalize. Devalue. No reason to have to know your name. You're not worth my time. The only Dude worth knowing was The Big Lebowski.

I responded in my most cool and appropriate up to date Laura-conferred relationship based fashion while holding out my fist for a knock. "Mike, my name is Lou. Glad you could make it."

Mike knocked and went back to, "Like, dude, I need some smoke. Marianne won't let me light up in her car. "

Maybe Mike thought I was the understanding therapeutic type. Like, wasn't there a legal age to be smoking? Guess not looking at the tattoos. Must have had them done out of state as parlors were illegal here. Mike reached into his pants pocket to show me he had the goods. Marlboro. Puke. I responded with a concrete answer. Laura would have been proud,

"Mike, At Valley Oak we have a No Smoking policy." You little twerp.

"That's fucked, Dude," he sneered, turned to Marianne. "Can we leave?"

"Now Mike," protested Marianne, in her proper pampering British smile.

"Screw this place," Mike interrupted. "I've been here, seen it, and it sucks. Unless there's some babes up the stairs."

"Michael, please." Marianne went from unruffled to exasperated in a heartbeat. First time I'd ever seen her vent. "You can either put your cigarettes away and be civil or the next place we visit will be one hundred miles from here."

I totally agreed. Way to go Marianne! Give him that tough love talk. Knock the little asshole back! Like, who the hell are you? You want to leave? Not a problem. The door opens outward. Take a long hike on a short pier. I caught myself.

Where was I coming from? Relax. Take a breath. Hold it. Think Zen. Count to Zenmillion. Should I expect something different from Mike? This is who he was. This is why Marianne brought him in. She hadn't made him get back in the car. She's still willing to work with him. Give him an out to keep his dignity. What's the problem with me? Why was I so angry? I have a lifetime of history with this type of student. Even lived with them. I'm supposed to be able to find a hook. A way in. That's what relationships are about. Right Laura? This guy is not going to deliver my paper or mow my lawn. He comes with lots of baggage and they were packed in disarray long before I had the pleasure of meeting up with him.

I reminded myself that this was a skill that I was working on. Didn't Laura continue to reframe my statements into a more professional and positive appraisal of our students? Couldn't I someday get a clue and not take this so personally? Step back. Process. The guy did not even know me. Valley Oak was just another bus stop for Mike. This wasn't about me and him. I need to not take every little detail like it was for my benefit. A blip on Mike's windshield is what I am. Maybe I could profit from a cortical implant or a med review? Someday, somehow, I just might learn how to deflect my eagerness to set behavioral boundaries at students who presented like hunkering salivating junkyard dogs.

(Goodness gracious and glory be, there is a glimmer of relationship hope for Lou.)

I wondered if Marianne had rolled him out to check for weapons? Enough. Let it go. That I had pronated students and taught intrusive behavioral interventions for the past eight years without a concern for alternatives and believing with heart and soul what we were doing was the right way, the safe way, the only way and, more importantly, the legal way. I can look back and understand that I had tunnel vision. No wonder I was considered a control freak by the students. Like there weren't more stars in the heavens than I could see.

The good old days. How I yearned for them. Ignorance was bliss. Did I concern myself with the student's feelings in being stabilized in a restraint? Afraid not. Did I care if there were bruises or cuts? Came with the territory for both staff and students. Restraints were harsh. And necessary.

Currently, due to my "personal growth," Laura would say that I was improving and there was hope for my being able to work within the Relationship Model. I just need to try to take a step back and find out what's really going on. I hear Laura's counseling, Lou, why is it that Mike greeted you with his need for a smoke? What is going on for him? How would you feel walking into Valley Oak as a fourteen year old with Marianne as your guide? If I'm the one getting ticked off then what's on my plate? Why do I need to be filled with so much anger? What was my problem? I mean, I may not know Mike and he may not work out, but I was certainly not reaching out with the helping hand. Where's his acting out coming from? What's churning inside him? Wonder if he has ever had a positive role model? If not me, then who? Where's the teacher in me saying "come on in!" Mike, glad you could make it! Hey, what are you interested in because we can do it! Heard tell you made All-Stars two years in a row. Take the negative statements as a dialogue door opening to offer you a way in. Did you know that we pay well for laughing at my jokes? What brand of cancer sticks would you like some assistance kicking the addiction to?"

All teachers deal with control and vulnerability. Not inner thought processes. Let the shrinks take care of that realm. Control first. Then teach. I mean, what country would listen to the US if we didn't have nukes and a way to deploy them. Not to mention germ warfare.

Take in how teachers prepare for the new school year and new students. First off, they need to find and identify the targets. Know your enemy. For sure, their prior teachers have forewarned you with teacher lunchroom horror stories that were funny then, but now these eleven year old psychopaths are headed at you.

How much mental anguish do we teachers spend on the one or two students in a class that challenge our authority? Get them out. If not at another school then at least into special education. This is all because the last question a teacher ever wants to answer is, "WHY DON'T YOU HAVE CONTROL OF YOUR CLASS!?" Lack of control is a teacher's nightmare! Whatever type of teacher you are, that's number one priority! Ask me if I have ever lain awake at night ruminating about how to garner control, reinforce it, and by any means, keep it. Like how the Roman Emperors employed The Coliseum during Pax Romana.

When I was on the West Coast, there was a writer for the San Francisco Chronicle, who often included an illustration with an apt statement regarding the Roman Pax. One of his best (I believe his name was Art Hoppe) was of these two gladiators lying wasted in The Coliseum as several drooling lions crept towards them. One gladiator says to the other "Someday we'll look back on this and laugh…"

Whew. Now those Romans had control. Again, for a teacher, after control, one might even teach. Then too, control might be the prime lesson of public education. Teachers state the terms. Students make their choice. You have to hear the music if you're going to learn to dance.

I do understand the perspective Lou is coming from as the role I held in the supervision of my younger brothers was reinforced by my Father's belt. My Father seldom employed the belt to redirect my brothers' misbehavior, but the belt hung on the closet door in the laundry room and it could be seen every time the brothers entered or left the back porch. When one of the brothers would question my authority, we all knew the bottom line.

In my quest of The Relationship Model the role of "the belt" is a concern. Should humanity be capable of dialoguing to manage and resolve differences or did there need to be a nuclear deterrent present to gain everyone's attention? Did the role of The Teacher need "a belt" to reinforce social expectations? Should James, who had been Valley Oaks only restraint, have been allowed to smash the pumpkin onto my computer? (Since the restraint, James had not required physical redirection and he was working towards a positive transition.)

Was not the impact of the "Quiet Room" or "Restraint" the same boundary at Valley Oak as my father's belt had been in my home? Did The Relationship Model demand a hard-core physically intrusive bottom line in order to be relevant?

Over the past ten years or so I have been able to physically control (As Laura would state, positively redirect) my "bad" students through physically assertive team control prone restraints or the promise thereof. Hey, it wasn't on me. Not something I made up. The Intrusive Behavioral Model that was employed to bring about control was not my invention. The concept had been around forever. Or, what was that Roman Coliseum all about?

During my years of being the student, the model was brought down by the public school teacher, though in a much user friendly manner. I remember Mr. Padovan throwing erasers at us in fourth grade. In fifth grade I got my first swat from Mr. Smith for blowing spit bubbles. OK. It just wasn't the bubbles themselves. I would tap the girl who sat in front of me on the shoulder, Martha Udall I recall, and she would turn around her nose popping my bubble. I recall that Mrs. Sherrick warned me and kept me after class a couple of times before she sent me to the principal. I quit after the swat. I wonder what would happen to Mr. Smith and his paddle today?

No longer can teachers and administrators bring about corporal punishment as they deem fit. Now, in order to offer a hands-on Behavioral Model, one must be PART (Physical Assault Restraint Training) or CPI (Crisis Prevention Institute) or some like skill trained. The interventions are basic industrial standard. Police, Fire, National Guard, they were all trained in variations of the interventions we employed at Valley Oak. Seminars were offered throughout the year all over the United States. I was the Certified PART Trainer on our site. I had attended a one-week seminar that taught the PART techniques. I admit. I was surprised to learn that the main instructional thrust was that the last thing you wanted to bring about was a restraint. All sorts of dialogue models were presented as alternatives to placing hands on. The first three days of the seminar were entirely devoted to internalizing the mindset needed to avoid a prone or other manner of restraint. Then why to set boundaries, how to set boundaries, when to set boundaries, where to set boundaries, how to reinforce boundaries, etcetera.

Think about it. Are you the type of person who needs a four person prone restraint in order to meet up with the everyday social norms of life? Like coming to a complete stop at a red light? If so, get ready for some on-going harsh experiences

Over the years of training I became a bit jaded at the attention paid to developing dialogue and recognizing stages of individual escalation. I came to view PART as the insurance industry's response to law suits involving restraints. If a program or staff could say that they were following PART directed techniques, then PART would supply the attorneys and take on the legal responsibilities brought on by a lawsuit. It was simply up to staff to follow the PART guidelines and protocols when implementing supportive expectations for escalating students. Twice I had gone to court on abuse charges from parents and students. Both times PART had defended my actions and I was acquitted. I appreciated their back up and the court experience was not one I'd choose to repeat.

Mike Adams. I refocused and came back to the reality of standing in the entry with Marianne and the anti-Christ. OK OK. There I go again. Mike was alright. My negative reaction wasn't about him, at least for now. My past experiences had to be exorcized. Mike was just being himself. I needed to simply accept that I still had a long way to go with the guy I saw in my mirror. Personal acceptance of responsibility was always the toughest thing to do. Not only to look at, but to make the good changes. I took a breath and exhaled my anger. What Mike was tossing my way was not personal. I knew that. He was just acting out what he knew. How he learned to cope. Yeah. That's it…

A Relationship Model Program was just more difficult to implement. Boundaries were not as clear. Staff had to make their own decisions, which we hoped would be the right ones. Rules and regulations just weren't written in stone like an Intrusive Behavioral Program. Students continually prod and prodded as to how far they could go? What they could get away with. I knew that I felt that the Relationship offering was a better program for the students. Getting into its mindset was tough for me. I hoped that I could make the transition.

The issues that Lou was having with Mike were not all about Lou. I had agreed with Marianne to admit Mike in spite of my reservations concerning his conduct disordered behavior. As Lou has stated, Mike was simply being himself in a social environment that did not present clear behavioral boundaries nor programs that would, from Mike's perspective, not meet his needs. What degree of emotional disturbance Mike held was difficult to determine as he completely masked his vulnerability and emotional issues through aggressive acting out. I thought of Mike as being a wolf amongst a flock of sheep.

Though I would not admit the concern to Lou, I was very aware of the part I played in admitting Mike to Valley Oak. I was new to the role of administrator/gate keeper where I held the final word. I had always been able to consult with peers and await answers from above. I felt immense pressure from Mental Health and Marianne to try and meet Mike's immense social emotional and educational needs within the county. Out of county placement was definitely expensive and, historically, did not bode well for the student upon returning to his district of reference. Residential room and board would cost between four and five thousand dollars per month. The cost of a non public school would be near three thousand dollars per month. I felt assured that Marianne was looking out for what was best for Mike, offering the "least restrictive environment," but her supervisors had to be watching the monetary consequences.

Then too, from the financial side of Valley Oak I felt the need to keep our census up. Each student was being offered a thirty-six thousand dollar federally supported scholarship to improve their social skills and emotional stability during the school day. On a personal note, attached to this was the fact that, as a contract provider, I was no longer receiving benefits in a county program with guaranteed vacation time, sick leave, 401, or personal leave. I had chosen to participate with Valley Oak because I was coming in on the ground floor and was able to actualize a significant influence on program development.

An additional concern was that I had known Mike at a younger, more vulnerable age when I had been with Bay County. Now, the challenge for me was to assist Mike in being assimilated into the relationship community of Valley Oak. I had to be prepared for a gradual transition as Mike was extremely guarded and not in an emotional place to allow Valley Oak to impact his tough guy exterior with relationship based social norms. The years of abandonment and alienation had layered Mike with a deep shield that had been erected to protect his vulnerable core. He had no way of knowing that this was no longer serving him well. Also, beyond Mike, I would have to contend with Lou.

I took a mental flash photo as Mike strutted past me, like so many punk angry White adolescent males. Peacock proud in his torn plaid woolen shirt worn two sizes too big, sleeves cut off and hanging down to cover his ripped, though freshly washed, Ben Davidson's. (Not the Raiders Defensive End). These had a belt on them that dangled around his calves with a chain, thick enough to hoist Old Ironside's anchor, snaked around to his right rear pocket. It was a miracle that his feet didn't get snagged in this ghetto gear and send him clanging to the floor. He sported a knobby shaven head complete with a braided Cossack lock and a face full of constellations of freckles. I wondered if Huck Finn presented this way in his community. Mike, however, had several P.O. sheets that read more like an up and coming Indian Jim. He was troubled if not hardened. One arrest for weapons during those four placements in Juvenile earned him a turn in the Youth Authority. He lived with his mom in a lower socioeconomic apartment complex. He was only fourteen, doing damage and wanting more. I never thought of Huck as a bully. I let Marianne handle Huck. I mean Mike.

Marianne, of course, was as dignified as ever. With Mary Poppins British detachment she scanned the map of James' bicycling progress across the New England countryside. Nodding her head she turned and gleamed a Mary Poppins smile at Mike and stated, "I explained to Mike that there were certain expectations that he would have to meet up with in order to be enrolled at Valley Oak." Marianne ignored Mike's guttural comment and cheerily went on. "Mike said that he was willing to have a go of it."

Mike walked outside and vertically sprang up landing lightly on the three foot front porch railing. He was agile.

"Only because I didn't want to go back to that shit hole of a Hall or a hundred miles from here."

"Now Mike," Marianne reasoned retaining her cosmic detachment, "No one bound and chained you to come here for this visit. You do have the option of home teaching while we determine an alternative placement."

Mike puckered up, "No fucking teacher's coming into my crib."

I made a mental note to remind myself to do a doctorate on the use of the word "fuck" by White male adolescents. For emphasis Mike sucked snot back into his into throat and hawked a huge lugie glob into the flowers below.

I wanted to puke. I hated Marianne and her years of sweet bullshit. And who the fuck is this Lou dude and Valley Oak crap? They are so into resurrecting my life. This thing about whether I'm conduct disordered or emotionally disturbed. What bullshit is that? Like, what are you going to catch me at being first? Acting weird or ripping life off? Both? Oh, OK. And you think, like, do I give a fuck? You stupid shits. How many times do you think I'm going to sit down in a chair and talk about my alcoholic druggie father beating the crap out of my dear mother? You want the time and date? Gee, Marianne, if we could only reunite for our special family celebrations! You don't think that I don't know this shit? Praise County Mental Health! The two broken bones I got that were never set right? For the record, since my father was right handed, they were my left ulna and clavicle. The fucking bum hand I got dealt from the bottom of the deck of life. Hey, I can handle it. No pro-blame-o. Like this learning thing. Who says I need a high school diploma? You ask me what I'm going to be like when I'm thirty-seven if I don't take school work serious. Thirty-seven? Is tomorrow Thursday? Like I know? Get real. Hey, like, dude,

I don't have better things to do than to improve my reading and math skills when I go home? Maybe you can get to know my buddy Corey, the friendly role model next door, who is expecting me to score some "hey mister" hooch or a steak for him at the A & P? Bummer for me if I don't come through. Oh yeh, work on my anger management skills while going through nicotine withdrawal. There's another good one. That's just real smart. How many Ph. D's did it take to think that one up? Marianne and Lou, what fuckheads. What a couple of dildos. Talk about a set up. If I don't meet with Marianne or go to school my PO is on the line giving me crap. That's why I'm here. That's why I agreed to visit this retard place. Is this ride over yet? Just so fucked up.

Throughout my work in special education I had found that students referred to my programs often had varying degrees of these two diagnoses ED or CD? CD or ED? One of being Emotionally Disturbed and the other Conduct Disordered. How to figure what was what between the ED/CD was up to the school psychologist. The bottom line for me was simpler: If a student would throw a brick through a window and then come tell me they did this and ask to speak with their therapist, then they were Emotionally Disturbed. I mean, do damage and want to talk about it? Like catch me, I did it! Anyone hear me? Here I am. Help! Someone save me from myself! I need some attention. Sounded ED to me.

Now, if the student threw the brick through the window, hoped that it clunked somebody on the way down, and no way-no how, nofuckingway—could you prove they did it, so what the fuck if you saw them you're wrong… they were Conduct Disordered. I looked over at Mike. I would have to be extremely aware of getting clunked.

Marianne smoothed out the silk laces on her blue lapel. Her starched raven hair was tightly bunned with a Monarch Butterfly clasp sprouting brilliant orange wings. She looked at me, smiled agreeably, and stated, "We are just here for a walk around and a chat with you, if you have the time Lou. Why don't you show us around?"

I felt Marianne's gaze and it was saying, "Lou, this is the reason your program is here. Not all the children in our county are going to present in the passive depressed mode of James or Sam. Pieces of cake, compared to Mike. Mike has been on my caseload for six years. He is no longer a latency aged six to ten year old. He has entered his adolescence carting all the full blown dysfunctional rage that an abusive home situation can provide. You need to give him an opportunity. How good are you with this abrasive un-nurtured youth who has no interest in social norms or dialogue to form appropriate relationships?"

I found myself saying, "Not a problem. Let's go into the office." I led the way and caught Mike scanning the kitchen and computer rooms where students were at work with staff. How Mike would do in our program was a crapshoot. He might still be young enough to accept our relationship model, work towards rewards, find the desire to transition back to his own local high school. I had seen stranger things occur. We sat down in Laura's old office, which I was taking over, as she was off site. I asked Mike what he had heard about our program.

"Got some hot honies here, besides Ms. Laura, Dude?"

"Excuse me?" was all I could muster.

Marianne explained, "Well, Lou, Ms. Laura was Mike's therapist when he attended the county day treatment program."

I kept it straight. "How'd you do with her?"

"You kidding me? Dude, she was cool."

I wondered why Laura had not mentioned to me that she had known Mike from day treatment.

Mike continued, "That's one positive about your program Dude, having a hot chick therapist."

God, I could feel myself blushing! I was letting Mike get to me. It was like I had a button on my forehead. I'm not sure if it was "the dude" or "hot therapist" or what.

Thankfully, Marianne intervened, "Mike, could you just say that you had a good relationship with Ms. Laura."

Mike paused, thought of some remark, then said, "Yeh, I can admit that. But, back to the facts. Dude, do you got any bitches here?"

I amazed myself with a straight answer, "Mike, as of right now, we have three female students and six males."

I looked at his pinched- tight adolescent erupting face. I was sure he knew from experience that special education programs were weighted towards males. Usually it was about ten to one. That we had three females was fairly amazing. Why? You ask why? Why were males the lucky ones to earn Valley Oak and other such programs? Are we like drones? Maybe the "dangling X" or just weaker genes? Could be. But, since you asked, here's my opinion.

Our history is against us. Males had just spent too much time out of the cave and on the hunt getting those gross motor muscles developed. Which sex holds the faster and stronger Olympic Records?? (OK, why Blacks?) Males were not restricted in movement by menstrual cycles and childbirth. Females had a lot of seated down time. You get restricted to the cave and what happens? You develop dialogue and relationships. You see a bone on the floor and you shout CROCHET HOOK! Get those fine motor skills down. Throw in the fact that, for whatever reason, females calcify cross the midline and mature one year ahead of males. So, who do you think is going to succeed in beginning "See Spot Run" reading, sit-in- your chair-get your binocular vision focused, classrooms? Curtain number three Monty! You got that right! Not the good old boys on the hunt. The winners are those with an evolution of fine-motored oral based crochet hooked communications skills! But that's alright. There's enough good stuff in life to go around. Just tell the guys what they've won!! Can you believe it? Yes, they have!! Zonkers! They have just won a Public School Lifetime Placement Award in Special Education!!!! Lucky stiffs. Maybe an Adjusted Diploma! Someday I could do my doctorate on this…

Mike continued to stick with his dude guns, "Look Dude, if I can't smoke, I ain't going to come to this school. I'll take the one hundred mile trip to a Timbuktu place where it's OK."

Whew, that solves a load gone there. Here I was concerned about this guy being a totally disruptive force. No smoke, no school, no problem. Next student please. Actually, smoking was an issue with several of our referrals. Joe Camel had gotten more than his share of this youthful population. I had found that it was best to be direct on our smoking policy. I looked at Mike,

"That's your decision Mike. We have a no smoking policy and that's just how it is. I tell you though, if you want some help in kicking those cancer sticks, this is the place.'"

Mike gave me a deadpan response, "Yeh, dude, like you'd spend the fifty bucks to get me patches."

Unbelievable. He was voicing interest. "Mike, we would do that. We've done it before. That's not a problem." Actually I had provided patches while in other programs and I had planned to bring the same into Valley Oak.

Marianne concurred that Valley Oak could assist students, with parental permission and physician consultation, in this manner. Mike looked at me, as if I might be something more than a dude, maybe a moneyed dude. Mike would be our tenth student. I really needed him to come in. There was a mortgage on my condo to take care of and a payroll to meet. I was not going to back off on the smoking policy to soothe his needs. We had been through all types of addiction with other students and other issues throughout my educational experience. Not only did I firmly believe in the policy, but if it wasn't smoking, it would be something else to come up against. Mike had to figure out what he wanted to do. No time like the present. We could offer the alternatives, they were his decisions.

I continued with gusto, "Think about it Mike, where else could you be paid by our Monetary Reward System to improve your health?"

I kept telling Laura that this was the toughest part, offering the student the opportunity to make decisions and allowing them to feel the power of their own conflict resolution. I was just trying to be more of a positive role model and let go of the need to control, run things, have all the answers. The thing was, if this was what my program was about, why was it so hard for me to do it? Why did I feel like such a hypocrite? It was like I was kissing the little twerp's ass to come into program. Why did I think of him in such pejorative depersonalized terms. Twirp, prick, punk. What was it in him that brought this out for me? Maybe I should be asking, what is it about me that holds onto and spews such venom? How much does Lou have to be in control and at what cost. Do I really need to be in charge or have the upper hand in order to feel good? Here, have some nicotine patches. Sure, let's sit down and talk about how we can meet your needs.

Yet, I really wanted to say, this is the program. You can work it or go say hello to your PO. Make your choice.

What the hell, I thought. I could see that Lou was really working through some anger issues with me. Even got him turning red over Ms. Laura. I could get into losing the cancer sticks. Marianne had nothing but good things to say about this place. Hate to say it, but Ms. Laura was good for me. Felt she heard what I was going through. Maybe I'll give this dump a shot.

I was seated at my desk on the second floor bedroom that had been converted into my office. I so enjoyed the Victorian. Two neighborhood cats had strolled in through my open window and found niches to curl into. From experience, I knew that they were after my sand tray, so I made sure to keep it covered when the window was open. I could overhear snippets of the conversation on the first floor taking place between Marianne, Mike, and Lou. I knew this was torture for Lou. He had not wanted Mike to come by for a visit. I recalled our conversation earlier in the morning, just before Marianne and Mike had arrived. Lou was starting to remind me of my Jack Russells. Both were stubborn and relentless.

"Lou," I struck a therapeutic pose, "Marianne is simply asking you to interview Mike. It's scheduled to happen within the hour." Lou continued staring at some cosmos on the ceiling. "It's important to keep an open mind during Mike's introduction to program."

Lou looked at me. He can turn so hostile! His eyes are capable of conveying the same distant flat hardness that fills my conduct disordered clients primal presentation. Wonder where that all comes from.

Lou responded with, "Then why read his file? Isn't that the first step?" He knew it was.

"What does his file present? How can you read about Mike's behaviors and not form an opinion?"

Exasperating! That's what Lou was. Always had some sort of sardonic comeback, especially when something was not occurring in a fashion he supported. "Lou, this is a time for professional judgment."

Lou exploded back at me, "I am being professional! I read the file. It is my professional judgment that he's not worth an interview."

I found myself twining my finger in my necklace, I consciously placed both my hands on my lap and continued, "Interviewing a perspective client is an expectation of our program by Mental Health. Turning a client down on a paper review would not be in our best interest. Although, unbeknownst to Lou, I had done this on numerous occasions.

Lou was scratching one of the stray tabby cat's ears and pulling its tail at the same time. All it did was purr. All the strays came up to Lou, they knew he was a soft touch.

"Well, Laura," he shrugged, "I guess you should interview him."

Nice try Lou. "Not my job definition," I tossed back at him. "You are the teacher. You are the educator." I paused. "Look, Lou, you read my intake comments. You know that I agree with you that Mike is not going to be an easy fit into our program and..." I held up my hand to stop Lou from interrupting. He was doing this more and more, "And, read my lips, It is imperative that you interview Mike."

"C'mon Laura! He's got a PO. He's been to the Hall and Back (Audie Murphy: Twice Medal of Honor Winner: WWII: To Hell and Back.) several times. He's headed the same direction as his brother."

Lou was about to cave in. It was time to play my trump card. Appeal to Lou's narcissism.

"That's right Lou. You are correct. He will be like his brother for sure unless Valley Oak gives him a shot."

Zingo. Now the money.

"Besides he would be our twelfth student."

He threw up his arms and headed for the door. "Okfine, bring him in," Lou grimaced. "And you don't have to add that he is a two time all-star. But he only has a thirty day trial!"

Over my career, I had worked with so many educators like Lou. They are able to construct their elaborate classroom rituals and did not want them tampered with, especially by a shrink. Their years of experience gave them a righteous perspective when evaluating a student's needs. They would argue against a new student with challenges coming their way as if Genghis Khan was knocking at the gate. So many times I had sat in staff meetings as teachers would justify their protestations to referred students. There were times I just wanted to pleasantly inquire as to what were they hired to do? Why had they chosen this public profession? I wanted to inform them that the Catholic Arch Diocese and the Peace Corp were always looking for a few good teachers.

From my experience, educators had a total disregard for the input of the mental health profession, even special education teachers who one would think would have some inkling about creative methods of supporting kids in alternative programs. Therapists were not welcomed into classrooms for observation or input. It was like we were some cancerous cell that needed to be contained if not eradicated. Educators just gave the impression that, within their grandiose curriculum offerings, there was no need for therapeutic insight. God, it must be great to have all the right answers! I had told Lou the old joke about how many narcissists it took to screw in a light bulb. Lou not only did not know the answer (one to hold it as the world turns around them), Lou didn't get the humor. Maybe it was too close to home.

I opened the door to my office to hear what further snippets I could from the intake conversation between Lou and Mike.

"Dude, I've been to schools like this where they smoke."

Fine with me. Ever think of attending them successfully? Time to move this intake to closure.

I casually stated, "I'm sure you have Mike, but that's a non-issue here, you can take it or leave it. There is no way to force you to come into our program. Just like Marianne has stated, it's on you. You need to be willing to accept the challenge." There, I said it. Your decision, you can live without us. We can live without you. Boy did that feel good. Knock the jerk back a bit. If it wasn't Valley Oak, good luck with whatever else you've got going. Yes! Score one for The Dude.

Although I thought myself so subtle, my frustrated flat lack of compassion comments perked Marianne up to the edge of her seat. Her abrupt glare at me stated she was feeling that I was setting Mike up to have him blow off program, she would be right. As much as I wanted student number twelve, I'd had enough. I'd done my part. Played it straight up. I had been doing so well, too, not one sarcastic comment or snide remark. Then too, I could feel Laura's heavy breathing on me. I could almost guarantee that her door was open and she was listening to this entire scene. She would condemn my effort as lackluster. Feeble. Laura would advise me that Mike's verbal objections were, in actuality, his initial attempts, albeit sordid, to engage in dialogue. Mike could have stalked out of Valley Oak and thumbed a ride home.

I took a breath. OK Laura, I'll give him another shot. Might be awkward, but here goes. I looked to see if I could draw Mike in. I knew I needed to present a positive voice that I did not feel.

"Mike," I began, "that part of program is set. We just do not believe that smoking is something healthy and to be engaged in during the school program. You want to smoke on your own time, that's up to you." I plunged on. "Mostly, our program is about not drawing lines. We work without quiet rooms, try to find things that interest students. Work those areas of interest into their school program."

Mike seemed to take this in. Then he jerked a thumb in the direction of James, "So dude, what do you do with that fat fuck in the kitchen?"

AAAAAAaaaaaaaaiiiiiihhhh!!!!! He just won't stop! I wanted to smack him real hard! Marianne was stifling a laugh. Mike was so good at targeting others. Mike, for sure, had me pegged. He had manipulated people like me all of his life. He wasn't the problem. It was everything else.

I attempted to keep my dude coolness. I looked towards James, who was rinsing off and placing lunch plates into the dishwasher, and replied, "If you are asking about James, I can tell you that he's earned the right to ride his bike three miles to the athletic club, work out on his own, and be back in time for lunch. Hopefully, we will start transitioning him back to his district high school in the Fall."

Mike scornfully laughed, "Whatever dude. What would I have to do if I came here?"

Oh, I don't know. Maybe sing me some Snoop Dog rap with resounding joy. Be prepared to tell me what to do. Improve my life with your insight. Allow me to cater to your needs. My problem was that Laura was again coming in with correct insight. Like, give me a break. Mike had, actually, verbally stated an interest as to program participation. By my maintaining a formal directness and not negatively reacting to his B.S, he was asking questions about program. Now what?

Marianne answered, visibly thankful for my positive resurrection and the pause to enter the conversation, "Lou is part of the IEP Team that determines your goals and objectives. He can inform you about program policies such as no quiet rooms and non smoking, but we will have an IEP meeting to determine what you will work on it program. Items like smoking can be modified at the IEP meeting to assist you in being more successful in program."

Well, Marianne got that right. As much as I wanted to play King Lou, I still had to work with the IEP Team.

Mike sauntered into the living room and we followed. "Dude, I can ride around town with no staff, like the fat boy?"

Is this Lou guy for real? Marianne had told me about the cash I could earn during the school day. How program went on activities from ball games to movies. That there were no time-out rooms. Restraints were the last thing done, not the first. I don't get it. It's like everything is wide open. Has to be a catch.

The thought of Mike's enrollment was becoming very unpleasant. He was going to be able to twist and maneuver situations in a skillful manner. Look at where the smoking policy was being compromised. Thanks Marianne. Pretty soon Valley Oak could be supplying clean needles.

I was stumbling through the intake interview. This was new territory. I was feeling my way through. I took out the caution flag, "Mike, those are things you can earn doing. You just do not walk into program and get offered the spokes to the city. There are some expectations that the IEP Team will ask you to meet up with."

I heard Lou's response and my faith of a just and noble universe was promoted. He had just taken the negative off of himself. Lou was learning that he did not need to be the enforcer coming up against a student. Place the onus on others like the IEP Team or the Judicial System or Educational Graduation Expectation or the Big Karma in the Sky. Learn to be a cheerleader and not to pass immediate restraining judgment. Keep yourself on the side of the positive. Offer the student a way for their needs to be met, for you to be on their side in approaching an issue of concern. Way to go Lou!!

Marianne gave me a perplexed look as if I were an alien from another planet. I don't think she could believe that I was being so insightfully agreeable. She nodded me a curt smile. I looked on as she took on the bad cop persona.

"And, Michael, you do know the boundaries. You have attended several IEP meetings. I know you've heard this earlier, but I must make very clear to you, that if you cannot be successful at Valley Oak, as we have stated, we will look for an out of county residential placement."

"I'm not stupid Marianne. I heard that the first ten times!" Mike spat out.

He hawked up a lugi, looked at the wastebasket, but didn't deposit. Charming. I wondered if I could assist him to say copulate? Out of county placement was a bummer for sure. I would rather stay in my own neighborhood than be shipped out to some other county. There could be worse things waiting for you at home than your natural parent, at least you knew where to hide. It gave me the thought that there might be something here that gets Mike's attention? Marianne knew it as well. The Choice would be Mike's and it was a clear behavioral boundary for someone who was a conduct disordered snot expectorating wannabe.

And, NO, this wasn't about me!

AUGUST 10 Hope?

"Watch this Lou, I can do four!!"

I walked out from the computer room to the front porch. It was a hot sultry day and the large front lawn of the Victorian was awash with spray from the water sprinkler shooting through the stretched fabric of our blue trampoline. Five students and three staff were spaced around the edge of the trampoline drenched in wet sunshine. The on-shore afternoon breeze had yet to billow the curtains from the open second floor window of the Victorian where Laura had set up her therapy room. Mike, barefoot and soaked, bounded. Getting his timing set to torque into a foreword-backward-forward-backward somersault routine. Pearl Jam blasted from the stereo.

I called out, "The crowd's here! Let see it!" I marveled at his confidence. I knew I was limited to one flop. Zero coordination at this point of life. Not to mention fear of re-injuring my spine. I was never able to land on my feet. Mike could do four flips. Switching directions. Keeping himself on the trampoline. It was like he was on a string. No training, just coordinated. Two-time all-star. I watched as he did his forward-back-forward-back routine, droplets shaking off him like a wet pit bull, landing on his feet and bracing to a stop.

"See that, Lou?" Dude was past history.

"Sure did, Mike. That's good stuff."

He was an athlete. Natural. Quick. Fast. Willing to take the risk. He had tanned during the summer activities, already hard bodied. His lean tautly muscled physique was poised to develop a body builder's structure. His zits had vaporized. To my amazement, during Mike's brief school attendance, the smoking issue had never become one. Mike was into being healthy. Feeling good, enjoying the positive attention he received for his efforts.

"I'll get another forward into it next week." He somersaulted down to the lawn as James used the footstool to roll on. Mike took his position to spot for James. "No cannonballs, James," Mike laughed, his new braces, that Maryanne assisted in acquiring, shined. James smiled down at him. James could only bounce on his knees as his weight would make his redirection impossible to stop him from crashing off the trampoline.

"Let's see some body slams!" Mike challenged. When Mike was involved in physical activity, he was into the scene with a focused aggressive joy that obscured negative issues. "Pin the sucker James!"

Our summer program was really geared to meet Mike's needs. During the summer session we focused on academics in the morning and then, in the afternoon, looked to do activities the students were interested in like biking, swimming, bowling, bringing out the trampoline, going for walks, or indoor activities such as computer and art. However, to be involved in these positive "leisure" activities, the student's morning needed to be successful. This was difficult enough for Mike, even in our laid-back summer program. He believed he had a right to speak what was on his mind anytime, anywhere. After all, this was America.

August 12   Honey Moon's Over

Mike feigned disbelief, "Why the fuck not?"

We were off-site, involved in Community Based Instruction. I calmly replied, "That's not an appropriate term."

Mike reeled, clowning thunderstruck indignation. "What's wrong with fuck? It's a natural act. My mother says it. My grandmother says it. They both did it or I wouldn't be here. I've said it since I was four. So, Lou, what's your fucking problem? I mean like it's not like calling someone a bitch. Right Lou? That's what you say. Now bitch is a bad word. Baaaaad,"

Mike shook his head like some craggy goat. He paused, then stated in a pontific re-stuttering of one of my statements, "Fill…fill….filled with sexualized historical pre..pre…prejudice." He was locked in. "Inotherwords, no bitch president. Way to keep the bitches down. In their place. Let them bitch. Can't use bitch. But fuck? What's wrong with fuck? Everyone fucks. Sometimes you get fucked. Even butt fucked. So what the fuck?"

"Thank you, Mike." Again, this could be doctoral research material.

He stood there lecturing me in a loud voice in the middle of Frank's Ace Hardware Store as if he were John Madden discussing the right type of pliers to purchase and why you should buy them from "The Helpful Hardware Man." I believed him, that his ancestral statements were accurate. Now, here he stood, as if on a podium, haranguing me with my logic on the prejudicial nature of language. Comparing fuck to bitch.

I sighed. I knew where this dialogue was going. "Mike, that doesn't make the term right, especially needing to present this in a social public forum."

He went into another tangent. "Lou, you're all the time telling me that might makes right."

Mike wasn't even angry. He's just enjoying this. Just such a game, but why here? Why in the middle of a social community? What does this do for him? He just gets so stoked, can see my embarrassment. He's on a roll.

Mike's voice is loud as he follows me past the electrical aisle as I try to make the exit. "Remember how you're always telling us about Humpty Dumpty and Alice. Right has nothing to do with it. You know what I think Lou?"

No, I did not nor did I really want to find out. I knew that Humpty wasn't put back together again.

Mike stood in front of me and whispered, "I think you got a problem with fucking." Now he spun in the air and slapped his hands together in joyous revelation. "That's it! I bet you got a personal problem with fucking, Lou. Maybe your plumbing is plugged up." He looked with concern at my crotch. "Don't you get fucked enough or are you just fucked up?"

Mike was having a real hoot.

Was this a multiple choice or true false test? I wondered how many times Mike had done this to an adult and gotten a toaster tossed at him.

Did he stay awake nights thinking the material up on his own for me? Mike's viewpoints were fairly insightful humor and I chose not to respond. However, Mike's ability to employ program principals and manipulate them to support his point of view did bring about an urge in me to put him in a duffel bag. Get out my favorite baseball bat and knock him into the corner for a double! Pardon me Laura, I meant to say, to redirect him in a positive manner and stabilize his escalating behavior by vesting him in developing an ownership for his actions. Getting to the basal root of what was stoking Mike's engine. Gee whiz, now I felt just a whole lot better. Thank the lord, the exit. I hurriedly pushed the glass door open with Mike yelping at my heels............

August 15 One More Customer

I had never thought of Red as the friendly bar tender, listening to customer's tales of woe. Yeah, I knew we had a special relationship, but I held that back. Another time. Another place. Red's only hard liquor was apple cider, fresh from the bottle, over ice. But, for sure, I knew he had a hell of a lot more insight into human nature than I did, especially on a day like today. Thank God it's Friday.

"Red, you have just got to see how this kid acts. I don't know what to do with him. It's the same stuff everyday." I whined with my mouth full of a Cajun Dog.

It was after hours. The red blinds on the front windows were three-quarters drawn, signaling last call for barbecue. Red had the plastic Russian Mustard squeeze containers lined up in front of him. They were shaped like basketballs. He had already washed them out and was setting them upside down on a clean white towel. He would fill them up the next morning. Red wasn't about to have some old condiments detract from his menu.

I put my dog down, swallowed a long drink of ice water. I had taken in too much Buzzard Breath Hot Sauce. It wasn't Red's hottest, but he wouldn't harass me for my choice, said he kept it around because one of his friend's made the brew up for wannabes like me.

"Red," I was imploring him for support. Some brotherhood of understanding, "Right in the middle of Frank's Hardware Store."

Red just kept on putting utensils away, seemingly unaware of the trauma of his lone closing hour's customer. Grudgingly, he looked over at me. Well Lou," he finally granted me some attention, "How'd the young man get in that hardware store?"

You have got to be kidding me? Say what? Red too? How'd the kid get there? Sounds like something Laura would put at me. Was it Mike's fault for going off on you in the hardware store? Of course not, you brought him there you moron! What should you expect? Please and thank you very much. I appreciate the opportunity to look at the tool displays? Jesus. H. Christ!!

"Lou," Red continued in his deep gravel tone, "I no more support the way Bobby Knight treats his troops than you do and you know that."

Red's right. I do know that.

"Now then, I can no more let go of Indiana Hoosier Red than you can the Red Sox and Ted Williams. Wish as we might to have idolized Stan is the Man." He tossed the cleaning rag into the basket from twenty feet away and continued, "The mystic forces of chance have given us our heroes and role models. We just gotta live with them the best we can." Red tossed his red hand towel into the deep sink. "We are where and who and what we are."

I had to admit, there were times when The Curse of The Babe weighed on my sense of allegiance, not to get into Williams never tipping his cap or owning for his Hispanic roots. But my support of physical restraints for students like Mike Adams was based on fact, not chance. Birthrights. Prisons weren't built to form relationships, unless Aryan Supremacy is a positive.

"C'mon Red. You know you are starting to sound like this...."

Red holds up his hand for pause and picks up the phone on the second ring, he shakes his head, smiling, hangs up the phone and walks past me to the door. I shrug and finish off my Cajun Dog. Good to the last chomp. Drain the ice water. I hear voices as he opens the door. Red's got another after last hour customer? Maybe delivery. Then, I hear the unmistakable clomp of wooden clogs on Red's tile floor. Tell me NO. Couldn't be? But there SHE was!

"Hey Lou. How's the food here?"

Laura Russo slid into the counter stool next to me. I was dumbstruck! My bastion. Port of refuge. What's next, is she going to show up in right field at Fenway with my buddies?

Red can see that I'm a bit blown away. He winks at Laura and utters, "I imagine the two of you are familiar with one another."

I nod.

Laura dead pans, "Sure, Red, I work with Lou at Valley Oak. In fact, I'm program director over there. Right Lou?"

I nod again. I don't know when I have last been caught so unaware. I feel like I was back in fifth grade at my first spring dance.

Red shakes my shoulder. He might be in his sixties but his grip is a claw. "Lou, you still with us?" He looks right into my eyes and lets go his hard deep laugh. "Guess you're surprised that Ms. Laura and I know one another."

I try to regain some sort of presence, "Red, you're always ten speeds ahead of me. I turn to Laura, "So, Ms. Laura, what do you need with me on a Friday afternoon?"

This time Red gives me a soft pop in my right shoulder that spins me half way around on my stool and growls at me, "That's no way to welcome a customer into my premises!"

"Awwww, go easy on him Red," laughs Laura. "He's still got a lot to learn."

Red stares hard into me. I know he could knock me into the cheap seats. I want to look away, then I see his creases flicker, "If you say so Miss Laura. I'll reel in the dogs."

I almost feel sorry for Lou. The sanctity of his relationship with Red had been breached. I know Red had become a much-revered father figure for Lou. Oh well, he would have had to know sooner or later.

"So," I manage, "How long have the two of you known each other?"

Red closes the doors to The General and salutes. "Miss Laura, how long have you been on the East Coast?"

Laura lifts her leather briefcase to the counter. Rests her chin on it. Ponders. I can see her counting. "Seems about fourteen years."

Red lets go a soft whistle. "That long that quick?"

"Lots of ribs." Laura laughs.

"Would you like some now?" Red asks. "Just gotta open up The General. I can hear them asking to come on out."

Laura begs off. "I have to get in my aerobics yet, Red! Anyway," she turns to me, "I came in to give Lou these two new referrals so he could look them over this weekend."

Laura uses both her hands to lift the thick cumulative folders out of her leather satchel, hands them to me. "See what you think Lou." She tosses her braided hair behind her back. "Gotta go. Time to sweat. Thanks for letting me in Red."

"Anytime, day or night for you Miss Laura." Red walks her to the door with both laughing as he closes it.

I stand in the doorway wiping my hands on my apron and watching as Lou carries away the two folders. He places them in the backseat of his beat up Honda and scratches Rudy, who is on the driver's seat, asking him to move on over. Hands him a rib full of meat. Lou places a wrapped bowl of my chili on his dash, waves, and I salute him back.

How long have I known Lou? Seemed like forever. Now, this Ms. Laura, she was special. She came into my barbecue while Lou was still on the West Coast. Why had I not let Lou know that Ms. Laura and I were friends? I smiled as I locked the door and pulled the shades all the way down.

I drove away from Red's and caught myself smiling in the mirror. I really enjoyed blindsiding Lou with my relationship with Red. Have to think about that some other time. I do acknowledge that Lou and Valley Oak are one in the same. How he transitioned from his restraint obsessed behavioristic background was paramount. Lou's perspective would define the Valley Oak program. He had not yet reached the point where he could consistently pro act to redirect himself from his classic polysyllabled obscure responses that encouraged a student with Mike's needs to model and sabotage. Giving it right back to Lou as he had done to all figures of authority throughout his life. I recalled how, for myself, upon first meeting Lou, I had been overwhelmed and impressed by his layered knowledge and insightful humor. However, slowly, over the following weeks, I had stepped back to assuage all that was transpiring in Lou and how he impacted program. Red and Marianne had offered additional perspectives.

Not that I have a complete chart, but Lou had disclosed to me aspects of his life with his adopted parents. Lou had several stories presenting how he was made to attend Catholic Church. One story was how he had decided not to attend church because he could not love a god that he did not know. This lasted about three weeks until his father told him, nice try, now get back to church. Lou's father was an agnostic. But Carina, Lou's mom, had been raised in the church and expected Lou to do the same until he was confirmed, then he could make his own decision. Lou had agreed, as long as he did not have to attend a Catholic school or be an altar boy.

If there was one thing Lou would have rather been than a teacher it was an athlete. Although Red would disagree, Lou told how he was not a superior athlete, but he worked hard and enjoyed the challenge. For instance, Lou described how, in his last year of elementary school, the sixth graders got to play work ups every morning before first bell. The tradition was that the first student at school who touched the ball monitor's door was first batter and so on. Lou, for the entire year of sixth grade, was always the first batter. He hit more home runs than any other sixth grader. Not because he was the best hitter, just the most consistent early riser.

My sports analogy for Lou is that he needs to become more like a Magic or Larry or Derek Jeter who assist those around them to do a better job. Lou needs to develop the inner confidence that will empower others to lay aside their protective masks and accept the relationships that life offers them. Easily said.

That, for whatever reason, I found myself thinking about Red and Lou was intriguing. There was just something about their relationship that I was totally not aware of, just their manner around each other. I had surprised Lou today, but Red and I went back several years. Why had not Red let Lou know of our friendship? The thoughts they exchanged with their eye contact were enigmatically beyond me. Well, that was a mystery but, for now, I had to shake my fat off!

August 18   How Much More..........

We were outside the men's locker room at the Five Star Bay County Health and Tennis Club. Mike continued, "Are you deaf or dumb? Hello? Lou? Knock, knock! Is this your fucking therapeutic disengagement moment? I thought your program was dialogued based. Dude, you can't fucking dialogue because there just isn't one goddamn reason why I can't go into the men's locker room and take a Jacuzzi. Like, am I going to get fucked? Am I going to see something new?"

I should mention that this whole "fucking dialogue" came about because Mike wanted to use the hot tub at the club. The Jacuzzi at the athletic club was in the men's locker room and you could make a choice to go in nude or wear a bathing suit, neither of which was OK for the Valley Oak program. It was part of our deal with the health club. We were not to use the indoor spa. End of story.

I felt people leaving our area of the club with looks of concern. Mutterings.

"How sad."

"Poor kid."

"Look at the father. What could you expect."

I approached Mike, trying some proximics and spoke softly, "Mike, we have talked about his issue. That you are choosing to get into your rights to use the spa at this level at our health club is something of a concern, just like at the hardware store."

Mike grabbed his crotch and limped around in a circle. "You think some of those gay guys are going to grab my dong or that I'm going to get excited watching some fifty-five year old fart get naked? Where the fuck did you get off?"

That he could just blurt this stuff out at anytime was disconcerting, just flat out embarrassing. Then too, I had to ask myself, why was I embarrassed? Was my manhood being assaulted because I could not "fix" his problem? Was I concerned that the other members thought that he was my kid? I wondered how many members were appreciating the father and son social interaction? Why had I thought that it was OK to go off-site with him? This was like the seventy-eighth time this had occurred. I admit the fact Red, I brought him here! It's on me and Conduct Disordered individuals need clear boundaries. They do not need breaks. You give them a break and they think you're a wuss.

I began a slow retreat towards the door. "Mike, we've always said, away from program, you can smoke your cigarettes or go into the Jacuzzi at the club. It's your life. You can do as you choose. In program, one of our rules is not to use the Jacuzzi at the club."

I took a moment and looked away. I knew I was beginning to vent and I would get "The Look" on. Lots of teachers pride themselves in "The Look." As in, when I get my look on, look out! The look can mean lots of things but, mostly the look means that the student needs to immediately make some marked behavioral improvement. The talking is over with. Get with program and get stabilized, or, yes, we can assist.

I had quickly learned that "The Look" did not work with the Conduct Disordered population. It was like these CD students had been there seen that and if that's all you got then you better go back and retool your stabilizing techniques. "The Look" had given way to the "Therapeutic Look Away," which I was now posturing for Mike, choosing not to engage in an optic battle. Just leave the nonverbal threats alone. Let him figure what to do. Of course, this pissed him off just as much. Then too, anything an adult did would piss someone like Mike off, and, yes I am sounding repetitive.

"This is old stuff, Mike. If you need to continue the conversation, we can do the review back at school."

At times like this Mike would get this incredulous look on his face, like he was talking common sense and I was just too stupid to get it. Pardon me, toofuckingstupid to get it. What was it with him? What was his reality? Did he not have the language skills to carry on a conversation that was not vindictive or sarcastic? Even his defense was offensive. I understood that this type of student processed events as if there was static on the radio station. Bad reception. Weak channels. A speech therapist might say pragmatics was the issue. Just could not do the encode/decode stuff at a level to match up with the social norm. They developed a narcissistic grandiosity to protect their vulnerable self-image. Toss in some ADHD. Dysfunctional family, and, presto-change-o, assaultive confrontational-verbal- endangerment.

We had referred Mike to our Speech Therapist. Mike would not allow our speech therapist to work with him or even test him. I had told Mike it could be worse. Like me, I had been in speech. Look at my language skills. This had been during the first through third grades. My issue was articulation. I had the "lazy l" syndrome and would tell someone, "It's too co'd outside to go to schoo', I to'd you so." Fortunately, way back then, the remedy for my issue was easily determined, I needed my tongue clipped. Of course, that hadn't been the cure, although I distinctly remember the operation. For years I would "awake" at night from the chloroformed induced sleep, unable to move with a whirlpool of orange, green, black, and red squares sucking me down into a deep whirlpool slumber that I could only stop by moving a leg. At these times I would awake and look for the liquid cherry jello that had been kept next to my bed during recovery.

I wondered if having Mike's brain clipped would allow him to consider other alternatives? Where were frontal lobotomies when you needed them?

"Hey Lou, do you mind if I go over and check out the new hand ball gloves?"

Did I miss something in the translation? I don't think so, but with Mike, it was no big deal. Like there wasn't even a negative interaction. Just, hey, can I check out those cool gloves? In a public forum had we not just been reviewing his rights to go into the Jacuzzi with naked old farts? I still didn't know if this was my fucking problem. Was I just fucked up? But for Mike the dance was over. Done. Just cut and dried. What Jacuzzi? What club? Move on. Was this the same person had informed the hardware store as to my need for a washer when employing a screw? Challenging my perspective of social norms? Nunca. Never happened. Like Lou, what was personal about what I just said? I'm fine. You got a problem? I don't. Maybe you should look at yourself. This could be about you.

At times like this I knew my ownership was a distinct possibility.

We walked through the main lobby of the club picking up James and one other student. They had earned the right to have been on their own at the club. With Mike, we were offering him a reward even if he had not earned the right. We had made the therapeutic decision to offer Mike positive experiences that he had not earned. The thought was that Mike would desire to improve his decision making as he experienced the positive aspects of Community Based Instruction. Got that Ms. Laura. This was a basic part of the Relationship Model. Right Ms. Laura? Due to Mike, everyone was calling Laura, Ms. Laura. Like there had been some coronation! Well, Ms. Laura, as you have so often presented, we had developed the rationale in our program that the students could not accept being successful without sabotaging their success. They could handle failure more readily because that's what had filled up their experience. Success was not part of their picture. Since failure was the natural state, the onus was on Valley Oak to present positive situations for them to experience, such as the Frank's Hardware Store or the health club, even if they had not earned the reward. Trying to break the cycle of failure and have the students trust success. So many of these experiences ended like the one with Mike where I came away feeling like I had been there before and had not learned anything. Here, beat me again. I can handle it. It's not personal. I know, I know, Ms. Laura. Forget IT, just move on.

We came out of the club into the heat of the early afternoon.

"Lou?"

"Yes, James?"

As a maroon '51 Mercury went by Mike spun around, jumping in the air. "What kind of bitchin' car is that?"

"Pardon me, Mike, James was asking me a question."

"What the fuck!" Mike stamped past us. "Answer his fat fucking boring goddamn question. Like I give a flying fart."

Here we go again. Mike just could not contain himself. From Jacuzzi to handball gloves to cars, something that would meet his need to gain attention. Something that would take care of the "I" in his world. Some form of nurturing that would soothe the wounded child. So how did I respond?

"You could say flying flagellate, the term has the same alliteration." When I look back and think, could I not have said, Mike, that's a sharp car. Gone back to James' boring question? Why did I need to throw unintelligible transformational terms at him? Why did I need to piss him off further?

"Where in the fuck are you coming from Lou? What the flying fart fuck are you going to do because I'm fucking going to say fart!"

I am totally done with Lou's fucking puny therapeutic bullshit. I can see in his eyes that he just wants to beat the crap out of me. Seen that look too many times. Have to catch me first. But all this bullshit about, how do I feel? What have I thought about? Did I consider this shit or that shit or like I give a shit. These fuckheads can send me one hundred miles somewhere. Walking around with fat boy and these other jerks is over. Enough of this crap.

I just shrugged, at least we were outside. We started towards the van and the safe haven of the Victorian. "That's right Mike, you can. You are making the point you can say those words. That you choose to instead of saying copulate or flagellate is up to you."

"Goddamn right I can and you can't stop me."

This polysyllabled dialogue approach was bringing me to the point of just being pissed off at this little punk. I needed to take on another tact. Certainly a review of my thought vocabulary beyond pissed off. It was time to try a behavioral boundary. I'd had it with being verbally assaulted.

"Mike, do you think that it might be in your best interest to have some assistance in being safe on the way home?"

God that was smart! Just brilliant Lou!! Why did I have to say that? All the students knew that being safe and offering assistance were code words to putting your ass down in an industrial strength prone restraint. What was I going to do to enforce it? Out in the community? A single staff? I just told him that he had gotten to me. That I was ready to kick his ass. I was tired of listening to his BS, just like his parents, just like his other teachers, just like all the adults in his world. What possessed me to challenge him over words out in public? For that matter, anywhere over this type of issue. Was he a danger to self or others? Maybe I was.

Mike just howled a laugh that doubled him over. "You going to run your fat ass in circles trying to restrain me?" He started gagging on the mental picture. James and the other student just stood there patiently, waiting for the latest episode to resolve itself.

That comment really hurt! Though I worked out consistently, I knew I could be thinner. I certainly couldn't catch Mike Adams if a Cajun Dog depended on it.

"That really hurt Mike." Try to use some humor around "I" phrases to diffuse this situation. "You know how much I work out. Just more difficult to stay in shape at my IQ." Maybe it wasn't too late to get back to being peripheral.

Mike began dancing in circles around our group as we walked to the van. I was not entirely sure how I had ended up in this situation, but I knew I was getting ready to call in on the cell phone and ask for assistance.

Mike started chanting, "Whatcha gonna do Lou? Whatcha gonna do? You' re so fat, I bet you jiggle when you screw!"

He looked over to Nick and James. "C'mon you guys. Join in!"

I was out of ideas. "We can choose not to bring you into program."

Mike roared. "Yeh, right. Shiver me timbers. Call an IEP! Give up the one hundred and thirty dollars per day you get for telling me not to say fuck. (Not to mention the seventeen dollars for transportation.) Give me a copulating break!"

For me, that sounded like a one hundred and forty-seven dollar fucking-copulated flagellated deal!

I called Marianne when we got back to the Victorian. We were way over the thirty day trial period with no discernable change in Mike's attitude. Sure there had been moments of hope and progress, but permanent change was wistful thinking. Marianne and I agreed the time had come for something more restrictive, like a hundred miles away. I knew Laura would support this direction before I went into self-destruct.

The thing was, I wasn't sure if Mike or myself who should take the hundred-mile hike.

Students such as Mike Adams depleted all resources in a Relationship Program. For instance, during his brief time with Valley Oak, Mike had wanted to become employed in a bike shop. Lou brought in bike books, videos on maintenance and repair, and had gone on twenty-mile bike rides with Mike to get use to what the road can bring at you. Mike changes his mind and decides that he wants to be a boxer. Lou arranges for him to go to the PAL gym and gain tutelage from the local Golden Glove contenders and other semi pros. Mike changes his mind and wants to take up hand ball.

Whatever is offered to students such as Mike just is never enough to meet their needs. Dialogue becomes a weapon for them to gain immediate rewards and to verbally assault and twist social norms. Mike or Lou or Valley Oak or Marianne or Mike's parents are not to blame. We are all in this together.

I recall my history professor evaluating my essay on Stalin. I had stated that Stalin's starving of millions was inhuman. My professor asked me that, given the atrocities throughout human history, were Stalin's actions actually what made humans human? That gave me pause but has not discouraged, but rather intensified, my desire to improve myself and my species.

For Mike, the change meant that he would have to be placed out of county in a more restrictive environment. One that would have clearer behavioristic expectations with student placements more in line with Mike's case history. Expectations that were written in black and white with scant room for dialogue. As Lou would say, a place that went clank. Mike may have been poorly served by coming into Valley Oak.

I was at a therapeutic impasse as to whether a referral, such as Mike with his Conduct Disordered history, could accept the relationship boundaries of a day treatment program such as Valley Oak. Historically, students such as Mike Adams, could not benefit from a Valley Oak Day Treatment program. Valley Oak could not service the needs of all of Bay County's referrals. Maybe I was just rationalizing our failure in assisting Mike. I just am not sure. What I do know is that for Lou, and Mike, not to mention my personal sanity, I needed to be more surgical with Valley Oak's intake policy.

Chapter 4

SHARON: TANGLED DEMONS

September 7, 1994

The howling wail piercingly reverberated throughout the staid Victorian. "He's my lover!! I love him! I am with his child! Doesn't anyone hear me?! (I do.) Blubbering. Coughing. Hacking gasp emitting. Breath sucking angst................. Aaaaaaaaaaaaaaaaaaa!!! Muuuuuuuutherrrr! Muuuutherrrrrr! Mooommmmyyyyyyyyyyyy! Help me! Heeeeelp meeeee!!

Sharon collapsed into a sob wringing heap on the dining room floor. Her long brown hair matted in disarrayed clumps of tangled contorted depression. Deep red welts with fingernail dug scabs marked her shoulders where a sleeveless yellow striped blouse had been tugged and tortured to tattered remnants. I stood ten feet away, blocking an exit to the other students, keeping my distance. This was not something I wanted to jump into. I knew this could be just the beginning. A prologue to a discordant harmony of terror she could only hear. Sharon was the maestro. She had the podium. She held the wand. We looked at one another, waiting. Not sure what to do. The staff didn't make a move because I was in charge. This was my program. If I didn't have a clue, no one else would. I knew, we had to be prepared to assist her in not doing harm to herself or others. Last Thursday had been helacious.............

While preparing for lunch Sharon had taken out two bay windows with a chair. She would have taken out two more if, while she had the chair raised, I hadn't called for team control and restrained her. We had to be concerned for the safety of all involved. Safety was the bottom line of rationale. I looked over at Marcia, who was quietly herding her crew of four students away from Sharon. Through the kitchen and screened porch. Out the backdoor towards the picnic tables. Away from the scene of escalation. They needed no prompting. I wished that I was going with them. I turned back to Sharon. Her turbulent history filled binders in several psyche ward file cabinets. The property damage she had committed on our site alone was in the thousands of dollars. Mike Adams even kept his distance from Sharon. Why had Laura brought her into Valley Oak? Sharon fought demons only she could summon.

We stood silent as the anguish slowly subsided. Sharon's sobbed wracked breathing diminished. Although she remained fragilely huddled, we could feel a gathering of herself. A billowing of emotion. This occurred after the tears and screaming, as she secured a second wind, began to emit low ominous moans. Her presence would become more focused. Awareness to the moment returned. Fortunately, this time, all the students had left the area. I motioned for staff to give Sharon more space. We drifted back towards the chairs and couches of the living room. Assuming detached postures that none felt. We awaited Sharon's unfurling. This was her ritualistic transition back. Back to her contorted reality, not ours. Hers. A stricken life for which she had erected a controlling shrieking shield to insulate herself from. To diminish her pain. Hide her heart, and, as with so many of our students, gain attention through dysfunctional needful asocial acts. Acts that had become internalized into daily operative behavior.

There was no longer any separation for Sharon as her fantasies had become reality as she, so like a Phoenix, slowly. Desperately. Eloquently unwound from the pyre of her collapsed corpse.

Where the fuck am I? Who the fuck are those assholes? What's staring at me?

The first sign of movement came as her pallid head gradually shifted, emerging to display random bruise marks. Scratches. Cuts. Lifting the marred orb disengaged from the torso embedded mound presenting dark, ringed, fear furtive eyes protruding through streaked sooted mascara. Charcoal lipstick smear lined lips drew a crooked smudge beneath a forever broken, splattered nose. Her hands raised to form a shield across her full eyebrows. Sharon could now recognize light and movement. She could see the room, details would come later. I could detect her drug-scarred focus latching on the various activities. There was Jack leaning against the doorway. Fred, with a leg up, stretched on the couch. Laura was in the entry hall, hands in her extended vest pockets.

Creatures......need to clear.....NO.......not things......people. People like me. I know them. Fred the Non-blinker...... Jack Hot Bod............ Lou the Cool...........Just hanging out. Waiting. That's it! Waiting for me. Waiting to see what I'll do.........what.........what should I do..........

None of us were looking directly at Sharon. Eye contact was a fatalistic challenge to do battle with her demons. A wave of the wand to unleash savage omens. No magic wand. This was too real. Too savage. We chose to defer. Waiting.

Laura cautiously, softly, stepped into the room. Sharon's visual search came to rest on our fish tank, ten feet from her. As Sharon scanned her eyes began to dart from fish to fish. The situation escalated became, suddenly, more volatile. I could feel the staff tense. Afraid. We knew the next event could be violent. If I could feel the vulnerability, so could Sharon. I caught a vision of Jack and Fred, both tight, wound up. Keeping their distance and posture. They were passive participants in Sharon's movements. I was too. I made sure that I continued to breathe regularly. I found myself praying that a restraint would not occur. I envisioned writhing fish spilled out on the carpet amidst broken glass and distraught staff. We had attempted other interventions that were not as physically intrusive. These had allowed Sharon to take out lamps. Mirrors. Windows. Computers. Endangered herself and others. We knew that the only way to stabilize her was to place hands-on.

Fear. I loathe their fear. I smell their fear seeping. These shitting excrement adults who think they can subdue me by pinning my physical body to the carpet. What fools! My powers go beyond their naïve awareness. There shall come a time when I will awaken all my senses and shatter their ignorant mortality..........

I had never been involved in a more difficult restraint.

"Team control!!!!!!!!"

I blinked, took my mind off tilt, realizing I had drifted. Sharon remained in front of me, contemplating the scene around her. Even in this state there was no denying her physical attractiveness. On community based activities she turned heads she was never aware of. Then too, how do

113

you wear a skin tight, cleavage exposing top, with wayward wanton eyes, and not get some wandering looks. Then too, where's the supervision? Sharon continued her ritualized stabilization. Slowly. Methodically. Smoothly. Her elbows lifted to align even with her forehead, palms flat toward the ceiling. Double jointed? Beneath this limbed canopy, her eyes quick scanned their shelter, glimmering recognition. Her eyelids fluttered in seizure signals. We tensed. Sharon arched her torso and straightened. I attempted to remain stoically passive. I leaned back. Outwardly calm, as if I was merely waiting for the light to change. Sharon took a full breath and forcibly leapt up to an extended stance straddle with her arms raised high. Wrists curled. ring adorned fingers spread wide, grimacing a shrieked proclamation, "Keith loved me. I am with his child!!"

Jack, Fred, Laura, and I remained comatose. Experience had taught us that our best intervention was to remain dispassionate. I wondered, who the hell was Keith? Couldn't be The Stones, that was Mick. He was pushing one hundred. Couldn't mean Keith Richards? Nirvana? I noted Jack nodding to Fred, they knew. I never could keep up with the current music trends. It now was the group. Pantera. Simplicity. Third Eye Blind. Foo Fighters. Who was in these groups? Where were the individuals? Where was Jim? James? Prince? Elvis? Janis? I could still name the four Beatles. How could I figure out their leading protagonists when I didn't know what had happened to mine? Again, my issue...................

"Sharon," Laura intoned entering her field of vision. Her layered pastel attire wafting a therapeutic demeanor. "Sharon, you are in the classroom. (Pausing.) You are at school. You are at Valley Oak." Laura paused, "We are getting ready for lunch"

Sharon looked for Laura's voice. Laura was trusted by Sharon.. Laura was a good object. I could see Sharon looking for Laura through the corona of her enveloped episode, reaching for the care and safety Laura provided. Laura had earned this trust by the countless visits made to Sharon's trailer home by the river. Laura had talked with Sharon's mother, neighbors, trailer park managers, and the menagerie of river life acquaintances. Laura had the ability to listen to all without devaluing. One came away feeling heard and understood. I knew that this did not mean that Laura agreed with a situation, but she just did not come right out and say it. In fact, Laura's tact had taken me a good while to figure out if I was being processed or given a straight answer. Mostly, I still didn't know...........

Sharon responded, "I'm OK now. I need to sit down." Sharon slowly knelt, crawled to the pillowed sofa. Her feet dragged along the floor. Mumbling, "What have I been saying? Where have I been? Where's Keith? Where's Jimi? Where are you?" She collapsed on the edge of a cushion. Her head fell back against the armrest. Her skin had been drained to a parlored chalk gray that left a moist mark on the flowered upholstery. I nodded to Jack and Fred. This one was over for now. Jimi and his flaming guitar were on break.....................

That Sharon's generation found Jimi and Morrison and so many others icons was another statement of how our generations crossed over. I never was a Sinatra or Como or Goodman fan. Now, Nat King Cole was cool. Even some Tony Bennet. Enough, back to program. Sharon was just a tornado touching down. The turbulence had subsided, for the moment...................

Back to serving lunch on the picnic tables. Late summer was presenting us with another warm balmy day. Culinary Arts had changed from baked to barbecued chicken and we would eat outside. I lingered in the high hallway listening to Sharon and Laura. Laura might need some assistance.

I stood beside Sharon. I appreciated Lou's concern, but I wish that he could have left with the others. The living room was not the best place to stabilize Sharon, someone could just walk in, but there was no moving her now. Sharon could not see Lou from her position. She should be alright. I sat down at the end of the couch, leaning back into a pillow. I tried to present a calm that I did not hold within. Sharon scared me.

Sharon immediately launched into her favorite boyfriend fantasies. She shook her massive curls as if to rid herself of the remembrance of the prior decompensation. The event had not happened. Did not exist. She would not admit the episode back to her reality until she had the need. An addict induced craving to rave in her tongue at the demands of the real world. She was a junkie whose paraphernalia was stored in her mind. She did not need needles to distort life.

Sharon began her liturgy while taking my offered tissue, "I waited for Ronnie to get done with work so we could go to his place and kick it. He needed to take a shower and wash off the grease before we fucked.

Sometimes we just couldn't wait and we'd get it on in the shower. He has such a hardass bod."

I needed to keep our dialogue from getting too sexual right from the get go. Lou was, at best, naïve, to state that Sharon was not aware of turning heads. "How is Ronnie doing with his job?"

Just great." She supported her head by placing an elbow on the armrest of the sofa. Her flowing crumbled hair obscuring one eye. "He really likes working on engines. Frank says that he's a natural, just knows the right tools to use and everything. Almost doesn't need a torque wrench to tighten down."

I remained attentive as Sharon's eyes suddenly fluttered and she paused.

"Where was I? Oh, yeh, Ronnie. What I really like is his hair. He keeps it short. Says he's going to get it shaved. I don't know if I would like that. I like feeling the short bristles. They rub up hard and rough against my skin, just like his beard between my thighs. I can see lots of his friends think that his bean would be cool shaved, but I don't know. What do you think?"

She is asking me. Inviting me in. Coming more out of herself. Becoming more aware of social interaction. Looks like she is going to come through this one quickly. What a relief. I have two more students to meet with before school adjourns. What did I think of skinheads? Personally, I had never been attracted to men with shaved heads. Hated the Neo Nazi convict emblem. The shaven head was something swimmers and other athletes did, and that was up to them. Maybe I had not experienced enough in divergent relationships. That was OK. I could handle the loss. Maybe Michael Jordan was just hiding male patterned baldness.

I found myself responding, "Oh, I don't know. I do think that people should be able to wear their hair the way it makes them feel good."

Sharon folded her arms under her full ripening breasts and squeezed herself tight. Her nipples protruded, outlined by her tight knit sweater. She refused to wear a bra. I often observed the younger males openly gawking, especially when she was on the trampoline. She was such a pretty girl. If she could just pull herself together. That was my job.

"I wish my mother felt that way. She's always moving into my conversations with Ronnie. Sharon paused and then came back. Do you have a cigarette? I could really use one. Never mind, no one smokes here.

I should know that. But she keeps telling him to keep his hair long. Like he cares what she thinks. She needs to take care of herself."

Sharon was moving into her fears and anger towards Martha, her mother. I knew that there was no Ronnie. On other days she would talk of Dave or Mustafa or Dante and all of these characters ended up being moved on or removed by Martha. Martha was the ever hovering enmeshed clouded character in Sharon's life. Martha the Ever-present. Martha the Omnipotent. Martha the Mover. How do mothers avoid that determination? How does anyone?

August 3   Immobile

I recalled an earlier meeting with Martha the Mother. I sat across from her in the small, cramped cubicle around the RV's kitchen table. There was no bump out. The Winnebago was a statement of her life. An immobile mobile stuck in a mud hole mosquito infested white trash trailer park next to one of our nameless sloughs. Martha had purchased the gem with the last of her disability settlement from the state. Twelve years with the DMV that had ended with her "accidentally" falling and receiving compensation. There was the grandiose plan where, Sharon and she were going to set off to see the United States and make a better life for themselves. They were going to move on to a world that would hold none of their beleaguered histrionic past. One where they could be with and support one another.

Events had gone marvelously for them at the outset. The two visited every RV sales lot in their tri-county area. Twice Martha had secured vacations to Florida from the dealers with the promise that they would close when they returned. With their newly purchased clothing, chic hair styles, and six digit bank account the dealers were ready to grant any of their wishes.

Finally they had to make a decision and had ended up here. Only eighty miles from their starting point as Martha met a guy at a bar with a "good" fishing boat and decided that she really did not need Sharon to gain karma in her life. The boat sucked up the remaining liquid cash account.

"I tell you Laura, I get nothing but lies and "what I need" out of that child." Martha said this while blowing a billow of smoke towards the open hatch in the roof. She knew I would appreciate the dialogue more if she didn't smoke, her compromise was to blow her smoke towards a vent.

"If I got Laura everything she wanted, there wouldn't be food on the table."

"Or smokes for your health." I enjoined with. I had known Martha long enough to be comfortable with reality based conversation.

Martha laughed, "Got me there kiddo!" Even though Martha was two years younger than I, she always referred to me as the youngster. Looking at Martha, with her facial life experiences marking the moments of the daily struggle, one would think she was ten years older than I. I came back around to our discussion.

"Martha, the focus for you is on gaining a healthier life style for yourself. I made two appointments for you with Mental Health/Social Services contacts for job training, neither of which you followed up on."

Martha stubbed out her cigarette and banged another one out of the box. That she did not light the cigarette from her previous one before it was extinguished might represent improvement. (I smiled to myself as I thought of catching my brothers smoking in the basement and what they had been made to promise me in order not to inform mom and dad.) Where or what were the authorities in Martha's life that would assist her in addressing the addictions she was living with? I knew I would not be able to make progress with Sharon unless I could intervene with Martha. Martha went back into old refrains.

"Laura, you know I didn't want to chain Sharon to her bed. That was her bastard father, Ralph. She lit her sixth cigarette, on my count, since my arrival, inhaled and blew out the match. "Well, that son of a bitch got what he deserved. Being locked up for the next ten years. God damn him!"

I knew from experience that this was Martha's way of saying that she was through with our conversation for that day. When she went back to her past with Ralph and how he, alone, had abused Sharon and made life a living hell for the two of them. Ralph was the one responsible for making the meth available and, since he was her husband, she became a codependent. Martha would then beseech me to forgive her and assist her in developing a healthier lifestyle. I would give her names and phone numbers with the promise that I would be back to check up on Sharon and her progress.

When I wrote up my notes on the conversations with Martha, I would be consistently disappointed with my inability to have any measureable impact on their lifestyle. As brilliant and introspective as my reputation was presented to be, there are moments when I would trade all of my LCSW credentials for a Jenn Aire Range and reruns of <u>All My Children</u>.

Driving home, I came back to Sharon. I could feel the helpless depths as her eyes wandered in and out of focus. I did have the ability to bring her back and have her acknowledge the needs of her present reality. Sharon so wanted me to be able to work with her towards better decisions and a physical and emotionally healthier life

Sharon's life had turned a corner and had become much more desperate. She was no longer a child as Planned Parenthood had unequivocally reported, but she was with child. I wondered if she had shared this information with Martha as Sharon was positive of going to term. Although Sharon was not certain of the father, she was willing, at this time, to accept the responsibility. In fact, when she was informed of her positive testing, she was overwhelmed with joy. I had to admit, one of Sharon's male fantasies was real or that an immaculate conception had occurred.

September 7   Culinary Arts

The darting fish would never know how close they had come to the carpet. Lou had left us alone, thank goodness. There was just the sounds coming from lunch being set up on the picnic tables. As Sharon began to edge away, I looked for a safer subject. "I talked to Martha. She mentioned moving. Something about relatives in the Morgantown area?"

"She's always moving. Probably would tomorrow if Ronnie could fire up the motor on the Winnebago. I hate that fucking piece of crap."

Sharon was becoming listless. Some food would be good for her.

"Sharon, what say we get some lunch?"

She staggered up off the couch, leaving a moistened facial imprint, "I'm starved. What are we having today?"

That was a good question. For sure, whatever we were having would be healthy and tantalizing. I always had to be aware of stuffing myself. The Culinary Arts Program had come to play a central vital role at Valley Oak.

Lou believed that food should not be an issue in program. Oranges, apples, bananas, and other seasonal fruits were always kept on display. Students could have them any time of the day that they wanted. They could be in the middle of a math lesson and ask if they could have an orange and the answer was always yes. Sometimes different fruits like kiwi and papaya were brought in. So far, the students' favorite was the mango! They loved to just suck on that huge seed. It was like a lollipop for them.

Program did its own shopping as part of Culinary Arts. We did this at the University Co-Op, which always had a bountiful supply of fresh organic fruits and vegetables in unique displays. The first thing Lou did, each Monday morning, was to get the two students whose turn it was to be our Culinary Artists that week to meet with Jack. The three of them had to figure out the daily diverse activities of program for the coming week. Where were we going off-site? Who would be here for lunch? How many might be earning Lunch Bunch? When they got the numbers determined, then they had to plan the meals.

Lou had come up with the name Culinary Arts due to a store in town having the same name. Culinary Arts just presented a better image than Let's Eat Food Production. Jack, our head chef, had been a fortunate hire for Valley Oak. He was a Culinary Artist, frustrated as he might be by our limitations. He had majored in nutrition and had begun his apprenticeship in the food industry at one of the local bar and grills. Gradually, over five years, he had worked his way to being a "Chef in Training" at one of the trendier white table cloth restaurants in our town. In fact, I remembered him from his chef days due to his height, he was six foot five, with a full beard. When Jack had been hired for our program, Lou discussed with him where he would like to see the food preparation taken. Lou never wanted food to be an issue for our students like one might experience in so many of their homes. He wanted the availability of fresh fruit, nutritious lunches that they could be prepared with Jack's supervision, and the involvement of the students in the planning, purchasing, preparation, and clean-up of the entire process that became known as Culinary Arts.

Jack agreed that this was a great idea. (Thank you, Jack.) One of his many insights was to add a special dessert to the menu each week. This was a "naughty" item that had nothing to do with health and nutrition, just tasted great. During the week, as students planned the meals, they would talk about what kind of dessert to prepare for Friday, Desert Day. This was Jack's forte. He was in his element watching the students blend whip cream and chocolate or lay down a flaky piecrust or combining kiwi and limes and some frozen concoction.

I sat down at the Costco picnic table waiting for Sharon and Laura to join us. Laura was magical in her ability to enter in and center individuals. I was proof of that. I looked around the table, everyone else was waiting as well. We did not begin lunch until everyone had come to table. There were times when situations occurred and not everyone was present but, for the most part, this was a ritualized aspect of our school day.

We were all seated at one long table, actually, there were three of the fold-ups joined together under two brightly patterned tablecloths. Twelve students and five staff now comprised the Valley Oak Program. James, due to his size, always sat at the head of the table. Sam and Mike were there, talking with students and staff seated near them. How we had grown from one to twelve students in less than six months had amazed me. The first five students had been placed by Marianne, but all the rest had come from districts outside of our immediate area. Caused me wonder what would happen if we advertised. We were now transporting students from districts twenty-five miles away. We were reaching our use permit maximum in the Victorian. All the rooms were loaded with computers and program related materials. We would need another therapist room, a room for IEP and family meetings, and, with reluctance, I was beginning to take a harder look at a rural site. I had always talked about having Valley Oak on a rural site. Red had bought up the old Founder's site, but the Victorian was such a jewel. I remained the only teacher and we had to be hiring another real soon as twelve was the use permit limit for one teacher.

Sharon, scrubbed fresh, radiant, came out on the back porch, bounding down the steps to our picnic table. "Barbecued chicken," she gushed. "I think I could swallow a whole one!"

We began our ritual.

"James, could you please pass the chicken?"

"Certainly Sam, the opportunity would be a pleasure."

"Howling Dogs are having a concert this week."

"Sharon, could I please have the watermelon?"

121

"Is that the group your cousin plays base?"

"Where they at?"

"Sure Sam. Let me wipe my hands first."

"Yeh, he does. It's at Dickens' Park on Saturday."

"Jack, could I please have the potato salad after you?"

"I hear Foo Fighters are coming our way?"

"No kidding."

"Not a problem Laura."

"They're playing at the Civic Center on Friday."

"Thanks."

"Did you know Foo Fighters go their name from the UFO's that pilots saw during World War II?"

"The garlic bread is hot. I'll just pass it around the table."

"That's gnarly. I thought they got it from Kung Fu?"

"Lou, how can a Canadian team win the World Series? It's Un-American."

"Different spelling."

"That's good watermelon."

"Yeh, it's seedless."

"Do you put salt on yours?"

"James, it's about time it became a World Series."

"Kinda like witch which."

"Mark, please put your napkin on your lap."

"The seeds are just so small you don't notice them."

"Jack, could you please pass the milk?"

"Thank you."

I took in the table, "Has everyone been served? Chicken all around? James, could you do the honor?"

A moment of silence followed as James stated, "Thank you for what we have."

Please, thank you, first names, napkins on laps, and the arms of Culinary Arts embraced our program whole as the table burst into animated life...................

October 9   A New Site

I was living a dream. A dream born from a nightmare. First the dream, that had become my go to reality. Here I am, driving out to work at my own school in the country. Valley Oak would never be as picture perfect as the scene I was taking in. Slowing down along a pasture in my newly purchased used Ford pick up to savor the fragrance of yesterday's fresh cut alfalfa will do for a start. Rudy roaming his truck bed domain, freed from the confines of the Honda, challenging any blackbird. Sticking his head in the sliding rear window to make sure I'm still there. I could see the John Deere Mowers that were ambling down the dirt roads to take up where they had finished the prior evening. Early morning Fall sun was beginning to stream in as clouds of vapor mist rose from the cut fields, It'll do. Moments like this I waxed grandiose and dreamed about the baseball diamond that we would build on the new site. Field of Dreams had actualized the fantasy that I held for building a high school diamond that students in our program could help erect, maintain, sell concessions, and invite local schools and leagues to play on. Field of Dreams had let me know that there are more whacko people out there besides myself.

For the past twenty odd years, wherever I had taught, I had made baseball a central theme of the language arts and computational programs. Every year I would revise and add something else. Currently, I was using computers to make team banners and would construct a map of the US on the ceiling. By the end of the unit, my room would look like a jungle. To me, the Theme of Baseball gave our students an area to dialogue about that did not focus on their abuse and neglect issues. America talked baseball. James, bless his pea pickin' Tennessee Ernie Ford exercise bike heart, was headed into St. Louis. Land of The Cardinals and Stan the Man. Branch Rickey. Baseball was an accepted topic. Even Laura, with all those San Francisco brothers, had been raised hating the LA Dodgers. Wonder if her dad had ever coached? But to know and share that Randy Cummings invented the curve ball and that Harvard U. determined the curving sphere was "too much of a deception" to offer a batter. Harvard refused to allow their pitchers to employ that pitch nor play teams that did.

I was able to give the students a slice of history that not everyone held. That the famous Cubbie double play combination that had the "Giants hitting into a double," only made seven double plays one year. I played and replayed the Ken Burns video series one inning, one month, at a time. My students could sing. "Did You See Jackie Robinson Hit That Ball," and understand why he stood up to his court martial. I knew, when we put the diamond up, there would be a "Green Monster" in left, just like at Fenway.

That I had the time to ponder these visions. no longer having to be involved in transportation on a daily basis, was a joy to me. Almost two years of being a driver, teaching the students, having administration meetings, taking on custodial responsibilities and all that small business can bring at you was giving way to more focused responsibilities of being in the classroom. Unbelievably, we had even hired a part time secretary, Mary, to answer the phones during the school day.

I continued to personally wrestle with why I had decided upon Founders, sure Red had advocated for the site, but there were lots of other empty, neglected farms in The Greater Boston Area. Why the return? What was in the coming back for me? Back to what?

This fact was what my rural vision born nightmare had sprang from here. The nightmare was mine. The nightmare began with the death of my parents and my being placed in The Founder's Orphanage. I wasn't placed at the farm site to begin with, that was later, but I had been here. No doubt about that. No one knew this part of my history, not even my buddies. No one, that is, but Red. This was when I first began to meet up with him. Red had kept me focused. Given me a direction and stayed with me following my surgery. Some premonition, some deep negative fateful magnetized harborage held me and brought me back.

Through some deep foreboding shadow from the time I had suffered my injury, I had known that I would resurrect my past. Red had said that the return to roots was a respectable, honorable action to perform. Was I on a mission? Seeking some righteous retribution. Deranged?

Staff was making the move from The Victorian to Founders with me. No one sought other employment, but there was not a lot of joy in Mudville with the change. That they were willing to take the leap was the expression of their dedication, enjoyment of what Valley Oak was about.

Program and life at The Victorian was just such good stuff. The level of comfortability we had cultured with so many more alternatives we could take on if we just stayed put. Why make a move and why, of all places and programs, to hook up with Founders? That's what they couldn't fathom. I wasn't prepared to get into disclosing my history. Not now. Now forever.

I pulled over to a stop. Left the engine on and got out. Walked around to Rudy. We were on a knoll looking towards the Founder's property. The site now was only about twenty percent the size it was when I was there. Five acre parcels with trophy homes dotted the landscape around Founders. From this distance all appeared lush and intact. I scratched Rudy's ears.

"You don't think I'm so dumb do you fella?

Rudy shook his head in agreement with me. Guys had to stick together. I bounced up and down a couple of times. Old habits linger on, clearing my head. No time to dwell on the past. I needed to focus and energize with so much to be done.

October 11 Ugh

I was smoldering as, here I was, THE unflappable, impeccable Laura Russo, pillar and, if I had not accepted Lou's offer to Direct Valley Oaks Therapeutic Component, next esteemed Director of Bay County Mental Health, driving out to Sharon's in my five year old Subaru Outback that was badly in need of a tune up, new wind shield wipers, and something had gone out with my heating system. Like my vehicle, I felt on the brink of blowing a fuse with only myself to blame for not staying with Bay County Mental Health. I was just about set to search out a good therapist and look into my hubris. At least, if I had decided to stay with BCMH, I would be driving a late model county car with the state taking care of the exorbitant cost of gasoline and maintenance. Great benefits including all the plush upgrades for seminars in the Bahamas! I took my small car towel and wiped the fog off my front inside windshield. I told myself to ease up and take a cleansing breath. I needed to stop the whining and just admit that I was personally disappointed, excuse me, LIVID with Lou in that he had scarcely discussed his decision to move the program with me. There were distinct moments when I was forced to realize that I was the Director of Valley Oak in name only. Marianne had suggested that I purchase a cleaver and employ it in a manner to get Lou's attention. With all the fragile egos of our students at stake, including mine, who was he to make a deal to move the Valley Oak School out onto some rural residential grounds. God, he could be an ass hole!! Pardon me, a REAL ASSHOLE!!! There, now I felt better.

I knew I should be concentrating on the road. I did not want to miss the turn to Sharon and Martha's trailer court. They were so symbiotic that I had considered combining their names into Shartha. Here it was, 6:30 a.m., and I was on my way to pick Sharon up for her SSI meeting. The SSI sign up was crucial, but I couldn't stop thinking about the fate of Valley Oaks.

Why had I not been aware of how serious Lou was in terms of establishing Valley Oak on a rural site? Granted, Lou does own the business and he has the right to make such decisions without anyone's input. Maybe I was just licking my egocentric wounds for not being more involved because, as much as Lou would become oppositional and problematic, I knew he valued my opinion. A strength of Lou, which was not at first evident, was his ability to compromise or set up a win-win situation through direct dialogue, with his being indulgent to the other's point of view One of the main reasons I had decided to come aboard Valley Oak was because it was not a beauracractic state business immersed in politicking. But, what kind of awareness did I have of this Lou Thompson and his personal devils and angels that had allowed Valley Oak to flourish? My Bay County friends had asked with concern what I might know of Lou Thompson and how much faith I had placed in Marianne's insight. I sighed, obviously not a lot and everything!

From my perspective, Valley Oak was just beginning to mesh with a reputation that, after two years was being besieged with referrals from thirty miles away. We were good and on a curve to only improve! Were Lou's priorities focused on becoming bigger with better in the background? Maybe just bigger and more money? I might be therapeutically projecting as I could feel my left eye begin to twitch, which it always did that when I was under stress and I was not wearing my necklaces. I began to notice the symptom about three years ago and wrote the twitch off too one of the signs of aging with wisdom. I hoped, anyway, because right now I did not feel that confidence in my decision making. I should have had better insight into Lou's character after working with this individual for the past twenty-six months. Somehow I just did not foresee that a move of this magnitude would occur and certainly not this quickly.

One moment Valley Oak gothic rustic and homey, tree nestled and the next, aging decadent surreal. The impact on our students, the stress to staff, the changes in day-care routine, the phone numbers to contact for emergencies, and all the other minute encumbrances that a business bears with change. Does any boss, even the "Sir Knighted Lou," ultimately have concerns about their staff when the direction comes down to what they wanted to actualize? The students? How could Lou choose to leave The Victorian and The University womb for this godforsaken desolate weed strewn overgrown excuse for a cremated residential program?

Moreover, the rumor filled history that was embedded with this Founder's rural site would make good fodder for a gothic novel or a sci-fi thriller. That the high-hallowed halls of Valley Oak were now to be located on a rural single storied flat structure that had weeds growing on the roof was an abomination. Granted, there were the fifteen acres for Lou's grandiose baseball diamond, but the site was run down, dilapidated, an eyesore, and I just found myself becoming angrier thinking about the reality. Again and again, why had I not been more adamant against the move and what, if anything, could I have done to keep us stabilized in our enriched nurturing Victorian?

I gave Rudy a final back scratch and got back in the truck. I had always wanted a pick up I could bang around in. Uncool about the gas mileage, but I rationalized that, being rural, program could certainly use one. Having a Valley Oak gas card was a positive. I needed to remember to get one for Laura as I turned off into the entry for Founders. I had driven past the site a few times, but you couldn't see much from the road due to thick foliage and trees. That had been the same even when I had lived there. Gave program a lot of privacy. Now I knew the foliage also kept the violence and restraints from being seen from passing cars.

"Well, here goes Rudy," I said to him as he stuck his head in the rear window and I turned off on the broken up asphalt road. The entry was still damp from and earlier thundershower. This was it. I prepared myself. I had heard so much. Envisioned. Dreamt. Goodbadugly of this moment for the past twenty-five years. Now, here the past came present. I rumbled across the small wooden rickety bridge, came into what was now Founder's Rural Home Settlement.

I turned to Rudy and mumbled, "I-don't-f'ing-believe this." I stopped the truck. Turned off the engine and just sat there. There was no human activity in this area. Some meandering chickens by a shed. Flock of geese out in the far pasture. The first of the group homes, the one where I had lived for four years, was completely boarded up. Warped disintegrating moss streaked plywood covered the windows. Vegetation grew as high as the sloped roof and completely covered the entrance to the front door. A lawn was sprouting on the remaining shingles with roots dangling down to the growth below. The sheds and out buildings were caved in. Fences that had penned in the livestock were collapsed. The place had gone to seed!

Red, what the hell have you gotten me into? Why hadn't I come and checked this place out? Such a deal I have for you. Red had smiled his smile, I now understood why.

I knew the history of Founders as only a former resident can, like way too much. I accepted that Founders was based on some noble ideals. I knew that this site was owned by a local Founders Community Organization that had, in the forties following World War II, purchased seventy-five acres of rolling verdant farmland with groves of pines. Visions of furthering their commitment to community service. In the fifties Founders had purchased an additional seventy-five acre site and erected two, seven thousand square foot residential homes as the cornerstones of the site. They sought to establish a rural program to supplement their industrial strength orphanage that was based in Boston. The homes were single story of cement block construction. Each residence containing seven bedrooms, that could accommodate upwards of fourteen clients. The kitchen in each residence was provided with, at that time, state of the art equipment. There was an indoor recreational area with ping pong, pool, weights, countless board games, books, magazines. Just about what any activity an adolescent might yearn for in their own home. The living rooms were enormous and each had a formal sitting area and fireplace. Wonder if they had televisions back at the start?

I had to admit, at the outset, with one hundred and fifty acres, the property was set up to be a first class self-sufficient residential facility that would rival any in New England. There were fruit trees, green houses, livestock areas, beehives, and, most importantly, a staff skilled and dedicated to the management of such an operation.

"Hey Lou!" I startled as Jerome Kelly banged on the side of the truck and laughed at nailing me in my thoughts. I joined in and climbed out. Jerome was the Rural Settlement Director for Founders. I knew him from our slow pitch softball league. We had agreed to meet and get together on starting to plan on how to bring Valley Oak out here to The Founder's site.

We knocked knuckles and JK welcomed me with, "No doubt I am pleased to assume that you are impressed with my neighborhood."

"I tell you JK, the place supersedes all my expectations."

"Yes indeed, mine too," He mused. "Let me get my machete and we can take a look at your new school building."

Jerome Kelly, JK, was well known in Bay County. Red had "recruited" him as the number one rated high school guard in Georgia over fifteen years ago. JK turned into an excellent college level athlete. He was fourth in lifetime assists for The U. I had, once, made the mistake of saying that his size had held him back from the pros, which JK disputed pointing out he had three inches on Spud Webb.

"Is it safe to let Rudy out?"

"Gotta watch out for lions and tigers and bears, but he should be ok."

I dropped the tailgate and Rudy bounded out. At least he was excited about the possibilities of this place.

"Come around the back, we still have a way in without a jungle guide."

Although I had a fair idea on what had caused the slide over the years, I was wondering what JK's take was. "How long have you been with Founders?"

"This is just my third month." JK pointed a direction to the back and we headed that way. "Straight out, looking at this place, there's only one direction to go and I want to be part of the effort. Like I said, welcome to "my" neighborhood and I sure hope you might choose to settle in."

"So, Red talked you into Founders"

That stopped JK in his tracks. How'd you hear about that?"

"Did the same thing to me."

JK shook his head. "First he recruits me to play hoop up here and then he gets me into Founders. Seems he has a soft spot for this place."

JK knew nothing about my past. I planned to keep it that way. Red had said the two of us would hit it off. Red had brought his sly skills into play to land JK and have The Founder's Board give him a shot at The Settlement. As usual, I could tell that Red was right from the get go.

"I tell you JK, there's more to Red than barbecue sauce."

JK slapped his hands together for emphasis, "Don't we both know that."

I watched Rudy snorting through the thick growth. "JK, what do you think happened to this place? Once upon a time it's rumored that there were some good things happening out here."

JK paused, "I hear the same. I understand that all the homes around our fences are on property that Founders sold off because state funding had dropped to a trickle."

Every now and then I would read something about Founder's activities in the paper and they were seldom positive. I asked, "Is all that stuff true about clients going AWOL and breaking into homes and stealing cars?"

"And that's just the tip of iceberg." JK grimaced. "Once they drove a D4 Cat into a home. Fortunately, no one was there. Another time they opened the irrigation gates and flooded six properties. I could go on."

That was enough I assured JK. I knew, from my experience that these were the items that made the papers. These activities involved the neighborhood. If the situation happened on site the event was all shut down. Even back when I was here staff cars were burned. Buildings trashed. Sexual abuse. But the concerns were always made whole. Those responsible had dues to pay.

I agreed with JK that the basis for the dysfunctionality was in the funding mode. Founder's was unable to bring aboard and retain the skilled staff necessary for a first class program. What Founder's ended up employing, for ten bucks an hour-zero benefits, was about anyone who did not have a criminal record and held a current driver's license.

JK jerked open the back door and I walked into the place I called home during four years of my life. I took a heavy breath and entered.

October 21   Out of My League

I sighed, blinked my eyes hard, and turned up the speed on my windshield wipers. The sky was beginning to open up with slushy blobs splotched on the windshield. I was not a morning person with eight o'clock alarms being my nemesis. That was morning to me, with coffee and cream please, and, could you make sure the shower's warm. So bleak and dreary but it was too early for snow to stick. I should be alright given the forecast was too warm for freezing rain. I dreaded the approach of winter with the numbing temperatures. My chains were still somewhere in the garage and I knew New England was telling me that the time was here and I should get them into the trunk. Everything in New England slowed down and, gradually, shut down when the full force of a Nor-eastern winter hit us. I had left thoughts of Coastal California far behind me as at least, there, you could choose to take on the winter snows in the Sierras.

Where was California when I needed regeneration?

For now, where was the sign for Sharon's trailer park? Although I had been here several times, I was unnerved trying to find the turn off in the dark, fortunately, I caught a glimpse of a blinking soft light on a faded sign or I would have missed the turn, Sam and Helen's Boat Park. Sharon said the park flooded every spring and one had to wonder if the trailers had outboards or life preservers. I thought back to my previous session with Sharon where I had given her all the rope I could as I attempted to gain another perspective of her inner processing. The session had not gone well.

I was in a nasty mood. I gave my hard ass stare at Ms. Laura Rosso, the Ms. Perfect "I've got everything you don't bitch." Her so nice and clean therapy room with everything just so. Like to tear this shit hole up.

There was something different going on with Sharon today that I just could not quite put my finger on. She was sitting, as usual, in the leather chair with one of my warm shawls wrapped around her, physically appearing as constrained and sedate as ever, but something was going on with her focus.

I was bored with our usual B.S. Wonder what goes on with Ms. Laura. I'd like to see her cringe. Maybe curl her toes a bit. See how she handles this, "I figured out who the father is."

"Well, that's news. Who is it?"

I took a match book out of my pants. Lit one. See how far I can push it, "I've known all along. Some things you just know for fact." Blew it out before she could bitch.

I decided to see where Sharon wanted to take this subject as there was an aggressiveness in her manner that had, until now, not entered our sessions. I waited for her to continue.

OK bottle Serene Blondie, here it comes. I began, "Ronnie, of course, is the dad. Like, he's the only one who could have been during that time. I know because we had this special place where we were doing it all the time. Sometimes twice. Morning and evening. Before and after his work. The place was just too cool. Ronnie found it. We couldn't have done it there during the mid-day in the summer because it got too hot. It was off the dirt road not far from the trailer park in a clearing. By a slough where we could swim and clean off. There was this big old '49, Ronnie said because he knows these things, Mercury. Said they use to be a fast kind of car which was why they were called a Mercury. Ronnie would sing me Cadillac Ranch and talk about James Dean. You know, that planet that goes so fast? Or is it the guy on the dime? Anyway, we would make times to meet there. I always made sure that I was the first one there. I'd get stark naked. Sometimes leave my cutoffs on but opened up. I'd sprawl out in the leather back seat with the door open. Just waiting. Thinking about how good it was going to get." Laura's just taking this in. Maybe she's getting off on it. "I'd hear Ronnie coming. He'd be whistling some old rock and roll song like Fire Lake. He could really whistle. Well, my nipples would start to harden up as I could see him coming up on the car. Sometimes we'd just jump into it and he'd just fuck me hard, but most times we'd kind of kick back. Smoke some weed or Ronnie would bring some shrooms. Never did meth. Didn't want to mess up my teeth. Coke was too expensive. We kept it mellow."

Usually, by this juncture, I had long since intervened and refocused our discussion into areas that were not sexualized. Later on, I will go over my decision to allow Sharon to continue to present her sexualized encounter with Ronnie, but, for now, the dialogue felt right to continue as Sharon might be pushing a boundary to see how far she can take me into her life during our therapy sessions. She might even think that she can startle me with the nature of her erotic topic, which would be difficult given my five years of clients from the Tenderloin of San Francisco.

"Lots of times I would take out the KY and.....Laura, you've heard the lie about ten inches and white." I continued my non-disclosing appraisal. "Anyway, what's ten inches and white? Nothing. Like the answers 'Nothing' except for Ronnie! I mean, I even measured it. He likes to claim a foot and I'd say no way! But what he could do with that rod!! I'd get him all lathered up and sit on top of him. That back seat had so much room. Get a rhythm going. So deep." If I don't watch it I'll start masturbating right here. Maybe I should. "As we got totally into it I'd put on this move. I call it The Swivel Saddle Move. Watch."

It took every fiber of my therapeutic will power not to shriek with laughter as Sharon suddenly, with practiced smoothness, lifted her legs over the back of the leather chair, locking them behind her neck, and rotated her body to have her back towards me.

"Absolutely awesome," I profoundly stated, remaining noncommittal.

Got her. Bet she's never seen The Swivel Saddle Move. I got it off of one of the porns Martha had brought home. "Yeh, that's just one of them. But with this one I got more because I'd grab his ankles, stretch out, and fuck him into the leather moist upholstery." Sharon shivered with the thought. "Sometimes I would tickle his feet or lick his toes." This was getting to be a bit too much information, even for me. "Then, just when I felt I had him, Ronnie would throw me off, wrap me in a ball, and just fuck me until I stopped howling with pleasure."

Enough, I decided that I needed to derail this locomotive before Sharon began sharing some of the other sexualized episodes. I made an obvious gesture of looking at the clock and asking, "So Ronnie's the determined father due to your not having any other relationships during this time?"

"Like I said, there weren't any others. Unless, well, maybe......"

October 23   Learning Curve

That was our last session before our current appointment and I would take care not to leave the dialogue so open ended as I should have known where Sharon would take her reality/fantasies.

I pulled over to a stop to check the time and make sure that I was not going to arrive too early. I had six minutes to wait so I turned off my wipers and listened to the heavy thumping downpour of rain cascading on my Subaru through the bare limbed trees. I found that I could not keep the issue with the move from coming forth in my thoughts, I decided to just process and, hopefully, clear my mind before picking up Sharon. Although my frustration was not serving any good purpose, except to raise my blood pressure, I continued to reflect on the Valley Oak move. Why had I not understood Lou's determined motivation as he had not been raised on a farm or from blue-collar values but Lou had always talked about wanting to be rural? In fact, I knew virtually nothing of fact concerning Lou's pre college life. I was pretty sure that Red was aware of Lou's background, but, whenever I probed, Red would turn the subject around on myself. What I did know was that Lou desired to develop a work ethic with our population that would assist them in being able to appreciate the effort that goes into putting a meal on the table. In a sense, being able to return to the goals of what Founders had started their program to be. With our current student population, I just was not sure of the level of grandiosity in Lou's thinking. Valley Oak is serving a population that is clinically determined to be emotionally disturbed, like capital ED, who are not programmed for row crop maintenance or cow milking and this population was not going to pick strawberries in the correct manner. The Puritan Ethic of "sweat of the brow" no longer held a place of respect within themselves or their culture as they were not Detroit Automatons who could see benefits coming down the line in forty years. Lou was coming up against an evolving social norm where emphasis was now on what you had and not how the cha-ching was gained. If you had bling, it was yours just like Halloween was ripping bags of candy off from little kids instead of knocking on doors and saying thank you. The asocial energy so represented everyday occurrences that were reflected all through our culture.

Thinking of sweets, I vividly remembered when I was attending USF when councilman and local neighborhood hero Dan White had murdered Mayor Willie Moscone and Supervisor Harvey Milk. He got five years for taking the lives, murdering two human beings because White had consumed Twinkies! Trick or Treat? A sugar rush made him do the murdering. We are talking about intelligent people buying into this warped mentality of developing a line of reasoning to license macabre asocial behavior.

I took a cleansing breath and told myself that, given voice to my inner frustrations, I was now in a better state of mind to meet with Sharon, if not a tandem with Martha. Not totally therapeutic of me, but I can handle the chastisement as I settled back in my seat and reminded myself to just take my time because the Immobile Winnebago was not going anywhere.

I started my engine, which took three tries, and suddenly thought that Halloween had to be coming up in a few days. My empty nest was no longer driven by my younger brothers' holidays and I perked up thinking that Halloween was coming up like next week, which, next to Christmas, was my favorite holiday display time. I needed to get my outdoor displays up as I could envision little goblins bumping around with all sorts of squeals of pleasure as their treasure increased.

Enough! Get focused! I needed to stop this free association and get back to the present reality of meeting up with Sharatha and the SSI dilemma because I had certainly made a mess of things the last time I had been here. I sped up my windshield wipers as fast as they could go and thought back to the time three weeks prior I had driven the same road as today to pick Sharon up for our initial visit to Social Services. That was a first for me as, in my embalmed life, I had never entered a Social Service building.

I recalled, that prior moment. Overwhelmingly distraught from getting up too early, too long a drive, too much listening to Sharon and, numbly, as we entered the impacted waiting area, saying to no one in particular, "Which line should we get into?"

Good question as we intruded upon detached, depressed muted mounds of heavy layer coated people seeking shelter from the season's first overture to winter. My egocentric personal survival thoughts wondering what were my chances of escaping without contacting some airborne communicable disease. I stood on my tiptoes, straining to see over the throng, towards the front where there was a semblance of order. I looked over the different service windows with an extended jumbled line reaching from each. The time was only 10:10, yet the entire room was clogged with humanity extending to the barrier of the back wall. With my jaded priorities, I just could not make myself get here by 8:00 and now we have to pay the price. The lines of bundled need in overcoats and wrapped with scarves was beginning to share its fragrance with me. People were sitting on the floor, some with their pets with nowhere else to go. Why was I so entirely unfamiliar with this situation as if this fact of American life were a new happening? Had I not experienced like environments when I was working The Tenderloin of San Francisco? How far away had I pushed the reality of being impoverished that the everyday factual reality of these desperate, depressed, people congregating around the well of social services seeking subsistence were a surprise? How did I come to accept myself as such a haughty high minded worldly therapist when I could not fathom such a reality check scene?

I heard Sharon asking me about which line to get into? I scanned the windows for a clue with the one holding the placard "Initial Requests" appearing to hold the most promise.

I shrugged motioning to Sharon. "I am not totally sure. Let's get in this one," I pointed. "This is our first time here so 'Initial Requests' seems to be the place to start."

Standing there, refraining myself from placing a handkerchief over my mouth, I wondered how Sharon was processing our situation.

God, Princess Laura doesn't have a fucking clue? Why did I agree to come here with this legally blonde brain drain? She and her layed back California easy does it bullshit. Oh, this line looks cute. What a dipshit. I bet this is her first time in a services building. I don't know who or what to ask, but I know my mom would never start at the end of the line! Mom would say that if you came here to stand in line you would never get out. Mom knows how to get their attention. She knows how to make them want to get her out. She's always so sure of what she needed. If you come here and suck your thumb and stand at the back of the line you're going to be here all day. Fuckenashit! I'll miss my time with Nick....or was it Ronnie's day? Why did I come here? What the fuck is this going to do for me? I need to get home. I need to get out this mess and lose this twit. Except I need a ride home. See if I can jump start this scene.

I could tell that Sharon was disengaging. Her shoulders had slumped and her eyes were glazed flat. She was leaving the room. No telling where she was going. This could just implode into one totally violent, ugly, nasty scene that I was totally unprepared for. What? Something bumped against my leg. I looked down. The bump was a two- year old toddler with an ear to ear grin. He was happy just to be here. He spun around, lurched, and clutching to stay upright, grabbed onto Sharon's pants. I tensed, prepared to do whatever needed to be done to refrain Sharon from launching the toddler across the multitude.

Sharon must have seen him coming, because she was not startled.

"What a gorgeous little guy! What a grip," Sharon laughed, holding onto his shoulders to keep him on balance as her long hair fell into his face. "Kind of young to be here for SSI."

Sharon gently spun him around and sent him careening back into the maze of lines. She did this so effortlessly. So maturely. We watched as an arm reached out and latched onto him.

"He's just too cool. I hope that my baby will have as much spunk."

I took an imperceptible glance at Sharon's swollen waistline. "Sharon, if he takes after you, there is no doubt he will be a whirling dervish." I stopped a person wearing a nametag and asked which line we should be in and she pointed me to one that happened to be the shortest, there were only ten people in front of us. We went over and queued up.

Fortunately, due to the bumping of the toddler, Sharon's mindset changed and, in the following forty-six minute stuck in a phone booth stream of monologue with a manic bipolar pregnant young woman that it took us to get to the front, I heard Sharon's entire litany of fathers from "Legend of Her Child." Wonder if she really knew who the father was, but I am sure she kept those around us entertained as well. Sharon just did not have a soft tone so that her volume allowed you and everyone else on the premises to certainly know what Sharon was thinking.

I thought back to whom did I think was hot when I was her age? Not that Sharon would take a breath to ask. Robert Redford for sure. Paul Newman, a tad old. John Travolta, when he was on Welcome Back Kotter, not any of his more recent stuff like Pulp Fiction. Vinnie was just so cool and fun, maybe how I thought of my dad from what I had heard of him as a young man. I did hold the entire collection of Clint Eastwood films, and some of his early Rawhide episodes as Rowdy Yates. I had seriously considered naming one of my Jack Russells Rowdy, maybe the next one.

Sharon's selection of past, present, and future lovers held no time or place constraints. She had everyone from Elvis to Johnny Depp and some boxer named "The Golden Boy." Such a menu that varied with the time of day. I liked Sharon and I cared for her success, but, in my best clinical observation, she was just one whacked out young lady as I reminded myself to include this professional insight into my next write up.

I was relieved when the line dwindled and, finally, our turn to check in. We confidently walked up to the window where the clerk's over rouged face read a road map of disinterest, as I hoped for some miracle to move us on through the day.

"Hi," I said far too brightly. "We have come here to apply for Social Security." Seemed like a basic, straightforward statement to make. "Sharon will be eighteen in two months."

The clerk did not look up.

I did not see any physical movement as I heard the words in a flat monotone, "Forms are in the back. Fill them out. Here's a pass so you don't have to stand in the line again."

She handed me a blue index card with the number seventeen on it. She looked through us, towards the next victim. Somehow I figured that she had made this statement more than once in her life.

I continued to present with all the professional dignity I could muster, "Pardon me," I continued, "After we fill them out and return them to you, what will occur next?" I could feel my face begin to flush as I accepted that we had stood in this line for forty-six minutes without attending to the expected paperwork. What a waste of time. She glanced up at me, as, obviously, my college career had made me too dimwitted to know the rules.

With resignation to having to dialogue she muttered, "You turn them back to me. We schedule an appointment."

My look told her that I was far more than dimwitted, I was simply middle class and clueless as to the expectations of passing through the SSI morass.

There was, almost, empathy as she continued, "The appointment will take place two to four weeks from this date. That's the way the system works."

She returned to her paperwork, hopeful of not having to further my education as she was bordering on the edge of being helpful. Sharon took my arm and we walked back to the form desk. I felt dazed. Codependent came to mind.

November 23 Second Chance

That was three weeks ago, seemed like six hundred, as finally, my neglected Subaru splashing through deep mud sucking sludge pot holes, I was pulling up in the pitch pouring darkness to Sharon and Martha's trailer space!

"Hi Laura!" Sharon was waving and standing under an umbrella outside the Winnebago waiting for me. Martha's shadow was in the screen door and I could see the orange glow from her cigarette.

The rain was lightening and, I determined, although the water was up at high tide, none of the trailers were floating out to the slough.

"I was wondering if you would get lost in the dark."

So had I. "Not a chance. Hop in and let's get this done. We'll get something hot on the way into town."

"Great, I'm starving." She always was.

"How about Jack in the Box. I have to eat for the two of us." She was now five months pregnant. "I love their breakfast burritos. You would think that Taco Bell would make better ones, I mean, that's what they do. But I like Jack because ......"

I let Sharon run on with her stream of consciousness dialogue. Per usual, allowed to set her own pace and subject, she would come around to things that were important to her. I knew that to ask her questions beyond how many breakfast burritos she would inhale, would cause her to pull into herself and become silent. Nothing worse for a therapist than a client's silence. Sharon ordered four beef breakfast burritos.

This time I was thoroughly prepared for the gray crumbled tattered neglect of the Human Resources Department of Bay County. We had our enrollment sheet in hand as we self-assuredly approached the appropriate window marked Today's Appointments, followed by November 23, in bold letters. Since I was commonly ten minutes late for everything, I was particularly pleased with being five minutes early for our eight-thirty time slot. I took a seat and watched as Sharon, when her name was called, strode up to the window. I mused that there were times she presented so intact that you questioned her placement in our program. Truly amazing what some good nurturing and a hot breakfast can do for one's psyche, I know the egg and ham biscuit helped me.

I never thought that part of my duties within the mental health label would include entering social security buildings at 8:00 in the morning to secure services for a pregnant client. Talk about professional boundaries! Somehow, the dream of a soft couch conducted therapy session in high ceiling wood paneled rooms was a fogged distant memory. At Valley Oak, therapy was where it happened.

I was scanning the room and wondering what next, when Sharon's knees folded and I could see her holding herself up by her elbows on the window counter. Not good! Holding my persona intact, it was all I could do not to rush up to the window to determine what was going on as, gradually, Sharon put her feet back on the vinyl floor and turned to totter back to me. I stood as she neared and I could see that she was in no state to discuss what had transpired. I walked her over and sat her down in one of the plastic chairs and I went back up to the window, cutting off the next person, prepared to do my best Martha imitation.

"Excuse me, but I am with the young woman who was just here." I had set my sights on a formidable confrontation but I only met professional empathy. Amazingly, the clerk simply nodded.

"I am really sorry, but what just occurred happens all the time."

She took out a laminated copy of an appointment time that had been highlighted on the appropriate sections.

"People see the appointment time and miss the section about needing to view the video prior to the appointment."

She pointed to the blue highlighted section. I could feel myself flushing with frustration.

"We are only fifteen minutes past the start of the video. We have driven here in this down pour from thirty miles distance! Could we not review what we missed?"

"That would make sense, but the department does not bend their policy. I am truly sorry. I can see how this affected your daughter."

Well, Sharon was not my daughter and, at the moment, I was sure she wished that Martha was here, Martha would not just have rescheduled. Martha would have……..

May 9 Therapeutic Trauma

Teachers teach, I have told that over and over to Laura. The negative comments that state, if you can't do it, then teach, were made by those who lacked the capacity to find the joy of the classroom. For me, that joy was everything.

I could only imagine the issues that come at a therapist. Not only does a therapist have to be able to communicate with the teacher, but with half of the free world ranging from food stamps to dental appointments. That's a load I had zero interest in taking on. I told Laura that I could have been interested if you could do therapy like when you were teaching batting practice.

As "Lou The Therapist" I could say something like, "Second knuckle to second knuckle."

"Like this Lou?"

"Yeh, that's got it. Make sure not to over grip. Keep the fingers loose."

"Should I choke up a bit?"

"That's your call. How's your dad doing?"

"Talked to him yesterday."

"And.................?"

"Well, he goes up for sentencing next week."

"How you doing with it?"

That's the way therapy should happen, I just couldn't sit in some chair staring at a person, but working on an engine or something active would be the way to go, I might handle that.

I know that I could not handle all the drama that had come down with Sharon. Laura was amazing with her patience and commitment. Right now she was with Sharon, at the hospital. Sharon had been knocked around, and, according to Laura, she would recover Nothing major. All the parts where were they should be. I would go on teaching my lesson on decimals as if there was nothing more important for my students than their understanding the role of that dancing little point in place value, especially with dollars and cents. I had to put thoughts of the accident on hold. If any of the students would ask me if I knew where Sharon was, my response would be like, who knows Now, Leo was another story. I waited for the phone to ring with good news.

I sat next to Sharon in the hospital bed. I had contacted both Valley Oak and left a message for Martha as to where I was and how Sharon was doing. Sharon was lapsing in and out of consciousness, listless, although color had returned to her pallid cheeks and her eyelids would sporadically twitch. I had always wanted a daughter, although Sharon was not the daughter I envisioned, as she emitted a soft moans, I had allowed myself to become emotionally attached to her well being. My involvement could not be clinically supported and Sharon was only being who she was. My efforts to assist her towards better decisions and a healthier life did not demand that Sharon be responsible to me. She had her own rhythm of life that, for that matter, I was basically interfering with the continuance. How much could she have changed? What did the future hold for her? Would it have taken me three visits with my own daughter to have gotten SSI? What else could I have done better?

There were bruises and abrasions on Sharon's arms and, I was told, up and down her torso, although nothing was broken. She had not injured herself in the auto accident but had fallen down a rocky embankment trying to get away from the police helicopter as her life contorted to unfold in surreal cataclysmic episodes. Her face had escaped injury, but Sharon remained in intensive care due to the hallucinogenic drugs she had ingested. Fortunately, her new born child was with Martha. I had been with her for two hours as Martha had yet to make an appearance and I began to drift.

In the stillness my mind floated back to an earlier session I had held with Sharon as so much, so rapidly with birth, death, loss reeling like a kaleidoscope. I had only know Sharon for five months when she had shared with me "the death." Sharon, as was her want, was rambling on and on…

"Then, after the movie, we went for a walk through town. Nick and I were getting tight. We were partners. Then, out of no where, Nick gets killed." Sharon was so calmly matter of fact, laying back in the reclining chair, eating an apple. Between bites, "We were walking along the levee road, you know, the one by the boathouses behind the trailers. This car comes up behind us. Doesn't honk or nothin'. Wham! Slams into the back of Nick. He flew in front of me. I saw the whole thing. Nick floated through the air without making a sound. His arms and legs were thrashing like the Scarecrow in Wizard of Oz. Then, thud! His head hit this sign post. Not a twitch. The car didn't even stop. Just sped up and kept going. Like so weird. Like, one moment we were walking along talking about the Black Eyed Peas coming into town and then POOF! He's gone……... Why do I so enjoy bullshitting Laura? Or was I? Sometimes I just get reality all fucked up. Can't tell lies from truth. So tangled………… "of course I hugged him and cried and screamed. I was so out of my mind. His head didn't bleed much. His hair was still combed back. He used so much jell. Just sort of hit with a thunk and snapped his neck. No blood and guts. He was sprawled with his feet in the water. If he could have been hit harder, maybe he could just have landed in the slough. That's what the police said. We should have known better, walking on the wrong side of the road in the dark. It was on a curve and there was just. Did I tell you who the driver was? You just won't believe it. It was Ronnie."

But, I did believe Sharon, I had to believe her, because this accident had happened and there was a Ronnie! The newspapers had run the whole story with Sharon bringing every scrap into program like it was show and tell. Ronnie and Nick were not fantasy characters and I had called the Bay County Sheriff's Department where had confirmed with me that the accident had occurred in the manner recited by Sharon. The two boys and "father" of Sharon's child were not conjured spirits of Sharon's imagination. The officer had stated that Sharon was walking along the wrong side of the levee road in the dark when her companion had been struck from behind and killed by a hit and run driver.

I had interrupted Sharon's torrent. "Are the police aware that you knew the driver?"

"Oh, sure. Like I told you, everyone knows that Ronnie's the father. They're talking as if Ronnie planned the murder, but it just happened. Ronnie and Nick were buds. Everyone knows they've partied with me lots of times. Hell, I've even done'em both a couple of different times. I just can't wait for this to get over with. Ronnie told me he's put down the first and last month's payment on an apartment for us that has a Jacuzzi and swimming pool. We're going to have a water baby. I can't wait to move in. He's going to be a great dad."

I had quickly surmised that fact and fiction were not going to be separated anytime soon with Sharon's denial of reality in creating a fantasy escape with an apartment and spa. Sharon's construct was so typical of her interaction with the negative facts reality offered her. Ronnie was not going to go anywhere until the judicial system passed judgment on his DUI and manslaughter charges that appeared to be pretty much open and shut case according to the officer I had contacted.

I recalled an English class that I had taken at USF. The discussion was on melodrama and tragedy in regards to Shakespeare's epics. The prof had made an aside comment, one that we would not be asked to site in our papers, but one that that had stuck with me. She had stated that "Melodrama was tragedy that happened to someone else." So true.

How many moments or months had passed and now, here Sharon was, out of her mind strapped into a hospital bed. The nurse came in and adjusted the suction tube from Sharon's mouth and checked the levels on her two IV's, one in each arm, with eight, I had counted them, electrode attachments to various machines. The nursing staff was not over wrought as they took it for granted that Sharon's crisis had passed and she had stabilized.

In a tired state of acknowledged glum I accepted that electrodes and IV's would continue to be a constant aspect of Sharon's life. The basic tenant was that I had met her far too late in her self-destructive mold and, I would like to let myself believe that, with an earlier involvement, Sharon would not be here with all her negative issues. I checked the time, acknowledging that I certainly must own for my personal fantasies and grandiosity. I had admitted that Sharon had moved away from my therapeutic attempts to stabilize and comfort, give reason for her to work towards a wholeness of well-being. I knew she had lost her will when Cody had been taken from her.

That event had taken place one month prior to her current hospitalization. Sharon's life, from that point, had been a swirling downward spiral that I could not enter into nor stabilize as I remembered Sharon shrieking the news to me.

"They took Cody from me! Can you believe the fuck? Nick's dead. Ronnie's in jail. That motherfucking social system of faggots! They just came in and made me hand him over. Like I was unfit or something. I raged at them Laura. I gave them nothing but shit."

Sharon expanded her eyes in a tortured replication of futility with tears being wiped away on her arm

"I told them that mother fucking nazi dickweeds had no right to fuck with me and tell me how to be a mom. What did they know except being motherfuckers! I grabbed a hammer to smash their puny balls. These fuckheads cuffed me and sat me in a chair and got Cody's things. Cody was screaming. I was screaming. The cuffs hurt. They cut into my wrists and I twisted around flinging blood all over those motherfucking thieves.

I told them I was HIV positive. Scared the bitches shitless. Steal my Cody! Take by baby!"

Sharon paused. I could tell that she was forming her next statement.

"I curse them. I curse them to be hand cuffed to their fucking cars as their own children are..."

Sharon stopped. She did not finish. She could not continue a curse to harm their children. I held her in my arms, rocking her, as tears sobbed on the back of my blouse. I hurt so much for her.

That Sharon's perspective of parenting was dysfunctional had proven to be an understatement for, although she and I reviewed videos, books, held meetings with Martha, the health clinic, and pregnant teen peers, I could not find a way to reach into her womb of motherhood. Following a normal birth, for which Martha and I were present, she simply refused to change her lifestyle. She would leave Cody with Martha, a friend, an acquaintance, or any stranger who would agree to care for him until she returned, and several times, due to substance abuse, she forgot who or where she had left him. Remorse? Stoned, sober, or drunk, she had none. Through all of this she continued to come to school and her main reasons, though, were not about education, but about guys and parties.

People in Sharon's trailer park struggled, but they were close knit, and they simply could not abide by her decisions with Cody and closed down on her. Sharon did not have transportation. Coming into our program was now a social event for her where she could posture the nurturing spirit without having to live the responsibility. Sharon no longer needed the manic escalations to gain attention. She had been through childbirth and our student population cared about Sharon and respected what they thought she was having to endure. The trailer park community had a fuller insight of Sharon's "mothering skills" and referred her to social services as a danger to her child.

Then there was Leo, and, if the facts had been known, Leo would not have gotten her keys for a car. Leo, along with every other male student in our program, was swept away by any attention Sharon might bestow in their direction and Leo was one of our most successful students. Leo had the social skills to get along with everyone, in fact he was one of those students you asked, why is he here as he never called negative attention to himself

Leo's mom worked as a secretary at Stuart's Used Cars where Leo often got work washing and waxing them. Leo knew where the keys were kept for the vehicles and where his mother kept the keys for the building in their home. He, also, knew the alarm code. With Leo's ability to gain admission to the car lot, he hatched the plan of making an impression on Sharon, so he took one of the cars and drove out to the trailer park. He had picked Sharon up and brought her back into town for a local party where, according to the police record, they were called to a loud disturbance around 12:30 A.M. They arrested six people for drugs, including hallucinogens, and alcohol. Leo had gotten Sharon into the car and attempted to get away, but a short chase had ensued with Leo crashing the '94 Camaro into a bridge piling. Sharon had been flung out of the car and, uninjured, she had gotten up, attempted to run, and had fallen down a thirty foot rock strewn embankment.

I had known Sharon for eleven months. The crushing weight of her life just kept shifting with more rapidity. I had washed her tears, laughed with her, and worked with her as best I might to have a better life. Now she was strapped down with tubes and wires. I knew I had twelve other children on my caseload and a new therapist I was breaking in. I knew I had to pick myself up. The time had arrived to say good-bye to Sharon.

I could hear Martha's histrionics echoing down the hall. I stroked Sharon's cheek.

I stood and prepared to sooth Martha.....................

Valley Oak School
Psycho/educational Intake Summary

Laura Rosso: LCSW

Name: Rick Hutton
DOB: 2/23/88

County of Residence: Granite
School District of Reference :Long Barn USD

Date: November 2, 1995

Physical Description: Rick is an attractive six feet four inch, slender, male Caucasian. He has worn prescription glasses since the age of four. Review of his school records present Rick as one who will choose to wear his clothing, accessories, and hair in many startling fashions. At intake, Rick was dressed entirely in black with black hair parted in the middle and slicked down on the sides to his shoulders. There was something disquieting about the manner in which he would fixate his gaze upon an object in the room or myself. It was as if there were thoughts occurring that I would not enjoy processing. Rick spoke in a polite soft voice in complete sentences. He asked several questions pertaining to dress code, food preparation, pets on site, and numbers of females in program. He appeared very comfortable with the Valley Oak environment.

Referring Criterion: Rick was referred to Valley Oak with a school history of poor peer relationships, inconsistent attendance, defiance of authority, depression, and a general inability to be successful during the school day. Rick's asocial nature had increased throughout his school attendance and there was concern that he might be entering adolescent schizophrenia. Although he had no history of animal abuse, there were several entries that presented Rick's fascination with animals and the notoriety from peers he gained by his intense focus on their environmental interaction. Of additional note, although he could not explain why, Rick brought a meat cleaver to his high school.

Family History: Rick was the second child of Patricia and Henry Hutton. Rick's sister, Suesan, is eight years older and was recently married. Henry was killed in an automobile accident when Rick was eight years old. It was at this time, as the family struggled to stabilize, that Rick's issues began to be presented. Rick had always been thin, ungainly, and worn glasses, but he had always been accepted by his peers and had several friends. Rick, at this time, began to isolate himself from his peers. He would not return phone calls, attend birthday parties, or participate in social events. Rick began collecting a series of pets such as rats, rabbits, snakes, lizards, contours, guinea pigs, hamsters, but never the typical dog or cat.

When Rick was ten, his sister married and moved out of state. The following year his mother, Patricia, was diagnosed with cancer of the colon. With less adult supervision, Rick was able to avoid attending school for long periods of time. Rick's teachers report that, when he attended, he was dysthymic and seldom participated in the class activities.

Psychiatric History: Rick has been hospitalized twice, both occasions occurring within the past eight months. The hospitalizations had been 5150's as Rick was determined to have undergone psychotic episodes while at Granite High School. Prior to these episodes, Rick had participated in the Bay County Mental Health Outreach Program. I had contacted his most recent clinician, Kenneth Underwood, who had three sessions with Rick over the past two years. Mr. Underwood supported the need for more services to be available to Rick and agreed that a medical review would be beneficial.

I have made a referral to Dr. Leer of Bay County Mental Health.

DSM:

Axis I:	295.30		Schizophrenia
			Paranoid Type

Axis II: None

Axis III: None

Axis IV: Mother morbidly ill; inadequate
             primary support group.

Axis V: GAF 30 (Past year)

Recommendations: Records document that Rick's illness has become more progressive as he has entered his adolescent years. I am not convinced that Valley Oak will be able to meet Rick's needs as the deterioration of his health is equaled by events in his home.

I do support a thirty day trial to review Rick's appropriateness for program with an IEP to convene at that time to determine placement.

Signed_____Date_____

Laura Rosso

Chapter 5

RICK: A GENTLE SHEPHERD

October 31

Halloween is for Ghouls. I like ghouls. They fuck around in the dead of night. Scare the shit out of everyone. Slimey and drooling. Devour anything and everything. Formless oozing shapes are my favorites. Fear nothing. Wonder if they really do fuck? Have sex? Are there baby ghouls? Halloween is so cool. Wish everyday was Halloween. Everyone wears a mask. I don't have to. My mask is real. No one can see me. Not even Lou. Lou cracks me up. Lou and his stupid Halloween jokes. Why don't witches have children? Their husbands have halloweenies! Hardee Har! Too funny. I like Lou. He does the best he can with what he's got.

I feel good. I look down at the hump in my zipper. Just the word fuck gets me hard. I gloat knowing I don't have a hollow weenie. I knead the hump with pleasure thinking of Sharon. I lust to knead Sharon's tits. Wonder what she's up to? Forget it. My vision is fluttering. I sigh. Indulge. Here I go again....

I arise in the sweet blooded red sweat stained saddle as the steed between my loins rears with cascading lightening arcs flaring the ground ahead. I know the way. I've been here before. They haven't. Arrows hiss around my shoulders as my growling gruel of a bonded hoard curse and howl at their penetrating impact. I raise my bloodied lance to mount a final crushing charge at the cringing foe. We hurl forward. There is no fear. They cannot touch me. I am filled with the lusting dread of which only shafts of light can impale my vengeance. I am upon them once again and thrust my lance through their hearts and loins bursting streams of savory human vitals upon me. My tongue salivates at the taste as I smash through their feeble lines and wickedly turn up my foaming cohort. They stand in mortal terror. Turn towards me with the vanquished knowing admittance that they will not share the dawn of another day. As expected, they flee, throwing down their weapons. I drop my lance. Lay hold of my lovingly long sword and thunder after them. Standing stiff legged in the stirrups I swiftly depart heads from thrashing torsos as conquering joy swells my writhing appetite. Only the awareness of the morning star dims my hunger as we return to our glorious work to mount the heads of the slain upon their spears. I am exhausted by the fruit of my labor. I need rest. I lay down as the casket closes. I am Vlad the Impaler.

The staff just did not want to believe that we were relocating out to the Founders' Rural Program. Laura was torched. En fuego. Too bad. I had an agenda. We were ready. Valley Oak was intact and needed space. Besides, Red totally agreed. Take that Laura. Maybe a chat with Red would cool your embers!

Friday afternoon after program rolled out I tossed my sleeping bag and Rudy into the back of the pick up and headed out onto The Cape. I had begged off going out to Martha's. Made up some story for the guys to get their permission to miss the Patriots-Buffalo game on Sunday. Somehow, I just always found my alone time to be a priority, especially when I need to clear my head. No place like the cast of characters you meet out in Provincetown to make any craziness you feel right at home.

Seems all the towns out on The Cape begin with East this, West that, North something else. Wonder why there are so many directional names? Rudy stuck his head through the sliding window, didn't offer any clues. I was taking The 6 all the way out to Provincetown. I wanted to watch the sun drop down with a brew on the sand, then have some fresh lobster at Lugo's. Damn though, why just me? I looked at Rudy meaning no offense. Like, I could accept not going with my married friends, those with the quote "significant other." They'd given up trying to hitch me up, just why I sought space from friends, activities had come to weigh a bit on me. I was closer to fifty than forty. Had yet to be with a woman for longer than two years. That was a marathon. Although Rudy was the only other guy in my life, besides Red, I always sought to be with a woman. That had never been an issue. Given the right lady, I certainly would not back off and, there had been several, but none had become The One. Than too, who am

I kidding? Like I am just Lou Cool and In Demand and able to snap my fingers to developing a quality relationship? Get real.

For me, my buddies were always available for good times, rock and roll. Bob Segar blasting. Metallica concerts. Barbecues. Every now and then they would launch into harassing me on my "alone" life style. But they knew my values, though their lady friends and wives could not stop trying to hook me up. Good friends. Their kids called me Uncle Lou. Give me right field at Fenway. Life was O.K, I could handle the pressure.

Not that I was against uncles and aunts and cousins. Having a family remained a personal goal. I admired the life style of mornings with ones you loved. Picnics. Little League. Block parties.

I could see the lights of Boston beginning to come through the sunset. I allowed myself to continue to dwell on my lingering solitude. Grant me awareness, like,I wasn't going to conceive children on my own. There were some preliminary expectations. Yet I always shied away when emotions needed to go beyond just having fun or a laugh. I had come to the conclusion that there was nothing more challenging, that took more work, more willingness to reach within yourself for another, than a one to one long term relationship.

Take Laura for instance. I smacked my forehead at my lack of insight! She's the issue! I mean, straight up. I have never been more attracted to a woman in my entire life. She has zero tolerance for my b.s. and, I know, there is respect there. Yet, can I get beyond one liners, talking shop with Laura and her friends at Jake's? Why could I not man up and say something like, "Laura, I have a table for two reserved Saturday at Barstow's. I am hoping you could join me."

"Lou, I would love to."

"I'll pick you up at seven."

"Great. Any chance you can leave Rudy at home?"

"I'm sure he'll understand."

WHY CAN'T I DO THIS?! Where are my priorities? What am I so fearful of?

I picked up a six pack of Boston Blackie Lager and went to my favorite quiet spot overlooking The Bay. Kick back, waves rolling in. I thought about how Birthdays, Christmas, Thanksgiving, were my favorite holidays, in that order. Now, I dread another B day. Christmas leaves me looking for reindeer on some ski slope. I am always invited to friends' family Thanksgiving gettogethers. I especially enjoy hanging with Red and celebrating with the day with whomever he invites. Nothing like spicy deep fried turkey!

Halloween still cracks me up that our students want to dress up and expect candy, candy, candy. Even the old tough guys. Staff gets into it too. We decorate the rooms. Hang cob webs. Throw in spiders and ghouls. Play weird noises. Past couple of years we even had a dunking bucket with staff taking the tank! Give awards for best costume. Best outfitted staff gets lunch for two at Red's.

Over the years I had settled on one costume. Take a guess…..I always come as "Bob the Builder." Easy enough to do with a yellow hard hat, red suspenders, boots, tool belt. Of course, we didn't allow blood, weapons, gruesome, sexualized types of costumes. The students still managed to get their point across. I always thought you could get an insight into a student's personality by how they got decked out. I'll leave Bob the Builder's pseudo persona personality for a shrink like Laura.

Personality, now, there's a thought. How do we become who we are? How do we get to where we want to be from where we were? The "cognito ergo sum" of Philosophy 4A. What's the process? Why do some make the social grade lickity split, others are forever looking for the starting line?

To me, the reason is like "no brainer" (Laura would agree I'd qualify.) What you do defines what you're about. I'm not suggesting that there aren't ever exceptions. I mean, there might be a sanitary engineer (garbage dude) who is into Brahms and chess. I'd bet they'd prefer a brew and a Red Sox game. Throw in a spicy dog and you've got Bob the Builder.

How do we come to do what we're doing? Leaving me out of this, one of my favorite techniques is to ask the question of a student. Put the thought to them. Where do you want to get to? What do you want to do? What do you want to be? I mean, I don't hit them hard like a parent might. Those aren't my exact staccato phrases. You get the point. Assist the student in developing a mental framework. Give them some brain steps, goals to attain. Try to get concrete with them, especially with themselves. Twenty years in the future does occur, just ask me.

For most of us, we have to let go of fame and Fortune Five Hundred. Get away from the grandiosity of game winning RBI's, walk off dingers, buzzer beaters. I went through this time, everyone does at some level. I mean, if you're into 4-H, you might want to raise the world's most gorgeously fat hog. You will have fantasies about the reward ceremony, the recognition. Only, look out for Charlotte. You and your Wilbur may need her to win those Blue Ribbons. Your arch enemy down the road, Frank might think he's got the best techniques for their hogs, maybe he has won three years in a row. Only you and Wilbur and Charlotte will show them. But, just like with game winning base hits, somewhere along the journey, you have to let the fantasy go. You do this because the world of fame is demanding. You have to raise a herd of hogs to feed your family. The price of corn can wipe out all profit. Be prepared to grind. You'll always have the pictures of Wilbur and the blue ribbons. I know I have mine, tucked away.

The issue for individuals like us is that, when they come up to this Tsunami wall of next level competitive skill, where do you go, when you can't cut the grade anymore? That St. Petered Out Principle. What can you do and feel good about? Where can you find success? Oh yeh, and, you can't go around blaming injuries, blaming people. Blaming the Gods of Your Universe. I say to get on with your life, first you need to look to yourself, check out the mirror.

If you are a woman and you want to be in charge of your country, better look to India or England or Israel. Hasn't happened in the good O'USA. Hilary's on the quest! Accept the arena you want to enter. Understand, though the time is becoming now. Maybe that a female will grab the top rung. No telling.

For sure, Barak, amazingly, got the ring. Maybe in my life time a woman. But hear what I say!. Figure out what you're up against. If you're bummed that the path takes you longer to do make up and hair, deal with responsibility. Just no whining. Seize the opportunity.

While you're on your quest, you will need to be aware of prejudice, like White Guys can't jump, which I confirmed by being an exception, at least once upon a time. Focus on what you're willing to take on. If you want to play for the Chicago Cubs, be ready to find a goat! Know your limitations. If you enjoy painting, just do mural. If you want to count on the mural for financial support, that's another issue, just don't murmur excuses. Harden yourself for societies' prejudice and devaluing. Prepare for some good moments waiting tables. Put aside your parents' expectations. At long last, you might open an art gallery and no one will come. So what? Define who you are and desire to become because you are about you. No one is going to care more about you that you. Final advice. Make your work your joy. One more time.........make your work your joy.

Take my decision to go into education. I love the arena that of being The Teacher. Maybe a teacher is like a builder. With Valley Oak I am able to hone in and develop a relationship with the individual student. I am not having to process one hundred and fifty students in core high school curriculum, meeting up with proficiency tests, gearing course credit to appropriate core levels and labels, correcting one hundred and fifty essays on Truth, handling the gate at football games. Supervising the parking lot during after game dances. I am not having to focus on my fifth graders acquiring the district determined skills to matriculate to sixth grade and being passed along even if hey do not know their multiplication facts, in a specified, data supported progress sheet. My role at Valley Oak is to get down to what's real for each student. What they want to do. Where they want to be. What can they achieve? ASSIST them in thinking in real terms. Hold on to their dreams, get them to talk about their dreams, listen to them. Let them know that what they have to say is important, because their thoughts matter. Make sure they know they are being heard. Then ask them, quietly, directly......

"What are you going to do to make this happen?"

Often times the pondered answer is something like, "I don't know Lou."

Honest response. I let that statement stand. Give some time for the student to think. To think for themselves. Parent and peer pressure need to take a back seat. I do too. Time is on them.

Sometimes, I'll come back with something like, "What are you going to do to get on with your life? What are you going to do for yourself?"

Have them feel the ownership. Don't look to your uncle in St. Louis. What are you going to do to make this happen? That's the key phrase. Get ready for YOU. Then, I listen.

"Well, what I'd really like to do is become a mortician, but my mom thinks that's stupid."

Yes! I might be a bit blown away by some of the dreams but I don't devalue, put up obstacles. Ask them concrete questions like: wherewhenhow. This is not a time for deflecting comments, like have your ever seen the movie Harold and Maude? (Great show.) It's on me to support the student in achieving their goal. What can we find out on the Internet or Google? What type of training do you need? Where can you learn the skills? What are the opportunities? Mom's a concern, so what can we put together that can address the "stupid" issue. I don't want the student to blame mom because one always needs to be looking in the mirror, the individual. Owning for who you are, accepting where you are at, what you need to do, what is your priority?

Then, GO FOR IT.................

Sure there's fear of failure. We all have it. I had it with starting up Valley Oak. It's just that, so many times, beg my Grey Papuan, you want to blame someone or something for your not cutting the mustard. You could do these things if, only? If they would have? If that could've? Oh yeh, gottcha. The woulda-choulda-shoulda shuffle. That's a good thing to keep in mind. You didn't do this. It's not your fault. That's cool. Just slack your ownership off. It's important to have someone to blame. Personally, I always keep a few in my hip pocket. Good to have the back up. But, is blaming going to get you anywhere besides a future of a personalized reserved barstool pedestal at Sal's Corner Bar? Is blaming going to move you off the street? Out of your parents' home? Get your day rolling? Float your boat? Because, if you don't make the move, get ready to stay put. Your future is on you. Yes, you do bet your life. (Was that Groucho?)

Talk about getting out of your parent's home, The Gonzalez Family lived next to mine through the age of twelve. I have such vivid memories of their interaction. In fact, they still are in the same house. At least the folks. Sure to be grandparents by now. Every now and then I drive by the place. There's an older couple living in mine. Probably around the age my folks would be. Keep the old place real neat. I totally respect the Gonzalez Family. There needs to be some kind of award for the stuff staying together families go through besides social security checks. Anyway, there is this summer day when I am finishing mowing the lawn and I am just sweeping down the sidewalk. Out of the Gonzalez house burst Greg and his father, Gary. Greg was the oldest of the four Gonzalez boys, Greg, Gene, George, and Gary Jr. Greg was five years older than me and was the local athletic hero. I must have been in fifth grade about then. Gary would pack us into the station wagon and take us to all of Greg's games. So, they come screaming at each other out the front door of the house letting the entire block in on their family dialogue, which wasn't that much of an unusual event.

Greg was yelling something like, "It's your god damn fault." (How it was such a strict Catholic family that Greg and his brothers would use God in vain I could never compute.) I always crossed myself when I heard him say this. I mean risking mortal sin and eternal damnation seemed a big deal.

Gary, "Like Hell!" Gary was getting into his best "I am The Father in The Home" form. He never hit his kids, seldom swore, but his twenty years of military training made The Great Santini an everyday living ritual. "Like Hell!" He was repeating himself, which was the signal that this conversation was going to hit ballistic real quick, pointing his finger in Greg's face, "I never had the disrespect for my family that you bring into this house!"

Greg, in full rage. Sweating. Veins popping. "Who asked for this house? Who asked for this life? Who asked to be your son? Who the hell are you! You're the one that brought me into this world! This is your god damn fault!" Greg then turned and stomped down the middle of our tree lined street.

Gary stood in the driveway, arms folded, shaking his head, then yelled down after him, "Hey kid! Hey, wait a second!"

Greg paused, but didn't turn around.

"Let's get this straight my son! Your mother and I were having a wonderful time and that you resulted in the interaction is your problem!"

Gary, went back into the house, slamming the door. I continued sweeping as Greg stomped down the street. I noticed George, Gene, and Gary Jr. his younger brothers, were looking over the back fence at the action. They smiled at me and waved. I shrugged and shook my head. Everything would be back together normal in another hour or so. Nobody got too excited about these events.

In the '80's, when "The Simpsons" came on, I thought of the Gonzalez.' Like the Gonzalez, the Simpson's always ended every episode as a family. The Simpson's are always on the couch, the Gonzalez are always around the dinner table. The Gonzalez were always made whole again because they were aware of and accepted the differences in one another, everything was in the open. This is not to say that they agreed on all of life's events, but they accepted. There might be some upheaval to the family fabric, however rumpled, they all shared the responsibility of who they were. The Simpsons. The Gonzalez'. Sly and the Family Stone are family.

I had forced myself to do this. This did not come easy. This being the accepting of responsibility. Your role in events. This is looking in the mirror and not blinking, blaming people, accepting responsibility. For instance, I like being right. I don't like going back and seeing what I could have done better. What might have worked for a better situation. But, if you don't check it out, take on the ownership, put down the blaming, how can you bring on the positive growth in the ways you consider important. Getting there is not going to happen.

I can recall one or two situations in my experience that I can look back on and wish that I had made a better decision. The kind of events that, when you think about reliving your life you say, for sure. Then you pause. Something does not quite check out. You think about a few things that did not come down so right. You think, OK, only if I could change that one night or skip everything about the fourth grade, then I would relive my life. Then I would be okfine. The thing is, lots of people get stuck on that one event or with a fourth grade mentality. They are unable to move on. They cannot grab the merry go 'round growth ring. All they can do is ride the up and down ponies and talk about how this and that happened and they and them and those are to blame. "If that asshole Coach Davis hadn't been such a turd, I would have been a professional baseball player." Yeh, right. Good to blame. Feels alright. Happens all the time. Stuck. Unable to look in the mirror, accept ownership. Move on..........

In Valley Oak's relationship based program an imperative is not to get stuck on stuck. Everyone's going to mess up, make mistakes. We all make errors in judgment that we regret. The important aspect is to learn and move on. Do better the next time. I know improvement does not come easy. No way. I try to model for staff some of my indiscriminate experiences, of which there are many to choose from.

One of my many poor decisions that I share with venting, frustrated staff is my infamous "Backpack Launch," to help get this point across.

I look back on the Backpack Launch event and still shudder, certainly humbled me. I can feel Laura nodding her approval.

The situation was as follows. Here was this student in my class, Billy Gains. Billy was around twelve and had tested, among other things, gifted. With gifts that went far beyond one plus one. Billy could utter some of the most sexualized, personally devastating accusations I have ever had tossed at me. Never a regret. Apology. He would refuse to accept redirection and could destroy any sense of classroom decorum. However, the talent that gave him the most Valley Oak School Yard Credibility was his ability to flagellate on command. He is the only student, human, I have ever met who could fart on command. Like he had a balloon for an intestine. We always wondered about what he ate at home. Big. Little. Squeak. Rapid fire. The worse were the silent ones. Smell!! Gag me! How many times we emptied classrooms due to his fart attack? The other students thought that he was just a gut buster and never got mad at Billy. Anyone who could bring down program was OK by them. Anyway, The Backpack Launch occurred when I was absorbing his verbal abuse. Asking that Billy leave the classroom. For some reason he chose to do so, walking out to the front sidewalk. From the "can I be stupid" section of my brain, I took the opportunity to make sure he did not return to my room. I then went over, picked up his backpack, opened the classroom door, and calmly launched the backpack about thirty yards after him. The alien bedecked backpack floated through the lower tree limbs, hit the cement sidewalk with a thud. Didn't even bounce.

Billy turned around and looked, totally blown away. He threw a hand to his forehead and screamed "My CD Player!" He then charged, screaming at me, bringing about a three person prone restraint.

The following day Laura and I, humbly, met with his mother and father to discuss the incident. They were very kind. They asked me what had taken so long for me to react in this manner? Shudder.

I had long ago accepted public education, specifically Valley Oak, allowed us to be with our students for a fraction of their life. Their real world, the one that counted, had different boundaries and expectations. Our students' homes would systematically employ physical interventions to redirect behavior, the slap-whap was a reality threat waiting to happen. (Again, Laura's father's belt). Getting your backpack launched by some bully, like me, would happen if you farted enough in his presence. Valley Oak's Relationship Program offered dialogue as an alternative to the physical intervention. Valley Oak was about breaking the cycle of violence and intimidation! With Billy, a gas mask, some Be-no would have helped.

I wondered if the Simpson's or Gonzalez's might have room for one more................

Personality: naturenurtureyinyangheridtyenvironment. How do we get on with coming out of that womb to face the onslaught of everyday life. (Make like a baby and head out. OK, bad joke.) What schemas do we develop to forge the relationships that will secure our safety net of wellbeing? How do we change the relationships to meet our needs? Did Gene, George, and Gary Jr. go through the same things as Greg? For me, I can look back on a lifetime of solid personal health, friendships, education, sports, with the realization that I can launch a child's backpack. Although someone might say that my middle class values are the reason I launched it. (Gotta find some blame!) I observe the students who come into my program and just marvel at their courage in acknowledging the dread of their own personal daily needs.................

November 18   Brazil

Rick Hutton. He was always looking in the mirror. Rick's flat affect completely shrouded his flourishing, if exotically dark, personality. I had never met anyone like him.

Done and Done! I sit on the far park bench across from St. Mary of Our Mothers' Catholic Church in Willow Glen. The magnolias are blooming. It's exactly 10:45. High mass. I felt the torque of the blast engulf me as dust and smoke billowed from the collapsed steepled roof. My hair blew back. Heat smacked my body. I could see the blood red smoke arise from several other like explosions. Fourteen if I could have seen them all. Fourteen for the fucking fourteen Stations of the Cross. Pray on that you Jesus Heathens. This time I will bear a blackened cross charred in my cauldron of fire. There were no screams. The scene was too soon for sirens. I had placed enough plastic explosive to insure that all within each fornicating Christian sacrilege would be obliterated. Vlad would be proud. I smiled. Wonder if he ever thought of learning Portuguese. Cars had stopped. People were standing stunned. I checked my plane ticket for Brazil and wandered off.

In a devoid of intonation alien muted mutter, "Lou."

"Yes Rick." It was a warm, soft, late autumn afternoon. Lunch break. I had my hands on my hips, hunched over, sweat soaked. Recovering from losing another full court basketball game. The four on four competition was continuing. I watched two of our students following their leashed rabbits further out in the pasture.

"Lou, I have been thinking."

I waited for Rick to tell me what he had been thinking about. He never rushed things. I had plenty of time to wait Rick out. We walked over. Took seats on the old brick barbecue behind the classroom. I knew I would never be capable of guessing what was of importance to Rick.

Rick shifted his silver studded dog collar, cleared his throat. "Lou, I decided I want to learn a foreign language."

I looked at Rick, thinking, that's cool, we can do that. We have both Spanish and French CD programs. Several of our staff have a foreign language background. I mused, how could Rick speak without moving his lips?

I wiped my face with a towel. Replied matter of factly, "Really Rick? Which one?"

Rick quickly responded. He must have really thought this idea out. "I think Portuguese."

The afternoon was a beautiful. Warm. Leisurely. New England Fall day. Ernie Banks, Mr. Cub, even in November, would want to play two. "Portuguese? How did you choose that language?" Rick always baffled me.

Rick answered slowly. Clearly. Lips imperceptivity moving. "I want to learn Portuguese because I plan to blow up all the churches in Willow Glen at 10:45 on Easter Sunday. Then, I want to escape to Brazil, where I can speak the language."

I just sat there. Cowabunga Buffalo Bob! Had I heard what I heard? Is this a pleasant time daydream of a seventeen-year-old? An objective in his life? Where was this coming from? I looked at him. In so many ways, Rick was age appropriate. Popular with his peer group. Even had played

Little League. I'm sure Laura had her clinical description of Rick. To me, Rick was a spiraling fantasy dwelling. Asperser paranoid. Blossoming schizophrenic classified adolescent. That's a load for a teacher, not to forget the student. But, due to the impact of Rick's fractured home life, he had vanquished his ego identity beneath a veneer of socially assaultive, maladjusted norms. Which included, amongst other issues, bringing a meat cleaver into his high school. Not acceptable Bay County Public Educational behavior. Now with Valley Oak, Rick was coming to trust the community acceptance of who, what he was going through. Everyone had work to do on themselves. However, Rick continued to select the road less taken by breaching social boundaries. What better way to start a conversation than destroying all the local churches. Fleeing to Brazil. I would bet that Rick was more for the Tribal Amazon that the Copa Copana Beach.

I chose the safe area. I didn't want to find out that he had a stash of dynamite in his basement. "Brazil?"

"Yeh," Rick was shyly smiling, smiling at the herd of goats being ushered past us to the near pasture.

I looked up as six geese wheeled in, set their wings, back fluttered into the neighbor's pond. I had heard that geese mated for life. "Geez Rick, why not Spanish. Most every country south of us speaks Spanish except Brazil."

Rick pondered for a moment. "I did think of that but I saw that movie about all the little Hitlers."

I asked, "Boys From Brazil?"

Rick edged nearer to me. Not touching, but close. He would often do this when he was into serious thought. Early on I had to stop myself from shifting further away.

"That's the one. Have you ever seen it?"

I nodded that I had, fairly disturbing movie. "Yeh, while back. What did you like about it?"

Rick took his glasses off and polished them on his black t-shirt. His black nails were bitten to the quick. "I want to meet the guy who did the cloning. I was hoping that he might clone me."

This was vintage Rick. He had some fairly disturbing ideas, especially for male power figures. Physically, Rick had the body structure of a Third World emaciated poster child. That he was all bones and sunken sockets could not be attributed to his lack of food intake, this boy could eat! Rick consumed food in a conspicuously obscene manner that relegated Christian Church decimation on Easter Sunday to the second page.

For instance, we would go into Red's for Lunch Bunch and people would slowly start watching Rick as he would voraciously consume Red's Famous Hot Pulled Pork Sandwich. I doubt that Rick was ever aware of the stares. Rick simply inhaled the morsel. He was always the first one done and looking for scraps. But there was much more to the act. Anyone who has ever had a pulled pork sandwich knows how difficult it is to bite clean through the item. I mean the good ones that are topped with onions, pepper, pickles. Sauce that slithers off of the thick French rolls. You just cannot take a chunk out of that beast without leaving pieces of meat. Other garnishes dangling around the edges or falling onto the table and your clothing. Not recommended for first time dinner dates. Rick was capable of chomping tooth to tooth. He was a Tyrannosaurus vacuum. Rick could take a devouring bite out of Red's Famous Pulled Pork Sandwich. Not leave anything hanging around or dropping on his shirt. Rick's bite was a surgical decapitating guillotine that Red's knife could not have duplicated. In fact Red had said this to Rick. Rick was one of Red's favorites because Rick would try any new hot sauce that Red offered. Nothing fazed Rick's taste buds. Rick would pile on the onions, peppers so much that Red began putting out a bowl of each when Rick showed up. Red had told Rick that he had never seen one of his Famous Hot Pulled Pork Sandwiches consumed with such a "tour de force" as Rick was able to give it. He asked Rick if he could take a picture of him assaulting the sandwich for his wall, but Rick was camera shy.

What would further catch the other patron's attention was Rick's approach to the food. He treated the sandwich as a bone to be revered. Savored. Honored. Ritualized. His long, slender, sinewy, cream colored hands caressed the morsel fondly as he longingly beheld the exquisite form. His mouth would slowly gape open, exposing a set of formidable choppers that would have done The Werewolf of London proud. Now, Red's Famous Hot Pulled Pork Sandwich was not famous because it was dainty. The Sandwich came in only one size, gargantuan. Red's was famous, as his entire menu will attest to, due to zest and size. I have never, Red concurs, have never seen anyone else who could wrap their mouth around the entire sandwich as Rick could. He was a boa constrictor with an unhinged jaw dropping to engorge the prey in ravenous rapture so deep that Rick's eyes would roll back while his eyelids fluttered in orgasmic pleasure. His lips would draw back in grimaced force as the rapier choppers, embedded in exposed gums, fell to cleanly dismember the appendage from the main body in a swift, surgical strike. The question was whether he chewed his food or swallowed whole?

I felt that was another good reason that our Lunch Bunch Platoon was allowed to come in a bit earlier. Not only did we get served quickly, but there were fewer customers to be made ill at ease by Rick's table manners. You just could not avoid watching him. Rick was such primeval paganistic predator. Rick never ordered anything but Red's Famous Hot Pulled Pork Sandwich. He never wanted to go anywhere but to Red's. He was always disappointed if Lunch Bunch had to go somewhere else. Then too, we all were.

"Brazil and Portuguese?" I restated.

Rick nodded. "That jerk dude The Pope dividing up the New World was stupid."

I agreed, "I doubt the Aztecs and Incas had future plans of speaking Spanish or Portuguese."

Rick did not respond. When I glanced at him I could see his eyelids were fluttering. I understood that Rick had moved on. I would stay with him until he returned, then, I would need to let Laura know about our conversations.

My therapy meetings with Rick always began on time. He never missed a therapy meeting as he was always punctual and desired to more fully understand himself. What were the determining factors in his evolving existence? What did his ritualistic transcendental thoughts signify? What was real? There was a soft knock at my door.

A hesitant, "Hi Laura."

"Good to see you Rick. Come on in."

Though gentle as the proverbial church mouse, Rick usually made me feel somewhat disconcerted. From our first meeting, there was a sunken distance in his eye contact that left me disquieted. I found myself nervously entering the concern on my note pad as I took a soft breath and began.

"So, Rick, is there anything I should ask about physical decisions in your life?"

"You noticed?" He giggled.

"Well, the red is quite catchy."

Rick had swirled and set his thick, shoulder length hair into five clumps. Each clump was cylindrically pointed as if an upside down ice cream cone had been used as the form roller. Each of these pinnacles was dyed a blood brilliant red with heavy droplets running to the base of each cylinder.

"I bet when Red sees you for Lunch Bunch he will ask if you dipped your hair in his barbecue sauce."

Rick gave a startled look and asked nervously, "You think so?"

"No, Rick, he will not. I was just making a joke." I laughed. At times Rick could be so concrete. So vulnerable. "Tell me Rick, what's up with the new style?" I had come to learn that, with Rick, he always had a purpose in mind.

"I am Vlad the Impaler."

That was a new one on me, at least, no demolished churches on Easter. Rick's current theme was more dialogue based as he was looking for what was the appropriate boundary for social discourse. Rick's probing of appropriate social boundaries was based on the fact that he never received consistent values from his family framework. Given his developmental reclusive social manner, Rick was stretching to earn peer recognition and form his personal id. Then too, there was a part of Rick that thoroughly enjoyed the shock value that some of his actions brought about. I had never heard of Vlad, but he had to be a step up from Adolph and the Boys From Brazil, Rick's former power figure of choice and, better the blood red hair than a moustache..

I ventured, "Tell me about Vlad."

Rick sat up straight and spoke with animation. "Vlad's this cool dude who cut off his enemies heads and impaled them on their spears."

I feigned astonishment. "Sounds ghastly."

"Yeh and lots of historians think he was the first Count Dracula. His castle is now a tourist spot in Eastern Europe. I plan to visit it."

I nodded, well, if he and Adolph did not share the same gene pool, they were both male power figures for Rick.

"How do you see yourself as Vlad?"

"Oh," Rick smiled, "I would skewer my enemies, cut off their heads, and impale them on their weapons."

"What enemies?" I had delved into Rick's fantasies with him, but they and never presented in terms of identified adversaries.

He immediately answered. "First would be my sister and her boyfriend. Hope they never get married. Then I would get John and Ronnie." He paused. "Third I would find that stupid Jack in the Box clown and tear him apart."

I had to suppress a smile. I had my own thoughts about that Jack in the Box character. They did have the best chicken tacos though.

"Seems like you have some definite ideas." Rick nodded. "Let's go through the list you just mentioned. We can start with your sister. What could she say to you that might make a difference?"

Rick's eyes began fluttering as he was entering a psychotic episode as another of his movies was seeking him. I would wait for Rick to come back from his personal venture and stabilize, then we could talk about where he had gone.

I relax into my mind with Laura. Laura is my goddess. I love her. If my goddess was not Sharon, Laura would be mine. She is so cool. I could never tell her. Maybe I could. Should I? Wonder what she would say? She notices everything I do. Asks me about how I feel. What I am thinking about. Her smell. The perfume. I figured that out. Every time I am with Laura I smell her sweetness. Wonder if she has boyfriends like Sharon? Maybe I can buy her perfume. Keep it close. Her nipples don't stick out like Sharon's. With Laura I dream of sitting under a blossoming tree on a spring day. We are naked. Just lounging in the sun warmed grass. She asks if there is anything she can do for me. What should I say? What should I ask for? Maybe I should ask Lou?

Not now. My minions harken. They bring my steed. I mount! Vlad rides forth!

May 21 Family!

Like I said, Rick was never stuck, he always came up with ideas. He just amazed me with his dust devil of thoughts. Always on the move. Always thinking. In his own personal, private, inscrutable way.

166

"Lou, can I go with you?" Over the months I had become accustomed to Rick's monotone.

"Sure Rick." I was headed into Willow Glen to pick up two of our students who were earning the right to transition to a less restrictive environment, which is IEP speak for returning to their regular district of reference high school. We worked with the referring school district to gradually include the student in stages. We had started a student back with as little as fifteen minutes one day per week with a staff present to offer support. The usual manner was to offer one period five days per week. Currently, five of our students were transitioning back to their school district of referral. This offering demanded that we dedicate one of our staff full time to transportation and others as needed, like my turn today. Thus far, the successful results made the effort worthwhile. I wondered why Rick wanted to come along. I was sure he would let me know as we headed into town.

We were rolling through the spring countryside. I enjoyed the winding two-lane road before we hit the interstate.

In flat no affect, "Lou."

"Yes, Rick."

"Lou, I've been thinking."

What Rick was thinking about could not always be shared. Laura was starting to get into some of his stuff. Rick talked about his rampaging movies with Laura, not the movies that one goes to see at theaters, but the ones that he experienced. He could see them with his eyes open or closed. They just came on, reel to reel full-length episodes. No admission charge. Monsters in ritualized taboo blooded orgies. Scary stuff. Not really compatible with returning to public school. Rick had given Laura permission to share them at staff meeting, which helped the staff get a handle on what was going on for him. With Rick's permission, of course.

"What have you been thinking, Rick?" I always talked straight with him. No humor. Just reality based dialogue. His interpretations did enough convoluting.

"I want to change my name."

"Really? To what?"

Rick was currently dressing all in black. Black boots. Black socks. Black belt. Black sweatshirt-black jacket-black dyed hair-black eye liner-black lip gloss. Names quickly ran past me like Black Plague. Black Blood, Black Bart. Boston Blackie.

"I'll give you a hint, take a look at my beard?"

I had noticed that Rick was growing out a goatee. Actually, the strands were a thin, wispy trailing of down that was almost two inches long. Like Charlie Chan. I visualized some other names: Black Beard. Black Fuzz. Black Chinny Chin Chin..........

"Black Reaper?" I ventured.

Rick looked directly at me, "Not even close. I want to change my name to Cuddles the Goat."

Nothing surprised me from Rick anymore. "That's a unique name Rick. How did you decide on that?" Maybe Cuddles the Goatee! Where would he go next?

Rick filled me in. He had been gazing at the herd of goats in the field next to our site and they just seemed to be so peaceful, pastoral, the moment was a gorgeous early spring day. The goats stood together, munching on the sweet emerging shoots, looking around now and then at the people action in our section.

We had constructed a soccer field and goal posts out of four-inch PVC pipe. Our games were huge. The field filled one section of our pasture. Everyone would play. From six years of age to me. Sadly I had to acknowledge that I was the oldest member of our staff participating. Even the little guys ran circles around me.

Rick never participated, he watched. This day he had fixated on the goat herd. Rick noticed as one of the larger goats raised up its head and bleated, then began heading towards a small, blue barn at the other side of their field. The rest of the goats had filed in behind. Slowly making their way to the barn. That was enough for Rick, he wanted to join the family, as Cuddles the Goat.

I sat there next to Lou. Should I tell Lou that I want Sharon to be the queen of the goat herd. I will be king. We will raise a flock. A flock? That's geese. I meant herd. Wonder if Lou would want to join? He could be a prince. Maybe a duke. Uncle for sure. Wonder how he would handle the honor. We would be safe. Have plenty of grass to eat. Our furry coats would keep us warm. Wonder what sorts of games goats play. Have to think about that. I've seen them fuck. Right out in the open. Like there's nothing to it. Wonder if guys ever fucked goats? Maybe that's why there's centaurs. Need to think about that. No way. (Shook my head.) Fucking a goat was too creepy. All that hair. I visualized Sharon as a goat. Somehow she had six luscious tits. The nipples were long and pointed. Ugh. Disgusting. Maybe a kangaroo would be better? I got up and walked away from Lou to think about the dilemma.

When I presented this information to Laura, she responded that Rick was trying to formulate a reunification with a family, his own was in such disarray. His father had died when he was nine. His mother was not well. Bedridden, in and out of hospitals. Rick's older sister's boyfriend had used a gun to extort money from Rick's mother. Now the jerk was serving time in the county jail. Laura did not believe that the mother would press charges due to the fear of her daughter harming her. Rick just wanted some peace and quiet, a place where he could feel cared for and nurtured. To Rick, the life of Cuddles the Goat was just that. Maybe he could be a goat herder? I was sure there was room for one more in Brazil.

June 14 Flashback

FOUNDERS RURAL RESIDENTIAL PROGRAM

Our animal husbandry program at Founders' Farm was becoming more of a force within Valley Oak. JK and I were coordinating efforts to maintain the livestock twenty-four seven. Prior to JK's arrival, there would have been zero hope of this happening. With his energy and supervision of the residential program site was gradually changing. Barns were being cleaned out and reframed. The wild growth was being chopped down and maintained. Things were going well, maybe the time had come to bring on some goats.

JK recalled, "Yeh, Lou, remember the first day we walked in?"

Did I? That first time JK and I came in the back door with all the plywood boarded up windows, jungle growth with the rush of foul mildew smelling fungus greeting our entrance. I was struck silent by the strangeness of merging into a period of my life I had put so far out of conscious thought.

"You sure you want to move your school into this dump?"

For sure I wasn't. "I tell you JK, if it wasn't for Red, I don't think either of us would be here."

"You got that right. At least the lights work."

JK had flicked on the hall lights as we walked by the bedrooms. Seven of them. During my five years I had been in all seven. I caught visions of my roommates. We walked out to the center of the home which was made up of the kitchen, dining room, and living room.

"There she be." JK turned all the lights on. "This is the same floor plan as the house we have now in use for our kids."

Although I knew the answers, I asked JK the basic questions about square feet, heating, appliances. I had already figured out how to divide the home up into classrooms. Where we could set up the therapists' rooms. All the time catching visions of my youth. The fireplace during the winter. Ping pong contests in the game room.

"Hey Lou. Let me show you the indoor gym." JK led the way pass the laundry room and, opening a double door, to a cement floor quarter length basketball court.

"How do you like that?"

"Amazing." Still here I thought. "The other house have one?"

"Nope, just this one. Heard the hoop was put in over thirty years ago because one of the kids was an all-state player. Made the court 'specially for him. Heard it was some super stud White Guy. Like you," JK laughed.

Yes they had. Staff had surprised me. I had been on a two week summer wilderness experience journey. Returned to my own basketball court. They had converted an open garage parking area into a raised roof basketball court. Just for me. I had been blown away. Of course, all that was Red's idea. I drifted back.........

"Lou! Lou! You've got to over play him on his strong side!"

I looked at Red. He had his scowl on. This was the quarterfinals. My first. I was the hot shot White sophomore who could not be stopped and I was getting my lunch handed to me. All game I had been getting tattooed by Grant's senior guard, J.J. Jerome. He'd waited all year to put a face on me and I was getting ugly.

Red did not let up, "You gonna play for Founders, you need to do more than score." Red took a breath, calmed himself. "Now, Lou, J.J. hasn't gone left all night. Over play to the right. Let's see what he's got."

I nodded, everyone was counting on me. "Wildcats!!" We broke huddle. Down 58-49 midway through the third quarter. Seemed like JJ had scored forty of their points.

"Spider!" Red called out. "You've got Lou's back!"

Spider nodded. He was my six foot eight jumping jack roommate. Only player who could out sky me. Spider was a senior. He'd been to the semifinals before. He hated the name Spider. He still had a total freaking fear of them. Only Red could call him that to his face without getting punched out.

JJ thumped the ball up court. He was nimble and smooth. Could play swing in college. Saw me overplaying him to his right, giving up the lane on the left. He looked right at me and smiled. Gave a glance to the off guard, with an ankle breaking crossover dribble made...............

"See that red mark at the top of the backboard?" JK pointed to a spot above the hoop. "Story goes that the White Boy touched that spot. Not bad for a six foot guard."

I nodded. I was six-three the day I did that mark. I stayed cool. "Did you ever hear about whatever happened to him?"

JK paused, "Not really. Long time ago. I think before Red was even coaching The Wildcats. Something about he got injured during a state tournament."

I sighed, "Life is a hard fall for high flying guards, no matter what the color."

"Ain't that the truth and don't I know it. That's why I stick with slow pitch softball."

"You and me both." I was glad to get off the basketball subject. My spine ached just thinking about the injury.

"You know Lou, we should get a ball team up from the residential staff here and Valley Oak."

"Sounds good to me." We walked out of the court to explore more of the building.

Red had foreseen that JK and I would do well as a team to get Founders back on track, at the same time our coordination gave Valley Oak a place to grow, with a stabilized residential population adding more students to the school program. JK and I began doing intakes together, with Laura's permission, of course. Founders' placements would also be IEP processed into the Valley Oak program. Our plan was for the behavioral expectations to be consistent between both programs. Also, staff could be interchanged, sharing information more readily between programs. Nowhere was our interaction better seen than in the animal husbandry-workability programs.

Valley Oak brought with the move a Workability Program. We had earned a Workability Grant of twenty-five thousand dollars that allowed us to pay students a minimum wage for developing employable skills. Get paid to come to school? What a concept! Also, Workability took the place of the Monetary Reward System that we had first established. Valley Oak did not even write the checks for Workability, straight from Massachusetts State Funds.

Along with the pigeons, rabbits, and chickens, we did have pet rats in program. Rick was especially fond of one, Rick had named him Mr. Peepers. Mr. Peepers was one of the older rats, he had been donated to us. Rats were not my favorite classroom pet. They smelled, didn't tend to live long. Worse of all, they were smart. If one got away, you could bet you would spend the next two weeks looking for the rodent. Everyday the students would come to school asking, "Have you caught Romeo?"

"Do you think he's OK?"

"Did he eat any of the food we left out?"

I mean, you would have thought that one of them who had gotten away. Gotten lost. Left out. Maybe that was the issue and once again, adult mismanagement.

"Lou,"

"Yes Rick."

"I don't think that Mr. Peepers is doing so well."

Rick placed Mr. Peepers down on the carpet. Mr. Peepers was not capable of running anywhere. He began dragging his hind legs. I could see what Rick meant. Mr. Peeper's body was shutting down on him. Rick stood there, arms folded, head hung down, gloom filled.

Rick continued to dress in black. Currently he had added cult appropriate items to his repertoire. Where leather fringe had previously dangled, metal had erupted. His black boots strutted silver studs jutting from the toe and heel. Black leather pants were torn in several places and held together with large, silver, safety pins dabbled with blood red paint.

The leather jacket must have weighed sixty pounds, more like a silver shield. Studs, silver plates, everywhere.........

Though, I admit, Rick had a heart, Rick conjured up The Tin Man. His ears were pierced in several places. Nose was pierced. Eyebrows were pierced. Lips were pierced. Tongue was pierced. I really did not want to know what was or was not else pierced. Rick's arsenal surpassed all expectations. Wonder what value the silver had on the open market.

Rick had gradually added items as he earned the Workability Program. Valley Oak had allowed Rick to wear these items because he was so successful in our program. Rick was popular with students. Worked hard. Followed directions. In fact, in two months, he would be eighteen, then his life was on him. Rick could decide if he wanted to go to school or not, sign his own IEP's. Maybe he would want to enroll in the local JC. Chronological age of eighteen allowed him to make those decisions.

"Lou, Mr. Peepers shouldn't have to suffer." Rick stroked Mr. Peeper's ears.

"What should we do?" Several other pets had undergone euthanasia.

Rick brandished a fiendish grin, "Let's get a hammer and smash his head! Can I cut off the hind quarters to wear around my neck?"

I just shook my head, somethings are just way beyond me. Later, Laura explained to me what Rick was processing. Laura let me know that Rick's mother was terminal. She could not leave her bed. The doctors stated she would not live past the next two weeks. Rick could not talk about her pain. How much he hated his sister and her boy friend. How they had caused his mother so much pain. Made her life unbearable by their mental abuse. Rick could not talk about how much he hurt, he wore the pain. He pierced himself in self-inflicted impalements of impotence. He destroyed those he loved. Vlad the Impaler could not have been more merciless.

I leered in the mirror. Mercy? Fuck that shit! Fuck them! They got as they gave. Fuck him! Had he shown my mother, my dear mother, any mercy when he splayed her open in the city square. His butchery hoards howling for lust. Mother had not told him where I was. What I was preparing to do. My plans. She who had given birth to me. Caressed me in joy. Shielded me after my Father's slaughter. I could love her no more than to slowly tear the sick bastard limb from limb. Watch the bloodied brain seep out. Sucked blood from his liver.

My revenge had occurred outside the city gates. They all watched. Watched what happened to someone who challenged me. I had begun by pulling his fingers out. One by one. How he had howled. He had looked on as I fed his body parts to my wolves. Then I tore each toe out. I hoped to see his kin come riding out through the gates, my minions waited in ambush. Sooner or later they would all get theirs! I twisted an arm and snapped the sinew and bone. Held the appendage above my head. Lapping the blood as it dribbled out. I laughed and tossed the fleshed bone to my devouring fiends.

Two days later Laura and I drove Rick home after school. Our main purpose was to drop by the hospital and support Rick in seeing his mother, we found her. Huddled. Tiny. Bald from the chemotherapy. Shrinking below a thin hospital sheet over her. She was heavily sedated. Her name was Rose. Rick could not touch her.

Her eyelids fluttered as she painfully breathed, "I feel small as a tack." Rose slowly laid back.

Rick did not have a hammer. He did not ask to save a body part. We left.

Rose died two days later.............

March 12

So, this is a funeral. I stood looking at my mother's casket. Wonder if I can watch it burn? Inhale the fumes. Maybe they can just burn her and I can keep the casket. The casket would make a cool bed. Just lay there with the top closed. That would be sweet.

August 3   Stampede!

Following Rick's mother's funeral, I thought of what life would be like to grow up without a family, searching to become Cuddles the Goat. Wearing the body part of a loved one.

Rick was disengaging further from the reality of his life. Rick had been such a normal little boy. One who loved dinosaurs, watched cartoons, looked forward to the cookies and milk his mother offered after school. Now Rick's reality was changing, a huge part that he had no control over was his heredity. Who knows from where or why. The onset of adolescent schizophrenia is tremulous. There is an obscure comment, a disconnected thought, a wonderment of how you got to where you were? Suddenly you are seeing pictures. Then movies. The movies might become full features

Thank the gods you might always came back, you could regain control of your own decision making, especially as a youth. The scariest part was that you were aware of what was going on. That you had been away, were now coming back. Returning to a focused reality. You could talk with Laura about Max the Behemoth, who dominated your movies with force, carnage. A rendering asunder of foes' body parts. How you admired him. Why you gave in to his dominance. How he took you away from the fragmented debris of your life to a world given over to omnipotent fantasy. How you relished the groveling of the vanquished to evolve into Vlad.

Laura knew too, knew that Rick was presenting all the clinical data of adolescent schizophrenia. Knew that the organic disease would gain ultimate control of Rick's thought processes as he entered adulthood. There was no stopping the onset. There were the medications. Psychotherapy to ease the transitions. The disease was here to take deep root to stay. Splintering established neural communication codes. Adolescent schizophrenia would make Max the Behemoth look like Cuddles the Goat. As an adult, full-blown schizophrenia was a one way dead end street.

"Lou."

"Yes, Rick." I had gotten so use to Rick seeking me out when I was alone.

"Is Sharon coming back?"

I knew the answer was no. I knew that Rick was infatuated with her. I took the middle ground. "Not immediately."

Word was that Martha was no longer at Sam and Helen's Trailer Park. Martha had sold the Winnebago. Sharon and she had packed up and moved to Florida. I was learning from Laura how not to be the bearer of negative information. Allow time to bring about the events that inform the individual. Allow the individual the time to process the events without an adult trying to come in to fix. Make alright. All better.

I began walking around the track. Rick kept pace, arms folded, body hunched over. He took long strides. "Oh, that's a bummer." He was disappointed. Rick's chin dropped below his dog collar.

Rick was always around Sharon. He might not be talking with her. Sharon might have been holding court with a group of peers, embellishing some exploit. Rick would be on the edge of the group, arms folded, wry smile on his blackened lips. When Sharon was through, walking off somewhere for a new audience, Rick would follow. Lacking an audience, Sharon talked to Rick. He never grew tired of listening.

"I hope she comes back. I want to fuck her real hard."

So matter of factly, Rick could have been blowing up all the churches in Willow Glen he was so calm. Our conversation was not within the general scope of student teacher dialogue. Did I look like a therapist?

"Rick, I would hope that there might be another way you could properly express your admiration for her."

Rick stood stumped for an instant. "I'm sorry, Lou. That was rude."

I agreed, "You might have just implied you would enjoy furthering a personal relationship."

Rick smiled. "That sounds like Lou. Kind of corny."

Rick was right. Corny? Where'd he come up with that? How about. I miss being around her? Something else besides the "f" word flying around in public. (No, I did not miss Mike Adams!)

Rick shrugged his metal pleated leather jacket, "Oh, alright, but everyone else has done Sharon. Didn't seem to matter as long as I wasn't the one."

I looked over at Rick. He was really in the dumpster. "What came down Rick?" He shook his head. We walked faster. I changed the subject to llamas.

Laura later explained, since the information was no longer confidential that, about a month ago, Rick had taken a bus out to Sharon's trailer park. Laura did not hear the story from Rick, Sharon had bragged how Rick was totally drooling over her. He had brought some mushrooms and meth for them to get loaded on. Rick told Sharon that he wanted to do the drugs, then have sex with her. Sharon was not into the sex. The drugs were OK. Rick was a good guy, she had plenty else to think about, like her child. She went out called a couple of her friends to come over, both guys. The four of them had gotten blasted. Sharon had sex with the two guys, not Rick. Sharon walked him back to the bus stop and kissed him good-bye. She liked Rick, just not that way. Made me recall that monster woman in East of Eden. Rick like Adam, you ask which Adam? Doesn't matter. Supreme Old Testament bummer impact.

That was not the only negative that was coming down on Rick, there was his codependent sister and her jerk boyfriend, fresh out of jail. They wanted to open a bookstore in one of the coastal villages. Be a cool place to hang out. Put in a coffee bar with Rick's money. Pay him back in a year. They had convinced Rick to give them his half of the inheritance, about six thousand dollars, so that they could open the bookstore. Rick said he had written them a check. He asked me if I thought his support was a good idea.

What do you say at times like this? Rick's life was simply ripping apart at the seams. The disease was progressing. His mother had died. Sharon had rejected him. His sister and boyfriend had ripped off his meager inheritance. How could he work through the cascading calamity? Where was the illuminating role model light to emerge from this muck hole of an existence? What's life like to be raised without a family support? Especially for Rick, a dad.

Sure I had wondered about my natural father. Who he was, why he left me. How did I end up at Founders, anyone would. I had never gone into the records to try and determine my natural parents were for two reasons. One was that I did not want to stir up the memories of my placement, that time was history, I wanted the past to stay that way. The second was that I did have parents, they had been as much mom and dad as any could have been. Even though our time was short, I remained filled with memories, some were more vivid than good, but that was not on my Dad. That was just about coming of age. Like the time John and I stampeded the herd of cattle. We were just boys.

John and I were about ten then. In the mid sixties cowboys were still a big thing. "Wyatt Earp, Rawhide, Have Gun Will Travel, Wagon Train, Colt 45, The Rifleman, Bat Masterson, Bonanza, Wanted Dead or Alive, Cheyenne," just filled the television evenings. Dad, John, and I were on a three day fishing vacation and staying at the Solari's cabin, which was next to the Collier Brothers Cattle Ranch. There were no other cabins on that side of the mountain, so that we were pretty much on our own.

One evening, after a day of fishing and rock throwing, I could never get the knack of fly fishing, John and I took out our BB guns. We were shooting anything that moved or got our interest when, off to the side of the narrow pock marked mountain road, a bull steps out of a gated backwoods trail. Behind the bull comes some cattle. Then more cattle. Then, before our very eyes, honest to god cowboys. John and I watched open mouthed as the cowboys whooped and hollered, just as we had seen on television. Hats in their hands, 'kerchiefs around their necks. No six guns though some had rifles. Rolled ropes slapping the lagging cows along. Big old dust cloud forming behind the herd as they made their way up the little used back road trail in front of the Collier's cattle pens. The herd kept growing. There had to be three to four hundred head on the asphalt road, more coming down the trail. The cowboys had just made the final turn for the corrals and dinner. They were beginning to parade right past us. John and I looked at each other, we shared one of those moments. One of those times that you do something you would never do alone. By ourselves we would not have had the guts. I said that I would do it if John would do it. He nodded. We crept down towards the road where the lead bull was trudging with the bell clanging on his neck. We went from bush to bush, hiding from the cowboys. They could not see us or we would be goners. We got up even with the lead bull, he was about thirty feet downhill from us. We could see the CB branded on his right rump. We started popping at it. We must have shot five or six times each, we could not believe that we were missing him! The bull was almost ready to turn for the corral. There was food and water waiting for the big guy. All of a sudden, zap! One of our BB's stings his hindquarters. He lets out a bellow. Raises up snorting, charges down the road. His big old bell on him clanging like Sunday Mass. The herd goes after him. Everything becomes a blur of dust. Bellowing cattle. Cowboys frantic yelling and whooping. John and I stumbling back to the cabin, praying to God that no one has seen us.

They saw us.

Later on in the early evening, one of the cowboys came up to the cabin and asked my Father if he might know anything about a couple of boys who had BB guns. My Dad said he did. The cowboy explained how the two boys had stampeded the entire Collier fall roundup herd. They were still bringing up strays. The time was around seven o'clock with dusk coming on. My Dad came over to John and I, looked at us, asked if we had done this? We put down our comic books, said that we had. My Dad just shook his head.

That night, after the worst tasting suppers I had ever forced down, my Dad told us that we had to walk over to the Collier Brothers Cattle Ranch. We had to find the foreman and give him our BB guns. Then we had to do a monstrous thing that I couldn't fathom, we had to tell him that he could do anything he wanted to us. Anything! His call. This was not just some scare tactic, Dad had not left the cabin to talk with anyone. This was for real. (Later I learned that Dad and the foreman, Gene, had known each other for years.)

John and I were petrified waiting for the moment of truth. We could see the campfires of the cowboys in the darkness around the cattle pens. All was just quiet, not even the cattle were mulling. It was around nine when we began creep over. We feared for our lives. Would they rope us and drag us? Dad wouldn't let them brand us. Would he?

Raising up from one of the camp fires, a tall, lanky, rugged Rowdy Yates cowboy came up to us. We told him we were the boys with the BB guns, which he might have guessed because we were holding them. That we were looking for the foreman. He said that he was the foreman. My voice completely broke into a high squeak as I related that he could have our guns. Do anything he wanted to us.

He looked us over, took a moment. Spoke in a measured tone, deep and gravelly, "You boys can keep your guns." He looked mean down at us. "Just, this better, not ever. I mean never. Happen again. Now, go on home."

That was my Dad. Lost Mom and Dad at the age of twelve.

I have never been much for country music. Some's O.K. More upbeat. That old joke about what you get if you play country music in reverse. You get your dog back, your car back, your house back, your money back, I couldn't get my Dad back, but this one song always reminded me of him and the stampede.

I should've been a cowboy.
I should've learned to rope and ride.
Carry my six shooter riding my pony on a cattle drive.
Stealing those young girl's hearts,
Just like Gene and Roy.
Singing those campfire songs.
I should've been a cowboy.
The singer's name escapes me right now.

"Rick, lets talk to Laura about Sharon."
Rick's dog collar nodded.
Lou ushered Rick into the room and left, softly closing the door.
"Hi Rick."
Lou's demeanor had told me there were concerns beyond his coping with and that it was time for Laura to wave a wand. I waited for a response as Rick took his seat, wand at the ready. Rick gently rocked back and forth.
"Oh, hi Laura." Rick replied as if he suddenly had awareness of my presence. I waited. Suddenly Rick was down on all fours!"
"Have I ever shown you that I can do fifty pushups?" He smiled up at me. "It's a piece of cake. Count them."
I obediently obeyed as Rick's long arms propelled him up and down as if he were bouncing off of a trampoline. "Forty-four, forty-five….Rick had not slowed down nor was he exhibiting any sign of strain. Abruptly he stopped and leapt to his feet."
"That's enough for now. Thanks for counting. He shook out his arms. Did I surprise you?"
How about flabbergasted me. "Rick, I had no idea that you worked out?"
He bashfully smiled with a touch of blush further reddening has face as he sat back down. Breathing slightly faster. In a cheerful, forthright manner he looked at me and stated, "Laura, it's time for Vlad to be impaled."
I sat back into my chair not knowing what to expect. Rick continued, "I need to take on the reality of my life. Like Lou always says, it's time for me to look in the mirror. I'm ready to move on."

Never, in all my therapeutic years, had I witnessed such a metamorphic transitional shedding of fabricated grandiosity. The Rick who sat before me was an individual I had never met nor latently considered possible. I attempted to maintain my professional composure, "Move on towards where?"

Rick drummed his fingers as if impatient with my inquiry, locking me with eye contact, "I need to get real. Find a job. Get off this residential reservation Look to get what's good for me. I will be turning eighteen. Valley Oak has been great and given me the ability to socially communicate at this level. I will be forever grateful and acknowledge........

Rick paused and with the fluttering hesitation I felt that he might be previewing an event when he said, "Gotcha Laura! You thought I was regressing." He burst out laughing! No chance! Nada. Time to get it together and move on."

Rick stood up, took off his dog collar, gently placed the armor on my desk, and with a nonchalant wave, ambled out of my office. I remained cemented in wonderment.

August 20   HUMBLE

I had not been in the Bay County Mental Health Building for four years. Thought back to my first visit with James and smiled. Four years and how many students, forty-two....three.......? Thirty-two who were still with Valley Oak. Three had graduated and transitioned back to their home school districts, and three had not made it. Not made it? I could almost take IT personally. (Laura would say I should.) I thought of the three. What could we, I, have done differently? Better choices? Pay you to go to school. Activities to interesting places. Individual therapy. Computers. Workability. Relationships...........

NOW, BRAND SPANKING NEW! ONLY AT VALLEY OAK. ASSITANCE TO ADULT SERVICES!!

Rick was the oldest student who had attended our program, recently turned eighteen. At this age he could now sign his own IEP's, decide to drop out of program, enter a higher education program of his choice, vote, buy cigarettes, get a tattoo, join a goat herd. A host of life altering considerations. Actually, through Federal Law 94-142, Rick could receive the services of our program until the chronological age of twenty-two. The further stay was made possible as long as The IEP Team determined program to be beneficial In our state, there were five ways a special education student could end their high school career in a positive manner: (1) Keep up with the units, academics, proficiency expectations of their class to earn a regular diploma; (2) Attend consistently, not meet up with the units, academics, proficiency expectations, graduate with alternative standards on their diploma; (3) Take the state General Education (GED) exam, gain a state diploma; (4) Turn eighteen decide to attend junior college. (5) Turn eighteen, decide to reject any form of public education, get on with the "real world."

Rick had grade level academic ability, was meeting all unit expectations towards graduation. He was looking forward to walking across the stage with his high school peers in June. Shaking hands with the local superintendent. Wearing a white pressed shirt and ties, as James had. All appeared to be a go as Valley Oak Rick's program specialist, Merced Miaramontes, had been communicating with the district graduation department for the past eight months. Making sure all would be in order. No loose ends. Rick's earning a regular high school diploma had even gone before the school board, where he had been unanimously approved. Rick was his district's first nonpublic school student to graduate, an achievement everyone applauded.

What brought Rick and myself to the Bay County Department of Mental Health/Social Services, was not about graduation from high school, our visit was about graduation into adulthood. In earning the right to make personal choices. The services that had supported Rick through public education, would no longer meet his needs. Time to move on. In moving on the social skills that Rick had worked so hard to develop would be challenged by the expectations of the adult world. Eileen Floyd was the Bay County coordinator of young adult services, she focused on transitioning students such as Rick, who would need continual support as they entered into the over eighteen on your own world.

We entered Eileen's office and introduced ourselves. Eileen was wearing jeans with her thick long gray hair tied in a single braid. Must have been about six feet tall. I had been told by Laura that Eileen had a direct no nonsense manner about her. No one liners Lou.

As we shook hands, Eileen began, "Rick, Lou tells me you're going to walk across the stage and graduate."

Rick nodded. No longer wore his dog collar, studded boots. No longer wore his black leather-metal jacket. Said that the jacket was "no longer my style."

"Lou says that you do not talk much, but you know what you want. So, if we are going to do anything today, I want you to tell me what you want."

Well, that was straight and direct. No mincing words here. I wonder how many times Eileen had held this type of conversation. We waited for Rick.

Eileen was patient, Rick looked up, his lips actually moved as he stated with clear intonation, "I want a place to live with people I respect and respect me. I want to go to junior college and learn how to become a mortician. I want to find a job to earn spending money." Then he looked right at Eileen. "I want to find a girlfriend, if you could help, I would appreciate all you could do."

Eileen nodded and smiled back, "Well, let's start with the most important thing, the girl friend."

Eileen went on to tell Rick about the social gatherings her program organized. They were based on several supervised adult homes in the area. The homes had four to eight adults living in each. The level of care being determined by the occupants. Men and women lived together in all the homes. Some homes had live in staff. Others might have a staff come by at dinner. Some would have staff who checked in on weekends. Just depended on what your level of need was. Transportation was coordinated between the homes in terms of school, work, social events. The group homes social events were held on Wednesday. On Saturday nights there were activities for instance: dancing with DJ's, bowling, movies as general forms of recreation. Some of the adults, of course, dated.

I was amazed, I had always understood that there were few services available once a student let go the umbrella of the IEP.

Rick asked, shrugging his shoulder to show his lack of understanding, "Is this all free, like school? Do I have to pay for anything?"

"No free lunch, you know." Eileen chuckled. "Your Social Security check covers the cost. You just sign the check over to the county and the SS takes care of all the services." Eileen paused, inquiring, "You have applied for your SS?"

Rick nodded. Laura had taken him through the hoops without the palpitating agitation of The Sharon Experience. What Laura had found out was that there was no real, except mental, harm done in Rick's sister stealing his inheritance. The amount small,. around six thousand dollars, but he would have had to spend the amount down to two thousand dollars before he could have started being awarded his SS. You think of people who are scrimping and squirming every penny to get along. They catch a windfall. that's nice. Sorry, no more Food Stamps (SNAP), Energy Assistance Program (EAS), and other benefits of being impoverished until you're scrimping and squirming again. Nothing personal, just the system.

Eileen's work program was handled through the vendor, HUMBLE Inc. (Home and Urban Members Building a Lifetime Environment.) HUMBLE, a non-profit, contracted with the state in a variety of manners through which their employees found work, the state found monetary relief. HUMBLE made a profit, enough to put back into their residential program and pay staff. HUMBLE supervised several assemblage component centers, where PVC parts might be put together for pool cleaners, air filters and other such tedious repetitive tasks. HUMBLE ran warehouses where workers were assigned to unload pellets, drove lift trucks, placed markings on specific containers. HUMBLE kept the roadsides of the interstate highways cleared of side rubbish, maintained the rest stops. What I knew was that HUMBLE was respected, offered a solid supervised service to the community.

One of the keys to HUMBLE was that the workers did not have to hold eight hour shifts. An individual participated for as long as they could, to the best of their ability. Six hours was all today? Cool, see ya tomorrow. Not feeling up to par? Why don't you clock in your two hours, call it a day? There will be plenty more tomorrow. Took all the grind it out frustration from the workday. Better still, HUMBLE provided transportation to and from work. When you were ready, HUMBLE was ready to assist. HUMBLE must have had as many drivers as they had supervisors, their blue and green vehicles were everywhere.

Eileen sat back in her office chair asked, "What do you think Rick? Are you ready for this step?"

Rick answered immediately, "Sure am. Time to move on. I'm ready to become an adult."

Eileen stretched her long arms. clasping them behind her head. looked over to me. "I am sure there will be lots of more questions, but if it's OK with Rick and yourself, I can fill out the paperwork with Rick and drop him off at residence after showing him around. As soon as he graduates, we can figure out a start date for Rick." Eileen turned to Rick with a warm smile, "OK with you Rick?"

Rick nodded. "Sounds good to me. Lou, I'll catch you at school tomorrow."

As I left the office with Eileen beginning to describe a supervised living home that she thought would work well for Rick. I noticed Rick straightening his shoulders.

Rick was being taken care of in an extended family manner. There would be a home. A couch for Rick to form relationships in his adult life. Perhaps, a relative of the Gonzalez or Simpsons might even live next door. As I closed the door heading down the corridor, I checked to make sure I had all my body parts. Seemed that Rick had found his herd.

September 6   Girl Friends

"Get real Laura. Schizophrenia is not a light bulb. You don't just snap it on and off."

"Geraldine's not only right, so's all the research." Martha Lee tossed back her cold Boston Blackie Lager and smacked her lips. "The kid just took off his dog collar and said seeya?"

"Look, I was as incredulous as either of you." I took another drag on my cigarette. I hated the fact that I was smoking again, but the burning drag tasted so sweet and I was in disrepair. Besides, my Seven & Seven needed the company. "The young man could have done a thousand push ups!"

"Girl, you are just plain crazy."

I wish I was but I had been there and witnessed Rick's transformation that had derailed all the literature in the field. Per always, I was sharing my cases, professionally, and personal issues with my two best friends, Geraldine and Martha Lee. Both had remained with Bay County Mental

Health and had done their utmost to dissuade me from hooking up with Valley Oak and, from their perspective, the notorious Lou Thompson.

"Well, I'll be damned. Would you look at this…." As Martha Lee stood up extending her hand, I turned to see Red approaching our table.

"Martha Lee, you needn't stand up on my behalf." Red nodded to us with his "so glad to see you" smile. "May I have the pleasure of sharing your company?"

"Hell, I was just stretching," Martha laughed, giving Red a hug.

Our waiter approached and Red ordered an ice tea.

"Ice tea? When will you accept adulthood?"

Red shrugged. He was impeccably attired in a three piece cream colored suit with soft blue pin stripes. He had his traditional red bow tie starched crisp. Geraldine leaned across the table, covered her conspirator lipped voice with cupped hands, and dramatically intoned, "Are you recruiting one of us?"

This broke us all up. Fridays were like this at Jake's Grill, our hang out. Great salads with a full bar. Oh yeh, fries, onion rings, burgers. Red was never upset with meeting us here as he considered salad to be rabbit food. Also, Jake's only hot sauce was Tabasco. We toasted one another and Red asked, "How's things?"

Maybe I felt brazen because I knew Red was here for more than twenty questions or, maybe my adrenaline was scorched because I was sipping on my second Seven and Seven when Red joined us but I let go as if I were at my family's dinner table.

"Things? What things? The plain fact that you are with three gorgeous women on a glowing Jake's Friday Evening, young enough to be your daughters and you ask about things?!" I attempted to look stern. "Red, you know you made a promise!" I raised my eyes to the tips of the tall elms that engulfed the patio decking and wrapped my arms around my face. I had never presented this passionate personal form in a public setting, not even among my dear friends, and I could feel a deep blush come over me.

"You go girl! Don't stop now!"

"Damn, look what you brought out in Miss Mary Poppins, Red!"

Good thing that we were a couple of hours into Friday at Jake's as our table pounding shrieking laughter flowed into the general mayhem of the establishment. No one even took any notice of us. When we caught our breath and returned to being civil Geraldine eyed Red and said, "Come on Red, like Blondie says, a promise is a promise. About time you gave us the down low on Lou."

"Gerri's right," Martha Lee demanded, "You promised last Friday or do you want to get Pollyanna's dander up again."

Red looked from one of us to the other. You might have thought we were asking for him to give up his barbecue recipe. "Why such a special interest in the young man?"

"Now Red, Geraldine chastised, "We've been down that road."

Just then Red's cell phone started playing "When The Caissons Come Marching Along," and Red, apologetically, excused himself from our table.

"I bet he has a button he pushes just to make his phone ring," Geraldine lamented. "Look at that," Geraldine made an inappropriate gesture to Red as he was signaling to us that he would have to leave our company.

"Someday we'll pin him down?"

"You really think he is ducking us?" I asked.

Geraldine and Martha Lee just sighed. "We have been trying to tap Red about Lou for the past nine years."

"That man knows Lou from somewhere," agreed Martha Lee.

"Well, if you have not been successful for the past nine years, why do you think Red would come forward today?"

Martha Lee and Geraldine just started in laughing again. "Girl friend," Geraldine sputtered, "Everyone knows you and Lou are sweet on each other."

Before I could utter my protest Geraldine put her fingers to her lips and lowered her eyes to our table. Martha Lee signaled our waiter for another round but held up three fingers for an additional Boston Blackie Lager. As I slowly did my crowd surveying scan without staring, I saw Lou gesturing to friends and trading insults as he gradually progressed towards our table.

.........the ball stuck, SMACK, in my right hand as JJ Jerome careened by me, an open lane to the hoop. With his crossover he had begun an "Earl The Pearl" tucked spin. My pick had been so clean and quick. JJ's flowing by me, the raucous crowd took a full second to grasp who had the ball. I was heading towards our basket. Our fans roared as I left my feet from the foul line for a two hand flush! Damn that felt good! But that was all. Like

Red demanded, back to D. We were still eight points back of the Grant Vikings. One turn did not make the game. I knew JJ Jerome was pissed and would come back hard at me.

JJ demanded the ball, bringing his dribble quickly up court. His team motioned to the weak side, giving JJ room to his right. JJ caught me off guard with, "Nice finish. See you got some hop." His compliment took me off my game. He got the edge going to the right. Even with my overplay. I could barely body up to him.

"Screen!"

Too late. I tried to push through. No chance. JJ rose up for his patented twelve foot soft kiss bank shot. Like a lay up for him. With me standing flat footed I watched in amazement as Spider came over, swatted the ball into the back court. I broke out again. This time being able to gather myself, finishing with a two hand reverse dunk that brought all the fans to their feet, even Viking fans caught the frenzy. You had to take a breath with the throw downs.

Spider clomped me on my back as JJ's team called for a time-out to stem our momentum and chuckled, "Got your back!"

Red brought us in with high fives and a nod.

"Evening ladies, might I join you?"

As I pulled back my chair, I caught the side glances they shared. Shattered my bravado. I felt like a mouse cornered by three cagey cats.

WHY OUR STUDENTS & STAFF
REQUIRE A SURVIVAL GUIDE!

"Mr. Preston, you've gotta do somethin' 'bout Troy's finger-sucking. Can you talk with him about it in therapy?"

This entreaty was offered by Lyent, one of the recently hired teacher-aides, just prior to Troy's retreat into the protection of my office. In his previous life, Lyent had shined as a professional athlete. I interpreted (to myself) that his identification with this eleven-year-old boy, a boy wielding a 75 M.P.H. fastball contributed to Lyent's sense of urgency.

Troy's presentations pulled for compassion and concern. In the classroom he often had two-to-three fingers deep in his mouth. When not clutching a pencil, his free hand compulsively fumbled the top of his ear. Troy's accompanying half-closed lizard lidded eyes, gave testament to its effectiveness. And the only reason other students refrained from teasing Troy for his slobbery fixation, was the fact that he could easily remove his fingers, ball them into a fist, and beat the shit out of them. Harvest Valley School teachers, staff, and therapists....we all observed Troy as a smart and sweet kid with vast potential. This this future Cy Young winner's oral fixation was also jacking his permanent teeth and breaking down the cartilage in his ear. What could we do about it? We needed a plan!

Later that afternoon, after our twenty some odd vans had dropped off the students at their homes, our staff came together for the weekly staff meeting. Curtis pitched his usual opening, "What else to go down on today's agenda?"

Immediately, "Troy and his sucking fingers," offered Lyent. Many other staff, even Troy's teacher, nodded in collective concern. Curtis scribbled the item on his pad, raised his eyebrows, and glance my way, "OK, got it. Troy's thumb-sucking."

First on the day's docket was clarification of cleaning policies concerning school's fleet of minivans...which led to a discussion about kids eating food on the van...which led to a discussion of Javonne (A new student who'd incurred a Diabetes 2 Diagnosis.) and his practice of imbibing an assortment of Hostess and Bimbo products during the morning commute....which led to a discussion on how we might disallow the copious amounts of Ranch Salad Dressing being consumed by students at lunch)Apparently it goes with everything.) because many of Javonne's classmates were on the verge of their own diagnosis.

Curtis intervened, "OK...alright...back to the agenda." He eyed Lyent with his Cheshire Cat smile, knowing the coming dialogue, "Troy's thumb-sucking."

Lyent swiveled in his seat towards me, "No disrespect Mr. Preston, but I saw Troy put his fingers in his mouth as soon as he left your office." Lyent turned towards the supportive staff challenging me, "Were you able to talk to him about it? Where's he going?"

Before I could answer, a teacher from another class offered, "Maybe we could get some of that bitter apple stuff…you know, that spray so dogs won't gnaw on themselves."

Another staff chimed in, "Or, what about those kind of dental devices…like an implant with a little hook or spike on it, so it hurts to put your fingers in your mouth."

This was one of those moments when I identified with Troy's need for oral something…but my fantasy involved 12-ounce bottles, preferably long necks. Freud wrote, "It almost looks like analysis (therapy) were the third of those "impossible" professions in which one can be quite sure of bringing about unsatisfying results. The other two, much older-established are the bringing up of children and the government of nations. "Working at Harvest Valley encapsulated all three of these impossible endeavors. The great challenge of being a therapist in an educational setting, was to maintain a therapeutic stance, not just for the kids who were on my caseload, but for the teachers and their supportive educational staff. Our students required a lot of therapeutic holding, and my psychic insulation was often worn thin by the end of the day. So…rather than respond to Lyent and his audience from a place of curiosity, psychoanalytic neutrality if you will, my defensive retort served to bolster my image as a new school hire from NYU.

With seething satirical venom, I responded, "These draconian interventions that are being mentioned ….they just may keep Troy from sticking his fingers down his throat. But, unless he is able to internalize more of a sense of security from the space we provide, he's likely to employ another orifice for self-soothing." To reinforce that I was being understood I added, "Sure, we can yank his fingers out of his mouth, but that may lead to sticking his thumb up his ass."

My hyperbole garnered a few laughs. (I knew I could count on Curtis.) Per usual, Kathleen's response was more…contained. She looked at me in a way that conveyed availability for what I had to say and a hope that I might rise to the occasion. She then looked empathetically at Lyent, whose eyes were bugging as if I'd just stuck my thumb up his ass in retaliation. I softened, "What I'm trying to say is, yes, I'm talking with Troy about his fingers, it this may take some time. And I appreciate that seeing Troy with his fingers down his throat is a difficult sight to behold. I wonder if we can talk a little bit about what comes up for us when we see Troy act like this?"

Prior, I had my graduate studies in social work, I too had been a teacher of a classroom of "emotionally disturbed students" (And I'd lasted less than a year.). And, before this, while in college, I'd also been a teacher's aide in a similar setting. Rather than earning a J.D., M.B.A., the degrees that followed the names of most in my family, I'd opted for earning an M.S.W. (Master's in Saving the World). I carried this sublimated rebellion into my career. I preferred work in the trenches over the comforts of hiding behind an analytic couch in a Park Avenue office. I was sensitive to the challenges that face teaching staff who are with a classroom full of these kids all day, rather than being psychically available for them individually for the fifty-minute hour. In my short tenure I appreciated the **relational culture** of Harvest Valley, and, yet, my own omnipotent exuberance contributed to moral rectitude that served to undermine our working as an integrated team.

A few days later I was in clinical supervision with Kathleen. This provided a safer forum for me to vent about the limitations of certain teaching staff and their reacting to certain limitations of difficult students. Kathleen's response was unexpected: "Preston, would you be interested in developing a training program, even making an accompanying manual, that might help the teachers and staff be more...more relationally informed as they work with the kids.

I took up this assignment with the vigor of an Eagle Scout. Ideas unfolded for an interactive training program, and I employed Kathleen's son to illustrate the manual. Trainings took place when the fleet of minivans had returned from their afternoon run. I was impressed and humbled by the degree of dedication shown by teachers and staff, who made themselves emotionally available after a crisis draining school day. I vividly remember Lyent's earnest questions as the manual and accompanying exercises prompted him to see how his own history, his own inter life...how these things contribute to how he approached Troy and the other students.

Twenty years later.....and I'm writing this prologue from my Beverly Hill's office...so much for "social-working class hero." Right. I've accrued more letters behind my name, and rather than a classroom, I sit near an analytic couch. When I reflect on the adventures I experienced with

Curtis, Kathleen, Lyent and, especially, the kids, I realize it was a privilege to work among wonderful people who were nothing short of heroic. And I now have a deeper appreciation of Kathleen's commissioning me to draft this "Survival Guide." Perhaps her motives were as much for my own development as they were for my educating teaching staff.

…such is the nature of the Relational Experience………
Dr. W. Preston Leer

192

THE
HARVEST VALLEY
EXPERIENCE

THE
HARVEST VALLEY
EXPERIENCE

A SURVIVAL GUIDE

A SURVIVAL GUIDE

THE HARVEST VALLEY EXPERIENCE:
A SURVIVAL GUIDE

"It was the best of times. It was the worst of time."
                                                    --Dickens

"(Sometimes my efforts feel)…no different from attempting to stop Niagara Falls with a postage stamp or trying to hold back a deluge of rain with a Scrap of paper."
                                                    --John Murray

"The toughest job you'll ever love."
                                        --Peace Corp Campaign

Working at Harvest Valley School will give you new appreciation for the above three statements.

The time you spend with these kids will challenge you in ways you've never imagined. After a week in the classroom you'll savor every minute of your weekends. But it's these same experiences, no matter how draining, stimulating, or unpredictable, that will have you coming back for more on Monday.

What this "Survival Guide" is NOT!

- It is not a definitive manual providing clear answers for every single situation that may arise. Believe us, we see new stuff every day.
- It is not an exhaustive list of commandments.

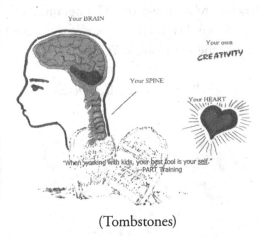

(Tombstones)

This guide presents some suggestions that will make your experiences at Harvest Valley School **much easier and satisfying.** Much of this information was gathered from people who've worked with this population for decades. Some of this advice comes from recently hired staff.

Your responsibility in completing this guide is to approach it with an open heart and mind. The payoff, in terms of working successfully with the students, will be well worth the effort.

First things first,--there are some essentials every Harvest Valley employee must utilize in order to be successful.

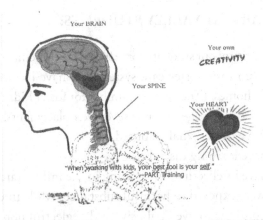

(Brain, heart, PART quote, tombstone, CREATIVITY.)

Harvest Valley is a "relationship-based" program. (We'll explore what this means later in the guide.) Therefore, one of the special requirements of working here is the ability to look at YOURSELF.

(Believe in yourself/face/etc.)

Every one of us contributes to the dynamic that occurs in van transportation, in the classroom, and on the playground. Working with this population of students will stir up powerful emotions in you.

The ability to step back and look inward, as you **relate** with the students, is vital. If you allow it, Harvest Valley School can be "a great place to learn"—about yourself.

WHO ARE HARVEST VALLEY STUDENTS?

The vast majority of our students come from very difficult circumstances:
- Many are in the foster care system and have lived in numerous different homes. (The average number for foster kids who enter the system under the age of ten is seventeen placements!)
- Many have been sexually abused.
- Some have learning disabilities.
- Some have intellectual functioning in the mild retardation range.
- Many were exposed to harmful substances while in utero.
- Many continue to live in abusive and neglectful homes.
- Some have spent time in psychiatric hospitals.
- Some have criminal records.

So....

When a student's <u>problem behaviors</u> drive you to the point of making you want to pull your hair out, the following mantra proves helpful:

"That's why they're here."

--J. Velardo (Former HVS teacher.)

After reading all of this, you may be asking, "Do emotionally disturbed students at Harvest Valley have anything *positive* going for them?"

Yes, they do. Every student you see here is a remarkable survivor. It's up to us to find their strength and help them to channel it in more positive ways.

ASK YOURSELF #1

It's time for a reality check. Remember the part of the manual that mentioned the importance of being able to understand <u>yourself?</u> Take some time and write your answers to the following questions.

Why did I choose to work at Harvest Valley School?

1._____

2._____

3._____

What strengths, talents, and experiences can I offer at Harvest Valley? (There may be more than three things.)

1. _____

2. _____

3. _____

What main goal do I, personally, hope to accomplish by working with these kids? _____

_____

_____

_____

What is a <u>relational</u> program?

The focus of Harvest Valley is **relational** (a.k.a. relationship-based). Behavior management is part of the program, but it is not the primary focus.

Harvest Valley is <u>not </u>a boot camp.

Sergeant Harvest sez:
"Get RELATIONAL!!!"

Harvest Valley is not juvenile hall. (Drill Sergeant)
(This means we are not cops.)

Rather than being strictly punitive, (law & order), we attempt to **dialogue** with the kids. The high staff-to-student ratio enables the students to learn from more functional relationships.

**We hope to teach Harvest Valley students
the following skills and traits:**

1. To learn to get attention in positive ways.
2. To learn how to more effectively communicate their needs and feelings.
3. To learn how to appreciate other peoples' physical and emotional boundaries.
4. To learn how to experience their anger in less destructive ways

What is a relational program? (cont.)

(Face) 2a

ASK YOURSELF #2

What special challenges may arise for anyone when working in a relational program?

1. _____
2. _____
3. _____

Harvest Valley School vs. Harvest Valley Treatment Program

Yes, Harvest Valley is a school. Academics are an integral part of the students' day. However, many of the students' academic problems are correlated with their being "emotionally disturbed." If you hired on with fantasies of playing an instrumental role in the education of future Rhodes Scholar, you are at the wrong place.

The thrust of Harvest Valley School is to provide an environment where the emotionally disturbed child can develop the **tools** and **insight** to better function in the world. Sure, we would like to see them make it into a "less restrictive" school setting. But, ultimately, it is our goal to try to <u>teach them how to live in healthier relationships </u>at school, at home, and in life.

In other words, if, after three months at Harvest Valley, a student is able to raise their hand **20%** of the time to get your attention---rather than cursing, fighting, or screaming----THAT'S REAL PROGRESS!

Great (and Realistic) Expectations

Think back to your written responses of what <u>you</u> hoped to accomplish while working at Harvest Valley. Most of us wish to work in a setting like this so we can **help others.** It is true that you could be working in a less stressful setting and making a lot more money. But you want to make a difference in these kids' lives. This is commendable. But there is one thing you must remember:

THE KIDS ARE NOT HERE TO MEET YOUR AGENDAS!

HARVEST VALLEY SURVIVAL MANTRAS

(Repeat daily for best results.)

1. Temper your expectations for a student with boatloads of patience.

2. Be prepared for **Glacial Changes:**
    Changes, for most of the kids, occur slowly. It's also common for a student to show improvement and, a month later, fall back into the same pattern of destructive behavior. Keep up the good fight and don't lost hope!

3. Try not to take it personally when a student screws up:
    We, as employees of Harvest Valley, are often much safer
    targets for the kids than abusive/neglectful people at home
    When you feel like you've been a saint to the kid and
    he calls you a "f'ing a—hole," try to remember it's not
    entirely about you.

4. Miracles do happen:
    The fact that some of these kids show up at school the
    following day is a feat bordering on the miraculous. Savor
    the 'small stuff"—It's a remarkable show if you let yourself
    watch.

When it comes to understanding our role in the process,
Gandhi shared a healthy perspective.

We can take credit for our work.....
but not the results of our work.

Great Expectations (cont.)

You will take part in amazing success stories at Harvest Valley. However, it's important that you come to terms with what you **will not and should not** expect from these students

Reality Checks:

1. **Do not expect validation from the kids.**

Seeking approval from your colleagues, your spouse, or your dog is appropriate. But, if you're looking for constant strokes from the kids, try selling ice cream.

2. **Do *not* expect immediate, consistent success in the students.**

This was touched on earlier when we talked about the rate of change being **GLACIAL.** Regression when a kid "back-slides," is part of the process. Although some of our students make it back into public school, a large number of them do not. We must be strong enough to continue supporting them when they come up short.

Your impact on these kids is significant. But keep in mind that we only have these students **six** hours a day, five days a week. This means that **138 out of 168** hours a week this emotionally disturbed kid is possibly in an environment that is less than conducive for positive social change. We must be realistic about our expectations of the students.

3. **Do *not* expect friendship from the students.**

Yes, we are a relationship-based program. You are adult employee---**you are not paid to be their peer.** Remember, it is not the students' responsibility to meet our own unmet needs. More of this issue will be explored in the "Boundaries" section of this manual.

(Face/mag.lens) 3a

ASK YOURSELF #3

Look over "Great Reality Checks." Of the three, which one may provide the biggest challenge for you? Why?

_____

_____

TRANSFERENCE & COUNTER TRANSFERENCE

This manual is not intended to be an interactive psychology course. But this next section tackles some important concepts that you must understand to work effectively at Harvest Valley. So, grab your coffee and take a deep breath as you tackle this next section where we'll discuss the phenomena of **transference** and **countertransference reactions.**

Originally coined by Sigmund Freud, transference reactions refer to a person's ***patterns*** of relating to their world

W.W.F.D.

???

When faced with challenging questions about transference and countertransference reactions, just ask yourself, what would Freud do?

TRANSFERENCE AND COUNTERTRANSFERENCE (cont.)

An **emotionally disturbed** child experiences significant abuse/neglect from early age.

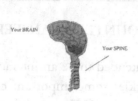

Primary caregivers (parents, proxy parents) parenting, provide unsafe environments, And/or actively abuse the child.

TEN YEARS, TEN FOSTER HOMES, AND THREE GROUP HOMES LATER, THE CHILD ARRIVES AT HARVEST VALLEY SCHOOL

The harvest Valley Student is untrusting, manipulative testing, reactive, just plain HELL-RAISING.

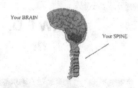

Teacher, HVS Staff Therapist. (Any authority figure.)

Transfers Feelings

Consider the unconscious pattern the child has developed in relating to his or her caregivers (which includes us):

The child **transfers** their rage, their mistrust, and their pain experienced from their *former* caregivers (and, in some cases, current guardians at home) onto **you.** How can this be when you aspire to be a "long-suffering, open-minded, objective person" in the child's life? Once again, it is about an entrenched pattern of relating to others that the child has developed in order to survive.

During transference **the child experiences you as if you are the person who hurt and neglected them.** Remember, as a functional adult, in a more structured environment, you are likely a safer target for the child's rage.

TRANFERENCE AND COUNTERTRANSFERENCE (cont.)

So, you gently ask a student if she needs some help on her class assignment and she creatively calls you and our mother every name in the book. This is where understanding your own countertransference reaction comes into play.

A **countertransference** refers to your reaction to someone's transference reaction toward you. Confusing? Let's approach this from a different angle.

<u>Signs When You Are Caught</u>
<u>In a Countertransference.</u>

1. When you are quick to raise your voice to get a child's attention.
2. When you **react** rather than **respond** to a kid's behavior.
3. When you threaten a student with a physical prone restraint.
4. When you are overly permissive to look the other way.
5. When you are overly rigid.
6. When you feel **betrayed** by a student.
7. When a student intimidates you.
8. When a particular kid really gets under your skin, and you just cannot put your finger on why.
9. When you feel your efforts toward a kid are a complete failure.

Knowledge is power. <u>Understanding the truth about your own reactions will set you free to better respond to a student's needs.</u> We all experience transference and countertransference reactions. It's being aware of them that enables us to relate to these kids and our colleagues in a more functional manner.

TRANSFERENCE & COUNTERTRANSFERENCE (cont.)

ASK YOURSELF #4

Think back on your experience, no matter how limited, at Harvest Valley. (If you're new, think back on your low life.) Write a detailed and specific account when a child may Have experienced a transference reaction toward you (i.e., when they related to you as though you had the attributes/behavior of a significant person in their past).

_____

_____

_____

_____

_____

What influences/experiences may have contributed to this student's transference reaction?

_____

_____

_____

_____

Good Job! Now think back on your own response to the student's actions toward you. In the heat of the moment, how did the student's treatment of you make you feel? What was your countertransference reaction?

_____

_____

_____

_____

_____

Okay......hindsight is 20/20. Armed with your heightened awareness, what might have been a more productive response to the student's transference reaction? _____

_____

_____

BOUNDARIES!!

It is inevitable. Attend any staff meeting at Harvest Valley and you'll hear someone alluding to **_boundaries._** A good understanding of boundaries is imperative to your success with these kids. Exercising healthy boundaries is as much a personality trait as it is an interpersonal skill—perhaps this is why it is a concept that warrants self-reflection and frequent discussion.

So, what does it mean when a person has *functional boundaries?* Perhaps the concept can be driven home with a quick **Healthy Boundary Quiz:**

HBq: Which of the following is the best example of healthy boundaries?
- A) Helping a student squeeze into his/her swimsuit before a field trip.
- B) Telling students how much beer you pounded with your buddies during the Super Bowl.
- C) Greeting the students with a hug as they enter the classroom.
- D) Mentioning to the students you're in a crummy mood because you were jilted by your lover.
- E) None of the above.

FOR THE LOVE OF GOD, please say you entered "E!" And yes, the incorrect answers were drawn from actual incidents in Harvest Valley history.

Your BRAIN

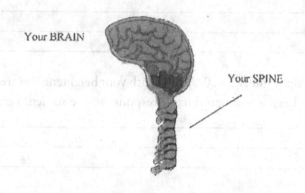

Your BRAIN

Your SPINE

Your SPINE

BOUNDARIES (cont.)

Healthy boundaries involve a person's sense of self and the dynamic of relating with others. For the sake of discussion, we will explore boundary issues as they occur in two realms: PHYSICAL & EMOTIONAL.

PHYSICAL BOUNDARIES

Most students at Harvest Valley show a rather poor understanding of physical boundaries. Why, you ask?

- Many are victims of sexual abuse.
- Many have experienced physical abuse.
- Many have observed domestic violence.
- Few have witnessed good examples of people respecting another's personal space.
- Some have a history of sexually perpetrating others.
- Some students have made allegations of being physically violated— even when the contact was intended to be supportive. (Perhaps this is reason enough to keep hugs to a minimum.)

Under the law Harvest Valley School is considered a "restrictive" environment. Whereas students in public schools may be allowed to hold hands, wrestle, and "play fight,--you know do the things kids do. Harvest Valley students are required to keep their hands to themselves. Yes, every kids thirst for love and affection and there is no denying hugs can be healing. But you will notice, given our students' lack of boundaries, many will attempt to hang off of you like ornaments. Our job is to *help them learn how to express their needs verbally and not physically.*

Boundaries (cont.)

(Face/mag.lens)

ASK YOURSELF #5

You've just read about the Harvest Valley School approach Addressing physical boundaries. What is your gut reacting to this edict? Do you agree with it? Why or why not?

_____

_____

_____

_____

In what situations might be it appropriate to hug a student?

_____

_____

_____

_____

EMOTIONAL BOUNDAIRES

It might take some effort for you to withhold daily hugs, but practicing good emotional boundaries can be even more challenging. Many people attracted to the "helping profession" have problems with this. But a lack of this skill often leads to burnout; or, worse yet, making poor decisions that may ultimately harm the kids we're trying to help

Naturally, as you get to know the students, they will want to know all about your families, your hobbies, your history, your likes and dislikes. Working in this setting demands you to be open and genuine, but not too self-disclosing.

BOUNDARIES (cont.)

So.......**ARE YOU CONFUSED YET??**

How do you maintain good boundaries in a RELATIONAL PROGRAM?

Let's attempt, to better understand emotional boundaries with some **Better Boundary Questions:**

BBQ #1: Would it be okay to share personal information such as my home address, email, or phone number?
BBA #1: No, it is not okay. For safety reasons alone, the students should never know any of this information.

BBQ #2: Is it okay if I make contact with a Harvest Valley student outside of the school environment?
BBA #2: Once again, the answer is no. Spending time with a student outside of school can create major problems.

How would you respond to. "Why did you go to Johnny's baseball game and not mine?" What would you do if you were with Jenn and she started screaming and cursing in your presence, but it's an activity not affiliated with the school? Would you inform her that she had "lost a point" on the behavior chart for Monday?

There are certain circumstances when one may make contact with a **former** student outside of the school environment. However, as long as you're employed at Harvest Valley, these (hopefully) rare situations must be approved by an administrator.

BOUNDARIES (cont.)

BBQ #3: A student asks you about the "trouble you used to get into when you were a kid." Is it harmful to tell them, now that you're mature and well-grounded, about your many youthful indiscretions?

BBA #3: Don't get hooked into this one. Sure you want the kids to know you're human. If you are a "reformed troubled kid" yourself, it's tempting to share personal parables. But would sharing your war stories *really* help the kids? Trust us, if one kid is told about the time you stole a six-pack from the Budweiser Truck, the entire school will be buzzing by the end of the day.

BBQ #4: You had a stressful weekend. You're behind on your bills, you were stood up by your date, and your hemorrhoids flared up. An insightful student asks about your weekend. Should you fill him in on your misery?

BBA #4: Please refrain. For 8 hours you must be able to leave your needs/issues/wants on the doorstep so that you can be a **sponge** for the needs/issues/wants of your charges—whose needs/issues/wants are unending. When it comes to disclosing information about yourself, it is helpful to always ask, "Is this information actually going to help this young person, or **is it about me** wanting to be heard?"

SpongeBob Squarepants
former HVS employee.
always exercised
healthy boundaries!

BOUNDARIES (cont.)

BBQ #5: A rather charismatic student, for who you care deeply, has had a rough month. You wish to motive him to improve his classroom behavior. So, you approach him during an unstructured break and make a "special deal" with him; You will give him your back issues of *Sports Illustrated* (Sans Swimsuit) if he improves his behavior. Kosher?

BBA #5: No, no, no! The classroom has a system to reward the students for improved behaviors. "Special deals" sabotage the student's understanding of structure, consequences, and communication. Your observations and ideas about each student are valued; share them at Team Meetings so we can all support the student.

(Face/mag.len) 6a

ASK YOURSELF #6

Enough of the BBQ's. Now it's time for you to respond with your own perspectives on emotional boundaries. Bear in mind that there is not always one right answer. However, hones responses will bear the most fruit in this exercise.

1) A student is directed to go to the "Resource Room" for throwing a book across the classroom. Then minutes later, after she has de-escalated, she approaches you and asks, "I want to go to softball tomorrow. Is there any way I can earn my points back?" What do you do?

_____

_____

_____

_____

What forces at work may motivate you to give the points back?

1. _____
2. _____
3. _____

BOUNDARIES (cont.)

2) A student approaches you with something that occurred at home that he wants you to keep "secret." How do you respond? _____
_____
_____
_____

3) You recently heard from a colleague that there might be some staffing changes in you classroom. A student asks you if the said staff is ever going to leave the class. What is your answer? _____
_____
_____
_____

Boundaries for Self

Perhaps it is most fitting to end this section of the guide with a few words on setting boundaries for yourself. The job is tough. You are asked to be a container for enormously powerful emotions with overflowing. You have to be able to give all day and, when you're running on empty, find some reserve as your shift ends to respond to loved ones who are asking, "Where's mine?

YOU MUST Have a Life Outside of Work!!

Recharging your battery will provide burnout insurance. Learn how to *leave our work at work*—especially in this business. You're little good to the kids when you're emotionally drained. As alluded to in the "Great (& Realistic) Expectations" section, good boundaries may help you to remain supportive even when your efforts feel futile. Healthy boundaries free you to experience amazing adventure that is yours at Harvest Valley School.

UNSTRUCTURED BREAKS
(Time outside of the classroom.)

Think back on your previous work experiences. Write down three things you liked to do during breaks:

1. _____
2. _____
3. _____

Now…, realize that as long as you're employed at Harvest Valley School you won't be able to do them? Why? Because from the time the kids enter the van until the time they are dropped off at home **you really don't have much of a break!** (We told you you'd savor your weekends.)

What Is An Unstructured Break?

An unstructured break is any time when students are not engaged in academics, therapy, or eating. Perhaps it could be l9ikened to "down time" or recess. These times also include transition between classes, boarding of vans, etc. It is during these time that staff must be the **most vigilant** and offer the **most supervision.** Remember….<u>these breaks are for the students.</u>

Harvest Valley is considered by the school system to be a "restrictive environment." The structure and safety for which Harvest Valley students yearn for does come at the expense of some of their liberties. Working during an unstructured break will allow you to lie our Orwell's greatest fear: **YOU WILL BE BIG BROTHER!** The only difference is that Harvest Valley School offers a relational spin to the process.

UNSTRUCTURED BREAKS (cont.)

Helpful Hints for "Breaks"

1) **Mingle with the kids on the playground.**
   Swing on the jungle gym. Shoot hoops. Play four square.
   Sit and chat….even listen!

2) **All students on computers must be loosely monitored.**
   Do we really need to go into this? Picture the moist
   crass web site imaginable—yep, a Harvest Valley student
   probably visited it when they were not being monitored.

3) **Exercise the concept of NUMBERS:**

Your physical presence needs to be utilized on the playground, off-site, and in the classroom. **There should always be one staff to no more than four students.** This makes it safer for the students and you. As soon as you find yourself alone with more than four students, <u>**it is your responsibility to get on the "walkie" and ask for support.**</u>

- Curtis & Kathleen have asked me to clarify:
  1) All staff are encouraged to take breaks as time allows.
  2) All staff are never "thanked" enough.

UNSTRUCTURED BREAKS (cont.)

Another spin on numbers:

- Three staff gathered together, chewing the fat, is a **crowd.** Which kids are you watching?
- Limit the number of basketball players. More than 3-on-3 is pushing it. No games of 21 with more than four kids! (Just trust us on this.)
- When you see a group of more than three kids gathered in a circle, drop it. Say "hi. At least mosey on over there and lend on ear. (We told you you'd be a Big Brother.

4) A word on **walkie-talkies**-use them! From the moment you arrive on school site, all staff and teachers should don this remarkable piece of technology.

A walkie is your "little friend" during unstructured breaks.

UNSTRUCTURED BREAKS (cont.)

5) (Walkies cont.) Communication is remarkably challenging when working with eighty E. D. kids. Given the lowered amount of structure, students are frequently more anxious during breaks. "Will this staff be able to protect me?" They'll test you by pushing the envelope right in front of your face. Utilize the walkie to communicate negative/positive consequences to homerooms.

Use the walkie to communicate when a student is going outside, entering the classroom, or asking to go to a different area. Avoid using it to broadcast certain personal information (e.g., the size of a bowel movement left by Johnny.) Please listen to the walkie at the end of the day

(Face mag.lens) 7a

ASK YOURSELF #7

Throughout Harvest Valley history, there have been incidents that were exacerbated when too few staff were overseeing too many students. What would keep you from using the walkie to call for staff support?

_____

_____

_____

_____

_____

UNSTRUCTURED BREAKS (cont.)

No Student Unattended

Remember the Big Brother reference? With the occasional exception of Workability students (Who will be donning a uniform during their off-site work.), **no student should <u>ever</u> be out of the watchful eyes and ears of a staff.** This includes moments when you need to leave the room briefly. (Use your "little friend" to call for support to keep the students covered.)

Not surprisingly, unstructured breaks provide ample opportunity for students with poor boundaries to exploit their urges. (The sexual escapades attempted at Harvest Valley would make Hugh Heffner blush.) Among our more violent students, boxing skills are often honed during these breaks. Computers...need we go into this one again? Any student working/playing on the computer needs your constant attention.

The adage, *"a stitch in time saves nine,"* rings true during unstructured breaks. Is a basketball game among student getting a little rough? Redirect those involved to take a breather before they erupt into fisticuffs. Is a group of students making fun of someone's shoes? Crash the party and dole out the consequences. Look, we're not looking for "shock and awe" on your part, but a little preemption can make a huge difference.

(face/lens) 8a

ASK YOURSELF #8

The first part of this guide explored man of the characteristics of an E.D. student. Given their needs, why must you be so vigilant in your supervision?

_____

_____

_____

_____

Sometimes "increased support" is read a "decreased freedom." How do you feel about playing such an intrusive function in these children's lives? _____

_____

UNSTRUCTURED BREAKS (cont.)

Toilet Time

Sometimes this can be a crappy place to work—literally. (One of Curtis' many nonessential facts was sharing that "taking a crap" came from the name of the inventor of the toilet.) It's not uncommon for students to take out their rage in the bathroom, often leaving the facilities in a sorry state. The annals of Harvest Valley lore have provided some disturbing bathroom epics. Many students have engaged in fireman fantasies (Gulliver) and hosed the place down. On an even more revolting note, some creative students have used their feces as finger paint. Grand experiments involving toilets and multiple rolls of paper have been a frequent favorite.

The Harvest Valley Bathroom Board has been developed as a practical protocol that has proven helpful for stabilizing students' fantasies in the restroom:

- When using the bathroom, a staff must accompany students. (See previous section.)
- Prior to the student's use, staff is to inspect the facilities.
- If the restroom is acceptable, pick up the clip board, allow the student to go in, shut the door, and sign your name and time.
- When the student is finished, thoroughly inspect the room as the student waits in the door way. If the room is acceptable, sign out on the sheet.
- Leave the bathroom locked.

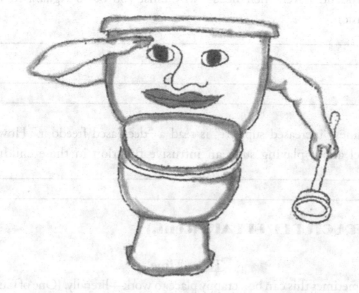

UNSTRUCTURED BREAKS (cont.)

<u>Toilet Time (cont.)</u>

The bathroom protocol strikes many as rather anal. Yes, it's a pain to have to inspect, sign in, and inspect again for every student. But this is a way of supporting the students to be less destructive with their anger. The students have come to expect the supervision. Besides, signing a sheet is a lot less intrusive than the alternative.

ASK YOURSELF #9

IMAGINE ACOMPANYING A STUDENT TO THE RESTROOM AND, PRIOR TO THE STUDEN USING THE FACILITIES, YOU NOTICE THAT SOMEONE HAS LEFT Lake Superior on the bathroom floor. What should you do?

_____
_____
_____
_____
_____
_____

POSITIVE REWARD PROGRAM

"Students will earn privileges, not lose them!" Lou Thompson (Following months of therapy.)

Lou KNEW the program would not work. ("Our Conduct Disordered, Assaultive student will blow it off.")

Laura KNEW the Positive Behavioral Program would prevail. ("Wanna bet?)

One of the challenging aspects to the Harvest Valley Program was constructing a Positive Reward System. The incentive program was based on rewarding the students for positive choices while, holding at the minimum, negative consequences for poor choices.

> "One thing unsuccessful students know
> how to do...is be unsuccessful."
> Pat Peterson: Program Specialist
> Lou (Curtis) & Laura (Kathleen) are the
> fictional characters in our novel
> INSCRIPTIONS ON A BELT.

THE CORE

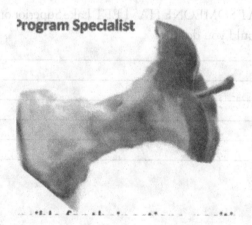

Program Specialist

Students were made to own the responsibility of their actions, positive & negative.

1) Students were given a clipboard to track their daily program progress. (**Lou, "Yeh Laura, I'll bet! Wanna see some flying saucers?"**)

2) Progress was based on:

   a. Goals and objectives of the student's IEP.

   b. On Mondays, students chose their Goals/Objectives to work on for the week.

   c. Three points could be earned for each class period, including transportation for a maximum total of 21 per day.

   i. Student determined 1 point.

   ii. Staff determined 1 point

   iii. If both agreed 1 more point was earned.

Lou (Becoming animated), "Get real Laura! Our kids will shred your will make confetti of your insipid point sheet!"

Laura, (Cucumber cool.) "I completely agree with you. No way around their initial frustrations." (Therapeutic pause….) "But get this Lou," (You Neanderthal Ignoramus.) "I am suggesting that their negative actions be limited and not ruin their opportunity for a positive day and here's how….."

1. "Students who do not **EARN** their points one period, may earn positive points in all the others. The negative is contained to that one period. Even a major escalation does not go beyond three points."

Lou (Eyeing the heavens.), "Spoken as a true therapist."

2. Students who average 20 points per day for the week (No one is *perfect.*) may still **EARN** Lunch Bunch at their favorite restaurant.

3. Students who average 18 points per day **EARN:**
   a. Off-site sports privileges
   b. Off-site work assignments
   c. Positive data towards transitioning back to their referring school district.

i. Data records are maintained for IEP meetings and presented in bar/graph form to illustrate the student's progress towards meeting their Goals and Objectives.

(Graduation Hats floating in the air ill.)

<u>WITH GRADUATION FROM HARVEST VALLEY STUDENTS EARN</u>

WITH GRADUATION FROM HARVEST VALLEY STUDENTS EARN

1. Celebration ceremony with family and friends at site of their choice.
2. A gift certificate of $150.00 to purchase an appropriate personal gift.
3. Full time enrollment in their neighborhood school.

- Inscribing their name on Lou's weight belt.

Lou, "Give it up Laura. This WILL NOT WORK!"

OUTCOME: PER USUAL, LAURA WAS RIGHT!

RESOURCE ROOM

(Time-Out Room/Consequence Room/Recoup
Room/Chill Room/Whatever Room...)

You may have worked in group homes or other settings that utilized a "time-out room." For those of you new to working with explosive youth, these rooms serve as a function of containment. They're intended to be a safe place where a kid who's consumed with rage can go hog wild: hit walls/ pee on the door/scream epitaphs—the sky's the limit. (Staff will protect the student from doing harm to themselves.)

Thankfully, you're not going to find one of these holding tanks here. After much deliberation, we concluded that a "time-out room" would not serve the needs of the Harvest Valley students. ("If you build it, they will come." Field of Dreams) Granted, it's true that from time to time there are students who are unable to de-escalate, and who are too unsafe to be in the classroom. But given our aspirations to operate a **relational** model, the practice of throwing the hell-raisers into a dungeon did not seem germane. Enter a *revolutionary new concept......*THE HARVEST VALLEY RESOURCE ROOM!

    Rrq #1: What is so special about the HVRR?

        RRA #1: The HVRR is to be a place of **LAST RESORT.** This room is a space where a student can de-escalate after he has engaged in **suspendable offense** and/or is unable to be redirected in a safe manner.

        The HVRR is not a place for a student to "take space." This option would have been offered to the student already. It is not a place for a student to complete in-school suspensions, van check-ins/check outs, therapy. Or aerobics.

    RRQ #2: What is the student expected to do in the Resource Room?

        RRA #2: They are there to be with their feelings and de-escalate to a place of being able to dialogue. However, this room is not the place to dialogue with the student. We repeat: STAFF IS NOT TO DIALOGUE WITH STUDENTS WHILE IN THE RESOURCE ROOM. The HVRR is a place where the student is to come to terms, personally own and stabilize their frustrations.

    RESOURCE ROOM (cont.)

        Dialogue with the student about the related incident is done outside of the HVRR, after the student has demonstrated that they are ready.

        Academic work should not be done in this room. If the student is able to engage in school work, the have de-escalated to the point that use of the HVRR is no longer appropriate.

RRQ #3: When is a student ready to leave the Resource Room? RRA #3: After dialoguing with the student, you should be able to gage whether the student is ready to rejoin the classroom environment. (This is only a test—are you awake?) No, this is where * **your judgment** comes in. After at least five minutes of silence, you may ask the student, "Are you ready to take some space outside or talk about it outside of the Resource Room?

Please, don't bring the student back into the classroom if conditions are not conducive for the student to remain deescalated. Take care to have addressed destructive dynamics between peers prior to bringing the stabilized student back into the mix. Recurrent visits to the Resource Room within the same day demand further team discussion.

Your Judgment: *The success of the RELATIONAL PROGRAM is based on QUALITY STAFF making QUALITY JUDGMENTS! A strict behavioristic program has intervention steps written in black and white. The basic tenant of the RELATIONAL PROGRAM is to place the decision making on the individual, both staff and student. The RELATIONAL PROGRAM DEMANDS QUALITY DECISIONS THAT WILL BE INTERNALIZED THROUGHOUT LIFE. If one desires a "more restrictive" program, our jails go "clank!"*

RESOURCE ROOM (cont.)

ROCKET SCIENCE RULES FOR THE RR

- Students must be accompanied by staff in the Resource Room.
- More than three students in the RR at a time spells disaster. Be creative and find space elsewhere.
- The RR is an inherently boring experience for staff. For the most part you must take a vow of silence, refrain from reading the sports section, playing solitaire, etc.

ASK YOURSELF #11

What factors may influence you to wish to dialogue with a student in the Resource Room?

_____

_____

_____

How can a lengthy conversation with a student in the Resource Room harm the student?

_____

_____

_____

_____

The student trashes the room, whips out a blade, and challenges anyone to get a piece of him. (The student is 6'4", 205, has been in program two weeks, and you pick the color.) What do you do?

_____

_____

_____

_____

- Our bottom line comment is that, sadly, as with governments where dialogue breaks down, you call for physical reinforcements. We offer the stated HVRR strategies with the desire to avoid a 911 call.

RESOURCE ROOM (cont.)

THIS PAGE IS PROVIDED FOR YOU TO OFFER AN ARTISTIC INTERPRETATION: THE TOPIC: ADVENTURES IN OBSERVING A STUDENT IN THE RESOURCE ROOM!

TRANSPORTATION: STAYBACK

Stayback (a.k.a. "Van Stayback) is intended to contain students who demonstrate they are too **unsafe** to travel home in their designated van. If you think back on your own school days, it's probably the closest thing to what you experienced as "after-school detention" without having to write on the chalkboard a' la Bart Simpson.

The decision for Stayback, while on the school site, involves multiple staff and, as available, the student's therapist. Being on the school site with a group of staff being involved in the negative consequence, is in stark contrast to the single driver making the decision to not transport the student to school in the morning. The driver's decision may be based on many issues: Gang related clothing, demanding to bring food on the van, throwing (yes) rocks/eggs/water balloons at the van upon arrival. I could venture on, but the issues in transportation warrant their personal survival guide. Stay tuned for _**Magic Bus: A**_

Van Driver's Survival Guide, but, for the record, a couple of events not to repeat:
1. "John, did you really pull over on I-95 and let DeShawn and Dante punch it out?"
2. "Mike, given appropriate behavior, have you been allowing the students to drive once you get into Quincy?"

(To be continued.)

<u>Recipes for Stayback:</u>
- The student appears unsafe to himself or others and he is unable to be redirected. (It should be noted that there have been students who were physically restrained in the morning and later de-escalated to the point where they were trusted for a safe van ride home in the afternoon.)
- The student already earned as much as a "level drop" and is continuing to engage in problem behaviors toward the end of the school day.
- On the way home the student is unable to be redirected y the van driver. In other words, the van does a 180 degree and lightens its load back on the school site.

At times, staff will utilize Stayback as a "level drop on steroids." We should be wary of students who ae prone to act out because **they desire to be on Stayback.** Staff should be judicious when utilizing this consequence.

During Stayback, the student is supervised by a teacher or their therapist. The student is to sit at their desk *silently* for one hour. They do not read, they do not play on the computer, they do not eat snacks, they do not draw the do not... Essentially, **they are not to be rewarded for engaging in behaviors that prove to be enjoyable or unsafe.** Following successful completion of an hour of compliant silence, they may earn the right to be transported home.

ASK YOURSELF #12

What factors might motivate a student to sabotage them self in order to be on Stayback?

_____

_____

_____

_____

(Van illustration of students acting-out with staff tuning out.)

Van transportation with Harvest Valley (All students are transported to and from program.) Provides non-stop stimulation for the adventure-seeker in all of us.

WHAT IS YOUR POSITION? (Proxemics)

Harkening back to the "stitch in time saves nine? Philosophy, paying attention to where you are physically in relation to the students can make a world of difference. This rather a **simple concept** to grasp, but finding the energy to apply it throughout the school day is **not always easy.**

- Position yourself among the students where there are the **fewest** number of your colleagues. If the teacher is in the front teaching, don't sit in the very back of the room with the other staff.

- When a student asks a question about their individual work, **approach them** before you offer an answer rather than voicing the answer across the room.
- When you notice a student struggling behaviorally and/or emotionally **approach them** rather than offering counsel from across the room.

As emphasized earlier in the guide, where you place yourself is especially important during unstructured breaks, during lunchtime, and in the vans. Sometimes your **proximity** to the students is just enough to support them to contain some of their dysfunctional impulses/

ASK YOURSELF #13

What factors could possibly keep you from actively positioning yourself effectively among the students?

_____

_____

HARVEST VALLEY 101

Harvest Valley Survival is, as formerly stated, not THE ANSWER to rescuing our society from the rage of these children. (THEY ARE CHILDREN!) Our hope is that we can provide a safe and caring environment were emotionally disturbed/conduct disordered youth can learn how to deal with their anger impulses in less destructive manners. Helping an individual to de-escalate is a skill that cannot be cultivated from an afternoon in-service meeting or how-to manual. However, you've made it this far in the HARVEST VALLEY SURVIVAL GUIDE! You've been encouraged to ask yourself some introspective questions that should inform your work.

As you continue with the reading of Inscriptions on a Belt, you will continue to gain perspectives on how to continue to develop and improve your art of working with these challenging students.

Final to do:
- Keep your eyes and ears open for student who are struggling. Approaching them before they blow out may defuse many nukes.
- Every child, every person, has a wish to be understood. Sometimes all the student needs is for one of us to listen.
- When you observe a student beginning to escalate, approach them and candidly. Invite them to take space: It seems like something's bothering you. If you take space you can take care of yourself and still have a successful day. OK?"
- Avoid power struggles. Don't draw a line in the sand. Be creative and be aware of your own countertransference reactions. Don't keep heaping on points in a scenario such as this: Staff: "Okay, you didn't earn that last point." Student, "I don't give a *&^$." Staff: "That's another point!" **Puullleezzze,** do not pile on!

In closing.........the most *EFFECTIVE EMPLOYEE* AT Harvest Valley School is the **person who can learn as much from these students as they do from themselves.** *The relational program can do a lot for you in the search for your* best self. It's a perk found in a business that can be so draining and toxic at times. *As mentioned at the beginning, this Survival Guide is not intended to offer all the answers you'll ever need. It is not a substitute for asking difficult questions in team meetings and supervision. It does not take the place of your own creativity. Hopefully, The Guide sheds some light on how to begin your adventure in this relational program. Congratulations for taking up the challenge of working at Harvest Valley! Put on your crash helmet, open your heart, and enjoy the experience.*

"So, you want to work at Harvest Valley?" Lou's two questions. **(TRUE)**

Lou: "My first questions is in two parts. You can go on a two week vacation, anywhere on Earth, where would you go AND what book would you bring with you that you have already read? _____

_____

_____

_____

Lou: "Last question. Who's your favorite cartoon character?

_____

_____

Lou: "Once you clear our background check, you can start. If you are still here in three months, look in the mirror and ask yourself why."

STATE OF CALIFORNIA ACCOMMODATIONS 2002
HARVEST VALLEY SCHOOL

Educational Program

"...focusing on literacy skills."

"...providing productive classrooms where students are engaged."

"...recreational activities are available for all age levels of students. The school even has athletic teams that compete with other schools. They offer a sports banquet where all of the athletes are awarded a trophy."

"...well-supervised students that enjoy their environment."

"...excellent interaction observed between students, teachers, and administration."

Staff

"...retention of staff longer than is normal, which indicates good job satisfaction." "...Providing comprehensive staff development. Staff meetings, conferences workshops,..."

"Staff (therapeutic and others) understands the principles of positive behavior intervention and have acted on them with Functional Analyses and BIPs..."

"...staffing the school at a level to provide for the successful operation of all functions."

"...instructional aides who are effective members of the instructional team."

"...developing a team model so all staff have the same overall purpose that

Transitional Services

"...providing transportation that gives opportunity to control the traveling environment."

"...returning a remarkable number of student to their districts of reference."

Valley Oak School
Psycho/educational Intake Summary

Laura Rosso: LCSW

Name: Reffti Lewis
DOB: 6/24/89

County of Residence: Granite
School District of Reference: Long Barn USD

Date: March 25, 1996

Physical Description: Reffti is an attractive well -developed eight-year-old African American youth. He is stylishly dressed with a new pair of Nikes, Levi Jeans, and a Fubu Jacket. He makes poor eye contact and shrugs his shoulders when asked even non-threatening questions of a conversational nature. The few words he spoke were from behind the fingers of his right hand.

Referring Criterion: Reffti was referred to program with a school history of verbal assault, physical assault, poor peer relationships, irregular school attendance and a general inability to be successful during the school day. Reffti's school experience began at age three in a Head Start Program. He repeated kindergarten at Coast Elementary and was placed in a self-contained special day class in the first grade. He was also referred to Bay County Mental Health at this time but was discharged when his mother did not follow through with treatment.

Family History: Reffti was born seven weeks prematurely. At the time of his birth his mother was addicted to crack cocaine. Reffti was removed from his unmarried mother's care and placed in three different foster homes during the first eighteen months of his life. He was returned to his mother after she successfully completed a drug rehabilitation program. Reffti's biological father has never been involved in his life and his whereabouts are unknown. Reffti now has a five-year-old step-brother, Jovonz. Natasha, Reffti's mother, reports that she cannot leave the two of them out of her sight for fear that Reffti will harm his brother. She notes that Reffti continually provokes Jovonz and will pinch and punch him when she is not looking. When Jovonz was an infant, Reffti attempted to smother him with a pillow. Natasha concedes that Reffti was out of her control at home and she did not know how to parent him.

Psychiatric History: Reffti was hospitalized nine months ago for another attempt to suffocate his younger brother with a pillow. He was placed on Ritalin for a diagnosed Attention Deficit Disorder and Imipramine for depression and bed wetting. Psychological testing indicates that poor impulse control, lack of empathy, and lower intellectual functioning makes Reffti at risk for misperceiving social cues and make judgments without considering consequences.

DSM: IV Diagnosis:

AXIS I: 314.01 Attention Deficit/Hyperactivity D/O combined type

              1.25 Major Depression in partial remission

AXIS II: 317.00 Mild Mental Retardation

AXIS III: V71.09

AXIS IV: History of removal from home; academic problems

AXIS V: 45 (Current)

Recommendations: As Reffti has been on home schooling since his discharge from the hospital eight and one half months ago, it is recommended that he be enrolled in Valley Oak School as soon as possible. A speech and language evaluation is also urged to determine if therapy will be useful in improving Reffti's processing and pragmatic skills. Finally, family therapy is strongly recommended to strengthen Natasha's parent skills and improve her relationship with her son.

Given Natasha's willingness to participate with program and Reffti's consistent attendance, I support Reffti's admittance to Valley Oak School.

Signed_____ Date_____

Laura Rosso

Chapter 6

REFFTI: A SAFE BED

February 3   Lunch Box

Cartoon break. Commercials are on. Time to act. Get my groove on. I'd planned this all out. It was a go. Slam dunk. Momma was down getting the wash going at the Laundromat. Ike was shoveling the snow off the front walkway before leaving for work. I was alone in the house, except for my dukie step-brother who was thumb sucking with The Electric Company. This was the same house where my Daddy used to live. Now this man. This Ike was here fucking my Momma and it wasn't right. Here them all the time laughing and groaning. Nasty stuff. Not in my daddy's house. Not in my Daddy's bed. Not with me in the house. Time to make them listen to me.

I went into the kitchen and opened the refrigerator door. It squeaked a bit. Nervous, I look around to make sure I was alone. There wasn't a sound except for Tweety, our Parakeet, and she wouldn't tell. Ike's bright green lunch pail beckoned me. I grabbed the lunch pail, damn it was heavy, quickly shut the squeaking refrigerator door, and scampered into the bathroom where I shut and bolted the door.

I hoisted the pail onto the counter and popped the latches. Inside were two thick ham sandwiches. I'm sure Momma had put some spicy jalapeno peppers on them. There was a small bottle of Wilbur's Cajun Fire. Ike liked his food spicy hot. There were some chips, his thermos of ice water, and two bananas. I took one of them out. There would be just enough room if I did it right. I'd saved up for two days. This was going to be a log. I dropped my PJ's and kicked them to the side. Didn't want to mark them up. No evidence. I straddled the bright green lunch pail and grunted. Slow it came. Hurt a bit. My turd came out long and hard. Curved right

240

into the other banana. Smelled so bad! Made me want to do some finger painting. I grabbed some air freshener and sprayed the lunch pail. Couldn't give it away until the time was ripe. Got that right. It'll be ripe alright. I made sure there were no marks on the side. Wiped it all down. Teach that motherfucker to screw my Momma in my Daddy's bed. I put the pail back into the refrigerator. I wished that I could be there when Ike opened it up at lunch. I checked out the area. All was good. Ike was just finishing the walk. I went into my room to get ready for school.

"Lou, got a second?"

"Sure Laura." I entered her office as she closed the door, serious talk. I braced myself for some verbally processed condemnation that was about to descend upon me. Like, what this time? What obscure human relationship infraction did I invoke?

Martha Lee and Geraldine have Lou pegged to a T. Just look at his puppy dog squirming tail between his legs entrance into my office. He might be head over heels for me like they contended, but I was not going to place my therapeutic directorship in jeopardy by asking Lou out, no matter how much grief Geraldine and ML gave me. I had seen Lou out and about and I knew he was not shy and any personal advancement would have to be from him. Then, what was I doing now, enticing him? Luring trepidation?

"What's up Laura?"

What could she want now? Not only was she The Director of Valley Oak, all the referring school districts asking for Gate Keeper Laura Rosso. Our reputation had continued to grow. Restraints were down to one a week, even with our student population increasing. We had one staff simply dedicated to returning students to referring school districts on a gradual basis. Founders Staff, JK couldn't get enough of Laura' insightful advice. Her Relationship Model had enveloped program. Hell, we might as well all be therapists.

Bet Lou is wondering why I asked him into my office and closed the door, which only occurred when there was a formidable issue to be discussed. Program was flowing quietly and I felt myself startle as I realized the main reason to close the door was to flirt with Lou! I smiled within myself, how deliciously unprofessional. Geraldine and Martha Lee would be proud.

I began, as professional as ever, "Lou, have you ever thought of becoming a therapist?"

He startled, shocked. "Say what. Some kind of joke? Have you gone bananas?"

Maybe oranges. What rhymes with orange, nothing. Old Lou joke. "Seriously Lou, have you noticed the scant few physical restraint forms we are needing to review in comparison with other day treatment programs you have worked in?"

I admired his reflective brown eyes as he squirmed for a response.

"Sure, in fact I was just thinking about that and the Relationship Program." Where is she going with this?

See how Lou takes a positive statement, "Well, I want to extend my compliments because the relationship culture that has become established at Valley Oak is due to you."

Laura's complimenting me? Say what?! Does she want a raise? I find myself beginning to perspire. "Well, thanks Laura, but I'm no smarter than the next person."

"We all know that," I laughed. Lou could be so cute when he was self-effacing.

What's she up to? Laura always has a hidden agenda. I can never figure out when I'm getting a straight answer. When I'm getting processed, she's always about five moves ahead of me. "Laura, it's your model. You brought The Relationship Culture on."

That could not be argued as Lou could not spell Relationship Model until he brought me into Valley Oak. I conceded, "Yes, I did, but the interaction would not have become program fabric without your actualizing the interventions."

"I appreciate that Laura." She was looking right into me. Those deep dwelling bright mystic blue eyes. I feel like a live bug under a magnifying glass, about to be pinned.

Neither I nor anyone else could ever bring out the past in Lou. Whenever conversation turned into that area he would deflect the direction. Let's see if I can get lucky. "Lou you are a natural therapist with your willing manner to take a step back and focus on the student's needs and hear them out. When did you decide to become a teacher?"

That's it! That's why Laura had asked to talk with me. She wanted to get into my personal history. She must be bored. No issues right now with program. Maybe Geraldine and Martha Lee have a bet going on with her. Grilling me at Jake's. Ply me with their so sweet words. See who can get me to talk. Well, I'm no rope a dope.

"Hey, can't say I always had the goal, just kind of happened. Like, how did you become a therapist?" Back on you Laura.

I could see Lou's eyes narrowing as he caught the drift of my interrogation, but I kept my benign smile glowing, "I will tell you if you tell me."

There she was, leaning back into that therapeutic crouch ready to pounce on my next phrase. Was Laura hitting on me? Playing truth and dare? How old are we? Should I just risk being ego slammed. Ask her out? I looked at my watch.

"We'll have to schedule in a weekend of therapy for that stuff."

This was just a warm up. I decided to let him go, this time. "I'll have my people get with your people."

"Cool, Rudy has a vet appointment that I'm late for." I bet I looked panicked heading for the escape door.

Lou was such a poor liar. He fumbled his way to the door and I stood and opened it up, lightly brushing up against him. I felt so sweetly wicked!

"Nice fragrance," I acknowledged before I could stop myself. I had never been this close and alone with Laura.

"Give Rudy a scratch for me." I closed the door forcing myself not to call my girl friends. This sizzling encounter would have to wait to be told Friday at Jakes.

Well, in a sense Laura was right. Her question was something I continually asked myself. How does one become a teacher? What sort of events occur where you say. I'm going to be a teacher, a fireman, Green Peace Envrionmentalistsavetheplanet. Garbage dude. A cowboy. You just can't wake up one morning say, yeh, that sounds cool. Think I'll be a teacher, how does the decision happen?

For me, I can talk for me. When. Why. That's easy. I said at age ten that I was going to be a teacher, if I failed at athletics. Developed fear of the fastball. Couldn't compete, failing at sports, didn't take more than the next seven years. Some bad luck. A bad back. Only the mirror to blame. Laura would further comment that my need for security was so great, that I developed an anal retentive tunneled vision to cocoon my future in. No college ball? Scholarships were still there for me following my rehab. I could have been a walk on anywhere in the country. Lots of people took up the gauntlet for me, especially Red.

Laura always had insight, teaching just seemed like a good life. What could be better than being a teacher? OK, walking down the street with people, turning to say, THERE GOES THE BEST DAMN HITTER IN BASEBALL! That would be cool. Ted Williams had his priorities buttoned down. But I could take teaching. Let go of childhood grandiosity, Why risk permanent disabilitating injury when you could share, talk about things that you enjoyed, believed in, Spearhead the enlightening of the emerging generation through righteous dialogue. Maybe coach a bit. You got all this vacation time. Talk about opportunities. Ten weeks every summer to do as you pleased, not to mention the two weeks at Christmas, one at Easter. You only had to work about one hundred and eighty days a year! Figure three hundred and sixty-four and every other day was a day off. Not too shabby!

Then too, it's an attitude thing. TinkertailorsoldierCEO. You have to like what you're doing. I remember saying in the teachers' staff room, towards the end of my first year of teaching, just two weeks until summer break!! Can't wait!! That first year had been a kick. Now came the summer break! Time to get rejuvenated for next year. Yes!! Europe, here I come. Whoa boy!! Brakes. One of the crusty, wizened lifers corrected me. No, she lamented, just ten weeks until we have to come back. Thud. Half empty? Half full? Take your pick. I let the crusty half empty educator's comment just blow by me. Anyone over thirty had to be jaded.

Teachers will say that they only make thirty-five thousand per year after four to five years of college. Look what the checker at the grocery store pulls in. They make as much or more than I do. All the prep time I put in with no compensation. I should have worked for UPS. They didn't go to college for five years. Just shows you where society places its values.

I say to these whining educators, GET A GRIP! That argument just never made much sense to me. Here's this teacher who works seventy-five to eighty days fewer than the clerk or UPS driver, makes the same money.

Complains about not having more. Is the home any happier with a few more bucks? Would a six per cent retroactive raise really make your day? If you want mo' money, work mo' days. Do summer school. Get another job, like who forced you to be a teacher? Write a best seller. Invent a new garden hose. Choosing to go into Education as a career has certain trade offs. One is that you will not be financially wealthy, unless you hit the Lotto. Otherwise, chill. Accept the profession of teaching for the joys that relationships can bring and put down the half empty cup.

So, I knew I would become a teacher. I could talk to students about things that were up front, personal. Take vacations. Get paid for all this good time. What could be better? I sure didn't want to go to law or medical school. Bookworm crawl through the youth of my life powering up to be something when I was fifty. Forget the wall plaques. Give me teaching. I'll earn my plaques there! Give me the sixties' forward social consciousness of taking on the real world for the betterment of All Kinds!!

There are some definite moats to be crossed prior to earning a credential. For instance, to become a credentialed teacher one must pass through the gauntlet of student teaching. My student teaching experience almost sent me to welding school. (No offense, I love the arc and bead.) I began working with junior high school students in a lower socioeconomic multiethnic English Reading class in Richmond, California. Such an oxymoron. Such a warm experience. I came in saying, "Hi, my name is Lou. You didn't have to call me Mr. Thompson. Lou was just fine. How you doing? So, what would you like to learn? Oh, you don't give a shit? Please, hold the fragrance. Ok, where were we? Want to discuss alternatives? Anyone thought of serving in the military? Was I as fucking stupid as I talked? How Socratic. I didn't really appreciate that language. Why didn't I leave so they could get their real teacher back?"

All this in the first five minutes.

I survived the initial onslaught because I quickly picked up <u>Essentials of Basic English</u>, first printing around my date of birth. Dog eared. Ripped pages. Turned to Chapter Three, page forty-seven, and began teaching sentence diagramming. Adjective modifies the Noun. Adverb modifies the verb. Asking theoretical question such as, what two letters do adverbs often end in? Oh, you don't remember? Remember, lots of them end in "ly." Drew the right lines. Lines that they were familiar with. It was the thing that teachers did. My students didn't understand all the lines. Smart kids knew this stuff. Never made sense to them, but it was what they were in school for. My Bob Dylan impression of Malcolm X. didn't get rave reviews. But the lines, the diagrams, the familiar chalkboard characters. The students' relationship with me immediately changed. I could hear them muttering over the sound of my chalk...

"God, he's smart."

"I didn't think he had a brain?"

"I thought he was stupid."

"This is OK. Let's give him a chance. He goes to the Big U. He seems alright. Just new, but he knows his stuff."

Maybe for them, but I wasn't going to spend nine months a year discussing sentence formation. Where was the Age of Aquarius? So much for revolutionizing the world through education. Maybe I could become a roadie with The Stones.

Fortunately for me, before I became a welder, I tried elementary teaching. I had always felt that elementary teaching was beneath my dignity. Who wants to sit around with a bunch of rug rats singing silly songs. Asking them what they had to share? What sort of challenge was it teaching a bunch of non-thinking thumb suckers? Anyone could teach reading. Write.....right?

Now, a quarter of a century later, most of my experience has been with these glorious rug rats. I loved them. I loved their unabashed joy coming into a room ready to learn. Just bright, happy, chattering, and willing. My first teaching experience had been in a small, rural, coastal village where I had taught a combination first through third for two years. It was at the end of the second year that I took a summer to ride my bike to Canada and back. (Good to know fact. The wind is at your back when you return.). During these peddling days I determined that I wanted to earn a Master's in Reading. I wanted to understand more about the process of reading that held so much responsibility for a child's success in public school.

It was while I was working on my master's that I first met up with the ED population, Emotionally Disturbed. There was an advertisement for a long-term sub that fit into my schedule. Additionally, the age group was five through seven, which is where I had my experience.

Piece of cake. Have some fun. Sing some songs. Employ some of my new theories. So where did I find myself? In a self-enclosed portable, way out back, like in Australia! No kangaroos, not that I should have been surprised.

There I was, sitting across the table from Martin, all six years and fifty-three pounds of chocolate pudding, who was giggling and tickling Joseph. It was time for lunch in the primary program of the county day treatment facility. The trays were being placed in front of each student and staff. We ate in our classrooms.

"Martin, no touching. You know that will earn you a time-out."

"So what Lou?!" He stuck his tongue out, flipped me off, and continued to poke at Joseph. Such a charming six-year old.

This was my third week. I was a mess. There were eight students and three teaching assistants plus myself. Additionally, we had three full time mental health therapists available for support. I wasn't much help. This was more like pie in the face than a piece of cake. It was moment-to-moment survival. Learning was on the back burner. Maybe I was learning how to survive. At lunch we sat around two, large kidney shaped tables. Since this was primary, my knees were higher than the table. You had to have a supple back to teach this age group.

"Everyone served?" I asked, looking around the two tables preparing to join a modest grace. Omygod! I could see them looking at each other. They're going to go off! Joseph, Josh, Steven, Martin, Xavier, Eric, James, Sean. They were going to bolt again!

"CHICKENBEEF!" They all screamed bouncing up joyously to heave their plates towards the ceiling. Applesauce, French fried potatoes, salad, and pieces of chicken showered the room. I grabbed Joseph as he spit at me. I placed Joseph in a basket restraint. Adrian, a TA, caught Xavier and James by the arms and walked them to the corner of the room. Sally had Martin in a five point prone. Josh, Steven, Eric, and Sean careened howling out the door screaming "JAILBREAK!!" with our staff in hot pursuit. At least they were outside! I leaned over Joseph wanting nothing less than to immerse him into the linoleum. He had caught me in the eye with his lugi. Yuk. Nasty. I wiped my eye as best I could on my shoulder, making sure to keep his elbows locked. Last week he had clawed me across my forehead. I still had scabs. I surveyed the classroom. Tables, chairs, food, drinks, in disarrayed shambles. So much for my afternoon lesson plans. I checked in with Sally and Adrian to make sure they were alright. It would take the next two hours just to reassemble the room. Our rule was that the students involved had to make things right. I calmly held Joseph more firmly as he attempted to twist and bite my wrist. Whatever was going on for them was beyond me. As for our hands-on survival stabilizing techniques per legal expectations, arrest us!

Their audacious behavior took me months to begin to figure out what was going on. Three months to be able to begin to establish relationships with this wild and crazy bunch of miscreant urchins. Three months to begin to internalize the relationship of the mental health/education team concept to a day treatment program in hour-long meetings following each school day. Three months so that I could come in and sing "Good Morning, Six Little Ducks, Ha-Ha This Way," giving them a sense of stability in the classroom and a break from the chaos that often enveloped their lives outside of our cocoon. Three months so that they trusted that I would be back the next day. Three months before they could start letting me know how they hurt without throwing their lunch plates in the air. Three months during which time I learned that this was where I wanted to teach.

April 3   Attachment Disorder

Primary teachers need to be energized with that Bunny Battery and have enthusiastic techniques that respond immediately to the ebb and flow of the classroom mood. A primary teacher needs to be a magician who sings with multicolor-consistent academic fundamentals flowing in a structured soothing manner all the while staying three steps ahead of the multitude. Primary teachers need to be Heather McCormick.

I hired Heather because I knew Lou did not relish getting back into the primary rhythm. Not that he would admit his limitations. Not that he was incapable of running a good program. Nothing personal Lou, but you just were not a twenty-two year old gymnastic child prodigy who had played four years of major college fast pitch softball while graduating on time with a clinical diagnosis of ADHD and agraphia. Basic ingredients for being a successful ED primary teacher. I marveled at Heather's workaholic enthusiastic dogma in the teaching of academics to our students. Academics that were such a struggle for her. If she could ring the bell, so could they. She not only expected appropriate behavior from her students, but she expected them to learn!

I watched from across the garden as Heather steered Reffti along the balance beam. He was a classic en-utero drug affected child. His psychological history was one of unfulfilled screams that tortured his mother as she entered rehab. There was no reference made regarding his father. What men had entered his mother's life were made to feel Reffti's wrath in scatological ways. I felt Natasha's wounds.

In one of our first sessions, as Natasha explained to me,

"Reffti would wait until my boyfriend and me were out of the room. Then, he would sneak in and urinate on the bed."

Natasha spoke clearly. She had discussed these events before. She was a strong person who had pulled her life back together. Her braided hair contributed to her looking like a teenager. (I was not ageing!) She would do whatever it took to do the same for her son.

"The worse thing," she laughed recalling the event. "The worse thing he ever did."

She paused. "Laura, why don't you call me Natti. All my friends do." I nodded.

"That I can laugh about this thing now is just amazing."

She relaxed back into the leather chair in my office.

"Reffti…….. are you ready for this Ms. Laura?"

She eyed me with a conspiratory smile that shed warmth, but, was I ready? I didn't know, I certainly could not have fathomed what Natti said next.

"Reffti opened up the lunch box of one of my boyfriends and dropped a dukie in it!"

My eyes must have gagged at the visualization of the act.

"That's not all, Laura, he wiped the edges so that there were no marks and sprayed box down with a bathroom scent. My boyfriend did not get the gift until he sat down at the work lunch table with his buddies!"

"Oh my God!" I exclaimed and grasped my knees. We both laughed in picturing that moment. This was our third session. Most of the initial hurdles had been passed. We were beginning to form a healthy relationship.

"My goodness Natti, did you ever see this man again?"

She nodded, "Matter of fact, I have been seeing him for the past four months."

"That's great. What's his name?"

"Ike." I waited. Natti continued, "He's a warm, good hearted Christian man. I met him through our church."

"Have Ike and Reffti done any better?"

"Not really. I have to meet Ike away from the home. Thank Heaven for my father. He comes over and stays with Reffti or takes him over to his house. They do a lot of fishing together, checkers, or dominoes. My Dad's a kind man. He has always been there for me."

I inwardly sighed. My father was present, but our relationship had always been a more surface one. There were my brothers, my mother, the church, the business, the relatives, and all of the related functions. Then too, if I had not been such a competent first child, my parents, who I love dearly, might have bestowed more attention to me. Outwardly, my maturation as a Straight A-Homecoming Queen-Heavenly Sent Role Model just evolved too easily to demand scrutiny, especially from my Father. For daughters, expectations were simply different during childhood. But I did miss that time with him. I wonder if he does now?

I empathized with Natti, "You must find the effort difficult with Reffti's rejection of your male friends."

Natti nodded. "It's just not them, but it's me as well. He does well with Grandpa, but no one else can get into him. The other psychologist I saw said that it was like some sort of alone disorder."

"Maybe an Attachment Disorder?" I offered.

Natti became animated. "That's it. That's what they called it. Where Reffti just cannot trust. He won't look you in the eye." Natti looked away. "Whatever you give him he destroys. He might ask for a Lego Set and the next thing I know is that the garbage disposal is clogged with plastic. He seems to have no conscience or remorse for his actions." Natti paused. "I accept and acknowledge that Reffti's issues have grown out of my substance abuse history. My early on parenting skills sucked. I just want for him to be able to improve and move on to a better life."

Attachment Disorders seemed to follow those children neurologically impaired by substance abuse. The womb and the first two years were so impactful. There never was enough for these children. So many of our student referrals came with this issue, whether it was a clinical diagnosis or not. They might be able to articulate what their needs were, but, when met, only gained momentary gratification. Lots of soft signs of autism.

I changed course. Tried to move into a more positive area." How has your father been successful with Reffti?"

Natti pursed her lips, searching for a phrase.

"I believe it's because Dad is just so calm and accepting."

"Calmer than he was with you as a child?"

Natti laughed. "Oh no! Daddy has always been a soother. Given time, he could take the bubbles out of a pot of boiling water." She gazed out the window to the pastures and soccer field, "He needed that to be able to live with my tormented mother for eighteen years. I wish I had more of him in me. Some of what goes on with Reffti has to be his reaction to how I carry on."

I lay huddled in my bed. I know I dare not walk out the door to where the party was happening. My butt still stung from an earlier whipping. I choked in a sob. No one cared. I wished my Daddy were still here. I had asked God to send him back if only for a little bit. Just to straighten Momma out. She had gone to pieces without him. Trying all sorts of different things that made her act weird. Brought people into the house that I was told were friends but I felt a nastiness from them. I wish I could live with my Grandpa. His house is always so quiet. Everything was neat. Had a place. I really liked it when he took me fishing. He had a couple of favorite fishing holes that were shaded. We always caught something to bring back for dinner. Most likely some Blue Gill and Cats. Grandpa cleaned them right there and tossed their insides back into the fishing hole. He said it brought in other fish for our next time back.

He had a harp that he played while we sat there. He said he would teach me how in a couple more years. I really liked to sing one of the songs he played. I couldn't remember all the words. He said the singer sang the blues about going fishing. His name was Taj Mahal. The song was "The Fisherman's Blues" and went something like:

"Betcha going fishin' all the time

Baby goin' fishin' too.

Bet your life, your sweet wife

Gonna catch more fish than you."

My favorite part was when he sang about how you goin' to cook them.

"Put 'em in a pot, put them in the pan

Honey cook 'em until they're nice and brown

Make a batch of butter milk whole cakes mama

And you chew them things and you chomp 'em on down.

I fell asleep singing to myself:

"Many fish bites if ya gots good bait

Here's a little tale I'd like to relate…

Natti was so willing to be involved. I wished all of my clients were like Natti. "That's interesting. How do you see yourself carrying on?"

Natti was opening herself. She was willing to make herself vulnerable in order to improve her life and what she could offer Reffti. Natti had presented situations that portrayed her as a self-indulgent, substance addicted, angry, single parent unable to quell her own needs, never mind those of Reffti. Even with her work through Rehab and The Calvary Baptist Church, Natti still found herself at the mercy of her emotions. Raw and open was how she put it.

I liked Natti as a person and found myself being empathetic and compassionate with her issues, which was not always the common thread in my adult clients. I respected the effort she made to reform her distraught life and Reffti's and we concluded the meeting with the intention to get together within ten days. I made the suggestion that she might consider asking Ike if he would be interested in participating with us. I had no illusions of Ike joining with Natti to form an intact family with Refft that would lead to complete peace and harmony. I had been involved in family therapy for twenty years and had come to expect interpersonal dysfunction as part of the territory.

As Natti left I thought of how I had wished that I had gone into teaching or a more uplifting field of endeavor. In school I had never envisioned the endless needy panorama of sad people who would fill my office with their personal melodrama. I had long aspired to gain the knowledge to assist others in addressing the traumas that were overwhelming their lives. I had realized many years ago that there was no recipe that was going to get me there. Bottom line, what heals is in the recipe of the relationship and relationships take time.

April   Sand Tray

"Bitch! Motherfuckin' Bitch! Get off me!"

I try to squirm and bite them. Tears streaming down my face. Fuck heads.

"Get off me Bitches!"

That hurts. Try to spit. Just runs down my chin.

"God damn let go of my arm you fuckin' niggahs!"

They won't talk. Bitches. That's the rule when you get face smashed. Took three of them, though, and I fucked up the room good.

"I'll kick you' asses bitches! Let go of me!!"

I can feel them change positions with staff switching and a new set of hands on me. I'll tire them out. They can't make me quit. I try to kick. No use. Too many of them and they're too strong. They've got me. I hate this shit. God Damn it why me? What the fuck did I do? It was that fucking Joshua who knocked the juice onto my new Snoop Dog shirt. Momma had brought it home special for me. Now it was stained and ruined. Lucky piece of shit got behind Miss Heather before I killed him.

"Motherfuckers let go!! I'm calm!"

Fucking carpet shit all over my mouth. Nasty. Sticking to my lips. Makes me want to puke.

"Get off! I'm going to puke!! Motherfuckers!!"

I did puke the other day. They just moved me over and placed my head on a towel. Do feel their pressure lessen. Still firm. I can breathe better. OK. Take a breath. Calm down. Got to get out of this. Only way is to stop screaming. Take it slow. Think about something else. Maybe think about fishing. Wonder what Grampa's doing? Is he under the shady tree? That's better...

Reading and academics in general were so difficult for Reffti, not to mention just being around other peers and adults. As I observed Reffti in our therapy session, he went through the various items to construct his sand tray story. I mused for a moment how I would feel about a child of mine being in a program such as Valley Oak. I know we did the best that one might in providing services for students with autism who had histories of physical assault, but what more could we provide? How would I feel?

I refocused on Reffti as he was deliberate, calculating in his approach to the sand tray placing a barn with sheep and cattle grazing nearby. In a corner he constructed a lake with scattered boulders and steered a boat on it. He looked through the figures finally settling on an adult male that he nestled into the boat. Reffti paused and stepped back to survey the scene he had constructed when, with a sudden movement he snatched a child from the figure shelf and perched him on a rock near the shore. The scene presented Reffti and his grandfather out and about on a fishing excursion.

As Reffti continued to select additional items, I surveyed. As with so many of his peers inflicted with attachment issues, he only chose a few people. None of the people were engaging in activities except for the two fishing. Of the others one was driving a jeep, another was standing by the barn, and the final one had a basketball. They were all facing away from one another with no exchange of eye contact or presenting an awareness of the other's presence. There was his personal dilemma right in the sand.

In addition to the layered distorted histrionic assaultive issues, was that Reffti's self-stimulation was increasing as a soothing mechanism. Often times staff would observe Reffti holding his hand in front of his face and manipulating his wrists and fingers like helicopter blades. Reffti would do this as a sudden impulse, as he could be walking down the sidewalk, holding hands with Natti, and suddenly go into a rabbit hopping finger frothing frenzy with his head twitching from side to side. Then, just as suddenly, Reffti would hold Natti's hand, give her a hug, and walk on as if nothing had happened. Heather had commented that his self-stemming had increased in the classroom to the point that he could not be on-task in the academic area unless two adults were seated next to him.

"So Reffti," I gently inquired. He startled, quivered at the intrusive sound of my voice interrupting his engrossment in the sand tray activity. "Tell me about the lake. Are there fish in it?" I moved nearer the tray.

I continued," Are there any fish jumping today."

He did not take his focus off of the tray.

After a long moment he nodded, "Yep. Big ones."

I bent down to his eye level of the sand tray, "Catch any yet?"

He pointed to the rowboat.

"Gramps got two from the boat. He's coming over to pick me up."

That Reffti was dialoguing was a positive step as I walked around to the other side of the tray and asked, "Did you just get to the lake?"

At this question Reffti turned away from me and began to further search through the objects on the shelf. Without turning around he stated, "Yeh, I was late."

Softly, not to accuse. "What made you late?"

Frowning. "I had to get the cows in the barn."

I looked over at the farm scene where Reffti had increased the number of cows to where there was now a herd, albeit in dysfunctional disarray as they lay on their sides or upside down. "There sure are a lot of cows. Are you going to be able to get them in the barn."

Reffti reached over and picked two more cows off of the shelf. He placed them right next to the barn. He could have placed them inside. The others remained in the field.

He scowled, "Too many for me. I got some of them in."

I supported his efforts. "Looks like you tried your best. You did a good job." I paused. "Is that how you got to go fishing with Gramps, by finishing some chores first?"

At that query Reffti gradually stood straight up reminding me that he was tall for his age. I had five shelves, three wide, filled with various figures and items for the sand tray that included everything from mystical monsters to railroad trains and Barbie Dolls.

I feel so pissed off. My vision is blurring. I feel hot. This is how it happens. I want to pull down those shelves. I know I shouldn't do it. That's what Laura and Heather keep telling me. Stay strong. Keep the cool. But I want to destroy this fucking sand tray shit. Just toss it over! I almost missed fishing with Grandpa because of the mess in the kitchen. Damn it. I could hear my head starting to hum and saw Ms. Laura's worried face. Don't come near me! Don't talk to me! I'll just want to fuck you up even if you are Ms. Laura. I'll close my eyes like they been telling me to do. Just breathe. Concentrate on breathing. Let the swarm calm down. Go fishing.....

I could feel Reffti's struggle as he closed his eyes and began the breathing technique that we had been working on. I moved to the side of the room, allowing for space, and sat in, what I called, my "Alice in Wonderland" chair. The chair could have been used at a medieval banquet hall with its huge back and leather arms. I waited as Reffti came back to the present, slowly opening his eyes and trusting that he had moved through the emotional issue. He began to scrutinize the second shelf which was mainly composed of household items. He chose a table, which he placed near the farmhouse upside down. Then he put some pots and pans around it. He sat down and picked up the table and set it upright with the pots and pans neatly spaced out on it.

I waited. After several seconds I asked.

"Did some things get messed up at home?"

Reffti confirmed by nodding. I knew that I was pushing his frustration level, but he had used the stabilizing techniques to work through his rage the first time and I wanted him to gain further confidence.

"Did you have to clean them up before fishing with Gramps?"

Again the slow nod with no eye contact. Furrows were creasing his forehead and I noted that his hands had balled into fists.

"Were you angry about something?"

Reffti, suddenly, lurched and spun around with a withering moan so base that I thought he was going to toss the sand tray over and assault me. He certainly was strong enough to perform both of those acts but, instead, Reffti turned his back to me raising his hands before his face. Before I could gather my wits he began to agitatedly stab and wave his fingers in front of his face while emitting a soft moan. I was bewildered. What to do? Like therapists always have the right answers! It was almost the symptoms of a petite mal seizure. Although Reffti was active, he was not frantic. There was more of a melodious rhythm in his voice. I decided to lean back in my chair. Give him time to ease his emotions. To come back in. I hoped he would accept the passive invitation.

Time passed as I sat in tortured silence............

May 4   That's Why We're Here

During the second meeting with Ike and Natti, I presented my experience with Reffti's escalation and his struggle to maintain in control of his emotions, to which Natti presented her frustrated anxiety by the tense clasping of her hands with Ike.

"That's just what happens to me," whispered Natti. "We will be sitting there, watching television. Nothing is going on. All of a sudden he is just all over the place. Hands in the air. Making sounds. Like someone flipped a switch. It's scary."

I nodded. "What do you do when this happens?"

She looked at Ike. "I've tried just about everything. Sometimes I yell. Sometimes I might hug him. Sometimes I walk out of the room. I just don't know, I'm at a loss."

Ike agreed, "There's just nothing that works that we can put our finger on."

We had discussed the breadth of Reffti's behavioral triggers. There did not seem to be any precursors to their escalating. Natti was not open to a medication review by a psychiatrist due to her previous experiences with substance abuse. We also discussed a referral to a neurologist.

I inquired, "What does Gramps do when he begins to act-out?"

Natti unfolded her hands and shrugged.

"Gramps just kind of pays Reffti no mind. Just keeps on doing what he was doing until Reffti settles in."

"Has Gramps always done that?"

"Far as I can remember," Natti caught herself in thought and laughed. "Hold it. I know what you're going to say, just why can't you do the same? Just let him calm down by himself."

I smiled and nodded at her insight.

"I wished to Lord I could."

Ike agreed, "We can be in church or out in public and people are looking at us like a freak show. It seems that we have to do something to get him out of the situation"

They were right that something needed to be done as Reffti's episodes occurred in every environment and were not about his needing to control. My family seldom had meals out at restaurants, but, many times, I have seen parents with agitated young children struggling to calm them or, one parent, removing the child from the table. The glares and disapproval of other diners followed their interventions.

"Why bring a young child to the restaurant?"

"Couldn't they have gotten a baby sitter?"

"What right do they have to ruin our evening?

"I wish someone would just tell them to leave."

I suspect that all families have experienced such an ordeal on one level or another. On that day Natti and Ike agreed to employ what we termed. "The Gramps Technique" for six weeks. The main premise would be that they would be there for Reffti but not get into his space or redirect him. Additionally, Ike and Natti would evaluate where they were going to socialize with Refft for, as much as church meant to them, Reffti might not have the attention span or frustration tolerance to be successful in that environment. The focus would be to think through where they were going to bring Reffti and to have a plan in place to assist him should he begin to have difficulty.

I knew Natti and Ike's developed confrontational manner with Reffti would be difficult to reteach, but it seemed a place to start, especially with Gramps modeling. Later that day, I shared with Heather the tone of the conversation I had with Natti and Ike.

Heather was pleased. "Seems they want to work with us."

"Yes they do," I agreed, "and Reffti is going to be a challenge."

"That's why we're here," Heather laughed, "Right?" As she tossed back her braided locks, I joined in the laughter because that was one of my lines...... "That's why we're here."

"Remember Dominic?"

How could I not? I watched as Heather prepared for her next day's program, mesmerized by the assured ease of energy that flowed through her movements. She was constructing a "mean e" vowel assignment with color coordination and asking me if I remembered Dominic? Like, no big deal. I have been doing this for years. Just another assignment. I wondered if Lou had any grasp of how lucky he was to have her as a teacher.

"Sure I remember Dominic. How could one forget?"

Heather snorted a guffaw the likes of which I had never associated with her. I am sure I reacted because she turned a bright crimson, coughing, and apologized.

"C'mon Heather, like I've never made weirder sounds."

She momentarily got hold of herself. "Dominic made Reffti seem like cement."

"Did he ever," I heartily agreed. "That child was a riot! I believe that I was joining in her laughter so hard that we contortedly doubled over at the memory of Dominic in his hunting vest, I mean his "Smart Jacket."

Heather pointed to one of the cupboards, "I've still got the weights, all we need is another hunting vest."

I shook my head and added, "Remember how he always said, "slow and steady wins the race," whenever we tried to get him to speed up!"

Dominic was seven years old and weighed one hundred and nine pounds. He could not take a step without twirling his hands in the air as if to seek balance from some mystical trapeze strands. Even with the assistance of a plethora of medications, he was unable to attend to any form of academic class work. As with Reffti, we were at a loss of how to involve him in program as his parents had engaged several psychiatrists and attended multiple clinics with little success. Finally at an IEP, the program specialist, Patricia Williams asked," Have you ever thought of weighting him down?"

We were all on good terms, so everyone had laughed. But Patricia was serious. There were studies to support and Patricia said that it had worked with several of her soft autistic elementary children. Why not try the weighted vest? So we had!

Valley Oak purchased a hunting vest, which Heather called a Smart Jacket, for Dominic where we placed weights into the various pockets "for smarts." Also, Heather augmented the outfit by placing one-pound wristbands on Dominic's arms for added smarts. The results were startling as, almost immediately, Dominic could now sit through an entire board presentation without jumping up to wave his arms in the air. He was able to follow the teacher's instructions and transcribe the information from the board with pencil and paper. When he went out to recess, he refused to take his Smart Vest off and, through staff pro-acting and Dominic's intimidating size, none of his peers ever made fun of his wearing the smart vest. Heather, slowly, over the following weeks, gradually took the weights out of the vest and Dominic wore it throughout the school day. In fact, he wanted to take the vest home and we felt sure that he probably would have slept with it.

Dominic was now back on a regular school site attending mainstream programs with Resource Specialist support. His parents had sent us pictures of Dominic's Smart Vest neatly tucked away in a drawer in his bedroom.

Heather continued to flit about the room, preparing for the next class lesson following recess. As Heather moved the overhead projector into place, she shared how Jason and she, her husband of six months, were planning a bicycle tour of New Hampshire. I continued to marvel at her natural skill for Heather was a member of the new breed of teacher who did not need to take up the gauntlet of the "isms," from sex to race, or the turmoil following the sixties that Lou had felt the need to confront. Textbooks were no longer based on sentence outlining of Lou's student teaching experience and beginning reading programs were presented in multicultural equal rights of color coordinated matriculated language development. I am not glossing over that humanity had, within a generation, developed an all encompassing social consciousness that would mute the histrionics of the Conservative Christian or Militant Muslim, but issues were now openly discussed. A positive step had been taken towards universal suffrage through the impact of forthright electronic communication that was softly blending the needs of different peoples.

My random thought was broken by Reffti's entering the room and Heather doing an impromptu handstand, promptly turning it into a single arm stand, and challenging Reffti to the same. Wow! Not to devalue Heather's innate skill level, but I was awed by the years of consistent physical discipline and family support to make the move so effortless.

The social changes that had been required whether through Title Nine or a more accepting generation had provided for the opportunities and nurturing. I chided myself for holding an envious small minded thought as I wondered, if Heather had five younger brothers, what impact their presence might hold? I laughed at myself as I certainly would not give up one of my five brothers in order to do an effortless one arm handstand... would I?

August 11   Painted History

As the side door skidded open, I was surprised to see Red enter.

"Hiya Red!" It was always a pleasure when he dropped by my program. I happened to be in the converted indoor basketball gym.

"Hiya Lou." His low warm voice rumbled.

"What brings you our way?"

"Gotta keep stock of Founder's progress." He smiled with a twinkle. "Didn't interrupt anything did I?"

I pointed to the red mark on the backboard. "Still there. Right where you painted it."

"That it is." Red slid his arm around my shoulder conspiring, "You want to fly up their and touch it up?"

I laughed, "Sure, with a ladder!"

Red shook his head, "Back in The Day..." He let his statement hang there and then said with more seriousness. "Lou, what do you think about it being time to just face the past? Just let it be what it was?"

Red was getting to be as bad as Laura and her girl friends. I decided to take him to task. "Now Red, over the past three weeks you have brought the same subject up every time I've been with you. Why the change? You know that was part of the agreement you and I made that brought me back here and to work with Founders. There was to be ..."

Red cut me off. "Yeh yeh yeh and more yeh." He leaned against the open door as if to block my escape route. "But Lou, things change. We both know that."

"So what's changed," I demanded irritably. Red could always get me going. "What's changed except Laura and her friends in Bay County Mental Health are snooping around?"

Red stood up from the wall. There were times he appeared to be ten feet tall to me. I hated these moments because I knew he was going to lay down some truth on me that I might argue with but I could not come up against. He placed both his hands on my shoulders and said with Red seriousness, "Lou, I am as proud of knowing you as any father can be of a son. You and I know that." I nodded. "Life is what life is and you have overcome a world of sadness and ill fortune. You have a blessed ability to bring people together that needs to be shared with the larger community, not limited by the fear of your personal history."

I stopped him right there. "Now hold it Red."

"No, let me finish." He continued with a sigh, almost whispering in my ear. His grip firmer. "Until you allow your history to be one of public knowledge. One that you can embrace and share you will continue to carry it like a coating of armor....weighing you down." Red walked over to the doorway and looked out into the afternoon sun, "Trust me on this Lou. It's time to open up and share your story."

For a moment I wanted to get that ladder and erase the red mark, "Damn it Red! Why can't you just stick with barbecue sauce?"

Red eyed me with his tooth grinning smile, "That's just what I'm doing Lou." He chuckled to himself and wrapped his hands behind his back. "Now, how about taking me on a tour of the place so I can get a fresh look."

As we walked out, JK hailed us. Red greeted JK with, "Great work on the bridge. Hardly heard a creak coming across."

JK beamed, "Yeh, we got some eight by eights set on pillars."

"Saw the redwood guard rails."

JK elbowed me, "Valley Oak added them with their Workability Program."

We continue our walk towards Founders main building. JK picked up a loose basketball. "Hey Lou, now that we got the softball team together, maybe we can look at some city league round ball."

I could see the corners of Red's lips kind of quiver and I knew what was coming. I wondered if JK and the ball just happened to be here at the same time.

"JK, Lou ever show you how he can spin a basketball and pass the sphere behind his back finger to finger, no look?"

JK stumble stopped and looked from Red to me with hesitant realization, "How long...."

Red kept going, "About two years before he put that red mark up on the backboard."

JK slapped his forehead. "I'll be swallowed." He looked at me with wonderment. "You're The White Legend?"

I stopped. "Hey you two, I've got to get over and see our speech therapist.

Red put his hands to his hips, "Lou, you can't keep duckin'...."

"And, JK," I bantered walking away, "Ask Red who painted the red mark on the backboard."

I left JK in earnest conversation with Red as I sought out Benjamin Marengo, our speech therapist. I found him sitting on a fruit box next to the chicken coop with Reffti and performing his magic. Benjamin would never call it magic. He would say that he was merely holding a mirror so that his student could see how really smart they were because, otherwise, they wouldn't believe that they were!

Benjamin spotted me. "Come on over Lou." He looked at Reffti. "Let's show Lou how smart we are."

Reffti smiled happy to show off. "OK!"

"Let's first show Lou how our body makes the short vowel sounds? You ready?"

Reffti nodded.

"Here we go." Benjamin put his thumb and forefinger around his throat and Reffti did the same as both said "aaaaaaaaaaaaaaaa."

"Now our chin." Both placed their right hands on their chin and moved them inward with the "eeeeeeeeee" sound. They kept the hand their as their chins now went out with the "iiiiiiiiiiii" sound.

"Good job Reffti. Now, the wind tunnel." Ben and Reffti made a circular shape with their two hands in front of their mounts and emitted the "ooooooooooo" short vowel.

"OK Reffti, what's the final number of this act?" Challenged Benjamin.

"Gotta lift the weights!"

"That's right!" Together they pretended to be hoisting a barbell of heavy weights into the air as they went "uuuuuuuuuuuuuuuuu.."

I applauded. "That's great guys."

"Thank you. Thank you, but we've only just begun. Now Reffti, let me have your left hand. Let's show Lou the sounds of our fingers."

Reffti held out his left hand. Ben touched his thumb. Reffti made the short vowel sound for A. Benjamin touched his index and Reffti made the short sound for E. Benjamin then went through the fingers of Reffti's left hand. Had Reffti do the fingers-sounds backwards. Then Ben chose fingers at random. If his finger decoding was any clue, Reffti knew his short vowel sounds.

Benjamin Marengo believed he could teach any person on the face of the earth, plus a few extra terrestrials, to read. Benjamin was almost sixty years young. We had not hired him, he had hired us. He called one day saying that he knew that we needed his services. He was right. We had just had our fifth Speech Therapist find a reason to leave. Like they would have too? Speech Therapists found working in a farmhouse with emotionally disturbed children on articulation and pragmatic issues not to be their cup of tea? No thank you. An air-conditioned clinic was preferred. Even a public school site anywhere over Valley Oak. Even at forty-five dollars per hour the assignment was not worth their time. It was however, worth it too Benjamin. Though, additionally, he asked for transportation mileage since he lived sixty-three miles away in one of the more remote boroughs of our state.

Benjamin had told me the story of how he didn't finish high school. He was living in rural Montana and had found it prudent to punch one of this teachers out. This was in his sophomore year. Benjamin was almost six foot four that year and was tired of being ridiculed for his speech impediment. I thought that being Black in Montana might have been equally trying. He decided to stay on and work the family farm his family had run from the time of a great grandfather being a Buffalo Soldier," until the seven-day a week strain of directing a dairy herd drove him to join the military and, ultimately, be admitted to the Green Beret. He lasted five weeks as a waist gunner on a Huey, which was three more than the average, before he was shot four times through his left arm. Miraculously, no bones were shattered. He spent over a year in Japan rehabilitating, earning his high school degree, and determining that the reason he had not learned to read at grade level was due to the incompetent teaching of phonics. He returned to the United States, earned his degree in Speech Pathology, and was hired by Lippencott to promote their phonic reading program. In this capacity he had risen to the stature of national prominence, developed reading programs for school districts across the country, suffered a stress related breakdown, and returned to Montana where he had been a fly fishing guide.

"Now Reffti, lets show Lou the "ap family.""

Reffti grinned ear to ear as Benjamin pulled out his flash cards of the ap family. One side had a picture and the other the word. First Benjamin said them and handed the cards to Reffti. "Cap, gap, lap, map, nap, rap, (Which was his self-made flash card with some rappers on one side.), sap, tap." Then Reffti took the cards and read them back to Ben.

"OK Reffti, backwards now." Reffti turned around so he could not see the cards. Benjamin laid them out in front of him. Reffti started confidently, "Lap, map, rap, nap, cap," and Benjamin gave him the card each time he said one of the words. Reffti paused. Benjamin prompted. "Remember my teeth?"

"Gap," Reffti stated.

"How about what is on a tree?"

"Sap."

"Very good! Now the last one. Ready?" Reffti nodded. Benjamin began tap dancing, he was pretty good!

"TAP! Taptaptap!!!!!!" Reffti shouted. "My turn now."

"It is now my turn," intoned Benjamin.

Reffti grinned and said, "It is now my turn."

"Make eye contact with me Reffti."

Reffti stared him straight in the eye. "It is now my turn."

"Yes it is indeedee it is."

Benjamin handed him the flash cards and turned around. Reffti laid them out in front of him just as Benjamin had. Benjamin began, "Cap, tap…" while Reffti handed him each correct card. I nodded and gave a thumbs up to Reffti as I stood up and gently left the room.

I went into the main building where I walked into Laura's office as Natti and Ike were meeting with Laura. They greeted me enthusiastically.

"I just can't believe the changes in the past six weeks."

"It is a miracle," Ike agreed.

"Reffti comes home and he wants to read labels. He gets out his story books and goes over and over them. It's like a different world."

I nodded. "Benjamin Marengo is such a good teacher. I'm learning a lot from him."

Laura commented in her consummate therapeutic tone, "As you know Lou, for the past two months Natti and Ike have been working with Reffti is a less intrusive way. I think their empowering him to work through his issues added with the confidence he is gaining in academics is allowing him to stabilize many of his behaviors."

"Worse than that, Laura," Natti laughed slapping Laura's thigh, "I'm even understanding what you just said."

"No more lunch issues?" I asked Ike.

"Praise the Lord and knock on my metal lunch box, never again," Ike replied. "I have been learning a lot about fishing from Gramps. Still can't catch them the way that Reffti can."

I knew the feeling. There was a knock on Laura's office door. Reffti and Benjamin came in. Laura introduced Benjamin to Natti and Ike. The four of them exuded a warmth like they were long lost family at a reunion.

"Reffti just speaks the world of you Benjamin." Natti said. "He comes home and says, Benjamin taught me this and Benjamin taught me that."

Benjamin looked down at Reffti, "You telling on me that way?"

"Yes sir." Reffti asserted.

"Look me in the eye when you say that."

Reffti looked up into Benjamin's gap toothed smile, "Yes sir." He said with a full on grin.

Natti and Ike invited Benjamin to go out for an ice cream with Reffti and themselves. Benjamin winced, he was an ice cream fanatic, and said that he still had four more students to see before the end of the school day, but he would make sure to schedule it in the next time. We said good-byes as Benjamin walked Natti, Ike, and Reffti out to their car.

"Such a change," Lou marveled. "From spontaneous combustion to model child."

Laura eyed me, "Not quite that far, but in the right direction." She paused. "Lou, on another subject, I continue to be impressed at how our students improve their academics."

I was too. I remembered the program days when I had earned the nickname of "The Wallet." Going way overboard in activities to develop relationships between students and staff. We would hold a morning meeting in the living room of The Victorian. Staff would say what might be going on in the area. Students, who had earned the right to participate, would talk about what they would like to do. Maybe get some model cars to put together. Go ice-skating. Maybe fishing. We'd talk about it and figure it out. Then, I would reach into my wallet and hand out the necessary funds. Somehow reading, writing, and 'rithmetic did not prominently figure into our curriculum, except for those who had to stay back on site with me. Slow death for us all.

Those days were now long past. Now we had quarterly scheduled class subjects, course curriculum, credits toward graduation, and enough structure that, in any moment, I expected bells to start ringing. As scary as it sounded, we were becoming a traditional school and, even scarier, the students were being more successful!!

"Lou," Laura continued with a measured articulation that warned she wanted me to pay attention, "What do you think about offering a reading lab that is based on Benjamin's Jacobs' phonics program to our middle adolescent group?"

Laura knew how I felt, but I responded "Laura, you know what I think about going "aaaa, eeee, iiiii" with older students. If they didn't get it when they were seven, why continue to punish them?" Laura was always pushing, maybe dragging me in a direction I did not want to go. From allowing James to have his own room to what, teaching phonics to street toughs?

"Look at it this way, like Benjamin says, maybe they just were not taught correctly. Maybe they were not receptive or ready to be taught."

I started to head for the door, "Yeh, right, and maybe I'm the Tooth Fairy. Benjamin's great for Reffti and some other one on ones, but not as a program direction. Our older students need social skills for work success. They need to have hands on experiences that will provide some money in their pocket. They've already failed at phonics, why have them fail again?

Why have them struggle with 'ch'-'e'-'ck'-'ing' when they could memorize checking? I just don't see the point."

As I left the room, Laura gave me one of her understanding smiles, Gag me.

I knew that she was just beginning. Laura would continue to bring up her view. But no way, no how, never, nunca, and you will never see me do it. Would I teach phonics to adolescents!

November 21   Community

The Thanksgiving Feast at Valley Oak was a feast to behold. Gradually, over the years, The Feast had evolved to include parents with students and staff bringing in special dishes from home. Valley Oak supplied the turkey, ham, yams, greens, cranberry, and pies. All the other side dishes came from the homes of our staff and students. Everyone tried to put out their best dish. I had a recipe from my mother that was my favorite type of pie. When the students would ask what I was going to bring and I told them, they would always go, yuuuuuuuck! That's nasty. My pie and, I could never make it as good as my mother's, was a Sour Cream Raisin Double Batch Caramel Walnut Almond Meringue Pie! Try saying that three times fast. When the student would try the pie, the yuck changed to, can I have some more please? It is one great pie.

Valley Oak now completely occupied one of the Founder's residential homes. In the Great Room of this seven thousand square foot building, we were able to assemble the nearly one hundred and twenty chairs and tables necessary for all attending. There were ribbons and bunting and fall colors galore to add to the festive feeling. For me, as an adult, this was my favorite time of year. There was just such a feeling of good will and community as everyone dressed in their Sunday best and eagerly awaited the saying of grace to begin passing the plates around the tables. Today's grace was being offered by the Reverend James Montgomery of the Calvary Baptist Christian Church, which Reffti and his family attended.

I looked on as the Reverend James stood. He was in his late twenties, tall, and wore a splendid light gray double vested suit for the festivities. With the Reverend's standing, the room slowly fell silent.

The Reverend bowed his head and began, "Let us pray. We thank you Lord for bringing us here, together, on this day to enjoy the fruits of our labor in your name." Reverend James raised his head. "I, personally, am honored to offer our prayers amidst such a wonderful group of people. In being amongst you prior to our meal, I had the opportunity to meet many of you and view the work going on at Valley Oak. Splendid work being attended to by students, staff, and parents in a manner that brings joy to my heart." The Reverend James paused, smiled to Reffti, Natti, and Ike. Nodded to Heather who sat with them. "In particular, I would like to offer my personal testimony as to the success of one of my parishioners at Valley Oak, because, I recall, he had such personal issues that he was not able to attend our church on The Lord's Day." Reffti hid his head in mock embarrassment. "Now, through the work of his teacher, family, and others, he not only attends on the Lord's Day, but he has joined us for Bible Study and has led our congregation in prayer. Before we embark on this blessed feast, I ask that Reffti stand up and we recognize his efforts."

With coaxing from Ike and Natti, Reffti stood and the entire Valley Oak program warmly applauded him. "Now," The Reverend continued, "Before I wear out my welcome by going on too long." He raised his slender arms in an elegant heavenly gesture, "Thank you Lord, for bringing me to Valley Oak, to behold a community of people working together to provide for Your Children and may The Feast be blessed in Your Name. Amen."

"Amen," chorused from all as the sounds of plates, silverware, and voices began to fill the room.

I watched as Reffti and his family filled their plates and passed the food, offering my personal,

Amen!

269

Valley Oak School
Psycho/educational Intake Summary

Laura Rosso: LCSW

Name: <u>Jake Oh</u>
DOB: <u>2/5/80</u>

County of Residence: Lincoln
School District of Reference: Lincoln

Date: January 18, 1997

Physical Description: Jake is a tall, large boned, seventeen year old Asian male. Medical records state that all developmental milestones were met within normal limits, although there were concerns noted regarding gross motor integration. Jake has stated, "Why run when you can walk? Why walk when you can stand? Why stand when you can sit? Why sit when you can sleep?" Jake has strong verbal skills and his fine motor skills are exhibited by his drawings. He has stated that he looks forward to a career as Asian animae artist.

Referring Criterion: Jake was placed out of county by CPS at the age of ten. CPS records state that Jake's father was physically abusive and that mom was unable to protect which led to the removal. Jake's behavioral issues were eventually not containable in the public school setting and, at the age of eleven, he was placed in the first, of what would be several, Non-Public School Programs. Referring concerns included verbal opposition and assault, poor peer relationships, an inability to follow staff direction, and a general lack of success during the school day.

Family History: Jake is the eldest and male child born to Raymond and Alysson Yen (Anglicized names have been adopted). Issues began to develop between Jake and his father due to their differing cultural expectations. Raymond, whose homeland was Korea, was not embracing Western culture while Jake, was acquiring the idioms and social norm of his parents' new country. Jake steadily offered more verbal opposition to

Raymond, who responded through corporeal punishment in the form of switches, belts, and paddles. These occurrences escalated to CPS reports and, ultimately, the removal of Jake from his home for his own protection. At this time, Jake has been able to return home for special occasions such as birthdays, weddings, and holidays.

Psychiatric History: No history in cumulative records.

DSM IV Diagnosis:

AXIS I:	Attention Deficit/Hyperactivity Disorder Combined Type
AXIS II:	V71.09 no diagnosis
AXIS III:	None
AXIS IV:	Out of home placement: history of physical abuse.
AXIS V:	GAF – 40 Current

Recommendations: Throughout his many school placements Jake has consistently been receptive to therapeutic relationships. With Jake's return to his county of origin, the expectation is to be able to engage Jake's parents, Raymond and Aleeta, in family therapy. If the family members can actively engage in this process, there is greater hope for success with Jake's reunification with his family and ultimate success.

Given Jake's willingness to participate with program and his parent's willingness to be involved in family therapy, I support Jake's admission to Valley Oak.

Signed_____Date_____
Laura Rosso

Chapter 7

JAKE: THE AMERICAN DREAM

FEBRUARY 4   Culture Wars

Hyun-Ki and Hyun-Shik. Fuck them. My twin younger tit sucking brothers. They know when I get them alone I will crush their slick combed-back hairy extra large Grade A heads like chicken eggs. They will cry for mercy and none shall be granted. Father will be somewhere CEOing in New England. I love my mother and I will not cause her angst but, when she goes out to shop until she drops, I will have my revenge. They are fucked. They know it. I will stuff rags into their toothy mouths and duct tape them shut. She will not know. The bruises I leave will be internal. They will take months to gain the courage to fuck with me again. They will learn not to lie on me, the worms. Even their names are an embarrassment. Everyone laughs when they hear them over the squawk box at high school. In English their names mean "wise" and "clever." I am sure my father thought that he was wise and clever for conceiving two more sons. Two for the price of one. Right now their ugly mugs are contorted in stifled giggles as I await my punishment. Let them enjoy their moment. They will need to relish the time. I am patient. I can wait. Their time will come and it will be soon enough.

Ah, here comes my most revered big money father with his wicked willow branch. I begin to rise from the chair and bend at the waist to accept the punishment of the whip upon my back. I am so fucking fed up with having to endure this humiliating pain from this miniature man. I feel a haze of rage blurring my vision.

"Bullshit," I suddenly scream out turning toward my pint sized father and snatch the willow whip from his hand. His eyes go wide with surprise and then terror fills him and he runs into the kitchen seeking the protection of my mother, I am more than twice his size. Almost three times in bulk. I have had enough beatings. For what? For what? Disagree with an elder? Using a fork at family traditions instead of sticks? For dressing like an American? For playing a Game Boy in church? For......? I snap the willow in three parts and turn for my brothers. They have wisely fled.

As I gather my heavy hooded New England Patriot parka and gloves, I see my mother's head cautiously peer around the kitchen doorway. Somehow the thought of how Koreans have such large swollen heads spins through my mind. Mine was gigantic. I blew her a kiss as I headed for the door.

"Jake," she hesitantly calls after me in her singsong voice. I appreciate that she chooses English to speak to me. "Jake, please do not be late for dinner."

I smile a good bye and softly close the door after me. I have thought about this moment for several months. Once I defy my father, I will not be able to reenter the home and my extended family will be closed to me. With my reputation there will not be a home in our Korean community that will offer me comfort. I can handle that. After several snow crunching blocks, I stop and hunker down to wait for the light rail that will take me to Founders.

May 15   Off Key

This was my third meeting with Raymond and Allyson Oh. Although Raymond and Allyson were not their actual Korean names, they asked me to use their Americanized names to ease communication. I had found the sessions to be difficult, but not due to a language barrier as both parents were fluent in English. In fact they were also fluent in French and Russian, which was certainly a multilingual skill I lacked. Although Raymond presented as the gregariously confident head account CEO for Samsung of New England, I had noted the respectful glances and questions he would share with Allyson. My insight told me that Raymond did not gain his lofty position on his worth alone. The communication difficulty that I was attempting to resolve was based on Raymond's continual deflecting of questions through humor, sarcasm, or denial. In many ways I felt I was starting all over with Lou Thompson, massaging Raymond's ego in order to get to the issues that had overwhelmed Jake and the well-being of the Oh family. (I look to the name of choice, Ray Man=Raymond.) For the third meeting, I decided that I would focus my efforts through Allyson.

I had gestimated that Allyson was around five feet tall, wore her hair in a formal bun, and sat with an erect posture on the edge of the sofa that gave her an air of haughtiness, which she was not. Although every aspect of her attire spoke of high end purchases in chic stores that I only walk by with an ardent gaze, she was down to earth and practical, a good match for Raymond's verbosity. Allyson had attended universities in France and the United States and held a masters in economics from Duke. I am sure that Raymond and she held conversations in multiple languages concerning Samsung stock futures that were far beyond my grasp.

"Allyson," I pointedly began by addressing her and not Raymond as I had in the prior two meetings, "given that your twin sons have Korean names, how did you determine to change that expectation for Jake?"

Allyson's thoughtful pause gave way to Raymond's barging in with, "Jake does have a Korean name but, like ourselves, we choose not to use it."

I nodded and continued to look to Allyson for a response. After a few quiet moments she offered, "Goodness Laura, there were so many factors and, could you call me Ally, all my friends do?"

"Certainly and I could hardly imagine all of the family issues around naming," I enjoined. "How many years has it been since you left Korea?"

Again Raymond answered, "Seventeen years we have been settled in New England to be tortured by our season tickets to Red Sox games."

I bet Lou would like to make friends of the Ohs. Allyson added, "Jake was born here, at St. Mary's."

That surprised me. I asked, "What did you call him when you first held him?"

Ally laughed before admitting, "I had so many girl names, but I called him Bon-hwa."

Again, Raymond interceded, "I called him Jake, but Bon-hwa is his given Korean name."

"The name sounds warmly romantic. what does Bon-hwa mean?"

Allyson unfolded her arms from her lap. "In our language Bon-hwa means "glorious.""

Well, got them to go this far with some basic information rather that Raymond's flippant one liners, "So, how did you go from Bon-hwa to Jake?"

Allyson glanced at Raymond and stated, "I will take credit for the change...."

"I wished she had paid in cash."

I ignored Raymond's comment. "What prompted the change?"

I had come to respect Allyson as she, obviously, long ago in their early relationship, had seen through and accepted Raymond's façade of brashness and was confident in her own individuality.

She smiled and stated with a maternal sighing shrug, "The name had become so tiresome in the playgroups I attended with Jake's brothers to be forever explaining their names and meanings. Although our upper socioeconomic peers were "ever so open" to our sons participating in birthday and soccer events, their names were a continual hurdle. I saw us as being in America for the long term and did not want to continue with the name issue." Allyson hesitantly paused and went on. "I, we, were not sure that was the best decision."

Raymond sadly shook his head in agreement, "You should see the melee that occurs when we go back to the family in Seoul."

I proffered my therapeutic nod and acknowledged to myself that this might have been the first direct statement I had heard from Raymond in our three meetings. "What happens then?"

Before answering, Allyson placed a hand on Raymond's arm and looked at him in a manner that stated she would address the question. "This has been a very difficult area for us to reconcile or talk about as Jake is so......so.... reluctant to admit that he is Korean."

I noted that Raymond was beginning to perspire as he added, "Jake will not answer to or respect his Korean name. He will argue with the elders, which is forbidden, showing them no respect. He will only communicate in English, although he is fluent in Korean.

Allyson momentarily closed her eyes stating, "The family has come to the juncture of asking us not to bring Jake with us to Korea for our visits."

Raymond was not the number one Samsung Executive for New England due to limited cortical functioning, "Laura, not to change the subject, but, was not your question directed to how we determined to select the name of Jacob?" Raymond was putting a stop to my entering further into the Oh's personal issues, for the time being, and bringing us back to a topic in a safe area.

Allyson seemed to appreciate Raymond's intervention as she placed her hands back together on her lap and smiled, "the name was entirely Raymond's decision."

"You agreed."

"Of course husband of mine, because you are always correct.

Raymond beamed, "Jacob, Biblical of course, means "he who supplants."

I gave a perplexed look as I knew that in the Old Testament Jacob is considered the father of the Twelve Tribes of Israel, but "supplants?"

"Raymond," Allyson chastised, "you did not know that at the time."

Raymond feigned displeasure with the correction stating, "I find it so difficult to tell a good tale when Allyson is present, but she is correct, I actually named him Jacob because "Jacob's Ladder" was my favorite church hymn."

"Please Laura," Allyson begged, "Do not ask him to sing."

Raymond began the hymn in a stuttering high pitched discordance that brought to mind a sound that I had heard from somewhere else, then it came to me. Jake had the same high falsetto squeal! I sat back and smiled, looking forward to further sessions with the Ohs.

June 24   King Rudy

This was not happening.

"Power to the People!"

I was not the bad guy. I wore the white hat.

"Power to the Peeeeooopppplll!"

Off key. Good emotion. Why was I the target? I had never voted for Reagan. Then too, I had never voted for any Republican.

Closer they crept, "Power to the Peeeeeooopppplle!!"

I held these sixties words sacred. How else could I have graduated from Berkeley in the seventies without the groundwork? People's Park and The Movement were alive and well for me in the seventies. I continually thank them for all the Pass/Fail classes.

Now they broke into two groups. Left side chanting, "We're on Strike!"

Right side in unison, "We're going to SHUTITDOWN!!"

Back and forth. Over and over. Activity stopped around the immediate area as the crowd of on lookers grew larger. I watched in thunderstruck disorientation. Shutwhatdown? A gorgeous early summer day with high banked cumulus clouds wafting in from the Atlantic. Maybe some late thundershowers. In front and around me, twenty-five or so of our stalwart students were stalking in a circle with painted placards in front of the administrative office, which I had planned to enter. Why was I so lucky to walk into this? And where, in God's name, were the staff!?

I could make out Jake's high pitched voice ranting, "Real loud now so Lou can hear you. Remember people, Lou is audio-orally challenged!" Jake Oh was orchestrating, "Turn your hearing aide up Lou!"

Audio-orally? One funny guy, I was ten yards away.

Jake turned to his cohorts, "Keep your formation. Don't let administrative imperial powers intimidate you! We are The People!!"

Whose people? What people? The people? Them people? The Village People? Not my people. Your People? You're People? YO! PEOPLE!?

They chanted the historically cathartic slogan again. Jake choreographing.

"Power to the People!"

"Power to the Peeeoooppplle!"

Jake commanded, "SING IT STRONG!"

"Power to the Peeeeeooooppple!!

"We're on Strike!"

"We're going to SHUTITDOWN!!!!"

Somehow, in the mayhem of mongrel growling, I thought of one of the Cal Bear cheers, LSD! LSD! Look Sharp Defense!!

They were having one good time.

One of our students' most cherished staff, Cheryl, who had been with our program for six years, came up to me. She was wearing a homemade red hammer and sickle press badge on one shoulder and a peace sign on the other. I noticed the microphone attached to a recorder. As she stuck the mike in my face she rudely demanded, "Excuse me, and are you Mr. Lou Thompson?"

Not unless I had to be. I whispered to Cheryl, "Isn't the Red Menace history?" She replied grim faced, "Not at Valley Oak."

I closed my eyes, wishing this was a bad dream, "OK fine. Off the record and on the QT, this is cute but what's going on?"

"Just Civics in action," she smiled and gave me a wink. "Just go with it. They made all the staff promise not to tell. Jake's been planning this for weeks." Cheryl flipped her braided red locks as she turned towards the salivating group and barked, "C'mon over here and put some pressure on! Show'em what you got."

With that the circle halted, "Follow me! For Union Solidarity," Jake bellowed. With that the union menace formed a line headed towards me. Their song changed under Jake's hand signal to:

"You can't scare me I'm in the Union

I'm in the Union.

I'm in the Union.

You can't scare me, I'm in the Union

And

The Union, is just alright with me!"

Maybe we should have a school chorus. Glee club? Reality was coming back to imitate my classroom art. How many times had I demanded that my students sit and listen to some lyrical recitations of social historical import. Why had Ford worshipped Hitler? How many slaves were freed by the Emancipation Proclamation. Who was Saul Alinsky? Today we are reading excerpts from Norman Mailer's Why We Are in Vietnam. Forced these young emerging minds to listen to recorded speeches of FDR. Asked them to discern what political perspective the speeches were advocating. How all came down to power. Money. Power for whom? Who? Money from where? Where was Red's usufruct when I needed it?

The mob more shuffled than marched around Cheryl and me. Their placards read stuff like, "Down with King Lou."

"Lou means Lou-sey Wages." Jake must have thought that one up.

Another staff, Martin Hoak, came running up with the video recorder. Martin apologized to Cheryl, "Sorry for being late, the battery needed some more juice."

Martin gives me a patronizing smile, "Hi there Lou. How's it going?" I nod. I didn't like any of this.

Just this past week, Martin had been voted our Staff of the Year by his peers. Previous to that, he'd played ten years of cornerback in the Canadian Football League for the Calgary Roughriders. He'd been on two Grey Cup champions. Showed me a football with Warren Moon's signature on it that he had intercepted. Martin still held the Division Two High School single game and total career rushing records in New England.

Martin patted the camera, "Ready when you are Cheryl." Ready? Ready for what? What are they setting me up for.......?

Cheryl shares a conspiring grin with Martin, faces into the camera. "We are here, today, at the illustrious site of Valley Oak School with the owner, Mr. Lou Thompson, on a day fraught with agitated student rights expression."

Cheryl stoically looks on as Martin pans the multitude. Epitaphs resound from the surrounding student body. Cheryl turns to me as Martin pans us into the forefront, "Mr. Thompson. I am here with Mr. Lou Thompson. Mr. Thompson I know it is hard to get your thoughts together amidst this student havoc, but I need to ask you, as owner of Valley Oak, how do you explain the student unrest that has engulfed your program. Simply, what is going on? What do you understand to be the situation giving rise to this fervor? Our viewers would appreciate a direct response."

The strikers eased their "fervor" in order to hear the dialogue between Cheryl and myself. They edged in like ravenous vultures. Like snapping piranha. Like the Yankees in late September.

I squirmed, nothing like multiple choice journalistic ambushes. I tried to conjure up an appropriate response. Keep the presence of composure. Never give away the internal struggle. Don't let anyone in. Stolid. One of Red's first rules.

I looked directly into the camera and spoke clearly, confidently, "Cheryl," I knew from Psych 1A to lead with a personal name touch, "I truly cannot fathom the grounds for this protest of dissatisfaction as the Administration of Valley Oak is dedicated to discussing the stated concerns," With a "golly-gee" glance at the protestors, I continued, "We provide an enriched opportunity for student learning at Valley Oak where the expectations are front and foremost through the IEP process."

There, take that. My barrage of verbiage should quell the mass! However, I beheld Jake holding up a number one. All the strikers, acting as ONE, extended their palms biblically towards the heavens. Some were kneeling. Gandhi would have been proud of the supplicating throng. All were exhibiting appropriate body forms of dismay and anguish. Total eerie silence.

I continued presenting my perspective. My voice seeming to echo hollowly in the sudden quiet. "No one has met with Administration or even put forth a list of concerns." I looked around commandingly at the assemblage, doing my best Captain Ahab impersonation. "I am always prepared for a discussion of student needs." I added with determined vindication.

"Students know there is a sign up sheet next to Ms. Laura's office to speak their concerns. I always get with that student within that school day!" They knew I was available. No argument there.

Time to assert my authority, I place my hand over my heart, "Here I am, merely going about my duties, professionally addressing my responsibilities, when I am confronted," I pause for a dramatic denunciation, "I dare say accosted by this unruly mob of muckrakers making placard demands that have no grounds in reality."

Cheryl glowers at me, although I discern a twinkle and turns toward the strikers. "Is what Mr. Thompson says true? Have you not approached administration with your concerns?"

A vast taunt erupts from the union:

"All the time!"

"He never listens."

"Never responds!"

"He lies!"

"He's a capitalistic pig!"

"Dude only wants the cash for our attendance."

"He roots for the Yankees!"

Jake Oh steps, rather, lurches forward, proclaiming, "We have our grievances." Martin swings the camera over to Jake. Jake waves his handful of papers at the camera and hands me a sheet entitled Student List of Rightful Grievances Regarding the Mismanagement of the Valley Oak Administration.

I glance over the demands. Jake has talked with me in his personally oblique manner about a number of these concepts. Then too, Jake has questioned my attire as being inspired by an intimate personal relationship with Liberace.

Cheryl had kept me up to date on Jake's conniving and Martin had informed me that the anticipated event was occurring. I hear the ruckus outside my window and I watch as Lou verbally maneuvers through the discord. I am hopeful that Lou will be able to step back and accept how much this event and Lou, mean to Jake. Jake is choosing to verbally communicate his emotions in a positive manner rather than escalating to the point of snapping a willow stick and never coming home for dinner. I smile thinking of how, when Jake was just meeting up with Lou he had confronted him over his being an admirer of Liberace. No one, outside of my parents, would have the slightest insight into who Liberace was or what he stood for in his gaudy gay attire. Jake is reaching out to Lou, attempting to meet him in his own realm of non essential distorted references, a domain Lou has employed to shroud and deflect his own emotions and past history. A realm frequently inhabited by Jake's own father. I chuckle, to me, there were some chickens coming home to roost. I hoped that Lou was up to the challenge as the outcome of this seemingly meaningless charade could be critical to Jake's healing.

I shook my head at the list of demands. The list was comprised of true blue collar issues like:

1. Students may choose to have union representation.
   Where's Jimmy Hoffa when you need him?
2. Students may wear clothing as they deem appropriate. (Pants sagging; hats backward; explicit gang related/sexualized graphics & language; etc.)
   These guys never knew Rick Hutton.
3. Students will determine Earned Activity agenda.
   How far is Provincetown?
4. Students can bring in uncensored music of their choice to listen on vans and during breaks.
   Hey bro'. Su music, mi music.
5. Students' Workability Wage to be increased by 25% per year, retroactive to placement at Valley Oak, with a matching 401k from administration.
   Can I join?

6. Students can choose to be intimate, hold hands, touch, and have private unobserved times during the school day.
   We have eight females and forty-six males in our program. Are you ready to rumble, or, are you prepared to cross that human rights line? Conjugal visits anyone? Transgenders welcome!
7. Students can designate a smoking area.
   Several staff would appreciate that.
8. Students have the right to unrestricted use of the Internet.
   What? No Valley Oak Platinum VISA?
9. Students will choose the curriculum to be taught at Valley Oak.
   So, what is the IEP process?
10. Students have veto power with regard to staff hiring at Valley Oak.
    We'll form a union!

I'm glad they left their Bill of Rights at ten. Then too, Jake would probably get them to go after amendments. I scanned the mass of signed names at the bottom of the document, noting that Jake's thick scrawl would have done John Hancock proud.

In order to better voyeur and hear the dialogue, I completely open the sliding glass door from my office to the yard and it is all I can do not to burst out laughing. If Valley Oak ever put together a drama department, the surreal interaction presented the fodder for an epic comedy routine.

I raise my eyes from the document and inquire, "Is this all?"

Jake lumbers forward. He's shaped funny. Jake looks like he was made out of one of those books cut into thirds where you can choose to have a different head, torso, and legs for your character by flipping the pages. Jake has a huge, like gargantuan head with a mass of billowing black hair, which he blames on his Korean heritage. He always wet combs it in the morning. As the day evolves Jake's hair just got more disheveled and ended up looking like a dried out electrically charged mop. Sort of a Don King look. Maybe I should turn him on to some Dippity Doo. Then too, old school, "Brill Crème, a little dab will do ya." Jake's chest is tiny in comparison, with short arms sprouting out like emaciated tree limbs. The residential population had immediately given Jake the name of "Rex," as in Tyrannosaurus, because of the huge head and short arms and humongous legs. Not only were they long, they resembled uprooted tree trunks, like each must've weighed in over hundred pounds! When Jake was on the move, there was this mystic vibe that reverberated off of his presence, as you could sense, almost feel him coming across the school site before he came into view. Puddles quivered. Goats bleated. People would bolt for the safety of port-a-potties. (OK, a bit much.) Hilariously, the students would quiver and vibrate with laughter as he staggered past them. Jake was such an amiable target. Good thing there was no tail. Jake had size eighteen feet, second only to Thaddeus who'd checked in with a school record twenty-two. Jake was six foot five and still expanding. However, of all his physical idiosyncrasies, Jake's most challenging aspect was his total lack of gross motor integration. Jake bumped into things, knocked items off tables gripped walls for support. I have seen him turn around too quickly and fall backwards, wiping out six desks as he flayed for balance. Jake was a living breathing Tommy Boy. He was banned from the Valley Oak baseball team because he couldn't hold onto the bat when he swung. Admittedly, Jake was a force on the basketball court, once he gained position.

Though limited by his singular physical presentation, Jake was a very intuitively adroit verbal individual. Jake had tested out at an absurdly high IQ, which he seemed determined to employ to the misery of all staff, with special dedication to myself. In fact, at this precise moment, Jake was licking his six inch incisors to add this event to his reputation.

Jake approached me in a mock respectful manner with, "Please, Sir Lou, do not misinterpret or prejudge our intentions?"

How could I? I waited. Red had always counseled that one should determine the opponent before engaging.

"Your Highness."

I checked my watch to see what time it was getting to be.

"I mean Holiness."

I was no longer a Catholic.

"No disrespect."

Yeh, and I'm Pocahontas. I remained passive. Not responding to any of his platitudes. Jake would just give me some spin. Sooner or later he would get to the point.

"Your humble supplicants thank you for the audience."

I stood there, arms folded, awaiting the ritual of Jake's oral language dissertation when, from behind the barn, several students charged out with a bed sheet wrapped around sections of PVC pipe. There was only a slight breeze so that the students had to loosen their flag. All eyes were on the unfurling.

Cheryl nudged me, "You're going to love this."

"Yeh, I can hardly wait."

Jake held up two fingers and all the students started chanting, "Rudy.... Rudy......RUDY......RUDY!!!!"

I saw Rudy begrudgingly gather himself up in the shaded bed of the truck to answer the call.

With a brief gust from the breeze, the flag fluttered out. There, before me, was a twin bed sheet fully detailed drawing of Rudy. Rudy was seated on a kingly throne with a crown on his head. All the students faced The Flag of The Rudy Nation, humbly bowing to their waists. Cheryl was right, I had to love this!

Jake continued, "With the valued and honored insights of King Rudy, our savior, Your Esteemed Best Friend, we desire to make clear our resolute pursuit of having our rights honored and actualized." Jake formally saluted Rudy in the truck bed. "There are a few more basic premises to cover so you understand our full intent."

Jake gave his union buddies the two thumbs up, cleared his throat, teetered as if to topple, caught himself and regained his composure. He had a full set of choppers. Although they weren't six inches long, Rex fit him.

Jake intoned, "The main thrust is to fully communicate to you what will happen if our rightful grievances are not addressed."

This was taking longer than a Yankee ninth inning rally. I hoped Cheryl had all of this under control.

Jake continued, "Because, Sir Lou, if we do not get our needs met, we, The Knights of Rudy, are going to put you out of business!!"

The rebellion went crazy at this proclamation. They had been waiting, seething for this moment. Frenzied threatening promises bellowed from the multitude:

"We'll shut you down!"

"You're history!"

"Down for the count!"

"Toasted!"

"Get ready to sell hot dogs!"

They knew me far too well. Where was Top Dog of Berkeley when I needed it? (No offense Red.) Shouting, waving their placards, jumping up and down they extolled my demise. OK, Jake was in simulation mode of getting both feet off of the ground at the same time. Residential staff had now come out of their house to see what all the commotion was about:

"Lou loses!!"

"Hail King Rudy!

Someone shouted, "Look! Rudy's standing in the truck andwagging his tail!"

"He's totally with us!"

They began their chant of, "Rudy....Rudy.....RUDY...RUDY..!"

Anyway, good show. Done deal. Let's get on with it and put Valley Oak out of business. Send me to Fenway as a hot dog vendor. I caught Martin still swinging his camera around. He's filming all this for posterity!? What would they do? What could they do? Who knows? Not me for sure. I'm just the village idiot.

Should I put an end to this student nonsensical demonstration? Employ some Gestapo union busting tactics? Would I, could I, remain placid and process their manic force field of energy? What if some administrator from a referring school district drove up into this contorted melee? What if a parent happened to come through? What would they think? Are we a school or what? Who's in charge? I had already heard the concerns from some districts like, let's put the kids out to pasture at Valley Oak. I hear they have a great kite flying program. Just get them off our campus! What was today? Thursday? Was there ever just going to be any two days the same in this program? I doubted, not with students the like of Jake enrolled. Just working the angles, looking for the cracks as I remained stoic.

Raising his shrunken arms, Jake quieted the groups so that he could read from a prepared statement:

I pulled my chair up by the open sliding glass door to continue my observation, marveling at Lou's self-containment at the out of the ordinary student display. Lou's acquiescence and allowing of the students to express their needs without being redirected was remarkable given Lou's need to control issues. My ceaseless efforts in attempting to evolve Lou towards the framework of the Relationship Model were being actualized for me. I felt myself beaming like a proud parent.

Jake was beginning to work up a sweat, which didn't take much, as he quieted the crowd of onlookers, prostrated his anemic arms towards his audience, he began orating:

"If Valley Oak refuses to negotiate with us in good faith, we are prepared to go to the school districts that refer to Valley Oak and address our former student bodies."

Say what? Gain entrance to a mainstream program that has disbarred them?

"We're with you bro!"

"Right on Jake!"

"Clue the dude in!"

Jake scanned his audience. Other students from animal husbandry activities were walking up, staff included, wondering what the show was about.

Jake bellowed with articulation that would have done Teddy Roosevelt proud, if a bit squeaky. "The first goal will be to inform the students that they need to be successful in their classrooms," Jake paused, "We all know how to do that, am I right!?"

"Piece of cake!"

"No problemo!"

Jake was on a full throttle screech and yelled, "Give me an IEP objective Mark!"

Mark Sands bellowed out, "They need to have positive peer relationships!"

Jake held up his left arm and all students said in unison "ONE!"

"William, give us another!"

"Students must follow staff's first prompt!"

Again Jake held up his left arm with two fingers and the students belted out, "TWO!"

"Charlene, what next?" Demanded Jake.

Charlene hated school, which had, until this moment, included Valley Oak, cried out, "Be on task in the academic area!"

"THREE!"

"We need a staff in here for solidarity!" Jake pointed to Henry, one of our therapists. Was everyone with Jake? "Whataya got for us Henry"

Henry stepped forward and stated in a calm voice, "How about making socially appropriate decisions during unstructured time."

"FOUR!!!" Rang out across our yard.

I could now see where this was going, Jake and his sideways sense of humor. He could run any IEP I attended.

Jake motioned for quiet from his multitude exhorting, "With goals and supportive objectives such as these, all students will remain in public schools." Jake halted, enjoying the attention of his masses. "We, as the sacrificial lambs of Valley Oak, we will WILL them to remain in public school." Again pausing for dramatic impact. "We will take no prisoners." Jake held up his hand to correct himself," We will accept no referrals. We will have our day! We are the students! We are the future. We will be heard!!!"

Jake had his enthralled audience, his loose fitting palm embroidered Hawaiian shirt billowing out like a sail catching wind.

Jake ranted on, "With no referrals. No students." He smirked, haunching his shoulder. I thought of the T-Rex going after the jeep in Jurassic Park. "No students means no cash. No cash," Jake looked around triumphantly, "Means that there will be no Valley Oak. We will be free! FREE!! FREE AT LAST!"

"You tell him Jake!"

"You rock Sir Dudest!!"

"Sayonara Lou!"

I stood there mesmerized by Jake Yen, he did credit to ML King Jr. Did he think this up all by his lonesome? Cheryl and Martin stood by as passive reporters, trying not to play into Jake's good times. They had to be cracking up inside. This was outrageously funny. Put Valley Oak out of business by convincing students to be good? Preposterous. Outrageous. Who'd of thunk it Booboo? Too cool.

Martin bumped against me, paused with the video, "Quite a show, eh, Lou."

I had to agree, Cheryl added, "We tried to get a high school band to show up, but it was too hard to schedule."

Nodding, I added, "I'm surprised not to see some Masonic Shriners wheeling in on their zigzagging go carts."

Cheryl slapped her hands in frustration over not having thought of those speed demons.

Jake continued, "Fair warning is duly issued this twenty-fourth day of June, explicitly made, that we are supplying the Bay Tribune with the video tape documenting these events. We will make copies and send them to referring districts. Advocacy groups. Parent groups!! Jake stumbled back, kept his balance, caught a breath, then revved the crowd up by chanting. "No referrals! No referrals! No Referrals," Other students emptied out from all parts of the program and came into the mix. Without a clue they joined into the pandemonium.

"No referrals!"

"No referrals!!"

"No referrals!!"

Who said the sixties were dead? The entire school-residential programs were now clustered around the Flag of Rudy. Showing survival instinct, goats and cattle in bordering pastures sought further refuge in their barns from the disturbance.

I remained fixated to the chair in my office with the blinds pulled discreetly down, smiling to myself, being sure not to be caught glorying in such an unnatural event. Only at Valley Oak. Where to now Sir Lou?

I stood there, quietly just going with Jake. This was not my usual M.O. Enough would be enough. The mutiny would run its course. Maybe I was maturing! Molting? I simply was not going to add fuel to the fray. I was going to avoid being caught up in the verbal onslaught. Where would Jake go with this now? His crowd could not maintain the high pitched feeding frenzy for much longer.

The call was on Jake, his followers wanted results. Changes. Action. A disruptive protest to the forces of the imperial control of the Death Star Administration was simply the first step. I could just visualize them having a sit-in at our administrative office! Refusing to go home! Where was the tear gas?

Then too, ringing the lunch bell might even be more powerful.

For a moment, the raucous multitude, had to be seventy or so of them, were perched, undecided. The mood was shifting. Then, Jake took charge, claiming the momentum by declaring. "TO HONOR KING RUDY! FORWARD! To the truck!!"

With the unfurled, as the afternoon wind was picking up, King Rudy Banner leading the way, the student demonstrators gathered around Rudy in the truck, chanting Rudy's name. Rudy responded by attempting to douse several faces with his tongue. They might have stayed there all day if Jack had not started smacking the clanging lunch bell with all his strength.

With high fives and Rudy hugs, amidst laughter, the victorious dissidents dispersed for lunch.

I looked over at Cheryl and Martin, this had just been bizarre. Martin slapped my shoulder, "Pretty cool. Reminds me of winning the Grey Cup!" I remained a bit out of body blown away. "How long have you been planning this?"

"Jake came up to us about three weeks ago."

I didn't have the nerve to ask what tomorrow might bring.

June 25   Jumping Jack Flash

"Hey JK."

"Take a stump Lou."

We were meeting in the residential house for our weekly get together to review program and plan.

"That was quite an event Jake staged."

I eyed JK, "And you had no idea it was coming?"

JK gave me a look of amazed incredulity, "Lou, good buddy, would I hang you out to dry like that?"

"Just felt some breeze is all."

JK changed the subject. "Laura on the way?"

"She sends regrets." I sat perched on the faded yellow topped chrome edged table that had to be out of the fifties.

"Can't take the heat of the two of us?"

"Hell JK, we both know she can trash talk us without our having a clue."

290

"Amen to that." JK got serious. "Personally I'm glad for this moment." He looked edgy. "You know you've been ducking me on this Legend History.

I knew I had, just wasn't an area that I felt like going back into. Yeh, Red had let me know I needed to move past that time. He had teed me up for JK. JK deserved an honest answer, maybe my buddies did too. I was getting a bit long in the tooth to be such a mystery. I needed to take on my fear and get past the pain. Then too, what did I fear? I grimaced. I shifted on the table, time to own up. I looked directly at JK to let him know I was talking for real, "OK JK. Here goes ....but this is the first time I've ever talked about my past, with anyone but Red"

JK sat back, "You've gotta be kidding."

"Scouts honor."

"No way."

"Just felt life was better to leave things where they were."

"Well, barbecue and hot sauce me, Lou," JK gushed, "The name Jack Reynolds as in The Legend! It's just so unreal that it's you I'm sitting across from." He laughed, "If it wasn't for Red I'd have to say you were just fanning my engines."

"Wish I was."

JK couldn't stand still, started pacing back and forth. "The Legend of Jack Reynolds holds such sway in the area, even after twenty-five years from Founders. Just how the hell do you fit into the mix?"

JK was so excited that he swore, which he never did and grabbed a basketball off of the couch, tossing it to me with the demand, "Proof. I need some proof!" He placed his strong hand on my shoulder laughing.

"I know you're White, but this White Legend thing needs validation, even at your ripe age. Let me see that behind the back one finger spinning transfer that Red was telling me about or are you going to whimp out with an age thing?"

I was glad that I was letting go with JK. He was a good guy and had his own history with round ball and tough times. Squared away with a reality based sense of humor that wouldn't take my words into the melodramatic. I knew too he would keep to himself until I was ready.

JK prodded me, "Tell me Lou or should I call you Jumpin' Jack Flash?"

Those moments came flooding back to me in a rush. Power Memorial of New York. Kareem was Lou Alcindor at Power. Home and home games. Red had scoured the country and parts of Europe to bring Founders a nationally ranked team for my senior year. Spider had been gone for two years. We now had more talent, two deep at every position. I was the centerpiece. Jumping Jack Flash, JJR. The White Legend to be coroneted. My senior year scholarships were clogging the mail box. Jack Reynolds could fly and deliver.

Red was his calm self. "Lindsey," Red pointed to our off guard, "I want a back screen from you on their two guard."

Lindsey breathlessly nodded. We were about out of gas.

"Tiptop," who had taken over for Spider in the middle, "With the back screen set I want you out to the right elbow. They won't be ready for you to come so far out."

"Got it Red."

"Luke, you break off Tiptop and get the inbound from Jack."

Everyone was nodding. This was the ball game. Our last shot. We were down one. Ball in our court with six seconds on the clock. We had taken Power when they had come up to our home Founder's Court. Power and their six thousand five hundred and ninety-three standing room only fans wanted to even the record.

"Jack, break by Lindsey, fake towards Tiptop, and Luke will hit you at the top of the key." Red looked into me. "Gotta take the rock to the hole. Flush or get fouled, either way we win."

Red put his hand out in the middle of the huddle. Twelve players did the same. "TEAM!" We responded. "FOUNDERS!!." And broke huddle.

"Tiptop," Red motioned. "After Jack fakes to you, crash the board for the follow."

"Got it."

The crowd was standing and rocking. I lived for these moments. They had been good to me. Such a rush as I took the ball from the ref and two hand slapped to start the play. Lindsey with the back screen. Tiptop to the right elbow. Power in a bit of confusion as Tiptop left the basket with Luke breaking off Tiptop for the inbound. I bounce pass in and charge at Lindsey, spin and take two hard steps towards Tiptop. Back peddle to the top of the key. Luke's pass is waiting for me. I look up. Four seconds.

Shoulder down one dribble to the foul line. Tuck the ball like a fullback into the line. Hands swatting me. I lift up, rising towards the hoop. The crowd is gone. Me and the hoop. Players are a whirl of color. I glance towards a breaking Tiptop.

Power players are momentarily caught between the screens. Tiptop's crashing the boards just not enough to draw attention. Power knew to come at me. Their two, six-eight forwards and hulking sumo wrestler center converge as I rise with both hands above my head for the flush. I recall cameras flashing as I continue to surge.

I came back to JK, "Jumping Jack got stuffed back into the box against Power Memorial.

JK nodded sympathetically, "I heard that four vertebrate were compressed. Issues with spinal fluid."

"I was lucky my spinal cord stayed intact."

JK knew the pain as he'd rehabbed from injuries. Mine was career, ultimately almost life ending. Years before I could allow myself to be involved in a pick up game and risk any physical contact.

JK persisted, "But where did Lou Thompson come from? What happened to Jack Reynolds?"

"He disappeared. Evaporated," I shrugged. "Things happen."

JK wanted more, "That's the Leg....."

"Lou," the walkie crackled with intensity.

I pulled the walkie off of my belt, pushed the button, "Lou here."

"You're needed by the bridge."

"Be right there."

JK nodded with awareness, "Saved by the walkie."

"For the moment," I acknowledged. "But we'll pick the history up again."

"That we will Jumpin' Jack"

Damn, I still liked the sound of that name. I held the basketball that JK had challengingly, guard to guard, tossed me. I spun the challenge on a single finger, passed behind my back to the index of my left, no look flipped to JK as I headed out the door.

The White Legend was alive and well!

August 3   Moments of Fantasy

I was in the shed with Rudolph and Prancer, our two goats, checking on their feed and water. Their coats had been recently brushed. I was pleased to see that all was up to snuff as they distinctly ignored my presence. Our Animal Husbandry program was a success much in part to the Workability grant. Workability, how long had I striven to bring an offering such as this to the students? The state was now back into a vocation frame of mind and Valley Oak had been awarded, through Laura's fine writing, a Workability Grant of fifty-two thousand dollars. With this grant we were able to purchase curriculum that reinforced the students' hands on experiences. More over, pay them a minimum wage for work performed.

The model that we had developed involved students at the age of sixteen qualifying to work on-site in a variety of capacities such as: culinary arts, landscape management, vehicle maintenance, peer teaching, light construction, secretarial skills and other like activities. In these various jobs the students earned real cash, paid out every two weeks in the form of a check, from the State of Massachusetts.

Supporting our hands on experience was the academic class where the students organized their portfolio, through a variety of curriculum offerings. They furthered their language and computational skills in a marketable area of interest. In the student portfolio they had their: Social Security Number, School ID Picture, résumé, letters of recommendation, birth certificate, transcripts and other data that might be pertinent for a job application.

In class, they surveyed the internet for employment opportunities, networked with other students seeking like positions, began to accept more of their age appropriate social responsibilities.

When the portfolio information was compiled and the student had been successful in on-site work participation, Valley Oak sought off-site employment. Placements had been made at large stores such as: Wal-Mart, Target, Les Schwab Auto. We had learned that these larger operations actually had specific staff assigned to monitor our transitioning special needs students. At other sites, such as local lumber yards, bowling alleys, hair salons, Valley Oak had designated a staff job coach at the outset of their work assignments. As soon as the employer, coach, and student were confident that there would be success, Valley Oak would gradually diminish the job coaching role toward total student self-direction, just as we were doing with the public schools.

I was extremely proud of the Workability aspect of Valley Oak. Something like seventy-five percent (According to Laura) of students who had been placed had been hired at their work site. I never thought that our students' work ethic would prove out.

There was just something about landing a job that filled our kids with pride. Being able to get away from the school site and be on your own and meet the general public with the social awareness necessary to be successful. Move on towards Your Future. Using skills that no one gave you any credit for having developed. Strange stuff that you might not brag about like: Getting all the baskets in from the parking lot without banging a car, know the heavy items go to the bottom of the bag, keeping the plants nurtured in the garden section without over watering, carrying your own walkie, wearing a store vest with a badge that has your name. Just being able to impact your life in a manner that will further your own self-determination.

Like Workability wasn't enough, Valley Oak also participated in ROP (Regional Occupational Program) placements. Again, our sixteen year old students could earn the right to attend off site programs in a variety of fields ranging from cosmetology to welding. In fact, welding was the most popular with our students as, after six to eight weeks, they could earn a Journeyman's Certificate and qualify for work with pay ranging from twenty-two to thirty thousand dollars per year. We provided transportation to the ROP training sites. When the students earned their certificates, Valley Oak convened an IEP with the school district to determine an appropriate work/education program.

For the moment, Valley Oak was at peace. I decided to go out to the Animal Husbandry Shed, which welcomed me in with a quiet serenity. All the animals were out and about in the fields except Rudolph and Prancer. I leaned out on an open window taking in the student activities. As an afternoon shower came thundering in, I caught sight of Lou jogging towards his pick up. At such times I have allowed my mind to wander. I imagined Lou thinking......

.......the afternoon brought gusts of wind. Good pitcher's day at Fenway. I could hear distant rumbling of far off thunder. I looked out of the shed to see a darkened wall rapidly approaching. I had always enjoyed these summer cloud bursts, unless they rained on a Sox game. I decided to hang out in the shed as this one came in. The rattling of rain on the tin roof was a rhythm I enjoyed.

The rolling percussions were spooking Rudolph and Prancer out of their doldrums. Dawned on me that Rudy would be trying to climb inside the cab as he turned frantic at these Zeusian invasions. I turned to head out of the shed and rescue him when Laura stopped me in my tracks.

This is out and out crazy, but I am not going to stop now. I had seen Lou enter the shed and now was as good a time as ever.

I confidently approached him, "Hey Lou, did not mean to startle you." You might have thought that I was a Yankee by his look. "Where is the rush?"

Another flash of light, Lou held up his hand to me and counted to seven before the thunder cam in. Seven thousand feet or so and closing.

"I was going to save Rudy, he gets freaked out by lightening storms." I could smell the rain approaching. "I need to get him into the cab before he tears out the rear window."

How many times had Rudy come between us? This time I meant to see myself through. "I will walk with you."

Lou checked my shoes. "Good thing you don't have heels, because we're going to have to hustle."

Lou was in such a rush that it was all I could do to keep up as he opened the cab, jerked the rear window back, and Rudy, wide eyed and beginning to froth at the mouth, dove into the protection of the rear seat. Without asking permission I opened the passenger door and climbed in as heavy warm drops landed on me and began to splatter on the windshield. I sat a bit breathless as Lou turned to calm Rudy. Alone with Lou Thompson, sans Rudy, in his truck as a summer thundershower comes in upon us. The day dimmed gray as the thunder storm shadowed the sun. I must be in a day time dream soap opera. The girls would just howl. What would Sharon Moreno do?

I got Rudy quieted. Suddenly remembered that Laura was there? In the passenger seat! How did I end up with her in the truck? I managed, "Give you a lift?"

I could feel Lou begin to close down, just like he always did when we were together and personal thoughts might be shared. He started the engine but, before he could get the gear out of park, I reached over and pulled the keys from the ignition.

"What the hell are you doing Laura?" That got his attention!

I was asking myself the same question as I placed the keys in my shirt pocket. Where was I willing to take this moment? "Lou, the two of us need to talk and this is as good a time and place as any." I did not have the slightest clue as to what I was going to say!

Where is this woman coming from? This must be important. What have I missed lately? She's always ahead of me even when I think she's not. Look at her. I've never seen such a determined manner from Laura, not even when she is calling me down for my physical restraints. Something must have come down bad. Maybe she's had another job offer and is going to take it. I sigh, look out the windshield at the torrent coming down on my pickup, "OK Laura, you've got the keys, what's up?"

I coiled back stiffly against the passenger door and looked to Rudy for support before I uttered the impossible. I knew I had to be blunt so that he could not evade the directness. I straightened my shoulders for a life altering statement.............."Lou, I am in love with you..........." There, said the words. I felt myself trembling. My God, look at him just sit there like I had hit him with a baseball bat!

What? What did she just say? I don't believe what I just heard. Can't be! Laura's sitting in my truck telling me, she's in love with me? Crazy. Surreal. Kinda cool though. Gotta get a grip. "Look, Laura...."

I interrupt, "I am not going to deny what I just said, but I must state that there are some minor reservations."

Bingo. Knew it. What's the catch? I kept it light, "Therapeutic ones I suppose."

"Not really, just...."

"Look Laura," I broke in as I had held this conversation in fantasy moments with my mind wandering about Laura. Sometimes we would drift into a frenzied passion. Others, I took a deep breath,

"Laura, you just boggle my mind." She started to interrupt. "Now let me finish." Need to keep this situation in check.

"If there would be one dumb, stupid, insipid act that could derail the success of Valley Oak, numero uno would be for you and I to become involved."

Thou doth protest too much, "Lou, have I ever shared with you what a lousy liar you are?"

I looked out the window as the sheets of rain fell across the yard, small streams forming, "Innumerable times."

"Besides, your lip is quivering." I leaned over and kissed him on the cheek and nestled against his rain splattered damp shoulder. I continued in a, what I thought to be, a soft, conspiring tone, "One of my reservations is that I would like us…….. to take us slow."

I grumbled, "You mean no sexual pandemonium in front of Rudy with the truck rocking like a storm tossed raft at sea?"

Flirtingly I flicked his ear, "Well, now that you mention it," I was thinking that we could start with dinner?"

Lou turned and damply engulfed me in his arm, asking, "Tonight, courtesy of Valley Oak?"

"I accept."

"Pick you up around seven?"

"Sure. Next, you can take me to a Red Sox game with your buddies."

I looked at Laura, that would be a bit of a step. "You sure you can handle them?"

I snuggled further in, "Lou, I DO have five brothers."

I felt Rudy's breath on the back of my neck preparing for a tongue lick as the rain pelted harder. With the wind buffeting I…

"Ms. Laura! Come quick!

I whirled around, scraping my arm on the rough wood of the shed, jolting back to reality.

"Jesse's got a knife and he's says he's gonna kill everybody!!"

I lurched towards the door, not giving myself time to regret the end of my, to be continued, fantasy daydream.

August 15

Students, such as Jake, were not relegated to the realm of outlandish student protest to have their grandiosity needs fulfilled. The school day was their stage with an academic format offering a continuous contained audience and, Lou, for his part, had developed several innovative offerings that only added fuel to the students' grandiose synergy. My personal favorite was Mr. Peepers Jeopardy.

"Ladies and gentlemen." I scanned the contestants. "Boys and girls of all ages. You are welcomed to the longest running game show in the history of daytime television. Back," I pause to add to the suspense, although they all know what's coming, "for the thirty-second consecutive year of uninterrupted telecast. Welcome to MR. PEEPERS JEOPARDY!!!!!!!!"

I promenaded in front of the class. Such an honor is rarely bestowed on a demised rodent. Rick Hutton would have been proud. This was our students' favorite academic "challenge."

I geared the anticipation up, "Our first contestant hails from the de Vries diamond mines of South Africa, heir to over three hundred billion dollars in rare, sought after, gems. Foe of apartheid, an advocate of peace, justice and the democratic way, I give you Mr. Tony Furlow!"

Tony stands up, holds his hands over head and dances around like a prize fighter. Everyone applauds. Everyone likes him. Tony pump shakes my hand grateful for the notoriety. There are not many Black billionaires in South Africa.

I turn to focus on Jeff Fields. Meticulous. Well groomed. OCD. Jeff is into computers. I begin, "We have with us today, back by popular demand, for his third rite of passage trial with Mr. Peepers Jeopardy. That impervious chip off the old block, that impressive cyclone of modern wizard circuitry. Holding the patent to the only "Jeff 4QZ: chip in mass production on five continents, I give you the man who is synonymous with Silicon Valley success, Mr. Jeff "QZ" Fields.!!!!"

Jeff is an extremely self-conscious inwardly-focused, detached student who once brought his father's thirty-eight caliber to school for protection. (Not the best decision.) Jeff gradually stands, pulls himself partially erect and nods awareness with a soft smile to the warm reception from the other students.

In Mr. Peepers Jeopardy everyone pulls for one another. They demand each team member to be strong, to be counted on to win and, especially, to dominate and vanquish me. Personal agendas and petty feuds are put on hold. Them against me. Evil vs. Good. Total war, on a cerebral note. Nothing personal. I continue on.

I search the multitude. There are only seven students, for my next coronation. I pontificate, "From Cadiz, Spain, where the Atlantic refuses the Mediterranean at the Rock that is Gibraltar." I survey the room. All seven students are at enthralled attention as none was sure who was going to be next. I anointed Jane Radnisch with my next recognition.

"Currently, with over thirty-thousand acres of vineyards on the Iberian Peninsula producing the finest wine in Europe, a fleet of seventy-two cargo ships, oil rights in South America from the time of the Incas. For God, Gold, and Glory! Mr. Peepers Jeopardy welcomes that Daughter of a Conquistador, Jane Radnisch!!!!"

Fists began flailing as the students became rabid with tremendous unbridled enthusiasm. I was going to have to tone the energy down a bit. I know I got as much from Mr. Peepers as the students did, then too, maybe more.

I took a breath. Jake Oh would be next. I took my time, began slowly, "Our next contestant is not an individual bound by monetary reward or multitude adulation" I took on a somber demeanor. "From the pure headwaters of the sacred Ganges, he has sacrificed his family fortune for the sake of humanity, devoted himself to curing the incurable, food for the famished, hope for the multitude of miserable. He has accepted the gauntlet as a personal challenge to eradicate the Earth of plague, pestilence, famine, and report cards" I give a moment of sacred pause. "True, his noble effort has cost him the love and joy of the woman he was once betrothed to, yet, he carries on. I give you that hallowed man who transcends our time. He who walks where none have trod. That icon for all that we are or hope to be. The modern Siddhartha…Jake Oh!!!!"

Jake bows deeply in full acceptance. Quiet applause acknowledges his worth. They need his points to win. Jake cups high right fist with his left hand. A man of pure mystic peace.

I introduce the next three students in like fashion with each having their own persona. Each is made the lord of a domain that they cherish.

Might be motorcycles, could be painting, might be rap. Whatever realm, they participate in Mr. Peepers Jeopardy with a rich and famous flourish.

My current contestants were from one of the Workability classes. I had seven students in front of me for the current academic portion of their program. The subject could have been Language Arts of History as it didn't matter. The key to Mr. Peepers Jeopardy was to immerse the student in the product. To hook in the perspective mark.

On a grandiosity level, I thought that I may have missed my calling along the neon lights of the summer carnival tour. Hawking in those gullible hay seed farmers or bored suburbanites to witness Lester, The Two Headed Ukrainian Dragon. Capable of belching fire and eating whole pigs alive!! Chained to his left arm was the mesmerizing Kisha, abducted from her... Sometimes I just can't stop myself. I turned back to the board.

"Our categories today are: Want Ads, Salary, Transportation." I pause, and what, pray tell, is the endeared reverent name of this esteemed challenge.?"

With that, all the students chant in guttural voiced unison, "Mr. Peepers!"

I draw out the moment, slowly walking towards the back of the room. "Mr. Martin Hoak, could you please show our viewers and audience what our contestants are vying for?"

"Sure Lou." Martin reaches into the bottom of his base voice and imparts, "Today's contestants gain the flavor of Equatorial Zanzibar with a gallon of New England's own Ben and Jerry's Chunkie Monkey Ice Cream!"

Smug confidence oozes from all seven students. They eye each other conspiratorially awaiting the contest and are unnervingly quiet. They understand that inappropriate comments and escalations will cost them points and possible disqualification.

"Chunky Monkey," Martin beams with his benign smile, stroking the gallon container, "Nice and cold on a hot summer day."

"Thanks Martin." I approach, then suddenly turn away from the contestants. "Pardon me Martin."

"Yes Lou?" Martin knows the playbook.

"Have you discussed what befalls our contestants should they not reign victorious?"

Martin eyes the students with his mean grimace, "Let me remind them." Martin strokes his goatee, "First off, the losing team will clean the livestock pens.............."

"Anything else?"

Martin ponders, "Why yes Lou. As I recall, Staff receives two gallons of Chunky Monkey!"

A throttled groan is emitted by the students.

"Gag me with a spoon!"

"I'll root for the Yankees!"

Martin holds up his hand and asks, "Do our contestants as yet have a name?"

It's Jake's turn to be captain. The captain chooses the name his team will contend under.

I turn and look to him, "Captain?"

Jake clears his throat and rocks back and forth for drama. Coughs, states, "Capering Cadavers."

"Bad choice. "Strike one Jake. Keep it positive and alive." I put a K on the board.

Jake and his team are fully aware that to get a second strike will mean that I will choose their name. They do not want their team to be called Lilies of the Field...

"C'mon Jake."

"Stop foolin' 'round dude."

Jake mutters, "OKOK." He kneads his eyebrows and evilly arches them, "We shall wage conflict under the banner of the most famous group of our era, Metallica!" The students start to sing Enter Sandman. I cut them off.

"That'll do for now Jake. In fact, if you win, you can serenade staff with your song." Now I needed to come up with an appropriate antidote for Metallica. A nemesis. Today's teams are Metallica and, I am drawing a blank. What should I be?? I place my hands on my hips for deep concentration and I decide.

"The Boston Pops!!" I always wanted to be Arthur Fielder

"So be it." Martin writes Boston Pops vs. Metallica on the white board as he's the official scorekeeper.

302

The board is dry erase and a colorful grid has been assembled resembling that of Jeopardy. There are the five vertical columns headlined with Want Ads-Salary-Transportation- Mr. Peepers-Jobs. There are four squares below each title for a total of twenty questions. The tough part, for me, is playing Alex Trebeck and having to come up with the questions. Alex just has to read his questions. However, in the Valley Oak Jeopardy Game Format, I had to think them up on the spot. Not only on the spot but they needed to be garnished with humorous insightful interest at an appropriate "Goldilocks" level for each student. I always wanted to be Jerry Seinfeld.

I watched from the connecting hall as Lou wove his Jeopardy Spell and I thought about some of the teachers I had endured. I had always felt that many teachers were about control with the students needing them to be seated, raising their hands appropriately, saying please and thank you. I firmly held that teachers often lacked the concern to ask the student how they felt about the classroom expectations. Do your work. Earn your grades. Get a diploma. How often did teachers delve into the psyche of the student to gain their opinion or have interest in asking how they feel about what they are doing? How are things going? What do you think about? Admittedly, not all teachers were the banal creatures I was forced to learn the three "r's" from and, not surprisingly, the teachers that were able to establish a relationship were the ones you remembered. They were the ones who did not put their personal needs first, but looked to what was going on for the student.

As a therapist, I found the task rather easy to present how others might improve their functioning for I can certainly get into telling teachers how to teach. With Lou, it was different as his conviction of putting the student first had led me to accept his job offer. I no longer held that he was just full of the need to control as Lou's issues were more layered, which was why, the previous week, I had asked him to join the Ohs and myself for a therapy session.

There was a soft knock at my door as Lou entered. "Lou, you have met Raymond and Allyson Oh."

"Sure, good to see you both." Lou shook hands with Raymond and nodded differentially to Allyson. He took a seat off to the side.

"Lou, come on in and join the party."

Grudgingly he scooted his seat in. He looked about as comfortable as a Yankee fan in Fenway's right field bleachers.

Bringing Lou, even with all our preparation, was a bit dicey, but I was expecting him to stay only long enough to give testimony to the use of sarcasm in communication and its impact on Jake.

I turned to him and, although we had discussed the direction and hopeful outcome of his participation, I could not be sure where Lou would go. "Lou, the floor is yours."

I knew the Ohs. They were bright, prosperous people who knew BS when it comes their way. I know how Laura wants me to come on. I just need to be direct. I began,

"Straight up, there's nothing Jake would like more than to come home."

Raymond feigned shock and immediately fumed, "Right, which is why we should be honored that he eggs our car when we are having sessions with Laura."

Just a bit of anger. This is not going to be easy. I try again, "What I'm saying, which may sound weird, is that Jake is looking for a way to connect with you. He wants you to know he's here and.........."

Raymond interrupted, "Which is why he tells us he has more success here than he has ever had in his life." He took Allyson's hand. "Jake states that people respect him here and that he wants to graduate from Valley Oak. When he turns eighteen he will make his own life in America, without us."

Allyson, with all her stoicism, was beginning to weep and I reached over and handed her a box of tissue. My decision to bring Lou into the session was proving to be a disastrous miscalculation as the Oh's emotions were so raw and Lou was being brutally, from their point of view, blunt. No matter that Lou was attempting to explain Jake's desire to reunite.

I could see the dialogue was going to be between Raymond and me. Too much emotion for Allyson. I plunged ahead trying to reason, "Jake is doing just what adolescents do at his age. This is his way of moving away from you as he heads toward adulthood."

"Not for a Korean son of mine," Raymond spat out.

Whoa boy. In less than a minute I knew why Jake had to get his own space. "Raymond, trust me, no kid anywhere would rather spend their lives in a place like Founders than in their own home."

Raymond had processed enough. He had accepted Laura's role, but he was done with me. He put on his CEO tone. "With all due respect Lou, how would you know?"

Right, how would I know? I waited a moment before replying, trying to convince myself that what I was about to disclose was going to be OK, I took a deep breath. OK Red, here goes,

"Raymond, Allyson," I look at them, ignoring Laura, "I know what is going on for Jake because I lived at Founders for six years after my parents were killed in an automobile accident. I was twelve at the time of their deaths" I stopped there, creating a stunned silence.

I didn't see any purpose in going into how I was adopted by them, as an infant, from Founders. I glanced over at Laura. Her eyes were wide with startled wonder at the information. I could not concern myself with her reaction.

Raymond's demeanor immediately softened. He genuinely responded, "Lou, my, our sincere condolences. I cannot fathom what a difficult time that was for you."

"Thank you, Raymond, but our discussion is not about me. What I am trying to share with you is that, given my experiences, Jake is desperately desiring to find a way back into your family's good graces, to regain your respect while maintaining his own.

I was flabbergasted, shocked, by Lou's revelation of a youth spent at Founders. No brothers or sisters? No family? What had I yet to learn about this man? I knew I needed to refocus to the Ohs but I could feel my therapeutic skills dissolving.

Allyson straightened her shoulders and entered the conversation saying to Raymond, "So much of the anger and frustration is between Jake and yourself. Raymond, we, must find a way to heal the wound"

Raymond sorrowfully put his head into both of his hands. Allyson soothingly stroked his graying hair. I could see that Laura was still processing my block buster info. I needed to take hold of the session and move the dialogue forward to Jake. Maybe I should have been a therapist.

"Here's what I suggest." Hope this wasn't too off the wall. "If it's alright with Allyson and yourself, I'd like to go over to residence and get Jake. This might be a good time to take a first step towards the healing."

Raymond lifted his head up and gave me his full attention. "Will he come over?"

"I'm sure he will and I know you didn't ask but what I believe would be important is that you let Jake know that you miss him and that you want him to return home as soon as possible." Nothing like telling a CEO what to do, like I was all knowing.

I turned to Allyson who was expectant, though somber, at the direction of events, "Like you said, I believe this is between Raymond and Jake. Jake needs to hear this from Raymond." Quite a speech. "What do you think Laura?"

I was feeling totally incompetent as Lou had taken over the entire session due to my dysfunctional reaction to his mind blowing revelation.

The three of them simply nodded. "OK, I'll walk over and get Jake." Raymond slowly stood, "Lou, I would like to walk over with you."

As we walked across the yard to the residential house, Raymond stopped me, "Lou, however my relationship with Jake develops, I want to let you know how much Allyson and I are thankful for Valley Oak and Founders."

We shook hands as Jake, with the school day over and vigilant about his parents being on site, came out of the residential house to meet us. I turned to leave…

"Lou," Jake called, "I would appreciate it if you could stay with my father and I."

I glanced at Raymond, who gave his approval. "No problem," I responded hoping there would not be one.

Jake and Raymond stood facing one another. Jake's bulk seemed to drape over his father. Finally, Raymond broke the silence, "Jake, I want to tell you how much I have learned since you have been gone. How much….."

"Jake interrupted, "Fuck you and your money."

Raymond continued, "In the past I would have made some joke out of what you just said, now, I want to tell you how sorry and concerned I am that our relationship has reached this point."

Jake was not letting up, "What's this sorry shit about? You've never been sorry for any of your all mighty spewing bullshit. Afraid I'll egg your Lexus? Ruin the paint job?"

Raymond straightens his shoulders, looked directly at Jake, and through moistening eyes said, "Jake, I love you."

Jake rolled his eyes skyward, "Right, you love your fucking CEO self image."

If Raymond was rocked, he wasn't letting on. "I agree Jake. That has been my world and I have been wrong. I need ..."

Again Jake interrupted. Not in a loud angry voice, though condescending, "So Laura and Lou have gotten through to you? Made you look in the mirror and see the error of your ways? Made you come over here to tell me that you love me?" Jake scoffed, "Love has never been a traded commodity in our family."

I decided to give Raymond some support, "Jake, your father asked to come over with me and meet with you."

"Well rootie toot toot." Jake was quoting one of my more childish responses. I had to learn to leave these epitaphs in the past and not model them for the students.

"Jake," Raymond implored, "Lou, especially today, has helped me to see how much I need to work on. How much I need to look at myself for the issues that are between us."

Jake smiled at me, "Yeh, Lou and Rudy are OK."

Raymond boldly stepped closer to Jake, reached his arm up to Jake's shoulder, and pressed his forehead against him. "Jake, I want to be OK with you too. I want that more than anything else. I will need your help getting there. I need you back in your home with your family, with me."

Raymond's physical touch and words knocked Jake back. Jake was not prepared for his father presenting such a vulnerable, needy side. Raymond's physical contact had never been part of their relationship. Jake had only been touched by the whipping rod. Raymond stood there, his head in Jake's chest, trembling, for several moments.

Jake gently rubbed Raymond's shoulders, "If I come back, can I beat my brothers with the willow switch?"

In the past, I might have supported saying something like that. But, before Raymond might have answered in kind with sarcastic insight, I jumped in. "Hold it Jake. Not only you, but people, maybe more so guys like us, have got to stop the one-liners. We need to say what we feel in straight ahead language." I looked to both Jake and Raymond. "This is not easy for any of us who have made a life living in a sarcastic state." I looked from one to the other. "Time to get real. Right?"

As they both nodded I said, "Let's try this again."

Jake, gotta love him, reached out to his father, in his squeaky but sincere voice, "There's nothing more that I want than to come home. To come back into our family." Jake bent down and the two hugged.

Raymond laughed, "Am I too flip to say real men can hug."

"Not at all," as I made it a threesome.

Jake wiped his eyes. "Hey Dad, want to come into residence and I'll show you around, meet some of the staff."

"Sure, let's go."

Time for me to split. "Don't mind my begging off, I've seen it before."

"Tell Allyson, we will be over in a few."

I watched, with admitted envy, as the father and son walked, maybe lurched due to Jake's motor skills, arm in arm to the residence.

That cathartic event took place six weeks ago, Jake was now able to spend sleep overs at home and the visits were going so well that JK felt he would soon return home full time. I turned back to Lou and the Mr. Peepers Jeopardy game show.

The team captain always went first as I began my introduction. "Our first contestant representing Metallica is that man for all seasons. A faith healer of cosmic proportions. A person who sees a stick with one end, the indomitable JAKE OH! Jake, choose your topic."

Without hesitation, "Vanna, I'll take Transportation for five hundred."

Not only the wrong game show but still funny with good timing. "Jake, care to try again, appropriately?"

"OK, my apologies Lou, your legs wouldn't make the cut anyway. Ever consider trying out for Chorus Line?"

Like I said, one funny guy, I couldn't allow myself to play into this. Jake needed to continue to work on developing the confidence to carry on a straight dialogue and get that people would still like him. For myself, I did not need to model distracting humor for this young man.

"That's a point Jake. If you continue I am prepared to move on without your participation."

Jake looked toward the ceiling.

I let the sarcasm go, continued with Mr. Peepers. "Jake, it is understood and accepted that to drive a car you must have auto insurance." Jake nods in agreement. "Your quarterly premium is two hundred and twenty-five dollars. For your first score on the Peepers Jeopardy board, what is your total yearly premium?"

Terms such as quarterly and premium are lost on most of the student population. A few of the students could do this problem with a calculator. Jake could process the problem in his head. I know he can do this problem with ease. Make up for the point he has already cost his team. Jake takes his time, relishing the stage.

Stroking his chin as if he had a wispy beard, "Well, Lou, given that a quarter is one-fourth or divided into four parts that would mean four times two hundred and twenty-five." He closes his eyes. "Four times twenty-five is one hundred, and four times two hundred is eight hundred, eight plus one equals nine. Nine hundred dollars."

"Final answer?"

"Final."

Jake's cohorts can tell by my exaggerated facial expression that he's right. I'll give him a tougher one next time around. "Impressive. Very impressive calculations for the representative of the Mystical Subcontinent of India."

While Martin writes an M for Metallica in the first square under Transportation, I look around for my next participant. I had to remember their characters and be prepared to ornately elaborate. How about Jane? Yes, Jane, she was the aristocratic Spaniard.

"We now turn to the woman who was given her land from Caesar's Tenth Legion. Where Charleton Heston brought El Cid (I had shown the movie) to fame. Home to Hemingway and the priestess resplendent Senorita Jane Radnisch! Senorita," I bow, "The television audience awaits your selection."

"I'll take Jobs."

I pause, don't want to make the question too difficult, got to be within reach. I saunter to the side of the room, "Senorita Radnisch, when a person comes to you and applies for work, he must bring with him an article that describes his past experience. For the square, what is this article called?'

Several of her team members immediately know the answer. They know, however, if they give it out, Metallica will lose the point and I'll skip their turn in the rotation. Then, too, there's the Chunk Monkey. They contain themselves.

"Senorita Radnisch, you are on the clock. Ten seconds and counting." I mark the second hand on the classroom clock.

Her team members writhe.

"Resume!" Jane suddenly shouts out.

"Correctomundo! Score two for Metallica"

Martin writes another large M under Jobs.

"Way to go Jane."

"Never a doubt."

"Cool dudette. We got Boston Pops down two to zip.

I continued, "We turn out attention to the riches of Africa. To a man whose family is synonymous with wealth and power. A man whose country has pressed coal to its purest form, historically considered to be a woman's best friend. The owner of those priceless diamond mines near the womb of humanity, TONY FURLOW!"

Tony stands erect, gives a military salute.

"Mr. Furlow, your topic of choice if you please."

"I'll try Salary."

I need to come up with a point for Boston Pops. I can't make the question so difficult that everyone will know I'm blowing by Tony, just hard enough for him to miss. "Mr. Furlow," I begin," pacing in front of the desks, "You work five days a week every week of the year. You have a mean boss who will not allow you any sick, vacation, or holiday time. We are talking Mr. Scrooge. The question is, how many days do you work in a year?"

Jake could do this. Jake is doing in his head right now. Tony will not get this one.

Tony signals for time and asks, "Martin, may I please have a calculator?"

I stop this silliness, "Calculators are not allowed."

Jake raises his hand, "Lou, as I understand, use of a calculator is one of Mr. Furlow's IEP Accommodations."

I grab my forehead in mock dismay.

"Fine."

Tony plucks away at the numbers.

"You have ten seconds Mr. Furlow." No way. He still has to remember that there are fifty-two weeks in a year times five days per work week.

"Two hundred and sixty?"

Martin yells, "That's three for Metallica!"

"Chunky Monkey here we come!"

"Way to go Tony!!"

Students applaud.

Martin looks at me and smiles, "They're on a roll."

Yes they are and even more, they are learning more than academics, positive social interaction. Thanks Mr. Peepers!

August 28   Fairy Tales

"You did what?"

"Brought him into your office to flirt?"

"You shut the door?"

"What are you thinking of?"

"You have gone completely loca!"

Geraldine and Martha Lee were letting me have it with a torrent of disbelief in my assertiveness towards Lou Thompson.

"Girl, what got into you?"

"You're just going to be another scalp on his belt."

"Honey, you playin' your cards way out of hand."

"You need to see your own headshrinker."

I had so inquired of my former "headshrinker." Events were just getting beyond me and I had asked to come back in for a couple of "tune up" sessions. The fact is, she had supported my being direct with Lou. Dr. Baughman had submitted that my passivity was keeping me from living a genuine life. She directed me to take a risk, put my ego in check, and take a leap of faith toward making those dreams of mine my reality. Now, for my beloved friends, I held up my palms asking for them to calm their rhetoric and allow me into the conversation. Thankfully, Red joined our threesome. Martha Lee and Geraldine started up again.

"Red, did you hear what's going on between Laura and that Lou Thompson."

Geraldine challenged Red, "Look at the way he's smiling. Red, you have canary feathers all over your mouth! What do you know that we don't?"

"Word has it that they've had a dinner date." Martha Lee blurted.

Red ordered his usual, an ice tea, and leaned forward confidentially on our table. "I know about that dinner date." I could visualize some yellow canary feathers floating around. "Fact is, I had the honor of keeping my oven going after hours Wednesday night."

"You should have seen it," I added, "Red had a special table complete with a white table cloth and a candle.

Martha Lee and Geraldine just exchanged looks of disbelief.

"OK Red, you who knows all that comes down in our fair town, since when did you know that Lou had been placed at Founders?"

Red shuffled his silverware and napkin, accepted the ice tea from the waiter, took a sip.

"C'mon Red," demanded Geraldine, "We going to get the truth or a fairy tale."

"Ladies, the truth might be a fairy tale."

"Well, we're all set for a bedtime story!" With that my girlfriends folded their arms and looked at Red in no uncertain terms that he needed to produce.

Red took out his checkered pocket handkerchief and mopped his brow for effect. "OK, here the truth be, you remember when I use to coach the basketball team at Founders."

They both nodded. "Sure we do."

"You know we attended most of the games, as if you don't recall. We sat nine rows up behind your bench. Had some great teams way back then."

Red strummed the table and mused, "Remember the name Jack Reynolds?"

Martha Lee eyed Red, "So, what does Jumping Jack Flash have to do with Lou …"

Martha Lee stopped in mid sentence and exchanged a knowing look with Geraldine and slapped her thigh.

"I always told you that Lou Thompson sparked something from the past."

"That's the truth."

"But no one ever knew what became of Jack after the injury, except that he became The White Legend."

"Well friends," Red laughed, "The White Legend, a tad older, is back."

Geraldine slapped the table with both palms, "Red, this is just too much to believe."

"Well, I said the truth might be a fairy tale. In fact, here comes Prince Charming now."

I rose from my chair to give Lou a welcoming hug.

September 30

Admittedly, I adored Lou but I needed to keep my perspective as gate keeper and director of Valley Oak School. I had, long ago, accepted that Lou's intentions for Valley Oak were purely altruistic in that he truly desired to provide a program that met with each student's individual needs. He would laugh at me for being overwrought if I were to ask him to look at his own, issues with, what has become, The Realm of Valley Oak. Not that Lou has used Valley Oak to meet his emotional needs in a way that could be considered detrimental to the program. However, more to the point, how Lou has developed the culture of Valley Oak as the caring family he had lost and continues to yearn for. I would prod Lou, in his words, to look into the mirror, to accept how Valley Oak was providing substance for himself. How he was seeking to being enveloped in the warm fabric of an intact, albeit emotionally disturbed, community where he was key to the wellbeing of all. He would respond by saying something obscure like he had to find a replacement for his basketball acclaim or, make some other sarcastic comment to close down the conversation. Lou simply could not accept that he had created Valley Oak to meet his, Lou's, need to actualize his dream of being held closely and loved.

However, whenever I doubt Lou's ability to own his own stuff, I recall his participation with our student graduations. These events were

lavish affairs earned when the student met their IEP goals and were rewarded with the privilege of returning to their local school program. The student, at these graduations, chooses the restaurant or outdoor park barbecue location and invites upwards of fifteen students from the Valley Oak program to attend. There is no limit placed on the number adults and friends from their community, so that these ceremonies sometimes approach forty participants. (Of course, if it was barbecue, Red would be there as Chef in Charge.) A personal gift of approximately one hundred and fifty dollars is given to the student in order that they might choose clothing, music, or other physical items to take away from Valley Oak. Additionally, they are able to withdraw all of their Workability savings, which, for some, was a substantial amount of several hundred dollars.

Lou is the maestro of these events for he is the father figure or kind uncle bestowing recognition on a prodigal individual in his family. In program Lou is such an impenetrable icon of boundary setter that I was caught totally unprepared for his physical emotion at the first graduation I attended. Then too, knowing what I do now, I really should not have been.

Everyone attending a student's graduation is asked to stand up and recognize the student of honor by recalling some incident of note in the student's past. At times congratulating students could only wish their friend good luck, which was enough. Some students would take the stage and talk on and on, but Lou was always the last one to present.

It's my turn now. How I hate this. I always come unglued. I'd better stand up, everyone's waiting. I need to say something away from all the banter that has been Jake's and my relationship. Something straight ahead for sure. I began,

"Jake Oh, we are so proud of you." I look around the audience. Cheryl is already dabbing her eyes. Allyson's hugging her son. Raymond is standing behind them, beaming with pride. Jake motions to his two brothers to come join them.

I continue, "I personally am so proud of you." I am. "You have not only taken on the issues that separated you from school but your family as well. You have done so by understanding the way you used…" (Here it comes. I can feel myself choking up)" humor as a shield to keep people from becoming close to you. Like we all have." I reach to recall a moment, keep my cool, focus on Jake. "Remember the first question you asked me, something like, how did I escape the dinosaurs?" I have to explain this to those who had not heard the story, which gave me a moment to recover. That was close, need to keep going,

"Not knowing Jake well at that time, I didn't see where he was going with this line of questioning. Here's this new kid in program, asking me how did I escape the dinosaurs? Where was he coming from? Was he into dinosaurs? I had no clue so I had to ask Jake, why he would ask this of me?" I look over at Jake. I knew my eyes were waterlogged, at least I wasn't blubbering.

"Jake looks at me with that totally upfront, honest, squeaky gee whiz way of his and says, Lou, you are so wizened, I thought you must have been alive then." The crowd laughs, appreciating how the moment so represented who Jake was.

Jake calls out, "Don't forget to tell them how you use to load muskets in the Revolutionary War!"

The audience is laughing with me through my blurry vision. Get a grip on yourself! This graduation is not about you, it's about Jake. Keep yourself together. Calm the emotions. Pretend you are on the free throw line. I gulped a breath of air to regroup.

"Jake has entered a life style of different customs and expectations than that of his family. He has endured many difficult situations that were not of his personal choosing." I catch a glimpse of Laura and can tell she is enjoying my struggle to pay tribute to Jake. "Through these experiences, not only has Jake earned the right to return to public school, he has gained a deeper understanding of himself.

All the Ohs were standing shoulder to shoulder and holding hands.

I continued, "While attending Valley Oak, Jake has had a grade point average of 3.9." This fact part was easier for me. "He has been instrumental in the student council and, fortunately, speaking for all administration, will not be available for future labor negotiations.

"I'll be back. You can't bury me!" Jake laughed.

"We, of course, will look forward to future conversations." I picked up an envelope with a check inside. "Jake has a Workability reward check of two hundred and twenty-seven dollars to take with him."

Everyone applauded. Martin called out, "Chunky Monkey on Jake!"

"But more than that, more than the physical parting gifts of the Aerobic Air Walk (Valley Oaks' going away present.) for Jake's physical health, Jake is taking with him our relationships. Relationships that have been forged because Jake risked sharing with us who he was. Shared with us his hurt and his dreams. Allowing himself to be vulnerable in a way that brought forward a consciousness in Jake. He began to accept who he was and where he wanted to go and he worked at developing the social skills he needed to get there. With the support of his family and his friends here at Valley Oak, Jake is ready to move into the next chapter of his life.

I walked to a side table away from the cake. I picked up my weight belt and a plaque. "Jake has inscribed his name on The Graduation Belt. Jake is the twenty-eighth student to sign. Their names or initials are burned into the stained leather." I laid the belt over my shoulder. "Jake's picture will be in the Hallway of the Wall of Graduation." I held up the glossy eight by ten of Jake's gleaming smile, slicked back hair.

"Now Jake," This is hard for me as I hold up the Valley Oak Graduation Plaque. "Our graduation diploma reads,

Say Good Things To Your Teammates

Leave The Other Teams Alone,

And

Hit Away"

I observe as Jake accepts the plaque and embraces Lou. Lou hugs him back. The Natural, with my favorite Robert Redford, could not have made the statement with more poignancy. Jake bows as Lou leaves the front table and Jake's family allowing students to move in to stand close to them with congratulations. Cameras flash as a boom box begins to play Enter Sandman. Students join in. Even Raymond has learned the words.

I notice Lou, off to the side, awash in the warm afterglow, softly singing along, cherishing, even if he could not admit, the loving fabric of the culture he had created for himself.

Valley Oak School
Psycho/Educational Intake Summary

Laura Rosso: LCSW

Name: <u>Lou Eugene Thompson AKA Jack (Flash) Reynolds</u>
DOB: <u>8/15/57</u>

County of Residence: <u>Bay County</u>

School District of Reference: <u>Red Rock USD</u>

Date: August 18

Physical Description: Lou is a pleasant looking (Some might say hunk) 45 year old Caucasian male. He has thick dark wavy brown hair, giving over to specks of grey, brown eyes, an olive complexion, and strives to maintain his six feet -two, one hundred and ninety-five pound frame. Lou has stated that he will no longer participate in sports requiring lateral mobility as consistent muscle strains have negated his enthusiasm due to an earlier back injury. Lou's facial expression carries the New England cursed burden of Red Sox affliction and he awaits the reincarnation of Bill Russell, Bob Cousy, and Jungle Jim Luskatoff, to stabilize the world of basketball. (Not discounting Bobby Orr.)

Referring Criterion: Lou is a teacher who always desired to direct his own school. From his history of special education teaching positions, Lou acquired the information necessary to initiate a Non Public School for Emotionally Disturbed Students. In so doing, Lou brought himself into the therapeutic realm of a Relationship Based Day Treatment Program. The impact of the philosophical expectations of the Department of Education meeting up with those of the Department of Mental Health caused Lou to review his sense of well-being. When Lou's mental health insights called his personal perspectives into question it brought about a cosmic turmoil in his acceptance of the order of the universe. Lou has a history of a needing to be right and in total control evidencing grandiosity, a fragile self-image, passive aggressive tendencies, and a disconcerting fixation on the Boston

Red Sox. The anticipated therapeutic outcome will be for Lou to more fully immerse himself in authentic intimate relationships and, toward this end, to develop trust in others and himself.

Family History: There is much speculation as documentation has been negligible, if not convoluted. Lou, himself, has remained vague and has only offered discordant strands regarding his family and childhood. To this date, Lou has stated that he was raised through the Founders Program from ages twelve through eighteen due to the accidental death of his parents. During the time that he resided at Founder's Lou Thompson was known as Jack Reynolds whom, local folklore holds, was one of the finest basketball prospects to come out of Massachusetts. Lou's potential basketball career was erased due to a devastating injury. Following his rehabilitation, Lou went to the West Coast where, he contended, his history would not follow him. He graduated from UC Berkeley in the Teacher Credential Program five years later. It was during this time frame, for reasons thus far unknown, that he changed his name from Jack Reynolds to Lou Eugene Thompson.

Psychiatric History: To date, Lou's involvement with the therapeutic field has been limited to Valley Oak School. Until this time, Lou has stated that he had not experienced headaches, depression, insomnia, anxiety attacks, eating issues, or a propensity to root for the Yankees.

DSM:

AXIS I:	Traits of Obsessive Compulsive Personality Disorder as manifested by his need to repeat bad jokes in spite of the disinterest of the audience.
	Obsessions primarily revolve around the league standing of the Red Sox.
AXIS II:	Traits of Narcissistic Personality Disorder demonstrated by a rather intense desire for validation and/or admiration from peers as well as a persistent preoccupation with the grandiose fantasy of becoming the next Red Sox left fielder. In addition, Lou's occasional emotional outbursts (Narcissistic rage?) appears to derive from wounds pricked when he feels impotent (in the non-sexual sense) or misunderstood.
AXIS III:	None
AXIS IV:	None
AXIS V:	GAF – fluctuates according to the performance of the Red Sox.

RECOMMENDATIONS: Given the unknown history of the client, there is much to consider relevant to his being a successful participant in program. His lack of transparency is of major concern as events in his life appear to be contrived, if not fabricated. Contributing further to the lack of transparency is Lou's continual employment of sarcasm/humor to deflect his inner ego. In order for a Relationship Program to be successful, the prime role model, which Lou is for Valley Oak, needs to be capable of establishing a community based on trust and openness, which have been abundantly absent in Lou's past.

Given Lou's willingness to accept the perspective of a Relationship Based Program in order to meet the needs of the students and consistent program attendance, I support Lou's participation in Valley Oak School.

Signed_____Date_____
Laura Rosso

Chapter 8

THE LEGEND

February 25 Chocolate & Vanilla

This would not be the last time that I would wake up with Red sitting in the sun dozing by my hospital window. I head jerked alert out of a deranged space and now just collapsed back into the pillow with the ceiling slowly revolving above me. I felt wasted. There was a faraway dull deep pain in my back. I lay there trying to put together the visions. Flashing lights. Shouts. I remember myself floating, then darkness. Yeh, the Power Memorial game. Basketball. That was it. Vaguely I wondered if we'd won.

Like an echo I heard, "Nah, Tiptop missed both free throws." He hadn't budged. Red's eyes were still closed. He must've felt my movement. He knew I'd go back to the game.

He waved me off, "I know. I know, Lindsey should have been at the line." Red shook his head. "I gave the rock to Tiptop. He demanded payback."

That was the Tiptop I knew. He would keep Spider's and my legacy alive at Founders. He just couldn't sink free throws. I smiled, thinking of my own nickname for my roomie, Lurch, which he swore he'd give me a butt whipping if I called him that in public.

Red shifted in the worn stuffed chair, "Just don't always get the fairy tale ending."

Got that right.

Red groaned, leaned up and came over to me. He was shaking his head. His eyes looked like his name. "Jack, you're all pumped up on fluids and pain killers. You need to rest." He laid his hand on my shoulder.

I drifted back off. Whistles were blowing. Bodies flying. Never an end. Just cascading. I came in and out over the next five days. Every time

Red was there. Sometimes I caught a glimpse of a familiar body. Heard a voice. It was hard to say just who. Couldn't understand what they said. I remember Red saying the team had left to get back for school and league play.

I felt I was done. Hoop dreams were over. I hadn't heard the final word. Just a bad feeling all over my body. I somehow recollected that they said the damage was repairable, but would take a long rehab. My spine was intact, but four of my thoracic vertebrae had been compressed. I was glad they wouldn't have to cut on me. Small mercies as I grimaced within myself. I could no longer see the ceiling above my bed. The hospital room was looking like a gift shop. Get well balloons of all types and colors and flowers from fans and opposing teams filled the room. Red made sure that they got shared with patients who were not lucky enough to have the generous outpouring from friends.

As the days came and went I gradually was able to stay alert for a few hours at a time. The docs had me tied down pretty well so that there wasn't much to do but watch ESPN. The bedpan was embarrassing, but I wasn't on solid food so there wasn't much to it. Events just sort of evolved through a clouded mist.

Red set his schedule to be with me every other day. He acted like driving up and down I-95 listening to NPR and ESPN were the joys of his life. He said that he was through coaching. Turned the team over to the assistants. I knew that had to be difficult for him. Red said it wasn't nuthin'. He might start doing some recruiting for the U. Red said that my old nemesis JJ Jerome had dropped by to wish me well. JJ was coming off the bench as a sophomore up in Syracuse. JJ wanted to let me know that they were holding the scholarship offer open for me.

On my ninth day in recovery Power Memorial showed up. Each brought a rose and said some good things. I was still a bit groggy but I appreciated their support. They gave me the game ball with Founders having the winning score. They knew Tiptop shouldn't have taken the free throws. Nice touch. Said they would catch me on the rebound in the Fall. I hoped so....

Like Lou said, I was there for all the comings and goings. So many people dropping by at all hours that I felt it was All You Can Eat 4-$5 Day at Red's Barbecue. The barbecue was in good hands. I'd made enough sauce for the next month. My worry was about Jack. He didn't know the details of his injury and I wouldn't tell him, even if he asked for the truth, but his basketball days were done. He could not risk another fall. One good thing though, Jack would never have to worry about finances. His adopted parents, the Reynolds, had a trust fund set up for him from the day they adopted him. Then too, the insurance settlement from their auto accident had been generous. I'd made sure of that with some attorneys I knew. Money was not the issue. He would have a load of it when he turned eighteen. It would be Jack the man. His mind set. How he came through his rehab. How he dealt with both the mental and physical pain. Going from a front-page phenome to buying a ticket would be a rock hard journey.

I would have to keep my interest in Jack close to the vest. I had kept my involvement with Jack hidden through the activities of the Founder's program. That was good then. What direction our relationship would now take, I was unsure of. But my bond went way back with Jack. Way back to an oath I swore to his father. A father he never met or, as yet, knew of.

As Jack slept his way back to health, I settled back into my chair. Reminisced. So long, yet close....... .....

I recalled the moment when the knock on my apartment door had been sudden and forceful. I knew the pounder was Lou. He'd called to give me a heads up. He wouldn't tell me over the phone. Something was coming down. Something serious.

Lou Thompson and I went all the way back. We'd both been raised from the cradle by Founders. Done everything together. Had joined up with the military as soon as we turned eighteen and been shipped off to Korea. Vanilla and Chocolate. Truman made our taking showers together possible. That was in '51 and we had finished out hostilities there. Then we got recruited and trained by the FBI for a couple of years. Lou liked the cloak and dagger stuff and had re-upped. Me, I needed more out in the open action. I'd left and moved over to a new group in the army special forces which was referred to as the "Green Beret," which wasn't our official title until JFK made it so. We did a little bit of everything and I liked that. My final gig was with the Navy Seals in the early sixties when that group needed some experienced leadership.

Lou's banging on the door of my walk up fourth floor Dorchester apartment was beginning to knock the hinges off when I opened it before he caved the rickety wood in.

"What's the rush....." I stopped. In Lou's long arms he held an infant. Lou handed the child to me and I cradled the babe.

"Don't much look like you," I managed.

Lou socked me in the arm. "About time you became an uncle."

I shook my head. "I don't quite think Boston's ready for that."

Lou popped a beer from the fridge and sank into my one old stuffed sofa. Practically filled it up with his bulk. No fat, only size. Just about emptied the bottle in one pull. Belched. Looked into me. "Family will disown my son and give him up for adoption."

I had known for some time that there was a weight within Lou. He just wasn't his same self. So, this was it. He had fathered a child. A child that no one wanted except him. Deja vu. Lou couldn't parent him because he was so far-gone deep into shadows he could no longer even talk to me about his life. He had mentioned that his involvements were edgy. That I could be in danger just to be seen with him.

".........and you would like me to do----just what---?"

Lou was in an intense craze beyond any battlefield we'd been on. He was acting all cool, but I knew him. Life was tearing at him. He had a knife in his gut. "Red, I need you to swear an oath that you will look after my son."

Funny how things come to pass. Lou and I had sworn oaths together from childhood. In looking back we had laughed about many of them. Some were just too silly like about which girls we liked. There was no laughing now. There was decorum for our oath.

I handed the bundle of clothing back to Lou. "What would you want me to swear to?" I stood up and raised my right hand. This was not a moment to be foolin' with. Not like the oaths we took about our young girl loves. Myrna Stokes would just make me tongue tied when I was around her. Lou, he was so smooth, he always would find a way for me to have a conversation with her. To this day, I can savor the fragrance of her curly dark brown hair.

Lou looked into me. Then to his son and solemnly stated, "Swear by all the love you and I hold dear for each other, you will love and look after my son."

I repeated, "I swear by all the love you and I hold dear for each other, I will love and look over your son."

Lou's shoulders softened and he leaned back against the wall. "Thanks Red."

I offered the obvious, "You want me to bring him over to Founders?"

"They did alright by us." Lou shrugged.

"That they did," I agreed. In fact, they did right by about almost all the children who came through them.

"Red, love you and I gotta go." Lou turned to leave, stopped, caught himself. Smiled. "Yeh, his name. I should tell you. Same as mine. Louis. Louis Thompson."

Sounded good but the thought came to me that Lou had left something out. "Young man have a middle name?"

Lou thought a moment, then laughed and slapped me on the shoulder, "Sure, almost forgot. Same as yours Red, Eugene." He saw the look of horror on my face."

"It's OK Red, I'll never tell where it came from."

I repeated each name slowly, "Louis Eugene Thompson, That'll do."

Lou sighed. Walked over to me. We hugged. He was a good eight inches taller than me. Then Lou rubbed my head three times for luck.

"Just in case we need The Geni."

We laughed. Shook hands. Lou left with a soft kiss on his son's forehead. Holding Louis Eugene Thompson, I walked over to the window and pulled back the curtain, watching as Lou long strided down the far sidewalk. That was the last time I saw my best friend....

August 31 CBI's

"Lou."

"Yeh April?" I'm out in the shallow sand area of the lake playing water baseball with six students. The rules always change. The game was a kick. Today you had to hit a whiffle ball, swim to Cheryl, and get back before the ball got to the plate. The temp is hot and we're wet. We're on a Community Based Instruction Earned Activity. The previous day our Culinary Arts kitchen had barbecued chicken and put together some macaroni and potato salad for lunch at Marble Lake. The lake was a great family place to go. My parents had brought me here on picnics. Nothing but good memories. The shore and shallow end were clearly marked. Life guards kept watch. You could throw Frisbees and play all sorts of water games in the sandy bottom area. There were water cycles, paddleboats, and kayaks to rent and rove around the lake. Marble wasn't huge. Only about three miles in diameter. But the cold water was clear and refreshing on a hot summer day. Bold individuals, which, had not included me, dove with tanned hard bodies from the sheer rock crags on the north side. Not with my fear of heights. Bruce Springsteen would've liked this place. Thirty-four students had earned the activity. A Valley Oak record!! Most were out on the lake paddling around.

April called again to get my attention, "Lou, John needs you to talk with Richard and Vince. He says they're kicking over garbage cans and walking on the picnic tables, telling everyone to fuck off."

Should I have been surprised, "Let him know I'm on my way."

I head up to the situation. I know John must be at the end of his rope if he's transitioning Richard and Vince to me. I think this was their second Earned Activity in five months, tuff guy wannabees. But both had focused on making the Earned Activity to Marble Lake. This was a program favorite. I had already cautioned them once about ramming into other kayaks. What now?

Suesan is walking towards me with Richard. The only class he attends at Valley Oak is my Reading Lab as a TA. He's been more than good with me. He's been excellent. I couldn't run seven students without him. Everywhere else he is discordant. He accepts my direction because, as he says, I have learned to listen. Laura would be proud.

"What's up?" I toss out coming up to them.

Suesan scowls at Richard, "Something about throwing a paddle at the canoe full of other students."

Richard throws up his hands in gang signs, gets loud and shouts, "That's a fucking faggot lie."

Here we go. Wonder how he saw the scene? "So Richard, can we carry on this conversation more appropriately?"

He looks away, glowering. "No. Not with the fucking lying going on. Staff doesn't know what the fuck happened."

"I'm staff."

"Yeh, and you don't know dick."

Do I know Jane? Don't get sarcastic Lou. Stay focused.

Such a fragile ego. Need to find out who is lying about what. At least he isn't tossing trash cans. Let's do the review again. "So who's lying?"

"Staff."

"Which staff?"

"Pablo."

"What's he lying about?"

Richard gathers himself. All of five foot hard bodied six inches. We know each other through two years of conflicted confrontation. Looks at me and talks calmly. The dialogue is what I've worked with him to do. Step back. Take a breath. Is this a hill to die on? I tell Richard that, if I can back off, so can he. Richard responds, "I don't want to talk about crap right now. I'm through with this talk about how things are. Just fuck it.!"

He drops a lugie at his feet. Memories of good ol' Mike Adams. Too bad I didn't have the skills then that I have now, Mike might've made it. Richard almost made it through the statement without a sexualized explicative. Not bad. Need to reprocess. Model. Direct. Here I am to save the day! Memories of Mighty Mouse. Don't be flippant. Last thing you need is to model a cartoon character. Focus. Speak.

"Richard, you know we're about dialogue. Talking things through. How many times have you reminded me that my job is to understand your needs. That you were placed in our program precisely for the reasons you're now presenting?"

Richard's rocking back and forth on his heels.

Suesan gives me a "thank you god smile" and heads back to the vans. I stand with Richard. I know he enjoys the personal time. The "I only listen to Lou" posture.

I recant, "Richard, you know that I know what we both know. Can we move on? Are we beyond the posturing?"

A lip flickering smile of acknowledgement cuts through the anger of his eyes. I call Suesan over the walkie. "You want to start rounding up program for the trip home?" I sit down on a picnic table. Richard leans against a tree. We have our space and time, I wait.

Richard keeps to the same tune, rocking. "I don't care what you say. I just don't fucking want to talk about shit. Over and over and over. I just want to get home. Can we leave?"

No we can't. That's not how Valley Oak works. Richard knows it. I know it. We just remain there. We're not going to get on the road where escalations are life threatening. I count the butterflies. I can see the boats with staff and students headed into the dock. Behind Richard I can see Vince and John walk up to us from the lake edge. Vince has been in program just five months. He has a biker mom. A tough home. He commits property damage as a self-soothing technique. Give him six more months and he may gain some of Richard's skills. Give him two years and he might be a lifer at Ryker's Island. Give me two more years and I just might be a therapist.....

"Hey Lou."

"John." Keep positive. Avoid the fray. "Water sure felt good today."

"That be right."

"Gesturing at Richard, "so what happened."

Richard screws up his face, "Fucking bitches nothing happened. It's all bullshit from faggot staff. They got the fucking lifeguard to bring us in for no goddamn reason!"

Gee, here I thought he was stabilized. I should know Richard. I have been through this with him so many times. I am no longer the faggot staff. He has plenty of other targets and he's good at hitting them.

Keep with perspective. "So, Richard, why don't you tell John what happened? If you can do that then it would appear that you are ready to get in the van and go home."

Richard and Vince just shut down. Eyes squinty. Mouths tight. John jumps in, "I saw a paddle being tossed from one kayak to another." John knows he's right and doesn't want to process their bullshit. I'll remind John later to give them more time to respond. A way out. Now he was becoming the target. Just like their parents or any other authority figure. Whether his facts were right or not, John's manner was not going to move us in a positive direction.

Vince taunts, "You couldn't see shit from shore! How could you see the paddle fly through the air from where you were? You got Superman vision?"

John clutches his heart, feigning extreme tragedy, "Oh, excuse me." John laments. Totally downcast. Lips in a protruded pout. "I meant to say the paddle submerged underwater and suddenly appeared in the other kayak."

Sarcasm. Bad choice. Just the type of response Vince needs to turn the screw a bit nastier. "I don't need your fucking ass wipe crap. You can shove your lips up your hole."

I look at John. I don't want him to transfer Vince and Richard to me to stabilize. That's what Vince and Richard want. Ride home with me. Devalue staff. They're into playing up to me. Saying I'm worth listening to and the rest of staff isn't. It's splitting and something adolescents are far too good at. I look to John to turn his anger down. John gets the message. He nods. Turns to Vince and Richard and states straight out, "I hear you. The blow up's on me. Can you let it go?"

Vince and Richard just stand silent, which is a positive.

I add, "Let's get home..."

They nod and we do...

There are no further incidents. Back on site that afternoon John and I debrief the situation with three other staff. The first thing John admits to is that he got pissed off and sarcastic with Richard. He blew it. He needs to keep his cool. Keep his wits about him. John's only twenty-three. His brain was still under construction and I could take that into consideration. It's such a pisser when you know a student isn't being truthful and there's no way of getting to what it is or have them own it. As five of the present staff put the activity together, the "truth" was that Richard and Vince didn't want to use the double paddles that are given with the kayaks. They had taken theirs apart and were using them like a canoe paddle. Their choice was to take the extra paddle and "share" it with another kayak. This had caused the situation.

Had there been property damage?

No.

Had there been physical assault?

No.

Had there been a stressful situation?

Definitely.

Could John have chosen to let the lifeguard go out in his boat alone and bring Richard and Vince in?

Next time for sure.

Did everyone get home in one piece?

Thankfully, yes we did.

Lou has become such a strong and respected icon for both the Valley Oak staff and the students as he has almost completely transitioned to a Therapeutically Based Relationship Model. I think back through James, Mike Adams, Sharon, and a host of our other students who have participated with Lou in his metamorphosis from being a master of control to offering himself up as a vessel to hold the student's emotional torment and seek positive resolutions with them.

Now, I had to massage Lou for an even more daunting challenge.

A Memory: Coming of Age

Spider had my back, but he would be moving on. I had to accept that I had to count on myself. There was nobody else out there. Yeh, this local guy, Red, had taken an interest in me. That was plain to see. He was on the Founder's Oversight Committee and all that, and I would hear around how he would be checking up on me. Talking with staff. Every now and then I would catch him watching me. Not that he was strange. Red was a good guy. Brought us over to his place for barbecue every now and then. Volunteered to be the Founder's basketball coach.

I was finding out that basketball just might be my game. Even more than baseball. At thirteen I could compete with our varsity team players in pick up games. I was too young to be on the traveling squad, but I went to all the local contests. I'd had a growth spurt to six-one, with, like out of nowhere, my big deal was dunking.

I hadn't even been aware of my first dunk. The older players just stopped the pick up game and stared at me.

"Did you see that?'

"Shit. No way!"

"Lou dunked!" My bud Spider yelled to the world.

I just shrugged. I knew I had gotten some air, but...........Everyone gave me five.

"We need a name for this boy."

"White Jam?"

That was hooted down.

Spider stepped to the center of the foul line. "I got one." Everyone waited. "How about 'Jumpin' Jack Flash?'"

"Yeh!"

"Jumpin' Jack Flash!"

"The Stones would be proud."

That was the birth of "Jumping Jack Flash." I had the ability to sky that no one else on our team did! Amazing. Like, WOW! At thirteen I could do that with either hand. Got to show my stuff during warm ups. Real crowd pleaser. Hard to believe a White Boy with so much lift.

When I turned fourteen I could play varsity. Until then I had a lot of time on my hands to practice different types of dribble drills. Read all I could about Pistol Pete Maravich. Funny looking White Guy with the dangling socks. Scored more points during his college career than anyone else. Guy looked like the basketball was a yo-yo in his hand. Great court sense.

Red brought me in some books on Bob Cousy and the Celtics. Even the Harlem Globetrotters. When I watched Spider, I thought of Bill Russell. Russell always had the Celtics back, especially against Chamberlain. Those were some great games. The Jones boys, KC and Sam. I picked up Sam's bank shot. Just like a lay up he said. The shot wasn't quite that way for me, but I worked at it.

I was just so alone. Night would find me silently weeping into my pillow, longing for the family that had been take from me...

September 6   r-u-n

"Ready?"

"I'm going to beat you Benjamin!"

"We'll see. Gotta wait 'til I say go."

"I know that."

"Set." Both Benjamin Jacobs and seven-year old Orlando are bent over. A long stretch of thick green lawn is in front of them. Smiling. Both are crouched, Orlando creeping forward.

"Go!" yelled Benjamin.

Orlando flashed to an immediate lead. His short legs pumping. But there was distance to consider. Benjamin kept a practiced steady kind of hopalong gallop. I thought of an aging buffalo. Visions of Bob Marley and the Buffalo Soldiers. Orlando kept looking back over his shoulder as Benjamin slowly, steadily, closed the gap. Orlando's smile broke into gut squealing laughter that he couldn't stop. Suddenly Orlando tripped and was rolling over and over on the lawn. Benjamin "sprinted" by him, as only a sixty-three year old former track star could do. He clenched both his hands over his head as he touched the door to the Speech Therapy Room. Started doing a victory dance, like some football player who had just won the Super Bowl. Orlando, struggling, got up and laughed his way inside.

I marveled at Benjamin Jacobs. The man's enthusiasm was remarkable. All the things that he had done in his life and he continued to challenge students in ways that made learning fun. More than that, he taught them. Students learned from him. I had witnessed our students' self-esteem increase through their contact with Benjamin as our speech therapist. He could teach a rock to read. I know. I had tried to teach the same students. I had not succeeded. And, I had my masters in READING! He was a speech therapist?

What Lou is stating needs some grounding as Lou had worked his own marvels with countless students in his classes and programs. What had worked for Lou was not to be found in a textbook as Mr. Hobb's Jeopardy, geographically hanging baseball pennants, and Power Words were not an easily assimilated statewide curriculum. The coursework could not be passed on to colleagues for Lou was who he was and brought students along with him because of his sheer joy of teaching. Lou simply loved the realm he was lord of and shared his wealth with the entire populance. Benjamin brought a system and his system was basic. His system was traditional. His system was phonics.

Benjamin had, at the outset, won me over to his perspective by explaining that phonics were like tools in a woodshop. Each had a specific job to perform and needed to be used at the correct time of the word being constructed. Just made common sense.

I had kindly suggested that he bring that proposal to Lord of the Valley Oak Manor, Lou Thompson.

October 2   Left Coast

Berkeley. San Francisco Bay. West Coast. From my sixth floor cubicle room in Deutche Hall I could take in the sun setting behind the Golden Gate Bridge with the fog coming in. Calendar perfect. I loved it. Everything was new from where I saw the sun set to West Coast talk. Just sounded clipped and kind of bare compared to New England. I hadn't gotten into Oakland for barbecue, which my roommates said was the best in the Bay Area, but I had come upon Top Dog.

Completely opposite from Red's Barbecue, Top Dog was a hole in the wall place with five stools, a large grill, and fifteen types of dogs to choose from. The grill guys were a hoot. All sorts of off the wall comments. The dogs were awesome. They had Calabrese and German and even a Bird Dog for the veggies. My New York roomies said that the Dog could not compare with their Coney Island, but it was good enough for me. Wrap this up with a grilled bun, Hot Russian Mustard, chopped onions, maybe sauerkraut and I was a very happy guy.

Life was so wide open to me. I could come and go how I wanted. No one was looking over my shoulder. I'd hardly even thought about basketball. Baseball was another thing altogether. I could not believe my luck in baseball. Somehow the Oakland A's and Charley Finley had put together a championship team that no one watched!! That Fall we were able to walk in on game day and get World Series tickets against The Big Red Machine. Unbelievable in New England!!

Like Red had said, my inheritance had set me up financially. I could have lived outside the dorm but Red had counseled that it would be a good place to meet people. For that matter, I could have moved to Costa Rica and had a good life with my bank account. But I wanted more than sand in my toes. I wanted to get into education and become a teacher.

UC Berkeley was something else. Talk about a wake up call. I'd been around lots of eastern schools as I was being wooed for their basketball program. But walking onto a university campus for thirty-five thousand students and knowing you were going to be attending classes was humbling. You could see the boundary of the campus up on Grizzly Peak when you were at the bottom of Bancroft. Up there were Moon Rocks, where they split the atom, and there were eight other campuses around the state!

I had read that Berkeley flunked out half of the incoming Freshmen class. But I wanted to take it on. No one would know my Jack Flash history. I would just be Jack Reynolds. Guy with a bad back from the East Coast. Nothing about Founders. Whole new ballgame. I was ready!

Getting to know Bezerkley with roomies, who were different, but we were all Freshmen away from home and that was cool. We quickly got the hang of complaining about dorm food and there never being enough hot water for showers. The upheaval of the sixties was past but there were a lot of parts left over. People's Park was still there, kind of a major homeless-druggie hang out. Sure The Park wasn't what the sixties students had wanted but, as Red always said, it is what it is. Telegraph was filled with street vendors hawking all sorts of jewelry, paintings, logos, shirts, pottery. Reminded me of an ongoing craft faire. Up Strawberry Canyon and into Tilden Park there were over two hundred miles of hiking trails, which amazed me as I had thought of Berkeley as being a lot of cement.

Just being away from Founders was such a rush. Adding to this was one splurge I had allowed myself, which made me a popular guy. I purchased a 1970 VW Bus. Nothing psychedelic outrageous in its paint job as it was tan and white, but it got me and my buddies around. None of us were from the immediate Bay Area and we made it a priority to explore our surroundings. Of course we had to immediately go over to "The Haight" which had become a run down druggy area, but held a glow. Explored Golden Gate Park which ran out to the Pacific. We'd hit Broadway at night to check out the action, thinking we were hot stuff. Walked across the Golden Gate Bridge. Monterey, Santa Cruz, Stinson Beach with every weekend being a new frontier. One Friday night we took off for Lake Tahoe, which was a long slow climb up the Sierras in the loaded van. Spectacular coming down the cliff hanging Highway 50 for our first view. Of course we had to try to gamble and got run out.

Amidst checking out all the new territory we did have to take on the academics. Ever walk into a lecture hall with fifteen hundred other students knowing that a fourth would not return after Christmas break and another fourth would be gone by Spring? Wondering if you might be one of those not making the grade. Word was that Stanford was harder to get in but Berkeley was harder to stay. Reality was that my roomies and I took on our assignments intensely during the week. I had never been on the quarter system and the smash of a midterm after three weeks of school was a blow. I was able to pass all my classes but I could feel the dorm mood shift as students began to absorb the bad grade news. Two bum quarters and you went home. Boston was three thousand miles away and Founders was no longer home. I was totally oblivious to Red's keeping tabs on me.

What Jack is saying is all true. I know for a fact as I had employed a former Seal buddy, now a private investigator, to keep taps on Jack. Jack was having the time of his life. The West Coast move revitalized his spirts. He did not have to feel the history of his basketball exploits with the accompanying empathy, although well meant, that continued to drag him down. Sort of a bird out of the cage. I knew Jack's smarts went beyond the basketball court and he could handle any academic expectations that Berkeley would dish out.

What Jack is not sharing, though, is two fold. The first had to do with the constant back pain that he was enduring. Although he continued the prescribed exercises, the impact of the injury continued to be harsh. Given all of his new experiences, he was able to keep it in place. He kept the intensity of his struggle away from his friends and just gritted his teeth through his mornings as he painfully rolled out of bed and performed his therapeutic stretches.

To my dismay, although not surprise, is that Jack began using marijuana to put down the ongoing ache, or so he said. Maybe it was the pain. Maybe it was hanging out with his new friends. Don't matter. Readily available in all walks of life, Jack had smelled the aroma at Founders but never sought its use. Now, away from eyes, his need increased from before sleeping to, ultimately, wake and baking. The way I heard it, you could get high by just hitching a ride in his van.

The second concern was one that Jack was not aware of and, to this day, may still not be. Jack could not trust enough to form close relationships. I couldn't blame him. He'd been tossed aside from the get go. Never had the good fortune to know his father as I had. He had his adopting family taken from him with no one else standing by to step in. Unkind times. That he endured and flourished at Founders took luck, some caring oversight from afar, and a very resilient character.

Founders: A Rite

"Hey New Meat."

I was putting my bed together when Hank and Marcus walked in, closing the door.

"Time to pay some dues Jack Off."

I had been at Founders for one week. I had heard the rumors. Rituals. The new boys becoming initiated sex acts to older kids. Hank and Marcus had let me know that I would be theirs in time. The time was now.

"On your knees fuckhead."

I made for the door but Marcus grabbed my hair and chicken winged my arm forcing me to kneel.

"Get ready to open wide."

Hank stuffed a sock in my gasping mouth. I tried to kick out and Marcus dropped his knee into my back. I almost, thankfully, fainted from the pain.

"Sure you don't want to brown hole him first?"

"We'll save fudge packing for desert."

So much pain I couldn't cry out. No one would be there if I could. Staff was all outside with a barbecue. Then, the door swung open. It was my roommate, Spider. Probably going to join in.

Marcus snarled, "Stay the fuck out of this Spider."

Marcus ripped my hair backwards causing me to groan. The sock dropped out.

"He's ours. Dude, you can take your turn later."

"This is dues Spider. You're welcomed to thirds."

Spider didn't say a word. He just whipped around a baseball bat and laid Hank out on the floor with a blow to the head.

Marcus whined. "You fucking crazy niggah?!"

I cringed on the floor. Marcus still had me pinned down.

Spider was just so calm. Matter of fact. "Nothin' crazy with me niggah."

Spider pointed the bat at Marcus. "Let my roomie up."

Spider was younger than Marcus and Hank but he had them on size. He for sure had gotten their attention with his bat. Hank was beginning to moan.

"You have a count of three to decide. This shit stops now." Spider lifted his bat. "One......."

Marcus quickly let go of me and got down and helped Hank to stumble to his feet and get out of the room.

Spider tossed the bat onto my bed. "Got your back roomie."

All I could do was nod. This was not the last time. Spider always had my back. What Spider did for me I made sure I did for others. A baseball bat evened a lot of things up. Like Spider said, it was time the shit stopped.

September 10   Wrong Again

"Lou..."

"The answer remains no, Laura. Never. Uh-uh. Forget it." Like what I say is going to matter. "Try this," I silently scream, "Nnnnnnnnnnnooooooooo!" Not today. Not yesterday. Not tomorrow."

I cover my ears with my hands in mock fear as Lou continues his tirade.

"And not EVER! I'd rather go back to being a sub in a public school!"

I mean, who does she think she is? Coming into my classroom and saying the program could benefit by a more academic approach. Like students are referred to Valley Oak for academics! And say what?! Phonics? You're killing me Squints! Laura and her therapeutic tribe keep coming in saying Johnny needs this. Johnny could do that. What's your problem with Johnny? Don't you think you could do this with Johnny? Yeh, right, like Johnny's higher education material. Like why don't you try relating to Johnny for more than two hours per week on a one to one basis? See what he does to your classroom. How about your psyche? Nice suggestions but the real world has some impact! And, of all things, phonics? What past epoch is she coming from? I had come to expect such initial tormented indignant outbursts from Lou and they brought to mind my venting clients, as I knew Lou would need to present his righteous frustration before being able to process my line of reasoning. I just had to wait Lou out as I always did for, somehow, due to some Educational Genetic Defect, he had the ability to see the light with which Mental Health Relationship Based perspective offered and come around to my point of view. One of the main reasons, besides his good looks, that I was attracted to Lou was that he gave me hope for the male of the species.

I remained cool and looked out through Laura's window at the countryside. I knew better than to come into Laura's office at the end of the day. Seemed I was always given some new doctrine to chew on, but this subject really got me. I tried to keep to the straight and narrow with zip sarcasm.

Let's see if she can get this. I turned to her, "The last thing our students need is to be locked into a room going "d/o/g." Can you image Frank or Lesley sitting there for 'run Spot run?' I find myself starting to wave my arms. Need to calm the theatrics.

"Laura, they're sixteen years old. They've got business to take care of, people to see. Their real life is out there. Away from us. Just ask them!"

I hate her therapeutic unblinking blue eyed processing. Like she's listening! Anyone home? Hello? Anyone in there?

"Get this Laura, our students have a history of failure with employing letter to sound relationships. They break pencils. They scream obscenities. They throw books. They toss desks. They assault peers. They assault staff. They assault themselves! And, this is when they show up! There is no rhyme or reason to regurgitate them back into their cycle of frustration. If they could have learned from this method, they would have by now."

At some point I am going to have to tell Lou how sexy he is when he gets passionate about learning, but for now, I need to go easy with him as the acceptance of alternative learning offerings is a process.

Slowly plant thoughts. I walked over to where Lou was gazing out the window, definitely avoiding eye contact as, I am sure, he was steaming inside. I offered, "Golly, gee, Lou, maybe they weren't ready?"

What did Spinning Therapeutic Web Woman just say? Weren't ready! Weren't ready?? Maybe the Aztecs weren't ready for some Conquistadors! Maybe Wiley Coyote wasn't ready for the Road Runner. Just maybe I'm not ready for teaching phonics in a program I'm in charge of!?

"Look Laura, my entire master's thesis was focused on neural development as pertains to reading. It takes just as much brain matter to retain the sound byte "d" as it takes to recall "money. Which byte are our students more apt to recall at their age and life experiences? Are they going to sit in front of a computer and watch bunnies hop around on carrot word sounds? Are they going to sit in a class repeating letter burp and belch sounds? Get Real!!"

I talk to her and talk to her and talk to her and she just doesn't get it! Do I walk into her how do you feel Howdy Doody Buffalo Bob therapy sessions and tell her how to conduct them? Do I interfere with her inter/intra specific dialogues with families? Do I challenge her acceptance of student points of view even when they are off the wall? Do I????? Maybe I should. I don't think there's another subject that ticks me off more than Phonics and Laura knows it.

I know she's just waiting me out. Just like she always does. But I can't stop! Damn the woman!

I vent, "What right do you have to come into my world and start spouting off about a phonic based reading lab?"

This dialogue just makes me want to jump up and down!

"Laura, you do not know the difference between a phoneme and a morpheme. What is an "r" controlled vowel? Our students need their self-esteem raised by other means than a first grade Lippincott phonic workbook."

That was what Valley Oak was about. Determining the needs of students and employing creative methods to meet them. Phonics for emotionally disturbed conduct disordered wannabe adolescents? I'd rather be a cowboy. I flopped onto the couch.

Praise the lord he paused for a thought.

I seized the moment before he started doing something weird, like tossing my office. Time to sooth the beast. "C'mon Lou, sit down and let's talk this through."

He grunted and folded his arms while looking away. I gave him my most genuine smile and moved into his line of vision," Lou, you, yourself, have lavishly praised Benjamin Jacobs for the growth he has made with students in reading. Like you say, you hold a master's in reading and have taught primary, yet, you have directed Benjamin to work with Heather in establishing the elementary reading program." Keep the ego massage going. "To your good judgment, every district that has placed with us has complimented Heather on the academic work she has done and the growth of her students."

Let's see if he can process this thought. "Maybe we should have Benjamin train one of our teaching assistants to employ his techniques in a middle grade reading lab?"

I look at Laura. She was serious. When she said "maybe" it meant that this should happen. I knew what she was saying. She was telling me that it was my problem that our students were not benefiting from the academic offering of Valley Oak as much as they should. If I was hung up about phonics, get out of the way. It was working. What further proof did you need than the progress our students had made with Benjamin? Was I deaf or blind, maybe just stupid, all three? Maybe I should just go hang out in the shed with the goats.

I couldn't deny that Benjamin's students had made progress. In fact, it was mindboggling. It went against everything that I believed. All the changes we had made. For instance, I was no longer "the wallet" with daily activities being pulled out of it. We actually had a class schedule! We had limited our community-based instruction. We had orchestrated a time controlled modular program. We had purchased state adopted texts of high interest low vocabulary curricula in all the subject areas. However, even the Woodcock-Johnson R testing that we did, which categorically documented our students increased academic scores, had not supported an increase in reading skills for our more challenging students. In fact, as Laura had stated numerous times, we were not taking a direct approach to the students improving their reading skills except "feeling better" about themselves. Again, this was my problem because I was the obstacle hindering the establishment of a reading lab. Like learning to read was the answer to poverty, the war on drugs, and the Red Sox overcoming

The Curse of The Babe. I was so righteously indignant towards the failure of phonics for the student population that I revolted at its mere mention.

He's beginning to listen. There is a light in yonder castle window.

I continued, "Lou the most negative comments that others make about our program is that students are "put out to pasture" at Valley Oak. That we do well because we do not have the same expectations as a public school would hold for the student."

Lou's rolling his eyes, keep the positive going.

"Lou, I know you have given up "the wallet," we have four "academic" periods every day, and you have increased the academic focus by cutting down on Wednesday Earned Activity to every other week. We no longer do as much out and about types of activities. What I am asking is beyond this. What I am asking you to do is to take a step back from your own needs."

He's not going to like this. This is personal. Here goes.

"Look at Sally, Jesse, Damion, Crystal. All of them have improved their reading ability. Every one of them is enrolled with Benjamin. They all look forward to their time with him. What is he doing that is working so well that the rest of program is not?"

I hate it when I know I'm wrong.

May 6, Life Is Good

Secrets. We all have them. Not the good ones. Somewhere in our past. Bad things happened. Maybe, we caused them. That's why we keep them a secret. If they were good, we would share them. Sharing good secrets is cool. Bad secrets we keep inside. We should have known better. Made better decisions. Realized the consequences. Like, I remember this time that Lurch, I mean Tiptop, and I were catching these beautiful Monarch Butterflies. We would cup them in our hands so that we would not ruin their wings. I got the sick idea of throwing them into this spider's web. Which we did and, before we could make things right, this huge black spider swung down on the butterfly and wrapped it up. Yeh, I still remember it. I bet Lurch does too. Sometimes I feel like that butterfly...

I did a pretty good job of not inflicting pain on humans. There were some mean people that got my attention, but they earned it. What I did though was screw myself up. Took matters into my own hands. It wasn't Power Memorial with the shot clock winding down. I just had the ability to make some decisions that were not in my best interest. That sounds like Laura. To me, I just f'd up.

Without a doubt, the one that eats on me and I will keep to the grave, was heading into the Spring Quarter my first year at Berkeley, when I thought I had it going on. My GPA was a solid 3.4, I was hanging with my buddies, and there were ladies available. I also really liked my time alone. Maybe that's because of how I found myself at Founders. Having no family and needing to put together my own back up. Take care of my own needs. But I craved those moments when I could get out on my own and just be.

One of my favorite places was over in Marin County on Mt. Tamalpais looking out over Pt. Reyes. Tamalpais was named by the Spanish for a mythical sleeping princess, which at dusk you could see outlined beneath the glowing sky from the Berkeley Campus. What I enjoyed about Tamalpais was the state park where you could have a view of the coast from the Transamerica Building in San Francisco north to the Pt. Reyes Headlands. Down below I could look upon Stinson Beach/Bolinas Lagoon and out to the Farallon Islands. Toss in a crimson setting sun with cascading fog entering the Golden Gate, and Tamalpais was not a bad place to hang out.

Pt. Reyes, itself, is part of another Continental Plate. I have read that, with the continental shifts, give it fifty million years and Los Angeles will be where I am standing. Could I root for the Dodgers? On this day I had driven down into Stinson Beach and around the lagoon to the town of Bolinas. To me, as I entered it past a post card elementary school, I could have been back in New England. Doubt if they brought in lobsters from here. I cruised the downtown, which had a bar, grocery store, and, of all things, a Christian Science Reading Room. There were some boats tied up but not serious fishing trawlers. Those came out of San Francisco and, to the north, Bodega Bay.

On the way back to Highway 1, I noticed that there was a baseball game going on at the elementary school and decided to take a look. There were two full teams with fans and family on both sides. I soon found out it was The Surfers vs. The Hippies. Game for bragging rights that was played every Saturday, weather permitting, from Spring through the Fall.

I found a shaded spot on The Surfer's side of the field and sat down. The players were yelling all sorts of things at one another. A keg of beer was stationed in ice near third base. Nothing like slow pitch beer ball on a Saturday afternoon. No sooner than I had become comfortable, than one of The Surfer's approached me to see if I could fill in for an injured player. He said, since no one knew me, both sides would be able to agree. I said sure.

That late afternoon, sitting up in Mt. Tamalpais State Park, I slowly puffed on my bong and thought of how cool it was that I could crush two over the fence home runs without any practice. You should have seen the scene after the first one. The Hippies were all yelling that I was a ringer brought in from somebody's family. People were throwing things on the field. The Surfers were just laughing and shaking their hands like they were in a craps game and had won. When I slammed the game winning three run homer in the bottom of the last inning, I could not make it to first! I was carried off the field in jubilation. My back never felt better. They made me promise to return the following weekend. Shades of Jumpin' Jack…

Although I respected Red, there just was not anything tying me down to Founders and the East Coast, I took another hit. Smoke filled the van. I kept the windows up and inhaled. Red would not approve. I had not given in to trying out the heavy psychedelics. They were all plentifully available. Maybe over the summer when classes were not so intense. I had dabbled with peyote and mushrooms. They were nice. Since it was Saturday, I opened my copper container and took out a dried mushroom and slowly chewed on it like a piece of beef jerky. Slowly, between the marijuana and mushroom, I slipped into the cascading sunset over the Pacific thinking ………. life is good.……….

When I awoke, the stars were out and the half moon illuminated the carpet of fog that had moved in and surrounded Mt. Tamalpais. I checked my watch, 2:07 A.M. Saturday had become Sunday. I placed my bong and copper container into the hidden compartment of my gym bag, started the engine, and, after a moment of marveling at the beauty of the blinking skyscrapers in San Francisco rising through the fog, headed down the twisting narrow road into Mill Valley.

May 9   An Angel

The timing could not have been worse in terms of my getting away from the East Coast. Not only had I committed to coach a high school all star contest between Massachusetts and The Best of New England, but Founders was looking to me to be the guest speaker at their Spring Graduation. The doctors at UC Med in San Francisco had kept me informed as to Jack's recovery, which verged on miraculous considering the report of his van tumbling over and over down a ravine and ending up in someplace called Muir Woods. The medical team had made the decision to operate on Jack and place a supportive rod in his vertebrae. They felt that the slightest twitch might cause Jack's spinal cord to be cut. Although I heard about the operation after the fact, I certainly agreed. It was good to hear that he was out of ICU. Then too, Jack was over eighteen and would have to absorb the impact of his decisions. On the flight over to San Francisco, I determined that it was time that Jack knew his history...

An Angel, that's what she was. An Angel without wings. She hovered near me as I came in and out of my dreamy fog. She would sit next to me when I was awake and sooth the deranged tangle of my thoughts. What had I done? What kind of operation? How could I finish my classes? And, what I couldn't share with her, what had happened to my gym bag and drugs?

Around the sixth day of my recovery, my buddies were allowed to visit. There were no jokes. They were just glad to see me starting to pull through. They let me know that they had taken care of putting my course work on hold. More importantly, to me, they had picked up my gym bag and stowed it away. I hoped they meant everything.

I thanked them the best I could. They said they would be coming in and out as long as I was here.

"You have a nice group of friends."

I looked up, upon my Angel. She had bundled blond into graying thick hair with pristine blue eyes that looked far beyond the surface. If I ever have a daughter, I will name her Angel Palmyra. "Nurse Palmyra, were you ever an Angel?"

"Jack, do you know how many times you have asked me that question?"

She fluffed up my pillow and adjusted the bed.

I didn't. "It's just that I….," I hesitated as my back began to spasm.

Palmyra gave me a frown, "You know you are not to talk or move too much, that's why I had to shoo your friends out."

"Do Angels have daughters?"

Palmyra beamed, "If you were Italian, I would say yes."

"To meet your daughter I would gladly become…." Another spasm took hold.

Palmyra reached over and increased the pain drip dosage. "You sleep and dream of being Italian…………..or, at least Catholic."

I nodded.

"But first, just listen for the moment."

I nodded.

"A friend of yours, Red, has been calling three times a day. He is very concerned and says that he will be coming to see you very soon." Palmyra waited. "I see a smile on your lips, he must be a good friend."

I tried to nod as I drifted off.

"I will look forward to meeting him." Were the last words I heard as the fog settled into a consuming void.

Valley Oak November 15

I sat across from Benjamin Jacobs. Guru of the Green Beret Phonics Mystic……

I had purchased three hours of his time to assist me in setting up the fundamentals of a phonic based reading lab. I had asked him to go easy on me. I had observed his work with Reffti, now, I was the learner.

Benjamin was kind, "Lou, I know this is not your favorite thing to do. I realize Laura has really worked with you on how program can benefit from such an offering."

I laughed. That's for sure. "It's all true, but the reason I'm here is because what you do works. I've seen it work. I'm willing to try and place my prejudices behind me and get into phonics for adolescents."

I was saying this? Did I believe it?

"Benjamin, given the good stuff that comes from your approach, I can envision a reading program that offers the same core technique in the elementary as in the middle and secondary programs. I think it's important to have the consistency. Meet the students where their skill level, not their age determines."

Benjamin laughed and slapped the table, "Atta boy Lou, keep saying that until you internalize the mantra because I do too," Benjamin continued. "I want to run this by you, see what you think." (I felt like Laura was on a video cam.) He shifted in his seat. Took his glasses off. Wiped them. I braced for pontification. "There are three areas that I have determined as being germane to a student's reading success." He paused, "I feel that it's important for you to buy into my program approach if you are going to teach it."

I settled back in my chair. Benjamin finally found a fit for his glasses on his jagged nose. Made a final adjustment and began, "The first issue to be aware of is that our students have been taught incorrectly." Benjamin paused. I hoped this wasn't going to take the entire afternoon. I had afternoon Celtic tickets!

Benjamin continued, "You've heard me make that statement several times. The thematic reading programs of the seventies and until the present time have done a disservice as a method of teaching reading in public education. I agree that it can be more fun for the teachers to present creative thematic programs around Women's Suffrage, Martin Luther King, Ghandi, Baseball, you name it, but they have not given our students the tools they need to decode and encode our graphemic system"

He smiled and looked away for a moment, "I only hold your generation partially responsible for the desperate collapse of reading scores."

He let that sink in. I wasn't sure if he didn't mean it.

"Additionally, there is no reason why a phonics based program cannot present the same thematic information. But I digress, back to why phonics."

Benjamin placed a sheet of binder paper in front of me. He wrote down the vowels. "What are their names Lou?"

I got this, "Easy. "AEIOU."

He shook his head. "That's our first misconception. They are a/e/i/o/u like in apple and elephant. You know the drill. Now, place your hand on your throat. Say aaaaaaaaaa."

I did that. Just like Reffti. I said aaaaaaaaaaaa. I could feel my throat vibrate.

"You feel the aaaaa?"

"Yes."

"One more time."

"aaaaaaaaaa."

Benjamin smiled, "I'm going to give you kinesthetic-visual reinforcement for the short vowel sounds that our students need to be offered in order to begin to learn how to read. There are lots of ways of doing the concept, this is mine. I am saying kinesthetic-visual because most of our students are presented the letter sounds in an auditory manner. Some of our students cannot learn through the auditory modality. Their learning strength might be kinesthetic or visual. Look at how we make the e sound. Feel your mouth?" Benjamin held his thumb and index finder at the edges of his lips as his mouth curved downward and he emitted an eeeeeeee.

"Visually you can see the corners of my mouth turn down as I make the eeee sound. Now, I want you to take two fingers of your right hand and pull down on the corners of your mouth as you say eeeeeeeeee."

I did this feeling like a first time snowboarder.

"Now the aaa."

I grabbed my throat as if I were choking myself and went aaaaaa.

"Good job." Benjamin laughed. "You can feel. You can see. You can hear. Now for iiiiii." How do you think we visualize the short i sound?"

Beyond me. I made the iiiiiii sound…..no bells rang…."I give up."

"The secret's in the chin." Benjamin demonstrated. He held his thumb under his chin and said iiiiiiiiiiiiii. I could see his jaw jut out and his thumb move forward.

"Say iiiiiiii?"

"iiiiiiiiiiiiiiiiiiiiiiiiiiii"

"Hear the iiiiiiii?"

"Got it." Even though I felt like an idiot. How did he get the students to do these stunts?

"Feel the iiiiiiii."

I did iiiiiii again. "Feels like iiiiiiii."

"Good, now give me our three sounds and their signs."

I got them. The a with the throat, the e, with the mouth, and the i with the chin.

"Now give them to me in reverse order."

I got mixed up but made it through.

"Not as easy as it might seem, but there is hope for you if you practice."

I cleared my throat. "Thanks for the encouragement."

"Not at all." Benjamin face was flushed. He remained very serious about his favorite topic. "Lou, forgive my bombastic nature, I just love teaching teachers how to teach right. Now, here's the key to teaching our students how to read. Not every student. Not you and me. Not those of us who get the code. But for those on the outside. Those who only get static on their internal televisions. Here's what they need to do, they need to learn to hear with they eyes and see with their ears."

"Benjamin, give me a break."

"Think about it Lou! If your nose runs and your feet smell, are you put together right?"

Ben laughed at himself. "I tend to talk on but our students just do not get it through the normal means of learning! We must offer other means. These means need to be consistent and from another point of departure."

I nodded. Knowing nothing. I was but "The Grasshopper" awaiting further anointment.

Benjamin went back to the drill, "Enough philosophy! Now for ooooooooooooo. Think of being at the doctor's office. He's got that tongue depressor out. What are you going to say?"

Like I didn't have a clue.

Benjamin realized my plight. "Watch me.....Ooooooooooooooo?"

"Once more, with feeling."

"Oooooooooooooooo!"

"That's good. The last is everyone's favorite. I tell the students that they are being weight lifters. What does a weight lifter say when he's got something heavy to lift up?" Benjamin placed his hands above his shoulders as if to lift up a bar.

"Uuuuuuuuuuuuuu."

"There you have it."

"That's it?"

"Lift the weight Lou."

I did as told. "Uuuuuuuuuuuuuuu"

347

Benjamin leaned back, readjusted his glasses. "That's the foundation. Students need to hear the sound, see the sound, feel the sound."

"No smell?"

Benjamin laughed, "That's another approach for another time."

He continued, "All these senses contribute to the student's internalizing mechanisms. Teach the sounds, not the names." Benjamin looked at me and gave me a moment to take in the need for learning letter sounds as to confusing them with names.

I nodded acknowledgement.

"OK Lou, then on to issue number two." Ben paused a moment to reflect. "The second area builds upon learning the letter sounds and it is consistency. Just as in math where one and one always equals two, a consonant vowel consonant sequence always has the vowel making the short sound. This is called a closed vowel. A vowel that is followed by a consonant. It says a/e/i/o/u. Give me an exception to this rule."

I couldn't immediately come up with any.

Benjamin rewarded my silence. "That's right and that's the way we should present phonics! Don't worry, the English language has plenty. But not enough to impact on our beginning readers, if we are careful. We can set the format to teach phonics just like one plus one. Students need to learn to trust that format. Teachers need to learn to teach that format. Phonics is consistent. We internalize the consistent to process the inconsistencies."

I looked at Benjamin. He was more than getting my attention, teaching from areas of strength to weakness was an educational cornerstone.

"So Ben, you know I have always stayed away from phonics."

"Of course Lou, I never held it against you as a personal character flaw."

"Mucho gracias petron, but one of the reasons was that my perspective of the English language was that it had so many inconsistencies. I mean it's not only witch which are you?" Ben placed his chin on his hands as I launched into my basic complaint. "But there are hundreds of words like "red." Is that the color or have you read the book I just did? No, I have not read it and I don't plan to read it either. However, I do desire to learn how a reed grows, so I will read a book about a reed as long as it is not printed in red ink. However, I may have already read it."

Benjamin smiled, "Precisely, I couldn't agree with you more, Lou. Transformational generative grammar is a major human reading headache." Benjamin responded. "But, let's stick to phonics. We know the inconsistencies. They only make matters worse. Avoid them. Teach around them. Find programs that don't present them. Focus on the consistent. Make reading as simple as possible for your students." Benjamin drummed the table with his fingers as if to play a piano and said, "think of phonics this way. Think of your woodshop. Would you use a Phillips screwdriver when a straight edge screw needed to be attached? Would you use a chop saw on a piece of wood that needed to have a half inch taken from a four foot length? Would you....."

"Benjamin, I get the point!"

Benjamin stood up and walked over and tapped his phonic chart, "Remember, you and I did not need this alternative approach. We were able to take from the abstract and form the concrete. Our students need mortar upon mortar upon mortar, with some Super Glue tossed in. Which brings me to my third issue and one that is bedrock with Valley Oak, building self-esteem."

This had always been my major concern. "Benjamin, you know my line on this, you just can't sit there with a fourteen year old and go d/o/g. They're going to laugh in your face."

Benjamin pulled back as if physically assaulted and asked, "Do you see Crystal laughing? You see Damion laughing?"

As with Laura, I was getting nailed. I shrugged in acknowledgement of the fact that they were apt pupils.

Benjamin suddenly brought his fist down hard on the table, "Damn it Lou! Get with it!"

I shuddered and almost fell over, but Benjamin wasn't laughing. I suddenly had a vision of Red talking about Hoosier basketball and Bobby Knight.

"Our students need the tools. Just like your shop does. The tools are phonics AND it is that simple!"

Laura and Ben were tag teaming me. I caught my breath, "That's just the point Benjamin, I don't see any of your students blowing it off. I don't know why they aren't and I don't know why they're learning to read. I'm simply incredibly amazed."

Benjamin smiled at the accolade and held out his arms to the heavens. "Ready for the third part?"

"Amaze me."

"Self-esteem. It's the key component. You have been after righteous self-determination through an enriched relationship based program. From my perspective, here's what needs to be done.

Benjamin began speaking with rapid excited animation, "Do not teach dog and cat. You teach the student "mitten." You avoid the 'mit' and 'ten.' You teach a student 'tablet.' Not 'tab' and 'let.' You teach a student 'cabin' without 'cab' and 'in. You teach 'fan-tas-tic' not fan." Benjamin put his hands behind his head and rocked in his chair. "Teach them BIG words. Teach them things they did knot know they knew! Assist them in finding out how smart they really are!"

Benjamin knew he had me. He knew I could see with my ears and heard with my eyes, just as he did. Now, for Valley Oak.

"That's cool. OK, how and when do we set up the Reading Lab?"

"Look at it this way Lou, how soon can we let them know how smart they really are?"

January 20   Reading Lab

We had waited until the semester break to set up the reading lab. During this time the individual therapists and I had met with the students and their parents who were to be enrolled and talked with them about what we wanted to do with the reading lab. Try to pro act to the blow back on teaching first grade skills. What the focus would be. Need to accept academic levels. Not target others. Be supportive and on-task. All had agreed to give it a shot.

Now it was up to me. Events were closing in. It was time to produce. I had taught in small rooms in huge high schools. Small rooms didn't bother me. I made small rooms enormous. I had always thought of e. e. cummings and his Enormous Room. Cummings was a pacifist during WWI. He was assigned to drive ambulances and was caught by the Germans. He was housed in a small room with several other prisoners. Gradually, as the story unfolds, Cummings tells each prisoner's tale. By the time the book is over, the tiny room has become enormous due to the personalities. I could do that with a small room. I could make them enormous. But that had always been by assignment, not choice. This was my program. I made the assignments. Now, here I stood. My decision. I would be in a tiny room with no windows!

Benjamin and I had just stayed out of Lou's path and shook our heads as he accumulated what Lou believed to be necessary for the success of The Reading Lab. It was as though Lou was preparing for his room to be under siege with all the resources he was compiling. Benjamin and I processed with Lou that he was all right, chill out, he was doing a good thing, phonics will work and we will be there to support you.

The fact is, which is one of the reasons I respect Lou, that he is sacrificing his personal needs and insights to meet those of the students. Lou is not going to baseball games, he is not off on a twenty-mile bike ride, he is not showing a Charleton Heston epic to teach history but Lou is placing his needs on hold in order to teach the students in a manner they can most benefit from. He has done this in a myriad of ways since I began with Valley Oak. Lou has realized, and accepted, that no one except himself could entice our older students to enter a basic phonics reading lab program and he was taking the assignment very seriously. Lou has been upfront with the students and he has told them in no uncertain terms that this is not his first choice, but it is the best choice for them. For their part, the students have agreed as they trust Lou and accept his ability to quell their anxieties and nurture them on with their lives. Now is the time for Lou to teach...

May 16   An Angel and Red

I awoke in clean ironed sheets amidst a dream about my 'Angel's' daughter where I was learning to speak Italian and wondering why angels were Catholic and spoke Italian. These thoughts were dashed as I recognized Red resting his head on his thick chest. The sun was starting to break through the morning fog.

"Bet you were expecting an angel," he mumbled.

I wanted to jump out of bed and hug him. God it was good to see him again! We talked every now and then but to be back and feel his presence, support, just made me feel everything was going to turn out O.K.

A whiff of starched air filled the room as Angel Palmyra entered, "So, I see you have a real angel." She laughed. "Here I thought I was the only one."

I could see Jack stiffen as I came to his side, "Palmyra says you've been hitting on her."

As Red gathered his arms carefully around me all I could think to say was, "I am so glad to see you."

"Red shared a bit of your history with me Jack. I want you to know that I am impressed with how you have come through some really tough times."

It would be weeks before I would be able to raise up and put pressure on my spine. I looked into the overhead mirror that gave me a view of the room and Palmyra, "Well, you sure have eased the pain in this episode Nurse Palmyra."

Palmyra shared her radiant smile, "Well, I will leave the two of you to catch up." Before she walked out she added, "By the by, my Angel Italian Catholic daughter is a freshman at USF."

Red shook his head. "Flat on your back and still fishin', sounds like you are going to be just fine Jack."

My eyes began to moisten as Red moved his chair next to me and held my hand. Letting out a soft moan as he eased into the worn chair,

"I know boy, this is not how you wanted things." Red winced. "But things are what they are." We sat there like that for what seemed an eternity. Red waited as I got myself back together.

Finally, Red began, "I have been debriefed by your medical team and everyone is confident that you will make a full recovery." Red paused. Checked his watch. "Physically."

I knew where Red was going. "Your mental attitude is a concern." I sank back deep into my bed sheets. If I could've pulled the blankets over my head, I would've.

"I'm not here to lecture at you Jack, so stay with me."

I agreed. Red was serious. "Least I could do Red."

He shifted uncomfortably in his seat. "This has weighed on me for what seemed forever." Red took a long moment staring at his shoes. "What I'm about to tell you will be life changing."

What else? What have I not known that Red has? I asked, trying to lighten the mood, "Red, I would be proud to know that you're my father."

I could sense that Red didn't know whether to laugh or shut me down. There was a flare in his eyes that slipped into a smile.

"Damn Jack, where'd you think that one up?"

"Well, you always had your eye on me and besides, how else could I jump so high?

This time Red laughed. I could see him relax. What he was going to tell me must be a bit mind boggling mysterious.

The room was still. I could feel the machines checking my health. Red cleared his throat and said straight out, "Jack, I knew your real father."

My eyes must have gone wide. "Hold on Jack, let me tell you everything at once."

Red did. Blew my mind.

May 28   Red and Lou Thompson

I stayed with Jack for over a week. I would have stayed longer if need be. I answered all the questions Jack could think up as best I could. As the days moved on, I could feel his competitive resolve returning. The day came when I knew I could get back to my barbecue.

Jack asked, for the thirty thousandth time, "My given name is Louis Eugene Thompson?"

"That it is. I still have the birth certificate in my safe deposit box."

"Crazy stuff, Red." I paused and asked, "Can you send it out to me so I can make the change legal? I'd like to honor my father and, hopefully, yourself."

"Sounds good to me."

"And," I smiled, "I promise not to call you Eugene if you do the same for me."

"Bet on it," Red chuckled.

I looked at the clock. I new Red was getting ready to move on. "Another thing, how did my father's and your oath go again?"

Red stopped and pondered for a moment. "That was long ago, but not something one forgets." Red recited the words to me.

The bed sheets were becoming sticky with my sweat. I could feel my throat becoming taunt, emotional. "I'd like to say what I need to say from a more upright position."

As if she had been listening, The Angel wafted in and gently raised me up as far as I could tolerate. As she fluffed a pillow and asked, "How's that?"

"Good." I managed.

"Angel?"

"Yes my Lou."

I squirmed, but asked, "Could you stay for what I have to say to Red?"

"Of course!" Palmyra and Red held hands.

Red waited, "Take your time Lou."

My new name. Identity. A real past. I somberly began, "Red, by all the love you and my father held dear for one another, I promise never to bring shame to either of your names."

Red bent over and kissed my forehead, "You never have Lou."

Palmyra gently kissed Red's and my hands.

The next day I caught a flight back to the East Coast. As I hailed a cab outside my hotel, I tossed a copper canister that Nurse Angel Palmyra had given me into a city trash bin. Lou's friends had only found the gym bag. The Angel had mentioned that she had five sons and hoped that, should there come such a time, someone would look over them. I thanked her and, as Lou says, some secrets you keep, even the good ones.

February 3 Phonics for Adlescents

I never admitted this to Laura, she would have psychoanalyzed me to my grave, but I kept having these two dreams about the Reading Lab.

In one dream my first period class begins to stagger in. There is no joy in their Mudville expressions. Nick is in the class. Fifteen years old. He has put on sixty pounds in his two years in our program. Non-reader.

Monroe, all six foot two of him. Cannot stop drooling. Everyone teases him about it. Not in reading lab. Need to remind him to swallow.

Rachel. Sad. Tearful. Screaming when things do not go her way. Sexualized acting-out. Could almost be in an exceptional center.

Ramon. Eighteen years old. Working three days a week at Wal-Mart corralling carts and wants to improve his reading skills. Good stuff.

Jeffrey. Came into program two years ago is still unable to write his name. His aunt blames me for this. He's fourteen now and ready to begin transitioning back to his district. Benjamin has worked wonders with him.

Patrick. Good athlete. Left-handed flame-thrower. Cannot remember a vocabulary word to save his soul. Hates pencils. Here they come.

READYSETGO!!!!!!!!!!

"Where do I sit?"

"You can choose your seat."

"Why do I have to be in here?"

"I don't need no reading lab."

"Can I have a fruit?"

"I don't want to be in here with Monroe."

"Shut up beach ball."

"Fuck you slime lip."

"That's a point for each of you for swearing."

"I don't give a shit."

"Lou, I need to go to work in ten minutes."

"We'll get you there Ramon."

"Can I be on the computer."

"Not right now."

"Rachel, hear you been kissin' on Stan?"

"I have not you bootie head!"

"Kiss your own bootie."

"That's your second point Nick."

"Big f'n deal."

"Moving towards a step."

"My Mom says I don't have to listen to you."

"We've talked about that Jeffrey. You have any concerns, you can call her."

"I want a drink of water."

I model, "Any chance of trying, pardon me Lou, may I have a drink of water?"

"Pardon me Lou, may I have a drink of water?"

"Sure, thanks for asking."

"I need some fruit."

"Whom are you talking to?"

"Lou, may I please have a fruit?"

"Sure, napkins are on the refrigerator."

"What's in the refrigerator?"

"I do not believe that reading lab is about what's in the refrigerator."

"Stop kicking me!"

"I wasn't."

"You know you was!"

"Lou, can I use the restroom?"

"Yes. Use the one in our room. Not the one down the hall." Our room use to be the custodian's room. It was small but it had a private shower and restroom.

"Swallow, Marcus."

"You swallow your daddy's dick."

"At least my daddy has one."

"Uuuuuuummmmmm............they talking about nasty stuff!!"

"Monroe, Nick, would either of you care to take some space or see your therapist?"

"Fuck no."

"Me neither."

"I'm out of here. I'm not listening to this bullcrap."

I pick up my walkie. "Maurice, is there a staff available in your room to monitor Monroe who just walked out of the Reading Lab?"

"Not a problem Lou."

"Anybody else desire to have a step drop and walk out?" I look around the table. Usually calms down after the first casualty.

"I'm leaving too."

"That's your choice Rachel."

"Follow your drooling boyfriend retard."

"I'm no retard. I'll slap your face you white fagot fatso!"

"Ooooooh, I'm so scared, don't forget your spray can of lip gloss"

"You've had your step drop Nick. Ready for a level?"

"Ooooooh, I'm so scared."

"Scared or not it's up to you."

"Retard just said she was going to kick my fat white ass! You didn't do shit to her!"

I pick up my walkie. "Matt would you be able to assist me in my reading lab?

"Right there, Lou."

"You going to scare me with Matt's face?"

"Not at all. We are going to offer you the choice of taking some space with Matt or talking with your therapist." Matt enters. "What's the choice, Nick."

Nick ponders the alternatives. "I'll take a walk with Matt."

I signal Matt ten minutes.

The intercom rings. "Lou?"

"Yes."

"It's time for Ramon to be transported to Wal-Mart."

"He'll be right out."

"See ya Lou."

"Have a good one at Wal-Mart."

Jeffrey's therapist, Moncrief enters. Moncrief was raised on Barbados. Not only is he multi lingual and working on his doctorate, but he is a world class cricket player.

"Lou, I hope that I am not intruding?" He asks in his lilting Caribbean English.

"Never, Moncrief."

"I was wondering if I might have a word with young Jeffrey?"

Jeffrey leaps up at the opportunity to be rescued from Reading Lab.

"Jeffrey, I did not hear Lou excuse you."

"Sorry." Jeffrey sits back down.

Moncrief laughs, "So anxious to leave are they?"

"Just their first day too."

"Jeffrey, would you come with me please?"

"Sure Moncrief."

"Why's everybody leaving?"

The tension lightens.

"Not everyone, Rachel. Patrick, you and I are still here."

"Well, I don't want to be here!" She folds her arms and I thought her lip was going to hit the floor. "I don't want to be in this lousy old school!" She begins a wailing cry that pierces cement. I look at Patrick. He's oblivious. Sandra comes in from the next room.

"We're setting up for lunch. Maybe Rachel would like to help?"

Rachel rubs her eyes and nods. Small mercies. She leaves with Sandra. That leaves Patrick and me.

"Let's go over the spelling words for this week Patrick."

"Do I have to? There's no one else in here."

He's got that right.

"Get ready for a growth spurt Patrick."

The second dream was like this. First period: Reading Lab: Valley Oak School, as if a dream. The dream is always the same. Think that was from Risky Business. I had never thought of myself as Tom Cruise and Scientology is just whacked.

I stand in front of the class beginning the lesson. "Before getting into our new vocabulary for this week, I want a quick review of what we have done thus far."

"Nick, when I write cvc/cvc, what does that mean?"

"Means you have a word with four consonants and two vowels."

"One hundred percent correct!"

"What about the vowels Marcus? What can you tell us about them?"

"They're closed vowels. Make their short sound."

"Good job."

"What's a blend Jeffrey?"

"Two letters that make one sound."

"Correct!"

"What are we studying now Rachel?"

"R controlled vowels."

"Right!"

"What sound does ar make Ramon?"

"Says the sound of the letter r."

"Good."

"How about or?"

"Makes the sound of or like in store."

"Very good. Excellent, every one of you. You keep this up and I'll feel like I'm a teacher."

"Now, for this week, I'm going to cut you some slack. I'm going to teach you three more r controlled vowel letter combinations, but they all make the same sound! Three for the price of one!!" (Was that Jesus' deal?)

"Er, ir, and ur all make the same errrrrrrrr sound."

"Say er."

They all chorus in unison, "ER!"

"Er says er in her."

"Er says er in her."

"What does er say Marcus?"

"Er says er in her."

"Everyone, ir says errrrrrrrrrrrr in sir."

"Ir says errrrrrrrrr in sir."

"Ramon, what does ir say?"

"Ir says errrrrrrrrr in sir."

"Excellent."

"Last one. Ur says errrrrrrrrr in turn."

"Ur says errrrrrr in turn."

"Patrick, what does ur say?"

"Ur says errrrrrrrr in turn."

"Yes!"

"Now, Jeffrey, what sound does er, ir and ur make?"

"They all make the same sound, errrrrrrrrrr."

"I agree."

"Marcus, tell me what three r controlled vowels make the sound errrrrrrrrrrr."

"Er, ir, and ur."

"Terrific!"

I was so proud of how far this group had come. Their targeting was a thing of the past. They were engaging as a community to assist each other in growing. Sure, the harmony wasn't perfect, but if they could do this well throughout program, they would be ready to transition back towards the district schools WITH IMPROVED READING SKILLS!

"Remember, these three are hard to spell, but they're easy to read. Why Nick?"

"Because they all make the same sound."

"Exactly."

"Give me an example from the board Patrick." I had written several of each r controlled vowel on the board.

"Fur and fir. One's a tree and the other is on an animal."

"How do you know?"

"F-u-r is animal and f-i-r is a tree."

"How do you know?"

"Because you told me."

The power of being a teacher. I could be telling them that fur was a tree and that fir was on the animal. They would accept my word. I could be tossing in some of my oblique insightful humor that would break down the lesson and confuse the students. Not one joke. Not one quip. Not one pun.

Just straight ahead by the book teacher directed lessons.

"That's true, I agreed. "but how could you figure it out in the context of a sentence."

"If fur comes in front of the word wolf, I know that it is not the fir that is with the tree."

"Right! Lots of times the context the word is used in will tell you the spelling and meaning. But, what's the most important thing Rachael?"

"To be able to read the word."

"Yes." She was so with it!

"Marcus, is spelling the word the same as reading the word."

"No."

"Correct."

"Ramon, is writing the word the same as reading the word?"

"'fraid not."

"Jeffrey, is reading the word aloud the same as reading to yourself?"

"Nope."

"You all are correct! Now, tell me what reading is." I pointed to the six-inch high bold acrylic letter phrase pasted to the board. No one made a sound. Everyone read the phrase. The phrase read, I READ FOR MY FUTURE!

"Denise," who is my TA, "How are The Greasers and the Socs getting along?

"Can I go with Denise?"

"I want to!"

"We are on Pony Boy is meeting up with Cherri. Sparks are going to fly."

"Who do you have with you today?"

"Marcus, Rachel, and Patrick. Patrick, could you gather up four copies and meet us in the reading room, please."

"Sure thing Denise." They walk out.

"Ramon, no Wal-Mart today. Correct?"

"Not today. Can I keep going on Level Three of Adventure Reading?"

"Sure, as soon as you and I read for ten minutes."

"No problemo."

"Jeffrey, we have added the letters e and i to homebase for this week. Use your middle fingers of each hand for these letters."

"OK Lou. If I get to twelve words per minute can I choose a reading game to play?"

"Good idea."

"Ramon, got your book?"

"Right here."

"What page did we stop on?"

"Forty-seven."

I bolted up and awake. I looked at my alarm clock. Read 2:38 A.M. I slowly realized that I had been dreaming. The dream was one of those dreams that you wake up from and you wonder where everything went. Then you realize that it was all a dream. Nightmare or Fairy Tale?

I smiled, this dream was slowly becoming reality......

December 2   Girl Friends 'til The End

"God, I'm glad it's Friday."

"You can say that again sweet heart."

I sat in my office with my girl friends, Martha Lee and Geraldine following an excruciating IEP that had to be reconvened due to my placing a two hour time limit on Valley Oak IEP's. I believed that if you could not come to some manageable resolution in two hours, take a breath and come back when the smoke had cleared.

"You down for Jake's with us or," Geraldine gave Martha Lee a knowing smug look, "do you have something else going on?"

"Yeh, right," I dead panned. The something else they meant was Lou Thompson. Over the past two months we had met for "business" dinners at some of the finest restaurants and "low down dumps" in our area, with each of us going home in separate cars.

"C'mon now girlfriend. No secrets."

We struggled into our long winter coats and gloves, ready for the blast of a frigid December storm. Heads down, we carefully stepped our way to Martha Lee's eleven year old Volvo, which she cared for as if the vehicle were a member of her family. Martha Lee was the last in as she scraped the light snow off the back and side windows.

"You girls make sure to shake that mush off your feet. Don't want my upholstery to be dirtied up."

"Yes, ma'am," we chorused. As we settled in with the heater turned up full, Martha Lee started the windshield wipers to clear the two inches of snow. Looking back, she hesitantly began to edge into the traffic.

"OK girl, let's get back to our topic."

"Got that right. You been coy with him or say what?" Martha Lee leaned back in the front seat, arched her eyebrows and began counting on her fingers, "One, two...almost three months."

"You two have to be doing something besides 'just business.'"

I looked at them, my two best friends, I had to be able to level with them. I sunk back into the back seat of the Volvo, sadly sighing, "if you think that IEP was rough, trying to figure out why I am so caught up with Lou Thompson is leaving me strung out and distraught."

This caught the two of them by surprise.

"You?"

"C'mon girl. Where's your strut?"

"What's he doing to you?"

"He just playing you?"

"We'll whip that boy's bottom!"

"Get his bootie in here now!"

My girlfriends, I had to love them. Lou taking advantage of me, how I wished. I laughed, "If that would help I would call him in here pronto."

"Well, if he don't need a trip to the wood shed, what in the good Lord's name is going on?"

For sure I wish I knew. "Lou has been the complete gentleman when we have been together. He…"

"Hold it right there," Geraldine and Martha Lee chorused. They nodded at each other knowingly.

"You go ML." sighed Geraldine.

"Well, Geraldine, for a woman who is pushing forty something…"

"Now GIRFRIENDS!" I shrilled.

We all laughed and then Martha cleared her throat and went on, "Let's see if I've got this thing right. You've been seeing the same person off and on over three months and your relationship remains," She looked to the ceiling, "Hmmmmmmm…." Martha Lee paused for the correct word, "Remains, as you put it, gentlemanly. We need to be told more of this tale."

"Let's put it to you this way honey pie." Here it comes, I thought. "Are your needs being met?

I knew I was blushing a deep scarlet but they were totally right for I wanted more from Lou than I was getting, both physically and emotionally.

"OK….OK…..I get your point and I agree." If possible, I sunk further back into the depths of the back seat.

Geraldine proclaimed in a confident voice, "Well, since we are all in agreement, just what are we three going to do about this Mr. Lou "The Gentleman" Thompson?"

I was open to any and ALL suggestions…

Valley Oak School
Psycho/educational Intake Summary

Laura Rosso: LCSW

Name: <u>Laura Rosso</u>
DOB: <u>7/25/51</u>

County of Residence: San Francisco
School District of Reference: San Francisco

Date: 5/8/99

Physical Description: Laura presents as the five foot six and one half-inch one hundred and twenty-five pound Risky Business Homecoming Queen that boyhood dreams conjured and her presence fulfilled. Laura's cascading blonde hair, pool deep blue eyes, given to a green hue, and photogenic smile, left one wondering of MTV enshrinement. With all the "Barbie Doll" enhancements, Laura's calm impeccable demeanor was primordially established by being the eldest of six children born to second generation Italian parents, Angelo and Palmyra Rosso. Her rigid parochial stance was due to her Catholic school tutelage and the experience of supervising five, younger, rowdy brothers. Laura's interests included Tai-Chi, sailing, family connections, organic gardening, and intense professional growth.

Referring Criterion: Laura has, historically, always done the "right thing." The restrictive Catholic family culture she had been raised under had demanded that she make the proper decision, adhere to social norms, and be a role model to her five siblings. Laura's impromptu decision to participate in Valley Oak and leave the safety net of the Bay County Mental Health umbrella was entirely out of character. Although there were suggestions that Laura's choice to leave the San Francisco Bay Area and her family culture might have given validity to Laura's ability to make radical resolutions. Interviewed Bay County Mental Health coworkers were alarmed by her abrupt departure and hinted at a "coming of age" dissatisfaction with her life's accomplishments contributing to a desire to experience risk. Laura's newly chosen path would lead her to an environment that would tax and challenge her intellectual interests as well as place herself in harm's way of a rogue personality, Lou Thompson. The consternation following Laura's decision would impact the well being of Bay County Mental Health for several months as she was being groomed for the upcoming Directorship of Bay County, although each and everyone of the staff wished Laura well in what appeared to be a personal quest for the "Holy Grail."

Family History: Laura was raised in the close knit Sunset neighborhood of San Francisco. Laura's father had earned his CPA credentials attending night school and was employed by the Bank of America in their Downtown Branch. Laura's mother returned to work, as a registered nurse at UC Berkeley's San Francisco location when Laura was twelve. Laura was given the task of supervising her younger brothers and, with the assistance of her large extended family, was able to coordinate everything from Little League to doctor appointments. Laura attended, as did her five brothers, The University of San Francisco and "chose" to live at home during the university years. Laura's parents continue to live in the original home, but Laura escaped for the East Coast when she was twenty-seven, as her youngest brother graduated from USF. Her comment to friends concerning the geographic change was that "she was ready to see an ocean where the sun rose rather than where it set."

Psychiatric History: Laura has been meeting with the same psychiatrist, Lynn O'Hare, for the past eight years. Laura referred herself with concerns of having an attachment disorder as she has had few male relationships and seldom dated. Coming from a gregarious Italian family, being more than physically attractive, and possessing strong social skills, her alienated status was cause for reflection. Laura's work consumed much of her energy as she attended state and national conventions representing Bay County, as well as donating time to the Battered Woman's Shelter. Laura's personal therapy sessions have decreased over the past three years to bimonthly as she has resolved her anxiety issues to the point that they no longer overtly interfere with her daily function. A major shift supporting her mental well being was Laura's choice to leave the Catholic Church and forming a bond with the Unitarian community, which caused her family to consistently pray for her.

DSM:

Axis I:	V62.81 Relationship Problem; NOS
Axis II:	Traits of Obsessive-Compulsive Personality D/O; (Diagnostic Features)
Axis III:	None
Axis IV:	Mundane social life; empty social calendar; fear of rogue personalities.
Axis V: GAF-65	Some difficulty in social functioning but, necessarily, coping pretty well.

Recommendations: Given Laura's desire to thrust herself out of the county mental health cocoon and into the pandemonium of non public emotionally disturbed day treatment education, including Mr. Lou Thompson, there is little left to say but... You go girl!

Signed_____Date_____
Martha Lee Rodriquez, LCSW

Signed_____ Date _____
Geraldine Moore, MSW

Chapter 9

VALLEY OAK: A PLEASURE

January 14   Make Believe

I found myself flitting nervously around my carefully appointed yard sale- purchased eclectic furniture feeling like a shy debutant preparing for her first date as I checked the aromatic candles. Not wanting to overdo the ambiance, I uncorked the wine, propped up the pillows, adjusted the lighting, nurtured the glowing fire place, and fidgeted with the volume of my treasured Robert Kern CD, to make my abode as homey as a welcoming New England cottage might be. I had even banished Bonnie and Clyde to their crates in the spare room. No yapping dogs to disrupt the tangled web I was preparing this evening.

No matter how veiled I attempted to qualify my intentions, I knew I was setting out to seduce that epitome of the male philanderer, Lou Thompson! If he was going to be gentlemanly hesitant in his overtures, contrary to all the girly gossamer gossip, then I would need to take the lead and provoke him with the incentives that would lure him into my silkened grasp. I felt so deliciously wicked!

I paused and took stock of my efforts. I truly loved my home, which was built in the 1870's, and passed down through generations of Italian family members, which is where my family name had served me well. All the Italian extended family of the original owners had opted for larger suburban homes. My cozy, two bedroom, bungalow was reclused on one of the neighborhood's many "not a through road" leaf engulfed sanctuaries that brought minimal traffic and welcomed privacy. The Tozi's had lamented its passing out of the family, but they were visibly pleased that their home was going to another "member of the familia."

Over the generations the Tozi's had maintained a large garden with an accompanying greenhouse that produced succulent tomatoes, squash, beans, and other delectables well into the New England winter. I had spent many a late afternoon, following a day of being encased in my chair at work, combing through my plantings, harvesting the wealth of the organically composted fertile soil that had been built up through the years. I also enjoyed the waist deep pond with the recycling waterfall tumbling into the pool with a wonderful rhythm that would lull me to wistful dreams through my open bedroom window.

One building I seldom journeyed into, except to clean out intrusive spiders and dust with my shop vacuum, was the shed where Augusto Tozi had left his formidable collection of woodworking tools. He had said that his children had no interest in them and that they were too dear to him to sell. The shed was also stocked with all types of nuts, bolts, nails, clamps, vises, in a labeled organized format, and several types of power tools that I could not name. Augusto charged me with keeping the tools orderly and serviceable and, with good grace, to encounter a man who would enjoy a winter's day with his stove's warming coals while constructing some needed project.

I promised Augusto that I would keep the shop shipshape and…to do my best about the guy thing………

There was a hesitant knock on my front screen door and I held myself back as not to seem too over anxious, as I cautiously opened the solid oak entrance to behold the man of my tool shed!

"Hey, Laura, nice place you got here."

"Thanks Lou,"

"If a bit hard to find."

"Well, I hope to make the visit worth your while." I laughed and winked him in with a brief glance into his soft olive eyes.

I helped Lou off with his coat savoring his musky cologne as I could feel him taking in the living room He handed me a gift wrapped bottle of wine. I took off the ribbons and discovered a bottle of the red and white checkered Paisano!

"Lou, you shouldn't have," I laughed.

"I spare no expense at your behest."

I gave him a gentle hug. "You are too gallant."

Lou bowed to the waist, then, to my wonderment, reopened the front door and brought in a bucket with TWO bottles of champagne perched in a silver canister of crushed ice, one of which he immediately opened with the cork popping off the ceiling! Heavens, what next?

"Have a seat while I pour our celebration," I commanded, doing my best to present a modest decorum.

As I went into the kitchen and opened the refrigerator for two, chilled glasses, I could see Lou trying to figure out where to settle. To ease, what I considered his discomfiture, I quickly returned and offered Lou his glass, he was still standing, so I tiptoed up and emboldenly offered a light kiss to his cheek. To my amazement and delight Lou placed our glasses of bubbly on the lamp table and in a swirling gentle grasp locked me in his arms and pulled me into him, compressing our bodies as his lips kissed my forehead, cheeks, ears, and sought my tongue, which I ravenously gave up seeking more. No words as I felt my emotions becoming undone and breathlessly aroused as Lou's hand wound through my loose hair and pulled my head back, dropping my beret to the carpet, while he nipped at my neck, his other hand expertly unhinging my bra. Intoxicated, I grabbed hold of his belt buckle and...

AWOKE!

Not again! How many times had my recurring fantasies found me laying distraught, embedded within my fluffed embroidered pillows, the sunlight of a Saturday morning beginning to reflect from my full length mirror! Dreamily, I found myself lounging back in time to the family Easter Dinner when I definitely decided that I needed an environmental change.

April 14 San Francisco The Family

"So," In his bottom of the ocean voice, "My loving daughter, what can I do?

"Papa, you can stop asking me."

I tossed the dish towel over my shoulder, pushed open the swinging door separating the kitchen from the dining room, and surveyed the carnage of our family three leaf extended table, and began cleaning the scattered remains of our Easter meal. My mother's traditional Rosemary Lamb was down to a few scraps with the accompanying mint jam dish empty, the seama was gone, so were the stuffed onions and zucchini. There was some polenta but the gravy was done. I ate one more of my mother's homemade potato gnocchi's, wiping her green garlic pesto sauce off my chin. Laden with platters, I swayed back into the kitchen. I had come to regret that Papa always helped with the dishes on these occasions and I wished he would just go out and join the brothers and other family members in trying to cheat one another in their traditional Pedro card games.

My Papa was as handsome as one could paint an Italian father with his luminous brown eyes, thick curling salt and pepper hair, and welcoming smile that exuded an enveloping joyfulness with all those he came in contact with. I was his only daughter, the jewel of his family, and, now at twenty-six years of age, coming to desire more space from the affectionate all embracing family love.

"Angelo, you going to do woman's work all night?" My brother Lorenzo called out from one of the card tables.

"C'mon Papa, take off the apron."

"Only when your sister tells me who she is going to marry!" Papa took me by the hand and, at the risk of shattering my mother's precious Holiday China, twirled me like a forked pasta into his arms. I squealed as a child in delight.

"Give it up Papa."

"But Papa, Laura is already married to the therapeutically undernourished, needy poor of America."

"Yeh, Papa, I hear we will be working at a soup kitchen in The Tenderloin next Thanksgiving!"

Everyone laughed and knew how much my Papa desired to see me married with bambinos. If they were not Italian, at least they would be Catholic!

"Hey Papa," shouted Albert, "Maybe you should walk with a sandwich sign down Columbus, advertising a deranged daughter available for matrimony."

More laughter as everyone raised their brandied cherries in a toast.

As I safely placed the platters gently in the sink, I gave myself up to my Papa's gentle hug. "Pay them no mind, my princess."

"Papa, I don't. But it's like this at every family gathering." I snuggled into his warm chest. He was always there for me, letting me know how much I meant to him. How much he enjoyed my happiness. It was just that my happiness had not come to include a husband and, for that matter, anything resembling dating. Not only was my family concerned, as they had given up setting me up with suitors, but I was beginning to question my sensibilities.

I attempted to change the subject. "Should I get out the Spumoni Ice Cream?"

"Wait until they have started to light their cigars and I sit down to play." Papa kissed my forehead.

I knew my family loved me and I adored them. I was already an aunt with two of my brothers, Geno and Marco, married and each with a daughter!

Sylvia, Marco's bride of three years, came up to me shaking her long brown curls, bemoaning, "Italian men, what can you do with them?"

"Wash their dishes and have their babies," Stephanie, my other sister-in-law chimed in.

Such complainers, "As both of you are finishing law school, I doubt that."

"True Laura, but you've got to let them know who's the boss." Stephanie laughed waving a rolling pin in the air.

My Mama entered.

"How did you survive having six children Palmyra?"

Mama paused taking the dish towel off of my shoulder, "Six? Is that all? Felt like sixty!"

Mama looked over at Papa. "Time for you to go out and start cheating your children and nephews at Pedro."

Reluctantly Papa kissed Mama on the check and slid the pasta bowls back into the deep cast iron double sink. "What Mama says goes." Papa bowed to us.

"Yeh, right just leave."

"At least we know where his sons get it from."

A welcoming chorus of camaraderie cheer echoed from the living room as Papa, with lit cigar, entered through the swinging kitchen door.

May 6, 2001   Valley Oak, A Pleasure

I thoroughly enjoyed the days that I came to Valley Oak with a cleared agenda, no IEP's, District Administration, or other formal commitments, attired in jeans and tennis shoes, leaving my therapeutic layered garbs in the closet. Not only I, but the staff as well, was pleased to see me wearing a more informal hat. Many of the students, especially the newer referrals, would do a double take when seeing me and ask questions like, had I lost my job? Glad to see that I was not judged by my clothing! I laughed, thinking how that had been a concern of The Little Prince.

Today was an early Spring sun warmed day with the random almond trees in their grand New England bloom, reminding me of the white blossomed orchards in the Central Valley of California that occurred two months earlier. For me, however the metamorphosis had happened, I found myself immersed in Valley Oak. The term I caught myself using more and more was that Valley Oak was "A Pleasure!" Valley Oak had become a carnival labyrinth of human and animal activity as I surveyed the fifteen acres that contained our creative energy. Right now, I was escaping my paperwork shrouded office for a survey of outside activity on a gorgeous spring day during lunch break. I took in a full deep breath of the fresh air thinking how The Founder's property had been transformed with the front five acres being mowed to a carpeted Bermuda shag by Workability and our flame painted John Deere, which seemed like to be in operation twenty-five hours a day. I could see Richard riding on it against the north end of the property, just tooling along, I could not hear the engine, as there was such a cacophony of sound coming from the smorgasbord of outside commotion.

I walked over to the soccer field, no longer shielded from the road and public view by the thick growth of trees, which we had cut and sold for firewood. Workability had used some of the same limbs and constructed two solid, albeit rustic, four by four-supported goal posts. JK had said that it would take a mob of anarchical English fanatics to tear these puppies down as I beheld Heather playing soccer goalie with three students taking turns drilling one in.

"Hey, Laura. Watch me blast one by her!" Monroe called. He was eight years old and had never seen a live goat before entering our program.

"Not a chance Monroe," taunted Heather. "You couldn't kick your way out of a paper bag!" Heather took a moment to more tightly bind her braided hair.

"Oh yeh? I already got me two goals!"

Heather looked over at me. She acknowledged, "The guy's good. I'm afraid to stop his ball. His foot's like a cannon."

I watched as Monroe, all of eight years old, gathered himself from twenty-feet away to attack the goal as his smile changed to fierce determination as he approached the soccer ball. Whump! He hit it solid towards the right upper corner of the goal. Heather sprung up and lunged to her right, landing hard on her shoulder, Heather really tried...

"Gooaaallll!" shrieked Tyler and Scott jumping up and down. Slapping high fives with Monroe.

"That's seven for our team!"

Heather explained as she picked up the netted soccer ball, wiping the smudged grass from her shoulder, "If they get ten goals, they get to go on the computers after break without having to do the boardwork."

"C'mon Heather! Quit stalling!"

"Let's go!"

"Whose turn is it?"

"Tyler's."

"Good luck Heather," I supported walking away. To be young and spry again...

"I'll need it, she sighed"

"Keep firing guys."

"Piece of cake Miss Laura."

"No problem."

Heather looked determined. "I could stop you guys sitting in a rocking chair!"

"Get ready for number eight!"

I strolled over towards Stan who was stroking softballs with a fungo, lazily backing up the outfielders to the two eighty-five foot mark on the fence that was constructed on four by eight three-quarter inch plywood with student painted illustrations of Ted Williams, Josh Gibson, and The Babe painted on them in cartoon form. The Ted Williams portrait was done to placate Lou, who promised that future portraits would be by vote. Stan was lobbing the flies up to the fence so that, when the fielders made the catch, they were robbing someone of a home run. Stan was even more of a baseball fanatic than Lou, if that were possible, as he had collected dirt, pardon me, sacred heritage, from every major league park. Stan had secured his job with Valley Oak by bestowing upon Lou a piece of the brick wall from Wrigley Field.

"Hey Stan."

"Hi, Miss Laura. Want to rip a few?"

"Not without some Geritol first." I recalled the days of family and neighborhood ball games in our street as, being the eldest, I had carried a big stick, even for being a girl. Those days of prodigious athletic fame were long gone.

Stan was good as he popped one between Frank in right and Jerry in center, making them look to each other and call it. It wasn't quite to the fence and Jerry came in a couple of steps and gloved it. He fired the ball back into Stan on a single bounce that Stan snatched and swung, launching another arcing pellet towards the large number 42, the Jackie Robinson mural.

Stan paused, nodded behind me where Lou was sauntering up.

"Hey Stan."

Lou gave me a smug look, I noted his lower lip was quivering. Something was up.

"Want to rip a few Lou? Guys would like to see us play some home run derby."

Lou held up his hands in total mock surrender.

I could not resist getting in a dig, "Yeh Lou, what was the score last time."

Jerry yelled from the outfield, Twenty-four to eleven Ms. Laura!"

Stan was that good. Lou bowed and, in a swoop, graciously led me away.

"The Angel called."

374

That stopped me in my tracks. "My own mother calls you more than she does me."

Lou ignored my complaint, pretending to be absorbed in the flight of one of Stan's arcing pellets. I had to smile, thinking back to the day I shared the delightfully audacious news regarding Lou with my family.......................

One Year Earlier   De Ja Vu

Palmyra answered the phone, "So my East Coast forgotten daughter, what is the news that so honors me with your call?"

In retrospect, I might have been more aware of the impact of my words as I blurted, "Mama, I am getting married."

Silence.........total silence........ then my Mother's laughter, "You got me there Laura. I deserved that for all the trouble I have given you."

I found myself trembling, "Mama, I am serious. I am getting married." I gasped as her phone thudded the wooden floor in the kitchen.

Mama picked the phone up. Her voice was an emotional rasp, "This is true what you tell me?"

"Yes Mama. I swear on the honor of our family."

Outside of religious vows, there was not a more sacred oath to be uttered within our inner circle.

"I believe you, but give me a moment." I could hear Mama opening a cabinet, a soft clinking of a glass being set on our kitchen table. "Now my daughter, allow me to calm my nerves before you tell me of what god is so lucky to charm you."

I waited as I knew she was having a sip of brandy. With a sigh of expectation or was it fear, "My daughter. I am ready."

I could see her with her shoulders erect crossing herself and praying for a Good Italian Catholic Man.

"Mama, you have already met him."

A long pause, then, "I know of none of our acquaintances who has left their family for your side of the country."

I knew I needed to not play games. The news of my marriage was enough to cause severe emotional distress. The next was preposterous fantasy, "Mama, the man is the Lou of Your Dreams."

I waited several moments of quiet before continuing, "Mama, Lou is the same young man you cared for years ago in the hospital."

Mama came back to me, "My cherished daughter who continues to torment me with fairy tales, tell me this..........."

I waited as I knew she was having a second sip of brandy. She began again, "Tell me this, does Lou have a friend who owns a barbecue."

My ever so politically correct Mother, "Yes Mama, he is Black, his name is Red, like his hair, and he owns a barbecue."

This time, both the phone and the glass hit the floor!

I came back to the present with Lou holding my shoulder with a bemused, yet concerned, twinkle in his eyes.

"You drift off somewhere?"

I nodded as we walked away from the ball diamond. I felt a bit flustered as Lou softly let go of my shoulder. I blushed admitting, "I was back calling Mama with the news I was marrying you."

Lou gave a soft laugh and added, "That was almost as good as the time I first met your family."

How true a statement that was! After kneeling in the remaining sawdust of Angelo's tool shed to ask for my hand, we had flown out to San Francisco to meet the extended Italian family.

Lou and I stood in front of my family's starch white yellow trimmed Sunset Home.

I turned to Lou, "You ready for this?"

Trying to show bravado, Lou answered, "One might ask, are they ready for me?" Of which I had little doubt.

Holding hands like high school sweet hearts, we mounted the six steps to the front porch and I, hesitantly, turned the knob to.................

.....having the door torn open. Welcoming arms pulling me in with Lou hanging on amidst a loud chorus of engulfing rancorous epitaphs!

"Hey Lou!

"Great to see you!"

"Time Laura got hitched!"

"Welcome aboard!"

The brothers and sisters-in-laws swarming, crushing our bodies in a frenzy of joy.

"Hey Lou, can you root for the Giants or are you East Coast?

Geno yells, "Finally get some height into the family!"

"Thanks for keeping Laura from a Nunnery!"

"Yeh Lou. Time for payback to Mother Superior!" (Which was the name my brothers always invoked when I was in charge of them.)

Sylvia reaches behind Lou and tousles his curls, then firmly pulls his head down to her level, giving him a thick red lip stick kiss on the cheek declaring! "That's one!"

Stephanie quickly slips through and lays another lipstick marker on Lou's other check. "That's two!"

They must have had the attack planned. I am unable to catch Lou's reaction to their vociferous welcome. I had warned Lou that events, of which I had no idea, would surely be prepared for his arrival.

Then The Brothers cleared an aisle for Papa to greet his future son-in-law. Papa came forward elegantly attired in a formal, three piece, light gray, pin striped suit with his starched white shirt. Collar open with no tie. Papa paused, framing his, momentary, head to toe appraisal before throwing his arms wide and holding Lou in a warm embrace stating, "Welcome to our home and our family!"

"Ritual time!" Yelled Albert.

"Circle up!"

The Brothers, including Papa, form a circle around Lou and chant their cherished male bonding welcome. Arms interlocked they begin....

"We are the guys!"

"Mighty, Mighty Guys!"

"I am a Guy!" (Pointing to themselves.)

"You are a Guy!" (Pointing to each other.)

"We are the Guys!" (Regripping one another.)

"THE MIGHTY MIGHTY GUYS!"

With ease three of the brothers hoist Lou onto their shoulders, Lou having to duck his head because of the ceiling. Then, suddenly, the family went quiet as I watched with horrid fascination as Papa held a hand up and pulled a white "wife beater," T-Shirt from inside his vest and proclaimed,

377

"Lou, as a new member to The Community of Male Valor, we bestow upon you the symbol of our dominant role in the home!"

Albert hands Lou a shot glass filled to the brim with brandy.

"A toast from Lou.............!"

Suddenly!

"Hold it one second!" My Mama commanded entering from the kitchen.

"Put my Lou down RIGHT NOW!"

"C'mon Mama!"

"Never let us have fun!"

The Brothers grudgingly complied as Mama wrapped her arms around Lou and, with astonished shock uttered, "My Lou, you are thin as a strand of dry spaghetti! Has Laura been starving you? Should I hospitalize you?"

Before Lou could reply, The Brothers raised him back on their shoulders and began to chant, "Toast! Toast! Toast!"

Lou begs forgiveness and asked, for the toast, to be placed by my side, which The Brothers allowed. He gently kissed Mama's and my cheek and, I noticed his lower lip quivering as he held up the brandy and proclaimed to all............"WE ARE THE GUYS!"

Chaos ensued as relatives and neighbors poured through doorways and pressed in to meet the man who had won my heart.

Lou acknowledged, "That was some welcome."

I nodded. I turned to him serious, like why could not my own Mama, call me? "OK, light of my Mama's life, why did she call?"

Lou did not immediately answer, which made me want to kick him. I found that he could, still, so easily irritate me!

"Well," he slowly began, drawing out the moment, "Mama wanted to know how I felt about two weddings."

I looked at Lou, showing that I did not understand the message.

"Allow me to clarify, how about a wedding on The East and West Coast?"

I found myself gushing, "That would be wonderful! Our East Coast friends could attend and Red could do the banquet!"

"That's just what Mama said. Lots of our friends just couldn't afford the flight and costs of a hotel. Also, Mama said that more of the family from Italy would be able to fly in."

"Sounds great! Do I have your permission to call Mama back and say let's do it?!"

Lou's walkie rang on.

"OK, I'll come right up."

He turned to me smiling, "You have my permission and I have to get over to the basketball court."

I gave Lou a brief side hug and watched as he jogged towards the basketball court. Looking around, I decided to go over to our bike shop.

Around the edges of our pasture bicycles sped and we had everything from BMX's and mountain bikes to Big Wheels. Workability had built some jumps, nothing life threatening, and Celia was monitoring the bike rack where students had to put them back rear wheel first and make sure there was no damage. Celia also made sure they limited the carnage and hung up their helmets.

I walked up to her as she was organizing the bicycle helmets by size, "Nice day, Celia."

"That it is Ms. Laura."

"Bikes running OK?" Their maintenance was always an ongoing issue for Workability and Celia.

"That they are. Workability has done a good job in keeping them going." Suddenly, feigning panic, Celia shouted, "Look out Ms. Laura! Here comes the Road Warrior!"

I spun around just in time to catch Trent bearing down on me, as, luckily, he showed mercy and skidded to a stop.

"Just kidding Ms.Laura." Trent was five. I could picture him flipping on a trampoline.

"Now, Trent, you could have given Ms. Laura a heart attack. You need to watch yourself on that rampaging bike."

Trent faked a forlorn apology, Yes, Celia. Sorry Ms. Laura."

"Thanks for stopping like you did Trent, but you know the importance of being careful." Trent threw his head back laughing and we shook our heads as Trent sped off peddling his training wheel balanced chariot in search of inflicting further havoc upon mortal beings.

"Hey, Ms. Laura! C'mon, we need you!"

I looked over to the basketball court where there was a four-on-four game going on. Our court, as with so many other things, had been constructed by our Workability component that had poured it in three eight yard cement truck sections, all on one hot day! We had adjustable hoops so that the elementary program could have some fun, and also, so people like me could dunk. One half of the court was painted with the major countries of the world so that, when we played Around the World, we really played around the world. The other half had a map of the United States where we would play games like "Out" while naming the states or their capitals. We didn't play Horse because the students could not stop from posturing that their "Ho" was better than your "Hor."

"What's up Quincy?" Even though I knew it would be someone doing him wrong.

"Greg won't pass the rock."

Quincy was one tough fourteen year old street smart bi-polar cookie. "Won't pass it or just won't pass it to you?"

"Do it matter?"

I looked over to Martin, who was the ref. He shrugged saying, "You know Quincy, hard for him to let go."

Quincy hollered, "Forget you Martin. You ref Ms. Laura. You be fair. Martin be calling that cheap stuff on me."

Every time Quincy played in a competitive game it was WW III, he not only had to win, but the game had to go down the way he thought it should. Quincy had to make THE pass, had to take THE shot, had to be THE MAN. So much of Quincy's need to be THE came out in my therapy sessions with him as, like many of our other students, the adults in the home life lacked the social and parenting values, whatever to blame, to provide consistent boundaries and positive human contact. The children were made to step up in order to control the chaos that filled their home environment for they could not trust the adults to make good decisions and, many times, their perspective was accurate. However, they were children, not small adults, and our students needed to feel safe and protected in order to enjoy their childhood, even if they were smarter than we were.

Martin challenged, "Quincy, you going to play or talk?"

"PLAY! Forget you Martin!" Quincy tramped back onto the court.

I decided to stick around and see what came down. I watched as Quincy took the inbound pass, made a smooth lead to Henry, cut around his opponent on a back screen, and broke open to the hoop. Henry, stepped back and dropped in a sweet twenty foot bank shot.

"Game!" called Martin, in game ending finality.

Quincy was going to steam blow with eyes cartoon-wide as his team had won but he hadn't gotten the ball back. He stomped towards Henry, who was three years older, a foot taller, and no one to fool with screaming, "Can't you pass!?"

Henry just smiled while high fiving his other teammates.

Then Quincy continued to trudge towards his homeroom, whining and moaning the entire way.

Martin looked at me and grinned. "Use to be a lot worse."

"Sure did," I agreed, recalling the automatic need for a prone restraint following a loss.

"Who's got next?" Martin called.

"We do," Sally hollered.

Martin asked, "You want in Ms. Laura until Quincy cools down?"

"Thanks, but I have to get some stuff out at the greenhouse."

"C'mon Ms. Laura. We'll let you guard Lou. He's weak."

Lou caught a toss from Sally, spun the ball from finger to finger, gave me a Cheshire Cat smile, just baiting me to step up.

"I'll make sure to have my tennis shoes the next time I come out," I promised crossing my heart as I headed towards the greenhouse. Wonder if they noticed it was with my left hand?

The greenhouse had been in operation for two years now and just about all of the plants that we had in our garden were started in boxes from seed and then transplanted. Just this year we had begun a hydroponics operation that was my claim to fame and I needed to keep an eye on its viability. I was still in a bit of awe over the effort and product that we had put together as I opened the door to the warmed greenhouse from our equipment storage shed where we kept the lawnmowers, rototillers, and various tools needed for our site maintenance. Without too much grandiosity, I hoped the time would come when our garden could, not only supply Culinary Arts, but we could have a vegetable and fruit stand next to the bridge.

I was greeted, not only by the steamy heat scented soil but, 'Look what I got Ms. Laura."

I shaded my eyes and looked out through one of the slant opened windows, "That's beautiful." Ashley and Mark were in the garden where they had caught a Praying Mantis in their butterfly net.

"Can we put the Mantis in the greenhouse to lay its eggs?"

"That's a good question."

"You're in charge of the greenhouse, right?"

They had me there. "I am one of many in charge and I want to make sure that Dustin, who knows a lot more than I do, is on board with the idea."

"The Mantis, "Ashley continued while in eye to eye contact with the green goblin, "could protect the plants from the bad insects."

"I agree. Why not get with Dustin and ask if it would be OK?"

I watched with delight as they ran off towards the horshoe pit where Dustin was playing a game with Ramsey. Dustin had worked with Parks and Rec for eight years before he had come to Valley Oak, stating that he needed some stimulation besides spreading pesticides in his workday. Through Workability he had helped construct planters, flowerbeds, the greenhouse, horseshoe pits, and, currently, was designing an exercise par course. We were glad to have him.

I reluctantly left the greenhouse when, "Duck Ms. Laura!"

Clunk!

A kite thudded down next to me, skidding to a stop

I heard a voice calling, "Sorry Ms, Laura. Can you help me get the thing up?"

I looked across the field. "Sure Shante. Just let me get into the wind." There was barely enough breeze to billow the kite out from where I stood as Shante wound the string into her.

"Ready?"

"Contact!" Shante ran into the wind with her long black hair flowing as the kite popped up to a safe height.

"Thanks Ms. Laura," she called over her shoulder running hard as she could into the light breeze. Happiness, Charlie Brown, is flying a kite for Shante who had survived a world of deprivation and familial drug addiction to find safe harbor in the Founder's Residential Program and Valley Oak School..

My pleasure Shante, I thought, letting the greenhouse go as I saw that Brown Bag was returning to site. Thursdays was Brown Bag Day, an addition to Lunch Bunch, which meant that those students who had earned it could go off site to a fast food or restaurant for lunch. Each Thursday was a different place like Taco Bell, Togo's, or an all you can eat Chinese buffet. Red's was off-limits as only Lunch Bunch could go there on Mondays. We allowed the students to spend up to five dollars that they may have earned from program's Workability and monetary reward system or brought from home for a Brown Bag lunch.

We had started Brown Bag because our students' goal was to transition back to their public schools and we had found that they had difficulty with the unstructured lunch scene in the various cafeterias. Several of the junior high and high schools from districts that referred to us had vendors such as Taco Bell or Subway in their cafeterias, so, on Thursdays, we encouraged students to bring a healthy "brown bag" lunch from home or go off-site and purchase their lunch. At the outset of Brown Bag, some students took the opportunity to bring in huge lunches filled with candy bars, potato chips, "non-alcoholic beer," sodas, or anything that did not look like an apple or granola bar. We had set out some expectations about what a "healthy" brown bag school lunch should consist of, which stopped the food displays and, now, about fifteen students a week attended the off site Brown Bag, and, when they returned to site, it was time for lunch break to end with homeroom being called, unless, of course, a major game was on the line.

"Home Room!" Martin called over the walkie. "Brown Bag is on site!"

I took in the transition as students punched their last tetherball and kicked their final Hacky Sack as, amidst laughter, program headed into the various classrooms. Valley Oak had grown to include seven classrooms with twelve students each, one teacher, three assistants, and one therapist for each room. When we sat down for our banquets our numbers had swelled to one hundred and thirty students and staff, which was as far as we could go with the current buildings.

I looked on as Lou came in from break, talking and joking with the students and staff around him. Lou was immersed in Valley Oak for he was now a part of the relationship based culture that formed the intrinsic fabric of our day treatment program. There was no doubt in my mind that Lou was the motivating creator of Valley Oak but his role was no longer the salient gatekeeper of all that was good or punitive, he was no longer firing from the hip or wallet to stabilize escalating situations as the Relationship Model had now been successfully incorporated into The Valley Oak Culture. In return, Lou, himself would state, that he was finding that students were seeking him out as a good object who cared about their personal well-being and had diminished targeting him in a physically challenging manner.

In the process of program growth and delegated responsibilities, Lou had chosen to become The Good Guy in The White Hat. This was not an easy transformation for an educator who needed to control his classroom, but it was a goal he had prioritized and attained. For instance, he was now seen as the key person who came up with creative ideas for our earned activities with students constantly bombarding him suggestions as to what was new and cool to do. Anyone for Laser Tag? Last Wednesday was typical as Lou and some students had conjured up an excursion Valley Oak had never experienced with a basic activity that was simple and the students had thoroughly enjoyed participating in. Their idea was to skip lunch on the activity day in exchange for Grand Slam Breakfast at Denny's and following breakfast, the group went to the IMAX Theater at the new mall for a 3-D experience. Everyone had thoroughly enjoyed the day and, as Lou would say, it was our pleasure and they had earned it.

Valley Oak's past Halloween is another example as, prior to this year, Lou had never supported the celebration of the gruesome pagan event in program as he felt that there were just too many negatives that could occur. So, what does he do this year, with the boundary of no bloody implements, students could dress as they wanted and staff joined in. The elementary program went Trick or Treating room to room and each classroom had two activities that ranged from fortune telling and face painting to timed races around the halls on "broom" decked out tricycles. There were prizes galore for everyone with the most astonishing event being Lou's renting a dunk tank for the day. Lou dressed up in a suit and said that, if it had not been for the scheduled IEP's that day, the students could dunk him. Then, he took off his coat and shoes and got onto the platform! Everyone, including myself, lined up to take their shots at him.

Now, that was a pleasure!

Throughout the cathartic six years that I have been with Valley Oak, I continue to thank my lucky stars for its existence for, in many ways, I feel like one of the students being offered the opportunity to improve my personal self-esteem and sense of well being. I am the one who is able to sit in an office with a swivel chair and attend board meetings while Lou is encrusted in his reading lab with no windows. I am the one who greets new families on intakes and represents the values of Valley Oak as Lou had gradually stepped back and supported my role with the realization that it was the one that most benefited program. His words were something like he was the salad, but I was the dressing!

Long gone, though not forgotten, is the moment I introduced myself as Lou Thompson, drawing dumbfounded looks from the attending IEP team members. I have tried to pass "brain fart" off as a lack of sleep and feeling the tension of family and district representatives attending the meeting, but there is no doubt that I had stated, when my turn came, that my name was Lou Thompson! I did not even comprehend what I said until Marianne advised me that the name Lou Thompson had been used by the individual seated next to myself. I have to admit, I certainly broke the tension and the meeting flowed smoothly from then on.

I am proud and honored to be entrusted with the lead responsibilities for Valley Oak and I value Lou's continued support of my perspective and views. This is not to say that, while enduring the onslaught of a Nor'east'er, I do not regret a California Zuma or Santa Cruz Beach, but I have developed a feeling of independent empowerment that has positively impacted my world away from Valley Oak.

I walked into the reading lab for homeroom where five of the seven students are seated. Lou and Tricia are going over the afternoon schedule while the other two students, Robert and Demetrius, had just arrived, strutting in from Brown Bag.

"Ms. Laura, is there baseball practice this afternoon?"

"I am sure there is Cory. You have a game tomorrow, right?"

"Yeh, we're playing Skyline. They're tough."

We were in a six-team league with other programs similar to ours. I say similar, because the other five programs had students whose aggressive actions were not consequenced by their not earning the right to participate in the league games, as Valley Oaks' were. In the four years and three sports we had been involved with in the league, we had won a total of six games. However, everyone commented that Valley Oak was the most socially appropriate team, which, even if our players would not agree, is what games and life are about.

"Should be a good game."

"I hope so," he nodded, Martin is having me play second base."

"Good luck tomorrow, Cory."

"Thanks Ms. Laura."

Over the walkie I heard Martin saying that they were ready to load for baseball practice, which was held in the local town at the city park softball complex. All of our students, not to mention staff, liked to try and rip one over the fence and I watched as Martin loaded five vans with twenty-one ballplayers, five staff, and all their gear. We would have had more but five students were on stayback due to behaviorally earned step and level drops during the week, and, of course, three were our best athletes.

"Baseball's ready to roll," Martin sent out over the walkie.

"Have a good one." Lou answered. "Let's go into third period."

I listened to the responses from the other rooms.

"Third period it is."

"We're ready."

"Switch is on Lou."

"Lock and load."

I watched as the vans lined up and headed out to the practice field thinking of the times program had attended Red Sox games. Lou always secured lower box tickets for us as he did not desire to sit in the middle of the rowdiness of right field. We would arrive early for the day game and park several blocks away setting up our barbecues for hot dogs and hamburgers. Before we set off for the park, students were given their choice of two granola bars, which were to hold them until the fourth inning. During the fourth, everyone was able to have a malted ice cream and were allowed to leave their seats unsupervised and roam Fenway to see what they could see. In all our times attending, not once did a negative situation arise from the trust we offered our students. Lou had commented that, since he could not play left field, he could not think of a better job than getting paid to watch a baseball game!

I paused as I headed down the hall to Larry's classroom with both sides of the hall being adorned with the thirty-two ten by twelve framed photographs of our Wall of Graduation students. Thirty-two students who had fully graduated from Valley Oak and transitioned back to their home districts and some, like Rick Hutton, had graduated from Valley Oak as a senior. Eileen had said that he was doing well with HUMBLE as he was in supervised living and had a girl friend who was attached to him at the hip. Sam was up there as well. He was attending junior college and working with Red part-time. Who knows, by now, he might even know how to mix the paint for the barbecue sauce. There was Dominic in his "smart jacket." I laughed at the thought of his strutting and tottering around in it. James, Valley Oak's first student, was sitting on his exercise bike. He said that he was going to continue to peddle across the U.S. I hoped he made it and, he would be, I thought for moment, twenty-three years old now! Good thing I was not aging.

Henry poked his head out from Larry's room. "Ms. Laura, see what I made."

Larry's room was huge as it had been the central room of the Founder's residence with the kitchen off to the side. In the kitchen Jack and two Workability students were finishing up the dishes from Culinary Arts. Another side area held program's ping-pong table and the entire area was over two thousand square feet. Three formidable beams ran across the room with the lowest one carpeted by caps from some of Lou's old Red Sox and Berkeley ones. Poor Lou, he was always moaning that the Red Sox had not won a World Series since Babe Ruth was a pitcher and the Golden Bears had not won a conference championship in a major sport since 1960, thank goodness for the Celtics and Bruins!

Larry was our newest teacher but he had three years of residential experience behind him. I had never heard Larry raise his voice as he was able to calmly stay with individuals until a situation was stabilized, which, I have no doubt, his six foot eight inch, two hundred and sixty pound frame contributed to.

"What do you have going here. Henry?"

"C'mon in and I'll show you."

In the afternoon program Larry and two other staff ran Your Art with the background of a Mozart concerto flowing through the creative endeavors. Some students were working on computer art programs. I looked at Henry's work as he was talented and took pride in his pencil etching of The Titanic.

"Very well done, Henry."

"Sally showed me how to shade it."

Henry was fixated on The Titanic and he had even made a clay sculpture of it painted in detail that now sat on the bottom of Larry's fish tank. Everyone was sitting around sketching as Sally was demonstrating a new technique from the board. Sally was a born artist who was with us part time because she had received a partial scholarship in art at a private college in Vermont.

I walked further down the hall and through the laundry room into Leonard's room which had been made from an enclosed patio and was almost as large as Larry's. I smiled looking upward to the basketball backboard with the red mark high above the hoop, which Red would not allow to be taken down. I remembered that I had, more than once, caught Lou gazing in far off thought at the mark. Leonard taught Science and Algebra, but his favorite was Literature as, for ten years, he had been a Professor of Greek Language at The University. He had tired of the endless publishing and ego battles and was enjoying the give and take of Valley Oak.

I keep asking myself, how do we manage to attract such talented people, even with a teacher shortage, who could pick and choose their jobs and for a good deal larger salary. Then too, there is that egocentric part of me that just was willing to acknowledge the heights and reputation our program had attained.

Leonard and his class are reading the classic To Kill a Mockingbird. I saw the DVD with Gregory Peck on the cover sitting on the television.

"Hey, Ms, Laura, you run this place. Tell Leonard to stop having us read this dumb old bird book."

Some students had the most oblique ways of saying hello, will you recognize me? "Russell, I do believe you are talking out and splitting staff and, besides To Kill a Mockingbird is one of my all time favorites."

Leonard added, "Russell is having a hard time accepting the role of Atticus as a single parent."

Russell adamantly shook his head, "No, it's just a stupid book. There's no action. People just talking and thinking and talking and thinking and thinking and talking."

Crrrrreee...WHAP! Everyone jerked around. The classroom pet, AWOL, our Iguana, had just leapt against the side of his ten foot square wire-meshed cage swinging his tail at the door, letting us know he wanted some attention. AWOL was almost two feet long. Often the students would sit in class with AWOL peering over their shoulder.

"See Ms. Laura, even AWOL's had enough."

"Russell, my call is that if more people learned to think and talk before they acted..."

"Forget it. Forget it, Ms. Laura. Forget I said anything. I should've known better than to talk with a therapist. Let's just read the book." Russell shook his head. "I wish Jake was still here."

Jake Yen and his promotion of human, especially student rights. I smiled at the thought of him as I walked out of Leonard's room across the site to the prefab set of offices that now housed Jeff's homeroom. Jeff ran the Workability Program and I could see one of the TA's, Joel, and three students off by the greenhouse, setting in the posts for a larger "range fed" chicken coop. I knew that Cheryl was off-site observing two other students at their job coaching positions. When I entered the room there were no students or staff, which was a good sign as it meant everyone was involved in some work assignment. I walked out the back door and observed the other members of Workability checking out the bicycles, where Jeff was, and washing and vacuuming our vans, with another student and staff under the chassis changing the oil. Everyone was involved and no one noticed me as I walked back through the room and went to Heather's, which was in what we called the Community Center.

The Community Center was just an old house where a long ago director of Founder's Residential Program had lived with his family. It was available when we came on-site and we had made it our second classroom and, as it had a kitchen, we served our lunches in it until we just got too large to handle everyone. Now, the Community Center was the elementary classroom and it was a great place because it had so many nooks and crannies for learning stations.

"How you doing Heather?" Her room was always so on-task. Tyler, Scott, and Monroe smiled up at me from their computers.

"Real good. These guys barely made it to the computers though," she said sternly.

I could see the boys giggling at each other.

"Pardon me Heather."

"Yes, Scott."

"Can I tell Ms. Laura that you only blocked two of our kicks?"

"I think you just did. Thank you very much," she laughed tussling his hair. "Take a look in the kitchen Miss Laura."

I walked around the wall to where Diane was mixing a cookie batter with Jalyn and Walter. "Whatcha making Jalyn," I asked.

"We're making cookie numbers." She seriously responded.

"Yeh, we're going to eat the numbers and then we'll remember what we ate," Walter agreed.

Diane added, "They be needing to add them correctly before any are eaten."

"Walter, you make sure you save me some of those numbers

"You got it, Ms. Laura."

Later, that day, I found a three on my desk.

I peeked into one of the adjoining rooms where Ellie was working with two students on multiplication facts.

I recalled how, when I was just tutoring for credit in college, I had a student from the Azores whose name, I will never forget, was Salvador Silva. He was just kind of a rolly-polly nice kid, with the problem being that, he was flunking fifth grade math. When I was referred to him, his class was working on division. I asked Sal if he knew his addition or subtraction facts for, if you could not compute these operations, how could you take on division? Salvador said he did not know them, but he knew his multiplication facts. Unbelievable, but he did and I asked him, how could you memorize your times but not the others? Sal said his parents did not allow him to watch television until he did! So much for enriched creative approaches. Sal earned a C on his final report card in math.

Now and again, I have wondered how Sal had gone on to teach his own children.

As I left the Community Center I saw Ricardo drive back on site with Gerald in his car. Ricardo had been with us for two years as a full-time therapist. It just boggled my mind that we had seven therapists, not counting myself, in the Valley Oak program.

"Hey Ricardo. How's it going Gerald?"

"Ricardo just took me to Red's for lunch!"

"Great. What did you choose for lunch?"

"I had the combination. Ummmm-ummm-ummm." Gerald rubbed his tummy like a genie was in there. "Chicken, ribs, and hot links."

"Yourself, Ricardo?"

"Oh, me?" Lou was always giving the therapists a bad time for "having" to endure lunch off-site at Red's. "I forced down one of Red's hot roast beef sandwiches."

Lou had told me that he always envisioned that therapy should be offered other than in the chair or on the couch in an office unadorned with personal artifacts. He thought that our type of students could have therapy while they were working on an auto engine, I could just visualize Lou as a therapeutic mechanic.

"Think we should take off the manifold?"

"Well, there was some milk in the oil. Moisture is getting in from somewhere. We'll need to take a look at the gasket. Could you hand me the seven-sixteenths box wrench?"

"Not the socket?"

"Nah, can't get leverage with the socket."

"Thanks." Lou shifts the angle to get the nut in sight. "On another subject, how're you doing with your Dad splitting?"

"Yeh. OK. Which manifold should we take off first?"

"Let's go with the left. I can see a gasket piece sticking out. How's your mom doing?"

"She's hanging in there. SSI is helping."

Of course, this never happened, maybe because our therapists did not have a background in auto mechanics, maybe going out and launching a rocket or having lunch at Red's was the equivalent of having a comfortable arena to form a relationship.

I had more firmly than ever come to believe in the formation of relationships was the basic component to a person's sense of well being. Those who supported the adage of," it is not what you know but who," were holding forth a cynical misinterpretation of the value of relationships. Life did come down to who you knew, who you got along with, who could you trust, who could trust you. Life was about relationships.

I mused, would you rather have a million dollars or ten friends...twenty friends, just how did one value a relationship? Would you rather be a happy fast food employee or an unhappy millionaire? Where did one get their sense of self-worth and I do not mean in the sense of, I have friends in New York that I haven't used yet. I am talking about someone you can share a sense of joy in life that is grounded in decent values and acts of kindness.

Relationships. Forming. Maintaining. Understanding. Accepting. That's what Valley Oak was about.

I shook my mind out of philosophical meanderings as I noticed that staff and students were leaving our various buildings, must be fourth period. With practice and job coaching going on, a good portion of our students were off-site. This certainly assisted the afternoon academics and switching times to go more smoothly as I walked back into the Reading Lab where we had three of our seven scheduled students. All three, Manuel, John, and Mitchell, had already been with Lou earlier in the day. In fact, Manuel and John would have been at practice except they had step drops during the week. All three had completed their board work, worksheets, oral reading, and had earned time on the computers. Students with Lou for the second time in a day could earn fifteen minutes of on-line time.

I observed as Lou taught.

"Lou, can I go on-line?"

"You know the rules Manuel. Who has earned the most points so far today gets the first start."

"That's always crack head John."

Lou consequenced. "That's a point Manuel."

"I don't give a fuck!"

"That's your decision." I noted that Lou did not need to inflame the moment by adding the loss of a point. Here we go again, I thought.

"I'm leaving."

Lou reminded Manual. "You know it's a step drop if you walk out of the room. You've had a good day. Why blow it off now"

Manuel paused. How far to go. "Ms. Laura, can I walk the track?"

No splitting staff here. "What do you think Lou?"

"Can you observe him Ms. Laura?"

"Sure." Even Lou called me Ms. Laura during the school day!

"Fine with me then."

Manuel walks out ahead of me and begins to trudge around the track. Posturing and threatening are just not the way to get your needs met in appropriate society and, heaven forbid, could even cost you time on the computer.

Manuel was on his second trip around the track when I went over and moved some water sprinklers and Manuel walked over.

"See the rainbow in the mist Ms. Laura?"

I looked into the spray. The breeze was blowing a fine mist. "Yes, I do."

"Where's the pot of gold?"

"Well, this is a small rainbow. Just some small gold under it."

"I don't see it."

"Well, Manuel, the way I understand how it works, you have got to catch the rainbow and you have to beware of the Leprechaun." Again, I thought of all the rainbows I had my younger brothers chase.

Manuel ran after the rainbow gleefully laughing as he dove and slid across the Bermuda grass.

"Ain't no gold!!"

"Nice try," I laughed. "Did you see the Leprechaun?"

Manual ran up to me, "Can I get on the computer when we go back in?"

"We can check with Lou. I am sure if you wait your turn and do your work that would be possible."

"OK. Let's go."

Manuel and I went back into the reading lab. About ten minutes later Celia took John into another room where they were reading Pardon Me, You're Stepping on my Eyeball! Manuel, finally, was able to earn his computer time. All was right in the world.

"Baseball's back on site." I heard Martin call over the walkie.

"Thanks Martin." Lou replied. "Let's go into homerooms."

All staff and students returned to homerooms where final announcements were made, papers handed out, behavior points reviewed, and preparations for van transportation put into order.

The coordinating of vans leaving site had always been a challenge as, at best, it had felt like controlled turmoil for the vans were made up of students from different rooms and there always was some sort of situation brewing. The coordination had taken a good two years as our numbers had swelled while employing different strategies, but our current method was working the best. We divided our eighteen vans into three groups with each van designated a specific place to park each day. Leonard would then call for the drivers of Round One to come out to their vans and, when all the drivers were accounted for, Leonard would call for the students in Round One.

"Round Two drivers," Leonard called over the walkie as the last van of Round One pulled off site.

Quincy came out and walked up to me. "Ms. Laura, you got to fire Martin."

"Why would you say that Quincy?"

"He's punk ass dope referee."

"Quincy," I acknowledge him, "As your therapist, need I take a point from you due to your choice of language?"

"Okokok, I just don't want Martin reffin' any of my games."

Besides being a homegrown super athlete in his day, Martin coached the backs at the local JC and refereed Division 5A basketball games in the area.

"Quincy, I admonished, "This is serious business. How do you want me to break the bad news to Martin?"

"Put it in the staff bulletin." Quincy paused. "Better yet, get an airplane to carry a banner behind it. Fly it around school tomorrow at lunch break."

"Great idea!" I beamed. "You got it Quincy."

"Thanks Ms. Laura, I knew I could count on you."

"See you tomorrow." I waved to him.

"I'll be lookin' for the banner."

"Not a problem." I thought for a moment. "Hey, Quincy, what should the banner say?"

Quincy stopped. He got his big gap toothy grin on. "Have it say... Have it say... MARTIN, Quincy loves you!!!"

I laughed as Quincy got in his van and I walked over and leaned against Lou's truck as Round Three vans were being filled. Lou came out with the last of the students, when he saw that I was by his beloved green, six speed manual, F-250 Super Duty Diesel and walked over to me. As I scratched Rudy's ears I could tell Lou was holding something back because his bottom lip would quiver. Someday I may tell him. I waited.

"Appreciate your dusting my truck off."

"Least I could do for such a gorgeous vehicle."

Lou and I waved to Martin, who drove the last van off site. "So, Lou, anything going on?"

He laughed. "Why, are my lips quivering?" Damn, I had forgotten that I had told him what his give away physical trait was.

"No," I professionally responded, "But you do have this tragic guilt look on your face."

We both laughed as Lou shouldered me into the side of the truck and then planted a kiss on my forehead.

"OK," he admitted, "Let's see if you're ready for this."

I stood straight, squared my shoulders, and took an overextended deep cleansing breath.

"Ready," I pronounced.

Lou took his time. Put his foot up on the bumper, rested an arm on the tailgate, looked around the school sit and, started to speak. Then stopped and smiled at his own antics. As I patiently waited, tapping my fingers on his door......

"Well," he finally began, "About a half hour ago I took a phone call from Long Barn School District. They were looking for Ms. Laura, Rosso, but staff could not track you down."

I could have been out on the track chasing rainbows with Manuel, I nodded for Lou to continue.

Lou scratched his hand, stretched. He was really enjoying this! He was waiting for me to come unglued and tell him to get on with it. Fat chance.

He looked at me, full of mischief. "What do you think about starting a second school on a regular school site in town?"

I was incredulous. "You have got to be kidding!"

"Nope."

"When?"

"Don't know, said that you would call them back and figure out the details."

This was startling news as we had been advocating for a transitional school site for our students. The site could also serve students as a half way point should districts choose to refer them towards our off site program.

"Is this something you would want to take on?"

Lou gave me one of his resentful "don't ask me if I'm sure what I said looks." Then replied, "Maybe we can recruit better and our teams would finally get some wins."

Why not indeed! "OK, I will go make the call." I could just imagine our students and program on a regular school site, how would the boundaries and expectations be maintained?

"Hey Laura!"

I turned back as Lou was climbing into his truck.

"Give me a call when you find out what school it is, I want to check out the restaurants in the area!"

I responded with a thumbs up. "Do you want a phone book?"

Lou shrugged, Nah, I think I'll just go scout out a place for a new Red's Barbecue."

With that Lou waved and began to drive off site. I paused realizing it was too late in the afternoon to call district administration and expect a response. I turned and watched Rudy bounding from side to side in the truck bed, thinking about how, that which had made Valley Oak was so dependent on the skills of Lou, but where Valley Oak was going was not neurosurgery. The successful impact of a relationship program with emotionally disturbed children was documented by the Valley Oak Wall of Graduation, the referrals from districts, the longevity of staff, and, now, the inquiry as to Valley Oaks willingness to, with the support of a local school district, expand its offering. Valley Oak now had the Grade A Educational Stamp of Approval.

As I held these thoughts, I stood there waiting, shaking my head knowingly, just to see how far Lou would play this out. He knew, I knew, that he was not going anywhere. As Lou hesitantly stopped and then went forward in OUR truck, I pondered if my entire future would be filled with such whimsical nonsense. Finally, he stopped the truck and turned back around, as I thought, atta boy Lou, like he was going to leave me stranded without my car. I leaned back against the warm stucco of the school building as he drove back up.

"Forget something?"

Lou deadpanned, "Rudy wants to know if you want a lift?"

"Depends on where to?"

Lou glanced back at Rudy as if to ask for assistance. "How about dinner out at some new place and then home."

I sauntered up to Lou as he is leaning out of the cab, "How about picking up some dinner at a superb take out and going home?

Lou covers his eyes. "You wouldn't mean Reds. Again?'

"Well, OK," I nodded, "But let's eat in and see if Red would be interested in opening up another barbecue."

Lou turned to Rudy, "Whata ya think big fella? She leading us on?" Rudy looks from one of us to the other, not knowing who to side with.

"Get real, haven't I always?!" I protested as I promenaded back into the office to get my things.

I pinched myself to make sure this time my dream was for real.

EPILOGUE: James

James greeted me as I entered the spacious locker room, "Hey Lou."

"Good to see you James." We shook hands. I noted that his fingers did separate.

Over nine years since James had walked across the stage at Adams High School, to the applause of students and hollers from family and friends, plus a mass of Valley Oak staff.

I stood back eyeing him up and down, "Lookin' good James.: He was too. Good skin tone, Nike matching maroon and silver workout togs, appeared to have dropped at least a hundred pounds. James had carried over four hundred during his heaviest at Valley Oak.

"Thanks, you too Lou."

James took a towel from the gym bag, wiped the perspiration from his face following the fifty-five minute step work out, adding,

"For your age."

"Thanks, I think James." I hated to admit the fact that I was now over fifty. We both laughed.

"Awwwwwww, you know I'm just kiddin' Lou."

"Well James, watching you do that step program is an inspiration to me to get going."

We left the locker room for the main lobby. In passing a petite young lady, in a form fitting mesh approached James.

In a sweet, coy voice, "Going to be here tomorrow James?"

"Sure Patricia

Giving me the once over, "How about bringing your friend?"

James laid a hand on my shoulder, smiling, "You know Lou, no time like the present to get started."

James paused," Pardon my manners Patricia. This is my OOOLLLLD friend, Lou. Lou, I have the pleasure of introducing you to Patricia."

I felt my hair turning grayer.

"The Lou you have told me so much about?"

"The one and only."

I got a word in, "Nice to meet you Patricia but I'll have to beg off getting started."

"Yeh…yeh…yeh…….." James grimaced. "That bad back still holding you down."

"Well, if you ever change your mind, we have plenty of room……."

James interrupted, "Especially for older guys."

Nailed.

Patricia sauntered off as James gave me a sly wink. A couple of club members gave James a "thumbs up" approval.

James pointed to a table in the lobby, "What say we sit down?"

James' awareness of the social nuances had always been part of his character. I thought good teeth, good social skills. We went over and sat down amidst the Maple Ridge Athletic Club's six fifty-two inch plasma screens.

Laura and I had kept in touch with James as he gradually moved up to being The Greeter at Max's Steak House, where James always made sure we sat at the best table. We had noted James' diminishing bulk, though we never brought the question up.

As we sat down, James lifted up on chair's arms.

"Remember the first time we met with Marianne?"

"Could I forget?"

James softly sat into the seat, "Go ahead Lou, you can or, better yet, take a guess."

I nodded, "Laura and I have noticed your shrinking suit size at Max's."

James stretched his arms out shaking his head, "The cost in clothing, especially suits, makes me want to find a weight and stay at it."

I agreed, "Thin does not mean happy."

I could see that James was waiting. "Two seventy-five?" I hazarded.

"You're forty-two pounds over!"

I slapped my forehead in astonishment, "Like a hundred and sixty pounds gone?!"

"One at a time." James patted his belly. "Hey, let's toast to my health with a drink."

James signaled a waitress.

"The usual James."

"Times two Cindy. Thanks."

Cindy brought over two ice teas with lemons. James toasted, "To our health." We clinked glasses. James took a small sip.

"So Lou, what brings you to my side of town?"

I sat my glass down, "First off James, I just want to congratulate you on how you are getting on with life. I know there are always issues but look at you, aerobics, breathing well, weight down, ladies checking you out. How did you bring this all together?"

"Well Lou," James gathered himself erect, "I know you're not fishing for compliments and, everyday, I thank my lucky star for bringing Valley Oak into my life."

James and I held silent eye contact, going back over the years of drenched sweatshirts, tsunami pool waves, blue green termites, threatening pumpkins, a room of his own. I held my glass up and we clinked again.

"Lou, as you've always said, good stuff."

Time for me to get to the point, "See what you think of this idea, Laura and I would like to bring back as many of the graduated Valley Oak students as we can contact for a gettogether."

James didn't hesitate, "That would be great. Lots of times I think about them. How they're doing."

I was pleased. Laura and I had decided to see how James responded to our idea. We'd had contact with him, thought he would approve. "James I just hope they're doing half as well as you."

James lit up, "Lou, you should see me bowl! I carry a one-seventy-three average in league."

"Impressive."

"We put together a team to represent Max's Steak House. Bowl on Monday nights when the restaurant is closed."

"Laura and I will have to come down and catch you one night."

James laughed and gushed, "Remember during our Earned Activities, 'Bowling With Burt?'"

Did I? "We still sing it in program."

James began and I joined in:

"I'm going bowling with my friend Burt.

I've got my bowling ball

And

My bowling shirt.

Bowling……is my kinda game.

On a good day I'll row me some strikes.

Maybe some spares, that's what I like

Bowling is my kinda game………"

We finished the song to a round of applause from members seated in our area. I gave James a hug. Promised to catch him on a Monday night with Burt.

EPILOGUE: Sam

"The usual Ms. Laura?"

"You got it Sam." I never ceased to marvel at the level of self-confidence Sam had attained over the course of years. When Sam had turned sixteen, knowing Red, he had the idea all thought out before, Red had hired Sam part time. Red had Sam do all the menial, back breaking jobs that the barbecue could offer. Sam never complained as he had scraped the platters, plates, utensils (Red refused to put in a dishwasher.) carried in the armloads of mesquite wood for The General's heat, scrubbed floors, washrooms, windows, and anything else that Red could think of as an obstacle to Sam's earning the right to be where he was now, Stoker of The General!

"Get a refill on the coffee?"

"Right with you Zip." Sam gently nourished The General's coals, grabbed the coffee pot, and gave the refill in one adept motion.

"Yours will be right up Ms. Laura."

"No hurry Sam." Still so formal. Ms. Laura. I did so enjoyed hanging out at Red's with the aroma of the barbecue and picking up the local's banter.

"Two World Series in my life time?"

"Hard to believe, all those years of suckin' wind."

"And Yankees."

"Got that right."

Zip cradled his coffee, "I mean the first one, down three nuthin' and behind in the fourth."

"That was sweet."

"Cards in four."

"How about that Pedrolia kid?"

"Swings like my old principal with a paddle."

Sam chimed in, "Sure didn't miss Manny."

Both men nod their heads in agreement as Sam adds a shake of spices to the coleslaw the expertly tosses the large bowl, goes to the register where he cashes two tables out, and turns to Sandra, his assistant, "Can you finish up Ms. Laura's order while I take a short break?"

"Sure, Sam."

Sandra asks, "Couple of bones for Rudy and The Jacks?"

"Much appreciated Sandra."

Sam keeps his apron on and comes around the counter to sit next to me with his tawny blond hair wrapped in a bun under a hair net, his blue eyes glimmering like milky way stars through his dusty skin. Sam was now a strapping young man whose high school graduation I had attended. I thought back, like wow! Three years ago. Sam noted me gazing at his saxophone case.

"Lessons are always available." He laughed sliding in on the stool next to me.

"Thanks Sam, you can count on me not to forget the offer when you are on tour."

Sam played saxophone and his twin brother, Seth, was on the drums for the RED HOTS, a local country bluesy band that was getting some major ink in our area, of course, Red sponsored them.

Sam answers me seriously, "Not sure I want the road life, Ms. Laura. Red says that, when I graduate college and I am still interested, in two years he would look to open another barbecue in Long Barn."

"That would make life easier for me, then I would not have to drive all the way across town for our gourmet meals."

Sam had thought his vision through, "Yeh, and, if Jack agreed, we could become a Workability CBI site for Valley Oak."

"Sam," I congratulated, "You sound like a full-fledged humanistic entrepreneur."

"Blame Red for that." Sam looked back over his shoulder to check on Sandra's handling of the barbecue.

Well, no time like the present for what I had been thinking. "Sam, Lou and I are wondering if you would have an interest in directing a music program at......"

I felt strong warm fingers on the back of my neck, "You wouldn't be thinkin' about stealin' my key employee? Now, would you, Ms. Laura?"

Caught in the act. Deny. Deny. Deny. "Red, how good to see you again." I turned and gave him a soft peck on his stubbled cheek.

Red just walked away grumbling under his breath, picked up a dish rag, and began wiping down the vacated tables. Sam actually blushed!

"Pay the fly on the wall no mind, Sam," I proclaimed.

"Yes'm. I just be yah stepandfetchit...." Red did a bit of soft shoe as he uttered these words, continuing to wipe down the tables. A laughing round of appreciative applause went up from the customers.

I turned to Sam, "Now, the real reason I came by is that we are putting together a ten year anniversary celebration for Valley Oak. We are hoping to get as many of the former students and families to attend as possible."

Sam smiled broadly, gushed excitedly, "You can count us in, Ms. Laura."

Red jumped on the comment, Sam, I may care for you dearly, but there ain't no us, as yet, in Red's Barbecue."

I batted my eyes and posed my best self-depreciating smile, "Now Red, you know the only reason people will attend our Gettogether is to savor your succulent fixin's."

Red strolled over to us, began wiping our table down. "Now, Ms. Laura," Red's white teeth gleamed. "You might have taken over Lou's business at Valley Oak with your sweet talk...........but, last time I checked, this here is still Red's Barbecue."

As Sandra placed my take out order and bag of bones on the counter, I stood up and gave Red a big smacking kiss on his cheek, and placed a twenty down to cover the bill and tip.

Red picked up the twenty, "Ms. Laura," admonished Red, "After such a loving bestowment as glazed my cheek, I cannot accept pay, but I can offer the gratuity to staff as a tip for having to stabilize your needs while in MY barbecue."

I gave Sam a hug. Kissed Red on his other cheek........and made my grand exit.........

EPILOGUE: Mike

I stood gazing at the framed portraits of the students in the hallway containing The Wall of Graduation. Ten years in. Ninety-seven students had attained graduation through Valley Oak. I was on my fourth weight belt! Some had transitioned back to their school district of reference, some had gone into the workforce, some had met district expectations and graduated from Valley Oak.

We had divided the students amongst staff to make contact about attending our ten year anniversary celebration. One student's picture was not there. His not being successful had always stuck with me.........Mike Adams.

Mike had attended Valley Oak before I had developed the relationship based skill approach. Mike certainly wasn't anymore difficult than other street savvy wannabe posers who had been referred to Valley Oak and attained graduation. Mike just came in when I was not willing to hear the pain in his acting out. What he was trying to say to me. I simply did not have the skills to provide him with a safe and dignified landing.

I decided to look him up...................

I was passed through three PO's before I caught up with his current supervisor, Andrea Boscou. She informed me that Mike's record was one of drug use, sale of drugs, petty crime. So far he had served over two years locked up. Currently, Mike was on her list to pick up as he had, on several occasions violated parole. I asked Andrea for a day's reprieve so that I could contact Mike. Andrea said OK, as long as I was done by tomorrow afternoon.

I drove over to Magnolia Street in Dorchester. I didn't bring Rudy with me as this was a hard area. I wondered if Red had last seen my Dad around here. Run down, rough and tumble area. I thought of West Side Story:

"My daddy beats my mommy.

My mommy clobbers me.

My grandpa is a commie.

My grandma pushes tea.

My sister wears a moustache.

My brother wears a dress.

Goodness, gracious, that's why I'm a mess."

I was humming Officer Krumke as I walked up to Mike's first floor apartment door. Garbage laying all around. Didn't see any needles. I had tried the phone number Andrea had given me, no luck. Scary neighborhood. A flimsy weather marred paneled door just about gave way when I knocked. There were sounds from inside.

Finally, "Someone get the fuckin' door!"

Nothing.

Then, "Who the fuck is it? Boscou? That you?"

Glad to hear that Mike's vocabulary had remained the same. "Mike, it's Lou Thompson."

Total silence. Some scraping of chairs. Closing of doors.

Mike opened the front door with a jaw dropping, "You shittin' me?"

So hard for me, in another space and time, not to encourage the term defecate. One of us had moved on.....

Mike thumbed me in with, "What the hell brings you around?"

I didn't expect a warm hug. Maybe a handshake. Quick glance of the room let me know that Mike was in his habitat. Couple of huge bongs in the center of the room. Still smoldering roaches in the ashtrays. Andrea had said that Mike was a poster card for meth addiction. Mike didn't disappoint. Scrawny body. Pocked mark face. Decayed teeth. Got my vote.

"Looks like you're having a party, didn't mean to make your friends leave."

Mike scoffed, "Them bitches all have PO's on their asses. Just playing it safe."

Mike laid back in a ratted out recliner. "You're welcome to join the party. Plenty for everyone."

"Appreciate the offer, but I can't stay long." Without asking I seated myself on a metal folding chair.

"Yeh. Well today or tomorrow is my last day. Might as well fly before Boscou comes by and seals me in."

Mike reached over, sucked down hard on a bong, blew circles out. I recalled the fragrance far too well.

"So Lou, what the fuck or...... should I say copulate?" Mike slapped both knees laughing. "You here to rehabilitate me?" Mike's pock mark sneer cut through the years.

I took my time, explained to Mike my reasons for making contact. Appreciated that he listened. When I finished Mike asked, "So whatever happened to the Fat Boy?"

"James is doing well. Carries a one-seventy-three bowling average. Holds down a first class job. Dropped one hundred and sixty pounds.

"Jesus H. Christ!" Mike collapsed back into the recliner. "That's more than I weigh."

Mike went on. "I see Sam working at Red's."

"Have you ever gone in?"

Mike snorted, "Not in my shape."

Mike lurched up, stumbled into the kitchen and came back with a beer. Took a long chug. Belched. Shook his head as if to clear thoughts out. "Lou, I have to admit there were some good times with the bike rides and trampoline."

"Sure were," I agreed.

Mike took another swallow adding, "I don't' think you need to be so copulating hard on yourself. I am what I am"

Knocked me back hearing Mike supporting me.

"Whatever happened to that whacked out chick. That bitch scared the shit out of me."

I thought, me too. "Sharon? Sent Laura a letter from Florida saying life was OK."

Mike gazed off, nodding.

I tossed out, "We're having a ten year anniversary celebration, any chance you might make it?"

Mike looked up, startled, replied with something approaching sarcastic remorse. "Love to Lou, but I bet I'll either be locked in or drugged out............"

I shifted on the metal seat to leave, Mike leaned forward in a soft voice, "How's Ms. Laura?"

"Doing well, she's now Mrs. Thompson."

Mike stood up, feigned falling over. "Good God Lou. Here I was feeling crappy about my life and you." Rubbing his eyes in mock disbelief, "But you.....MARRIED A THERAPIST!"

Mike, finally, got control of his howling, paused, put out his hand, "Please tell Miss Laura.......... you too Lou, "Thanks for all that you tried to do for me."

We shook, both of our eyes had moistened, I let go of Mike's hand, gave him a full strong hug. Clapped him on the back.

As I walked by the bed sheet covered front window, I heard, "LETS' GET THIS FUUUUUUUUCCKINGGG PARRRRDDDEEE ONNNNNNNN!"

I laid a marker down for myself to check in with Boscou. If Mike was locked up, I could get him released into my custody for the party. If Mike was out..........I would drag him over..............therapeutically.........

EPILOGUE: Sharon

Lou has the time frame right, as I recall that day, two years or so past, when I received a rumbled personal letter from Sharon Moreno. The postmark was from Key West, Florida, and I paid the postage due to receive the envelope. I had not immediately opened the letter, but waited until our program had left for the day as, I felt, sure the contents would be unsettling. I had allowed Sharon to take on a personal relationship with myself that was not professional and I had, most certainly, crossed therapist/client boundaries. As, even now, I looked at the envelope propped up on my desk during the day as a reminder to myself to keep personal needs away from those I served. (The letter I had placed in a file to make sure no one else might read.) I smiled to myself thinking of the numerous visits to the Wobegone Winnebago and my attempts to nurture Sharon through her transition of becoming a young mother, a young adult. Then too, I mused, was not I truly trying to nurture myself...........

In the calm of the late afternoon, with students back to their districts, vans accounted for, I had cut open an end of the envelope, out fluttered five scrap pieces of paper, written on both sides. I gradually put the jigsaw together.......

HI LAURA!!! XXXOOO

Seems so like yesterday. WOW, it's been seven years. Can you believe it? God it's gorgeous down here. You should come for a visit. I have lots of friends. I split with Martha.......like five years ago. The old hag kept hitting on my men. What a sucking bitch. But, like I was saying. Life is just great here. Like Heaven on Earth. Everything grows. Hate the spiders and snakes. Key West is so CRAZY. So laid back. I love it. Monroe, My Man, loves me. He is so cool. May go to Barbados. I'm working at a B&B. Get free room and breakfast. Mostly eat fruit. Monroe wants me to pole dance. No way. I've been used enough. My B&B has been knocked down four times by hurricanes. I've ridden a couple out but no biggies. Old

410

Timer, Jimmy Buffet is in town. Party time. Ever hear of Cheeseburgers In Paradise? Shoroo just came by and invited me to a party. Told me to leave Monroe out. Have to think about that. Hey, tell Lou I miss him. Haven't seen my son since the pigs took him. Hope he's well. Do you know where he could be? My ride just showed up. Gotta go!!!

LOL Sharon

What struck me about the letter was that there were no spelling errors! Clear, legible writing. Everything sounded like the Sharon I had known. Red had let me know that Sharon's son had, through Founders, been placed in a quality home out of state. I had, with resignation, demanded of myself to not follow up on the child's progress. What was his name? Cody?

Looking inward, I know that I feel a loss in that I have never had the opportunity to have a child of my own. I can accept responsibility for that absence. However, when the gift is so lightly taken and given away, I mourn for the unrealized. That I, from the intense and extended family relationship culture, had not been able to nurture a child bearing relationship that Sharon had so crassly abused, left me with an emptiness. Sharon had undergone an experience that I could, even with all the richness and joy of my life, only surmise and envy..............

EPILOGUE: Rick

Rick Hutton, true enough, had found a home with HUMBLE. I had called ahead, cleared with the house supervisor that Rick was in. That Rick was ok with visitors. The supervisor let me know that the co-ed/partners home was the least restrictive of the HUMBLE facilities. The basic expectation for participating in this home was for the individuals to apply and be approved by the current elected board of the home, all of whom lived there. Participants could come and go as they wished. The supervisor was only present once a week for the house council meetings. She put Rick on the line, Rick said that it would be cool to see me.

From Rick's flat tone, I didn't know what to expect. Over the years I had seen Rick around our town doing everything from landscaping to light carpentry. Obviously, if he wasn't with the same girlfriend, he had a significant other. Good for Rick. Living by choice in a communal setting. Shades of the sixties. I had waved, said hi, but never sat down with him to see how life was going. I looked forward to seeing Rick again.

I walked up the broad brick path, neatly kept, to the screened in front porch of Rick's home. In a way I felt like I was coming back to the Old Victorian, only in much better condition. Rick greeted me at the door and didn't stop with a handshake, but gave me a full on embrace. Rick was a good four inches taller than me. His body was no longer that of a thin frail rail.

Rick directed me to a side room that was set up for meetings such as ours. Rick was dressed in Levis with a long sleeve blue work shirt. His hair was no longer arranged in macabre designs, short with a part on the side. I noticed his leather shoes were shined. Before sitting, Rick asked if I would like some ice tea, which I did.

"Mind if I tag along into the kitchen?"

"Not at all."

I followed Rick down a narrow hallway that had doors leading to a large living room-dining room combination. Off to the side a window enclosed study, stairs to the upper floors, finally to the expansive kitchen in the back of the home.

"Quite a place you have here."

"Thanks Lou. We work hard at keeping it together."

Other house members were coming in and out. Rick introduced me to several as he filled a pitcher with ice. We went out on the back deck where Rick opened a nozzle on a five gallon container of sun tea, filling the pitcher.

"Want to sit out back Lou?"

"Sure."

I took a seat in a patio chair, looking out on the manicured lawn, colorful fauna that filled the boarders of the spacious backyard. There were several fruit trees against the back fence with three adults were setting up a volleyball net.

Nick caught my thought, "Wednesday is volleyball night." He smiled, Vicious competition."

I laughed, hearing Rick talk about vicious competition just seemed so far removed the solitary figure I had known. Just then a girl dressed in a Starbuck's uniform approached Rick, bent over, bestowed a warm full kiss. Rick's lips were left with a smudge of her dark red lipstick.

"Lou, like you to meet Sarah. Sarah, my friend Lou."

I stood and shook Sarah's large hand. She was almost the same height as myself with sultry brown eyes and a warm smile.

In a silk sweet voice, "So pleased to meet you Lou. Rick has talked about you forever over the years."

"We did share some good times together." I admitted. Suddenly, I felt self-conscious, added," Times like now I wish I had stayed in closer contact and, yet, it's just difficult for me to enter into another person's current life."

"Well," Sarah wrapped a hair net around her bunned auburn hair, "I'm glad we finally had the time to meet and I've got to get to work." Sarah turned to leave adding with a full smile, "Hope to see you again, soon."

Sarah gave Rick a kiss on the cheek and skipped down the back porch step and out through the arched honeysuckle covered back gate.

"Nice lady Rick."

Rick nodded, "Just celebrated our fourth anniversary.

"That's impressive. Same lady you first met with HUMBLE?"

413

Rick paused, then replied in the clear manner that I so well remembered of him, "Nah, she dumped me." Then Rick asked in his intrusive, though never meaning so, manner, "You ever been dumped Lou?"

I thought back, took a moment, Yeh, too many times to remember," I lied. I just never allowed anyone to get that close. I decided to get into why I'd come.

I sipped my ice tea, "Rick, Laura and I are looking to celebrate Valley Oaks' ten year anniversary. We'd like to invite as many of our graduates, their families, friends, back as we can contact."

Rick took a moment, then stated, almost with emotion, "That's a great idea."

"I have talked with James, Sam............"

Rick interrupted excitedly, "Will Sharon be coming?"

Still had a hold on him. Maybe all first loves do. "No. I hear she was somewhere in South Florida, don't know exactly where." Truth was, Sarah could be in Barbados. Her letter to Laura was years old. I quickly moved on. I knew that Rick would appreciate my new information.

"Red's doing the catering for the celebration."

Rick slowly smiled a smile, had I not know him, I would have said gruesome, as his face began to take on a warm glow like a florescent light bulb.

"That's way too cool!"

I asked, "Get by Red's much?"

Looking down, Rick shook his head. "Not since Valley Oak."

That surprised me, "I thought you'd be there everyday..."

Rick just shrugged, "I guess I just felt too embarrassed."

I knew where Rick was going, he had always been the focus of attention at Red's. I had an idea.

"You got a few minutes?"

"Plenty of time. Today's an off day for me."

"Great, let's you and me take a ride over to Red's."

Rick looked into me with wonderment, "Really?"

I crossed my heart. "Let's go."

We went out to the truck where Rick and Rudy shared a long lost hug. We got into the truck. Rick asked, "How old is Rudy?'

"Pushing twelve." I hoped Rick would not ask me for body parts.

Red was behind the counter and stoking The General as we entered. Red's eyes lit up. He came around the counter. In front of everyone gave Rick a warm embrace saying, "Do my eyes deceive me or has my favorite customer returned?"

The two made quite a sight as Rick towered over Red. Rick blushed.

Red would not accept payment for our lunch, though he did demand that he be allowed to take Rick's photo while dissecting his Pulled Pork Sandwich.

Rick, with a self-conscious smile, relented.

Today, when Rick or anyone else enters Red's Barbecue, there is an eleven by seventeen framed picture of RICK "THE CLEAVER" HUTTON severing a Pulled Pork Sandwich, in a state of ecstasy.................

EPILOGUE: Reffti

"Reverend James doesn't look a day older than when he gave the Turkey Blessing at Valley Oak."

"Amen to that."

"Such a handsome man."

"I'll bet the single ladies of his congregation say the same thing."

"Not to mention the married."

"Now girl friends" I admonished, "Let the preacher be."

"Make me wish I was twenty years younger……."

"How about thirty."

"Girl friends! Enough!!,"

The three of us, Martha Lee, Geraldine, and myself had decided to attend the Bay County First Baptist Church where Natti, Ike, and Reffti had continued to attend over the past eight years. Even with my twenty-first century perspective of human rights and relationships, I still found myself a fish out of water in an entirely Black African American attended service as we settled into one of the back pews.

Martha Lee read my thoughts whispering, "Just pretend you're at some High Holy Roman Mass with a bald white guy mumbling jumbo mumbo and you'll fit right in."

"At least you are cinnamon colored," I retorted.

Reverend James began he service by asking all brethren to turn to page forty-seven of the hymn book and join with the choir in singing "All Creatures of Our God." As we stood and began the song, I spotted Hatti and Ike standing tall in the second row and, as the choir entered through the front doors joining in the praise, we nudged each other as Reffti passed. We looked in wonderment as in recognizing Reffti, we beheld a handsome, tall, shoulders back young man with joy in his heart spiritually engaged with his community. I shed my reluctance and raised my voice level, joining in with the congregation in beseeching heavenly redemption!

Following the service we stood a bit to the side as members warmly greeted one another. Chatting about everything from the message of the day brought forth by Reverend James to the unthinkable of another Red Sox World Series. Natti and Ike approached us

"How you'll doin'?"

"Glad you could make it."

We exchanged hugs and laughed.

Amidst our long lost welcome we skimmed over the past years during which time Hatti and Ike had been married, which had been our last meeting. Reverend James joined us, sharing a resplendent welcome.

"Has it been six years?"

"That it has."

"Reverend," Martha Lee gushed, "You do not have one speck of gray hair!"

"All due to the healthy vittles my loving congregation bestows upon me."

Into our group sauntered Reffti, who was now, taller than Natti.

"Well, well." Welcomed Geraldine, giving Reffti an affectionate hug. "Last time I laid eyes on you, I could sit you on my knee."

Without missing a beat, Reffti replied, "If you like Ms. Geraldine, I can now return the favor."

"Listen to that boy talk.

"Ummm,ummm."

"Well we sure heard your voice in that choir and you can sing!"

"Ms. Laura, can I ask for a hug."

You don't have to ask," as I squeezed the young man I had know as a boy. Reffti was a good head taller than me! "What have you been feeding this young man?"

"Just the Lord's Banquet," smiled Reverend James.

Natti spoke up, "Reffti has been offered a music scholarship and, not just for his singing, but he has a special hand with the organ."

"That he does," agreed Reverend James, "Reffti is a role model for all the young people in our congregation."

I asked, "What do you most enjoy playing Reffti?"

Reffti squirmed a bit, answering, "I should say gospel......."

Reverend James interrupted, "I will not hold the truth against you."

Reffti brightened, "Just about everything. Jazz. Blues. Rap. I just kind of pick it up as I go along"

Ike offered, "Reffti has a magical ear."

Natti nodded, "That's no brag. Reffti can hear a rhythm and bring it back the first time."

"Well, most times," qualified Reffti.

Just then a thought hit me, "Did you know hat Red is sponsoring a Blues-Jazz band called the Red Hots?"

Reffti looked astonished, "Red's doing that?"

Geraldine commented, "We've heard them a couple of times."

"People say they have a future," added Martha Lee. "Have you heard them play?"

"Not yet. But I've seen their posters. Friends of mine say they're good."

I went on, "I was just talking with their saxophone player the other day. He mentioned they were looking for a keyboard player."

Reffti asked, "You don't mean Sam, do you?"

I nodded.

"Sam was at Valley Oak before Red's Barbecue?"

"Before your time Reffti"

"Well I can't wait to talk with him."

Reverend James spoke up, "Good enough. How about we all head on over to the picnic area where we can further on our discussion of formulating Reffti's future."

With laughter, we made our way with Ike and Hatti stopping every few feet to introduce us to their fellow churchgoers.

EPILOGUE: Jake

I dialed the number, after four, thunderous rings, the answering machine picked up with:

"Out of the night
When the full moon is bright.
Comes the thundering horseman
Known as ZORRO!
This bold......

Then the same squeaky high pitched voice I knew so well, "WHAAAZZZZZZUP LOU!?"

Jake OH, time had passed, his voice hadn't changed. We'd stayed in touch through the years. Jake had graduated in three years, a double major in Economics and Korean Culture from NYU. Then had done a year of law at Princeton. Jake moved to the West Coast to finish at Boalt Hall at UC Berkeley. He denied that he wanted to be closer to family. Stated the reason was for Top Dog. After his law degree, Raymond's influence got him assigned as an attaché to the American Consulate in Seoul...........

"Your phone messages always amaze me." Jake seemed to change them every other week.

"You approve."

"More to my liking than some of your Korean acid rock."

"Lou, this is the twenty-first century. You're going to have to let go of Perry Como."

For all of his smarts, Jake would remain his sacrilegious self, at least over the phone with me. Jake had e mailed me pictures of his attendance at family functions in full blown cultural Korean attire. Told me he had assumed a Korean name. The name, Jake, was for earlier friends like me.

"Jake, this twenty-first century is just mind boggling to me. I mean, like a World Series for The Sox, maybe a second one. Who'd a thunk it?"

419

"My prayers for your happiness to Hwang-gung, one of the Four Guardians, have been answered with his ascendance of the Red Sox. May you sleep well."

I could picture his left hand covering his right fist. "Jake, I and the rest of New England are forever in your debt.

Jake was in a jovial mood, "I keep telling you Lou, that for the real baseball you've got to come over to Korea. You can bring in your own food and booze. We have cheerleaders! Put those English soccer miscreants to shame."

"I'll be over on the next plane."

"Seriously Lou, my Dad now has the Samsung jet at his disposal. We can do this."

I'm sure Raymond would. That Jake was able to return to his family, develop a devout interest in Korean history, Korean culture, had given his parents, Raymond and Allyson, the joy of an eldest son whom they had believed forever astray.

"Need to check in with Red, also Laura, make sure they can spare me."

"We'll bestow upon you a traditional Korean welcome!"

"Jake, before you Shanghai me…………"

"No ethnic slurs upon my southern cousins."

Still tough to get a word in with this guy, "Jake, Laura and I are getting together a ten year anniversary celebration for Valley Oak. We'd like you and everyone else who can to make it to join in."

Jake actually paused for a brief moment, "Lou, count me aboard! Is King Rudy going to show?"

"Rudy asks about you every day. We don't have a firm date yet. I'll get back with you as soon as we get one.

"Super duper. I'll make sure my father's box seats at Fenway are available. I'd like to see how this new Pedroia kid is working out."

"Sure the Samsung Lions could use him. I hear The Lions are the Yankees of Korea."

"When you're big, you're big."

I caught Jake speaking Korean to someone.

"Lou, gotta go. Get back to me with that date."

Next time I called, *Enter Sandman,* greeted my ears…………

EPILOGUE: Lou & Laura

...............I was totally absorbed into The Belt. I did not notice Laura entering the shop until Rudy let out a huge sigh. I looked over, Bonnie and Clyde were licking his ears. Rudy just rolled his eyes as if to say, give me a break Lou.

"Hey hon."

Laura handed me a hot mug of New England coffee. "How are the toy boxes coming?" She gave me a hug and shooed the Jacks away from their torturing of Rudy.

"Coming along real good." I pointed to the two sanded maple tops. "Just getting ready to put on a clear coat of Varathane."

"The kids will probably use them to hide in."

We had adopted two children as infants. Of course, both were through Founders, Angel Palmyra and Jack Eugene were now five and six.

The wind rattled the window panes. I became aware of the storm's having arrived in a white blanket.

"Where are they now?"

Laura rubbed the moisture off a window pane and pointed to where the two were taking turns falling in the snow, flapping their arms and legs making fallen angels. I laughed as Angel Palmyra tossed a snowball on her spread out, defenseless brother, then turned and stumbled for the back porch door before her brother could get up.

Laura gave Rudy a rub. "I better get in there before Jack catches up with her."

"Don't forget your two beasts."

"Let's go Jacks. We know when we are not wanted."

I held up my mug, "Thanks for the coffee."

Bonnie and Clyde never listened to me, definitely took their cue from Laura. Gratefully, Rudy let out a sigh of relief as they trotted out the dog door.

As suddenly as the manic energy had entered, Rudy and I were left in the quiet of our glowing coals. I placed the coffee mug on the Franklin, keep the brew warm, ran my hand over the top of the maple toy box tops. Decided to give them one more damp swipe with the towel to bring the grain up. Hope I was doing Augustus proud. Needed to finish with a final sanding of two-twenty grit sand paper, that should do it.

The snow was piling up and burying the windows on the northeast side of the shop. Rudy's eyes were already twitching as I moistened the towel. I found myself back with The Belt. Fixating into two large, charred letters, **PG**. Almost burnt through. Pedro Garcia. He was.......